Rain No Evil

Rain No Evil

BASED ON TRUE EVENTS

Michele Savaunah Zirkle Marcum

Printed and designed by Bookerfly Press
www.BookerflyPress.com

ISBN Number: 978-1-945178-69-6

Printed in the United States of America

First Edition

www.rainnoevil.com

Dedication

I'm most grateful for the experiences I share in this book. First of all, to the Almighty who allowed a bit of Heaven to rain down on me. Second, to my family and friends who assured me I was sane when the world no longer made sense.

To my two boys whom I cherish more with every breath. To my current husband whose faith in me brings me tears of joy. To my dad and step-mom who fed me many a warm meal as they listened to my stories of the strange occurrences. To my mom who has shown me that true forgiveness is not only possible, but utterly essential in order to flourish. To my sister who stood with me, wet and wondering what her big sister had gotten her into this time. To Francie who spurred me through the final phases of writing this novel.

To the Catholic priest who is endeared to my heart for the peace he brought my family. And to the lady light-worker, my angel endowed with the whitest of light, whose influence on my life is profound in a way not describable in mere words—I hope I never run out of questions for you.

Most grateful to the various Panera Breads, Hardees and libraries that have provided a cozy respite in which to write. And to Michael Knost who took an interest in my manuscript. I'm tickled that you digged my story.

I cherish all the individuals who have encouraged me in the writing of this story that demanded it be told. I love you all.

Bless all those from whom I've learned invaluable lessons as I lived the life I describe. These lessons have helped me to become the person I am now, immensely happy and ineradicably loving and accepting of myself.

May the Omnipotent shine His divine light through us all. **And may it Rain No Evil**.

Table of Contents

Chapter One
THE TIN MAN

Something about his crooked grin snagged me. When his chestnut eyes winked my way, I knew we'd contracted to love each other—if not before that moment, then right then and there in the firehouse that on Saturdays transformed into the hottest teenage spot in town.

It seems like only yesterday Alex was clutching my waist on that dark dance floor that was spinning faster than we were dancing as the wine coolers I'd downed fizzed through my petite frame. The way Alex hovered over me while Tom Petty serenaded us with "Free Falling"—the way he bent to kiss me, I knew he was my appointed guardian.

Before we married, Alex would call me "Pooh Bear," as he ushered me into his Mustang, but now—

"Hold the damn thing still!" Alex yells above the sound of the heater blazing in the corner of the garage.

"I'm trying!" I say, shifting my balance on the ladder that's digging into my thigh. Benching 110 pounds—no problem, but balancing this huge slab of drywall above my head—impossible.

I search Alex's face for a glimpse of the compassion in those eyes that first loved me, but he's glaring at me from his side of the drywall.

He doesn't see the real me anymore. The real me—the compassionate, cheerful girl with a moral compass that points due North—has died a bit more every day since I became Alex's wife.

What would Alex do if I really weren't alive anymore? Bet when I'm gone—primed and stuffed with embalming fluid—he'll ooze eloquence like the other mourners who'll peer into my casket, saying to my beloved Alex, "Oh, she's so beautiful!"

Like I'm going to need a compliment then! What kind of sicko says that, anyway?

I'll hover above the casket and scream through the ethers at the do-gooder, "I'm not fucking pretty. I'm dead, damn it! I don't need to be attractive!"

I'll yell at Alex the loudest—tell him to redirect his compliments to one of his many girlfriends.

I don't want to be on this ladder, yet here I am, trying to help my Alex, Wooten County's very own walking-tall version of justice who's swung his hickory stick so long that he's callused not only the hand that once slid a ring on mine, he's callused his heart.

Screws from Alex's hand clink to the concrete floor as a cramp courses up my arm.

"Fuck a duck!" he says, sweat creasing his face like a crooked country road. He jams the screwdriver into the one remaining screw, gripping the trigger until the screw's as tight as my chest and swipes his arm across his forehead. "You got this?"

"I don't know if—"

But Alex is already backing down the ladder.

Pressing my toes harder on the rung, I stretch until my palms won't slide any farther toward Alex's side. I can't reach the edge, and the drywall droops.

Alex's head sways over the garage floor. "Dang it! Where'd they go?"

I feel my arms giving under the pressure, and a spasm shoots down my back, but I manage a shallow breath. I wish he'd hurry. He'll be so mad if I drop—

My arms cave under the weight, and I duck, shoving the drywall away from me. Chunks splinter onto the concrete, narrowly missing Alex's Harley.

The largest intact portion of drywall slams into his calf as he scampers to escape. He trips, his forearms smacking the front bumper of the four-wheeler as his knees hit the cement floor.

"What the hell are you doing!" he screams, scrambling to stand. "Are you fucking crazy?"

Grabbing the top ledge of the ladder, I freeze. My pride lies scattered among the broken drywall at Alex's feet. Doesn't he know how much I want to impress him with my strength?

Alex stares at me, nostrils flaring. "I said what the hell are you doing?" The remainder of his rant blows past me; the only discernible sound is the thumping in my ears.

This can't be happening again. Alex was so nice this morning; he kissed my neck and thanked me for breakfast.

Just when I think there's hope of him changing, he goes ballistic, like the assholes he arrests for domestic violence. Alex holds his tantrums to a roar, but what will I do if he gets physical and slings me against the wall like a ragdoll? Will I have the courage to leave him then?

"Almost hit my bike," he says, snatching the largest piece of drywall and leaning it against the weight-lifting bench. Clenched fists hang by his side, making the man who promised to love and cherish me look like Thor ready to battle the serpent.

Trembling, I cling to the ladder, hoping Alex won't sling me off it, but I'm not letting him see I'm afraid. "I told you to move it before we started."

"Damn it, Savvy! Can't you do anything right?" he says. "All I wanted was a little help today! That too much to ask?"

I hold firm to the ladder. I don't need this shit, don't need Alex. I imagine Ryan, a flame from the past, his arms around me, my face cradled in his hands. But I can't run back to Ryan. That's only a temporary fix, and I want a permanent solution—want my marriage to work—want Alex whispering in my ear every morning, "Love you, babe," but I don't possess the magic to make that happen.

Tears burn my eyes, and I turn my head. He hates it when I cry. "It was heavy!" I say, my legs twitching as I descend the ladder. "You know what? Fuck you! Fuck you, asshole!"

I storm out of the garage, pleased with myself for using the big-girl word *fuck,* and stomp up the side steps to the house.

Each room I pass through feels too close to him. I smack my chalky hands over my ears, attempting to drown Alex's voice, but the echo closes in on me. I need to get out of here.

Seconds later, I punch the button on the radio in the shower and launch a scream into space, sobbing as water pounds my back. I can't take this anymore. I deserve better. I close my eyes and scratch the lavender-scented loofah across my skin as if I can scrub away the insults.

Randy Travis croons through the radio how he's going to love someone forever and ever. I want to mute the memories of dancing with Alex and of the intimacy we once shared, but I listen and revel in my suffering as images of a happier us pour over me.

We've dug our heels into this mire of a marriage, anchoring each other through many monsoons, but rust has eroded our anchor with each flap of Alex's open mouth, and I feel lost at sea. I can't keep drifting. I need to change course. I raise my face, allowing the shower to wash my worthless tears down the drain.

"God," I say, collapsing into a shivering ball on the shower floor, "I just want Alex to treat me like he loves me, to stop screaming at me, but nothing I say penetrates his missile-proof head."

I hug my legs to my chest, warm water caressing my shoulders as I let hopelessness wash over me. All my prayers for a happy marriage were a waste of time. Just like me praying to an unseen God—an invisible being who's supposed to love me, yet permits Alex to flatten me with every word he speaks as if I'm a penny on a railroad track. I mean, where the hell is this God when I need help?

"God," I say, "Why can't you make Alex hear himself the way I hear him—force him to realize he speaks to me like I'm one of the criminals he arrests? If he could just hear himself, maybe he would be nice to me. Maybe we could enjoy each other again." I swipe my bangs out of my eyes and wring the water from my hair. "And as for the crap I hear at church about how when I feel alone You're actually carrying me, well . . ." I jab my finger toward heaven and shout into the empty air, "Bullshit!"

3

I push off the cold tile and stand as water slaps my face. "So, here's to the God I'm not sure is listening; since You can do anything, how about proving to me You're real! How about that?"

I sling the faucet off. If He *is* real, He got an earful today—Him and all His angels. I may go out in a blaze tomorrow, but I'll be damned if I'm squeaking out like a church mouse. If God does exist, I want to know so I can avoid the consequential hell I've convinced myself I deserve for committing adultery.

Growing up in a church pew, I'd have never considered questioning whether God actually existed or even dared to think it. But now? Now, I'm too scared to *not* question, because to not question means I'll never know the answer during this lifetime. It means I haven't searched hard enough for the spiritual path I'm supposed to follow and may never find.

If God's not real, Hell's not either, and I've been condemning myself for years for nothing. That would make me the judge of my own actions, and if I'm the one holding the gavel, this court's in recess. I need to examine the evidence, need to determine if I'm justified to screw around on Alex because he treats me like he hates me. Even more importantly, I need to decide if living with the tormented vacillation of trying to make Alex happy one day, failing, and screwing someone else the next, is worth it.

The song on the radio has Travis Tritt spelling the one word I want to find a little of right now—"T-R-O-U-B-L-E." Alex, that dickhead, is not gonna break me! I'll show him I can be happy without his love. Maybe I'll call Ryan—get a hug. Nothing wrong with that.

The hoodie feels soft on my skin still trickling with droplets I missed. I hustle down the stairs, each step creaking like it's mocking me for not having silenced them eight years ago when we first moved in, but delicate repairs require finesse and Alex is the demolition man.

I need an excuse to be by myself for a bit so I'll fake a store trip. I toss cans of veggies and boxes of cereal into plastic bags, tuck the bags into the trunk of my car parked outside, and head into the garage to face the renovation king.

When I step inside, Alex glances up and continues sawing a piece of drywall.

"Going to the store. Need anything?" I say, hoping he doesn't.

"Nope!" He grabs the slab off the sawhorses. "All I needed was your help and I definitely can't count on that."

I want to punch him in the gut—knock the wind out of his cocky ass—tell him he's not the only one who's disappointed, but there's no use for me to explain that I feel disrespected. He won't understand—just call me a bitch.

I turn to find a breath of freedom on the highway, leaving Alex fondling his precious drywall. I need somewhere quiet to think—to erase the recording of Alex's voice playing in my head.

As I roll along the concrete conveyor to wherever, West Virginia, sunlight reflecting from the ice-strewn river beckons me closer, so I slide on my shades and turn toward Ridgeland's levy. I ease into my favorite spot under the tree

4

noticing several druggies waiting their turn to exchange cash for hash through the open window of the maroon car at the upper end of the lot.

Despite the drug element, I'm more comfortable here than at home with my own husband. Here all I can hear are my thoughts, as frantic and desperate as they are, at least they're mine, not Alex's irrational, malicious ones.

A girl with scraggly hair walks to the maroon car. I wonder if she's more desperate than I am and what tragic events led her to drugs. Was it a sexually abusive father—growing up in a family of users—or maybe she lost her self-respect like me, let someone convince her that she is nothing and her opinion is as worthless as a crumb fed to an alligator. I need this cycle of love and hate between Alex and me to end.

Then a thought seizes me. It wouldn't take much for me to open my door and jump in line behind her. My hand goes to the car door. I'm no better than she is. She sticks drugs in her mouth to numb the pain. I used to stick dicks in mine to numb my mind, but the shame from those illicit encounters lingers even years later. A fix has to be less humiliating than being probed by a man who doesn't love me, or even worse, by some stranger I picked up at the market.

I look through the window and into the eyes, the empty eyes, of a girl who looks like the living corpse I imagine myself to be. I jerk my hand from the door. I'm not empty. I'm full. Somewhere inside the galaxy my head is spinning in, is the joyful girl who caught lightening bugs and giggled while they squirmed inside her hand. Somewhere there is the dreamer who scribbled her best-selling novel into her eighth grade tablet, wanting to leave something tangible for the generations to come.

My gaze lands on the Ohio River, the humble skyline of MuddSock Heights framing the opposite bank. The river seems to return my blank stare. It's not going anywhere. Just like me. I'm stuck. Stuck in a deceitful existence. I lie to be happy—lie to be loved. I move like the water that goes nowhere, but still fills the basin as it weaves around its banks and disappears around the bend.

I realize I'm holding my breath and preventing air from entering my lungs is not going to preserve me in a catacomb of peace, but the river—the glistening river seems to wink me near. I don't have to be here. I could be dead and then Alex would be sorry.

I'd like him to be sorry—sorry for just half the nasty, hateful words he's said to me over our fourteen years together.

A pickup pulls in beside me so I turn and lean my back against the door. The notion of numbingly cold water surrounding me, sucking me deeper into the icy darkness makes me shudder. A mirage of Ben and Isaac's faces floats by. My boys—what would happen to my boys? They're at their granddads right now, probably shooting BB guns and arguing over who's the most accurate shot.

They've grown up fast, but they're still my babies. I'll never leave them over some dumbass man like Mom did Luce and me and definitely not intentionally drown myself like I'm the weak house of twigs the wolf blew down. No siree—I'll screw every man in town to numb the pain before I'll slam myself into a wet coffin, leaving my boys motherless.

I don't need pot to feel better—one hug from Ryan and I'd be soaring. I'd call him right now, but I don't want to break my two-year good-girl streak and make a decision I'll regret.

A door slams. A young man rounds the front of the truck to my left and opens the door for a giggling, blonde-haired girl. He reaches up, grasping her waist as she wraps her legs around his hips and free-falls into his kiss.

Alex and I used to enjoy each other like that.

I watch the couple stroll hand-in-hand, stopping every few steps to smooch. I want to be the blonde with someone's arms around me. I want to feel woozy in love with Alex again, but the closest I may get to that feeling is the one I used to conjure when I was seeing other men. It was easier to pretend I was in love with them than it was to actually be in love with Alex. Caresses from men who had never belittled me or scorned me I accepted easily, stirring them inside my mind until they melted into that gooey in-love feeling I wanted.

That gooey recipe used to be instant and genuine with Alex, or so I thought. He used to touch me like a delicate flower whose petal may drop at any moment, like he cherished my skin, my heart, my whole being and I felt nourished, wanting to blossom into the most gorgeous flower he'd ever laid eyes on. I thought that feeling was all I needed, but what I really needed was for Alex to talk with me as an equal inquisitor in this world—for him to entertain my curious questions about the origins and purpose of life, my speculations of what God is or who He is. I needed Alex to share his thoughts and accept mine without dismissing the importance of my purposed conversations like they were as unnecessary as a toboggan at the Bahamas.

Physically, Alex satisfies me, but mentally he's a bully and a bore, and I'm not sure which is more pathetic. A bully I can tame with wit, but how do I inspire abstract conversation in a man who dismisses any notion beyond his understanding and scoffs at the idea that there is anything he can't control.

To avoid an argument, I often let him think I agree with him or that I'll do what he wants, but he can't really control me. Somewhere tucked inside of me is the seed of my existence that was placed there by a Higher Power—the seed full of potential for what I might become and it was planted in love.

I just need to figure out how nurture it so it can sprout, and I can grow it into liking myself again. If I could love myself again, I wouldn't have to seek love from Alex or any other man ever again.

Now when I'm having sex with Alex, I don't expect a soul-to-soul conversation either before or after. I let him manipulate my body and his for our mutual pleasure, but my mind is far from his reach, suspended in a sacred space I reserve for my deepest thoughts, for my quintessential questions that go unanswered such as who created God and why am I here.

My stream of consciousness fills the private space, providing refuge for my thoughts—thoughts that want to pull Alex close—that want to permit tenderness to enter the region of my brain that takes a battering every time his open mouth swats me like I'm a fly on his pie.

When the marvelous sensation of orgasm overtakes me, and Alex rares his head, victorious in believing he's conquered me—that I'm vulnerable and my passion for life indelibly tied to the performance his dick gave, I am safely locked in a room in my mind that Alex can't enter. One in which he can't cause me pleasure or pain.

Sitting here at the levy feeling sorry for myself is siphoning hope from my gut faster than the river's flowing. I have to believe that tomorrow may be the day Alex and I can locate the morsel we're missing that made us "us." I just have to find a way to feel better until we're able to do that.

I guess it couldn't hurt to call Ryan and just talk. I've got to do something to divert my attention from my marital problems and from the super-cuddly couple that are huddling so close on the bench that they appear to have one head.

I dial Ryan's number hoping he hasn't changed it since the last time we spoke.

The familiar, raspy voice on the line makes me hesitate. "Hi, Ryan, it's Savannah. Been a while, huh?"

"I'd say. Probably over a year. Man, I thought I'd never hear from you again."

"I know. I was trying to be good—" I can't suppress a giggle. "But . . ."

"Oh, good's not working for ya?" Ryan chuckles.

"Guess not. Things with Alex are . . ." My fingers caress the hard leather gearshift. "Well, could we meet and talk? I'd really like to see you."

"When?"

"How's now?" I say, wishing I hadn't seemed so eager.

"You always were crazy, girl," Ryan says. "I have Briana this weekend and she has a friend over, so we can't come here. Could you meet at the Super 8 in MuddSock Heights in say thirty?"

The boy on the bench squeezes the girl to his chest. They're getting high on hormones while a gaunt fellow hands a wad of bills for his fix to the arm extending out the window of the maroon car.

"Sure can," I say, wanting my own kind of buzz.

"Okay, you're on," Ryan says.

On—I suppose, like a cancer-filled dancing girl kicking her legs high to impress the audience while slowly dying, but if impressing people is an art—I'm Michelangelo—even if Alex doesn't think so.

I peer into the visor mirror. A dab of powder under my puffy eyes, dark cherry gloss on my lips, and I'm off.

I'm zipping across the bridge into Ohio, relieved to be on it rather than diving into the icy depths below, when a message pops up from Ryan telling me he's checked-in. Minutes later, I pull in the motel parking lot, bumping across the cracked blacktop until I wedge in between a van and a dumpster by the back door.

Cheesy-ass place—last time I was here with Kent I swore I'd never come here again. I wonder what he's been up to. Last time I saw Kent he was throwing candy from his church's float in the Christmas parade, his wife to his right, singing with a wagon full of children stacked on hay bales. He was never going to leave her for me, and I'm quite sure I didn't want him to.

Through my shades, the narrow hall is dark and welcoming like the deadly river, and I allow myself to be enticed to what awaits behind door number three.

When Ryan opens the door wearing only jeans and a smile, I step into my cube of paradise and collapse into his arms.

My purse slides off my shoulder and onto the floor as I nuzzle against his chest that's been hewn from an Olympic barbell. "I'm so tired of dealing with Alex," I say, pressing my waist to his, wanting to feel close to someone. "He just doesn't understand me."

Ryan squeezes me close. I close my eyes and imagine how we must look like the couple at the park, all snuggly and content.

Ryan relaxes his hold on me and I look up into his eyes that are mocha-colored like the coffee I like. I feel helpless as his fingers glide from my chin to my neck. I watch as he squeezes my breasts and yanks my hoodie over my head, his teeth tugging playfully at the bra strap draped loosely around my shoulder, exposing one nipple.

My skin tingles with goose-bumps as Ryan's fingertips play the entire length of my arms. Feeling like a cub being dragged along by its mama, I allow him to nibble my neck and nudge me closer to the bed with each skin-surfing bite.

I should stop him, but I may as well enjoy his sinfully pleasant touch. God's probably already pissed at me for this morning's tirade, and if that didn't damn me to the fiery pit, one more offense isn't going to either.

Ryan grabs my ass with both hands, tongue lapping at mine, each lick removing the morning's festering wounds. I smash my belly to his, arching the small of my back against the roughness of his hand as he unsnaps my bra.

I grasp his hands and wrap my mouth around his finger, sucking it like it's a creamsicle and gazing into his heat–filled eyes. He must enjoy watching my tongue swirl around his finger. I feel his attention streaming into me, sanding away the scars from Alex's verbal beating and polishing every cell with the hope I need.

With Ryan's hands on my waist, I step out of my jeans and my legs bump against the mattress. Shadows of our bodies dance on the green wall making me dizzy. I want to let go—not think anymore, just enjoy the sensation of being desired. This sure beats finding peace under a river current.

Ryan yanks off his jeans and pounces on me. I fall onto the bed, my legs open, exposing the tunnel to my heart that's contracting, wanting to be filled with Ryan's hard penis that's buried in my leg.

A growl in my ear startles me, but makes me want him even more.

His chest smashes my breasts as I reach up cupping his face in my hands, reveling in the sight of him poised above me. Intrigue radiates from the dark in his eyes while the smooth point of his hard-on presses on my clit—presses so hard it hurts.

I deserve to be hurt. I shouldn't be here, but the intoxicating feeling of being wanted overrides the sickness in my stomach, so I close my eyes and let him enter me. I hear another growl and realize he must want me bad. He moves faster, deeper, until his fountain of lust sprays into me, claiming me like a dog does a fire hydrant.

As he withdraws and rolls off my damp flesh, I lay still, my hand resting on my belly, wishing I could cling-wrap myself to the spongy mattress suspending my weight. Maybe I deserve to be stuck here—glued to this bed of shame.

I smooth my hand across the gritty sheet that reeks of a cigarette I didn't smoke. I cringe. Mine isn't the only grunge in this bed.

Ryan's hand stops mine, and lifts it to his mouth for a quick kiss. The glory of the transient moment has absconded, along with my earlier resolve to cultivate the divine seed that could, quite possibly, grow the love for myself I need.

I inhale a musty mix of sex and sweat. I feel miserable. I'm worth more than this two-bit motel. Sex with Alex is degrading too, but at least our bed is clean. Next time, it'll be the Hilton, or his house. I wrinkle my nose at the thought of a next time—of another encounter that makes me feel worse about myself than Alex does.

I squeeze Ryan's hand. It's not his fault that I feel this way. *I* called him. If I wasn't married, if I were free to love someone else, that someone could be Ryan.

He looks into my eyes and brushes my cheek with his fingers. For a second I imagine it's Alex touching me like this, but his words from earlier boom through the mirage I'm creating. "Can't you do anything right?"

I spring to my feet and slip into my panties. Once the sex is over, so's the sexy.

"You in a hurry, babe?" Ryan asks, standing up and wiping his dick on the blanket. "No double-dipping today?"

Not a chance of that in this skanky love-shack, I think, tugging on my hoodie and faking a smile. "It was amazing, love bear, but I'm out of practice, remember?"

Still holding his dick, he squeezes out the excess semen, letting it dribble onto the bed. "Love bear? Where'd that come from?"

"You growling at me," I say, bending down to retrieve my jeans.

"What you mean growling? I didn't growl at you." Ryan waddles past me holding his dick with one hand and swatting me on the rear with the other.

"Sure you did. Twice. You were into it."

"You must have been into it—you're hearing things, but you know your ass gets my rocks off," Ryan says over a commode flush. "Anytime you need to practice, you just call me."

"Will do," I say, satisfied to know I *am* good at something even if what I'm good at makes me more miserable than if I were good at nothing.

Love bear prances back into the room. "Gotta go," I whisper, sliding one arm around his back. "Text me later," I add, more out of a sense of obligation to than because I want him to.

Walking the dingy corridor I feel like I'm deep in the recesses of a swamp and treading toward the surface.

I can't believe I just let that happen. I only wanted his arms around me. Maybe I really am crazy even though I've never been diagnosed as such. One minute I'm wanting my marriage to work and the next I'm slithering out of a hotel where I met another man.

I push my sunglasses onto my face and exit out the back, edging around the trash bin and into my clean car.

I'm relieved to see Keagan's truck in the back driveway when I return home. Alex won't yell at me in front of his dad. I pop the trunk, snag the groceries I planted earlier, and with a triumphant stride for staying one step ahead of Alex, reach the kitchen door just as Alex and Keagan emerge from the garage.

Alex makes two of Keagan, towering over his dad's slender frame like a gorilla over a stork. "You just getting back?" Alex says, brushing white dust from his hands onto his bib overalls. "What the heck took you so long?"

"Long lines. Everyone in Wooten County who's on welfare got their checks this week, you know," I say, attempting to turn the doorknob with bags dangling from my wrists.

Keagan steps up behind me. "Here, dear," he says.

He holds the door open and winks at me. Big flirt. I thank him, shuffle through the wooden door and heave the bags onto the kitchen counter, smiling at the twice-bagged items that lend a new meaning to the word, "recycled."

Keagan drives off and Alex bounds in, flakes of drywall falling from his shirt. "I'm starving," he says rustling through the bags. "You fixing dinner?

I reach into the bag he's abandoned and flash a smile at the robust can of baked beans that seem proud to aid in my cover-up. "Grilled cheese and soup," I say.

"Soup! I'm talking about food—mashed potatoes, meatloaf. You buy any *real* food?" Alex peels open a bag of almonds, tosses a handful into his mouth and stares at me, crunching and waiting, I guess, for me to say his highness's sirloin will be served promptly.

Really! Does he expect me to ignore his outburst this morning—pretend I enjoyed his rant?

My eyes burn as I scan the cabinet for the soup labeled "Tomato." The boys will gobble up the warm food even if Alex refuses the only nourishment I can muster. I snap the can under the opener. "You're hungry and soup's quick."

"Forget it. I'll eat cereal. Fend for myself like usual." Alex slams the faucet lever forward at the sink, shoving his brawny hands under the spigot and splashing water up the wall.

"Boys upstairs?" I ask, stirring the soup.

Rain No Evil

"What?" Alex says, flicking the dust off his shoulders with a dry dishcloth. "Oh, yeah, upstairs."

"Alex," I say, watching the red soup bubbling like blood in the pan, "You act like you hate me. Do you?"

He scowls over the box of Captain Crunch in his hand. "Are you stupid?"

As he rambles on about how, after fourteen years of marriage, he should know I wouldn't help him with the construction project this morning because I never do, all I can do is stare at the word "Captain" on the box and think, "Oh Captain, My Captain, our fearful trip is done . . . the prize we sought is won . . ." and wonder what treasure I've earned from my marriage, if it's indeed over.

Abe Lincoln won freedom for the slaves while keeping the country intact, but I'm in unchartered water with Blackbeard for a captain and don't trust his guidance to find the love and acceptance I'm searching for. "I did want to help. It was just too heavy."

I scoot the pan off the burner and amble toward the table where Alex is sitting, hoping he'll see the tears trickling off my chin and say that, of course, he doesn't hate me, that he loves me more than he can possibly say in words, but all I get is "Oh, bullshit."

I'd like to smack that smug grin off his face. Arrogant bastard! He thinks he's invincible—so tough no one can hurt him.

Maybe no one can. Maybe he's the tin man.

That would make me Dorothy and right now I want to be anyone, but who I am. Makes me wonder—if I could click my heels and be anywhere; where would I be? Would I be alone, and would alone be better than staying with Alex?

I walk zombie-like to the laundry room in the basement and collapse into a pile of dirty laundry. I want to leave. I want to stay. I want to scream and cry. Why can't I make Alex understand that I just want him to love me—to love me even though I'm not perfect?

Love's supposed to be enough; yet, with him, nothing I do is ever enough. I stopped drinking—started working out, pumping iron and eating fish. Thought if I had a tighter tush, Alex would be happier and that would make me happier by proxy, but that theory's as dried-out as the tears on my face.

Pain sears through my hands. I look down and remove my fingernails that are embedded in my palms. I press my hands to my heart as if the pressure can keep it from pounding out of its cavity.

Guess living in my own warped world helps me relate to troubled teens at Ridgeland High who share stories about how cutting their flesh actually makes them feel better. I'd like to think that, as a teacher, I have better coping skills than they do—mutilating my body has never appealed to me, but my brain— that's a bobber of a toy.

In my search for self-worth, I've become addicted to controlling something in my life that Alex can't control. That something is sex with other men. Even when he found out about a few of the affairs I've had, he forgave me and rightfully so considering his gun-belt replaced his fidelity belt years ago.

But if he finds out I'm cheating again, he may leave me and he could get custody of the boys. He's chummy with most of the judges in the county.

A world without my boys—without Alex is petrifying, like the idea of free-falling through a black hole. Screwing around is not worth the risk of living in a separate house than my boys do, not worth the risk of being known in the community as "Templeton's Cheating Ex," nor possibly living the rest of my life alone, but I need to funnel this pain somewhere so that it doesn't soak the seed of hope inside me, rotting it before I can nourish it with the ability to survive that I have to believe God gave me.

I pull a soft gray sock from the pile beneath my sitting bones and blow my nose. These slashes I'm carving into my cerebrum may be more similar to those etched across the stomachs and wrists of my disturbed students than I care to admit. My struggle to prove to Alex that I can do something right has to be for a reason. Doesn't every struggle have to have a reason?

I have to figure out a way to find peace. I just hope it's not at the bottom of the damn river.

Chapter Two
Stool of Terror

As night settles, I climb in bed, turning away from Alex and curling my legs tight against my stomach. I drift off to sleep, entering a world where Ryan lies beside me. His fingers stroke my round hip, making me feel like he's relishing every moment he's near enough to touch me. His hands smooth my hair and graze my bare shoulders before pulling me closer for a kiss—a kiss I don't feel.

Somehow Ryan's gone, and I'm in a cramped, dingy room cradling a baby girl in my arms. Bringing the baby's smooth cheek to mine, I kiss the infant's fingers, inhaling the fragrance of new life and wondering why I'm taking care of this precious child. I scan the room for the baby's parents, but see no one. My bundle feels lighter. Looking down into my blanket-filled arms I see there's no baby. I scream, but the air is void of sound.

Gasping, I wake and glance at the red *2:30* glowing from my alarm clock. A feeling of weightlessness washes over me as my arms stretch above my head. My body rises effortlessly and floats to a tall stool sitting in front of my dresser—a stool I've never seen before. As soon as I realize it shouldn't be there, I'm sitting on it and watching a fog form around my dresser.

I'm not dreaming anymore. I'm really on this stool even though I don't understand how I got here. My body doesn't look or feel human. The solid, earthly consistency of my familiar physical body is now a transparent spirit form—a fluid motion of iridescent energy with swirls of light coursing throughout and radiating from within.

I stare at my hands, turning my palms over and over again, and watch the aura around them glow like the bioluminescent bay I kayaked through in Puerto Rico, awestruck that I control such extremities and that a single thought sets them into motion.

Michele Savaunah Zirkle Marcum

I am the aura. I am the light, yet I'm still me and I know I'm the observer of a truth not visible unless the veil between worlds is parted—like now. This is unreal, yet more real than any experience I've ever had in the third dimension.

I shudder. I'm not alone. Keeping my head bowed, I peer into the peripheral space to my left and right where sparkling white entities surround me. Somehow I know they are angels.

Without any physical contact or audible command, the angel directly in front of me insists that I raise my head and look into my dresser mirror. I sense the angel can read my thoughts as I silently plead with him to spare me the sight. I know what I will see—the most horrific me I've ever seen—my true self, but my will is irrelevant. I must obey.

My head begins tilting upward. I strain to stop it, but I can't re-gain control and within seconds I'm fixated on my reflection. My entire face looks crispy, carved like a pumpkin and deep-fried with charcoal black scars disfiguring my cheeks and forehead. The crown of my elongated head sways to the left and waves into a tapered point.

My eyes are locked into the windows to my soul, but my blue eyes aren't the only ones staring back at me in the mirror. A demon's gaze is boring through me. I want to escape—to scream and run, but I'm paralyzed as I stare at the grotesque face that's fused to mine. My face *is* a demon's face—pure evil.

I'm unable to bear the macabre vision another second and suddenly crash back into my physical body that's still lying on the bed. I jerk my head off the pillow and snap on the lamp feeling like I've just snorted an ammonia capsule for a record-breaking squat in a power-lifting meet. I scour the room for any remnant of evil emanating from my mirror, ready to scream at the first sight of any spirit, good or bad.

The stool I just sat in is gone. There are no angels or fog. Everything in the room is the same as before.

Everything—except me.

Have I gone mad like Ophelia in Hamlet? Or did I really just see a demon in my reflection? And if a demon's in my mirror, does that mean it has taken residence in my soul, or do demons just pop into people's mirrors on a whim? If it's really in here—inside of me—how long's it been here, and how the hell do I get rid of it?

A terrifying thought grips me. The demon might be able to hear my thoughts right now and, in an effort to prevent me from making it leave, could impale me or eject me from the bed and hurl me toward the ceiling like in a movie I saw about a possessed girl.

I shake Alex's shoulder. "Alex! Did you hear me get out of bed?"

"Huh?" he mumbles.

"You hear me get up?" I ask, still shaking him. I need someone to snap me out of this nightmare or trance.

"What? I'm sleeping." He says, brushing my hand away.

"I walked to the dresser, but not with my feet. Something evil is here," I say, leaning against the headboard and realizing I sound as insane as I feel.

14

Rain No Evil

Alex drapes his arm over my leg. "Oh, Sav. You're dreaming."

I remain silent, hoping it was just a dream, but it seemed real—as real to me as the purple tulips embroidered on the quilt beneath my hand. I need to write about what I just experienced. I dig my journal from the nightstand and something glittery falls off of it and onto the bed. I brush my hand across the sheet, but the glitter is gone. I rub my eyes thinking the bizarre things I'm seeing tonight could be a result of eating too late. Grandma Lennie always told me not to go to bed on a full stomach, but I just thought it was an old wives' tale.

The last entry was . . .

September 20, 2005

Alex and I rode the Harley to Huntington. Over a burger at the shop's diner, he told me about an old college buddy who's divorcing and his wife's getting a portion of his retirement. Alex told me, "When you divorce me just don't take my retirement." He says that all the time and I've asked him to stop joking about us getting a divorce, but he keeps joking about it anyway. Makes me wonder if he really wants one.

When we got outside, Alex grabbed my arm and French kissed me right there in the parking lot. It shocked me. For a moment, head hovering over that Harley, I felt special, like I did in high school when he ran past the cheerleaders after the football game to sling his helmet-laden arm over my shoulder—but then he spoke and broke the spell. "That's what you want me to do, right?" he asked. He doesn't understand that I just want him to be real and do what he feels like doing. I want him to want to kiss me—not feel obligated to. That's what I want.

It stormed on the way home. We drove under a shelter at the dam. Alex called Officer Pete and paced around the bike while we waited out the storm. I wanted him to just sit on the picnic table with me and talk or cuddle, but he just kept laughing with Pete and pacing while I watched the rain splatter onto the concrete, wanting to melt into a puddle myself so I could evaporate when the sun came out.

There's no need to actually disappear though—Alex can't really see me now. I can't explain to him how fragile I feel knowing his idea of who I am is the only opinion I value.

The last sentence sounds so weak—so not me, but maybe his strength counters my weakness, and maybe that's why I strive to meet his expectations in what he thinks a wife should be. I can't ever let Alex find this journal or let him know I'm desperate for his approval. He would think I'm pathetic and pathetic is worse than being the unhelpful bitch he thinks I am.

I write "March 18, 2006," in the journal and scratch out the scariest non-fiction notes I've ever written. I've recorded my dreams since I was a teen, but never had a supernatural event to chronicle until now.

I'm definitely not telling Alex I saw a demon in the mirror. He would tell his officer buddies how loony I am, and every time they would stop by to ridicule some dirtball's latest escapade, they'd say, "So, Savvy. You seen Satan's shadow lately?" and laugh at me, too. But I *am* willing to risk praying aloud in front of my stoic husband. Evil is present in this room—even if it's not in me.

I press my palms together close enough to my mouth that I can feel my breath and invoke aid from the God I can't see—from the One who may not even exist—because, my hope that He *does* is all I've got. Should my belief that a Supreme Being guides me here on Earth ever vanish, I would combust, like a punctured aerosol can, and dissipate into nothingness.

"Good Lord Jesus," I say, "please place angels around me and my family to protect us from the evil that's here. Any evil spirit that is in this house right now, I command you to leave in Jesus name." I toss in what I can remember from Psalms, "The Lord is my Shepherd. I will fear no evil. Thy rod and thy staff comfort me. Amen."

Alex hasn't moved his arm from my leg or cut a joke. He's either scared of whatever it is he thinks I saw or of me having lost my mind—or both.

I bury the journal deep in the drawer, click off the lamp, and ease down into the sheets, smiling at the thought of him being frightened—of anything.

In the morning, I smack the snooze pad feeling woozy like I drank from a trashcan-full of spiked grape Kool-Aid like I did in college. As I untangle my legs from the sheet's grasp, I wonder why my glutes are sore. I didn't hit the weights yesterday.

The image of a sweaty, climaxing Ryan flashes through my mind, and I realize how my hips got a workout without squatting. He made me feel wanted, and sex with him was magical. Now remorse is piling up like the blankets on my bed.

I bury my face in my pillow and breathe in the safe, clean smell of Downy. I'm glad I'm home even though living with Alex is challenging. I'm probably not easy to live with either. I'm selfish with my time. I'd rather read or shop or even clean house than hand Alex a wrench under the hood of a car and he knows that. What he *doesn't* know is my attempts to help him are made with great effort. I genuinely want him to have assistance on his building and repairing projects. I just don't want to be the one who has to provide it. Working with him requires communication, and communication with Alex entails him screaming and me crying. The entire cycle of attempting to understand what he wants from me and of him trying to articulate what he needs is exhausting.

I lumber toward the dresser, a vague sense of dread makes me stop . . . the dresser . . . the mirror—something happened last night. My memory snaps like rubber bands, stinging me with images of my demon reflection, making me feel like I'm bound to the stool of terror again.

Ever since we moved into this house, I've heard knocking in the wall directly behind my dresser, but blamed it on the clamorous, old water pipes located in the adjacent bathroom, not on a demon that's polite enough to knock and wait for an invitation to enter. If that's the case, I certainly didn't intend on extending one with yesterday's outburst in the shower.

With sunlight sneaking into the room through the parted curtains, it's hard to fathom that last night a gruesome face stared back at me in this mirror. I touch the glass. There's not even a fade of fog or of a demon in it now. Was I dreaming, or could there really be a demon in me?

I study my face for a lingering trace of the scars I saw last night, but only see a few creases that retinol can correct and I wonder if the scars I can't see today are visible in another realm.

Can the shame from auctioning my body like it's a Da Vinci knock-off create real dents in my moral flesh? If so, I don't know how to heal those. Maybe I can prevent them if I stop using sex with other men as a way of coping with my un-copasetic marriage.

"Aren't you going to get ready for church?" Alex strolls past naked and swats my rear on his way to the bathroom.

I feel cheaper than I did yesterday when Ryan smacked it. I promised Ryan nothing, but to Alex I pledged, "till death us do part." I'm a liar and a cheat even though I don't want to be.

If what I learned in my evangelical youth group is true, demons don't possess holy people, just sinners. Maybe it was warning me to stop compromising my values and prostituting my soul—and just in time for Sunday, redemption day. Think I'll head the warning—get my ass to church.

I scurry through the hall chanting my favorite morning revelry, "Rise and shine, sweetie pies. Rise and shine." Banging first on Ben's door, then Isaac's, I order them to get their sleepy butts out of bed. I hear a few rumblings of life inside Isaac's room as something that sounds like a pillow hits the door.

Silence greets me at Ben's door so I open it and flip on the overhead light saying, "Come on, sweet-pea, the world's spinning a billion miles an hour. Hop up and join the ride."

Ben tumbles over, his legs jutting over the edge of the bed until his feet touch the floor, so I pop into Isaac's room where he's sitting upright, cell phone in hand.

I accept the progress with a thumbs-up and burst into the bathroom where Alex sits texting on his semi-private throne.

Good. I get the shower first. I slide open the glass door and turn on the faucet.

"I was just getting in there," Alex says.

I smile and yell over the running water, "You snooze, you lose!"

"Snooze! Yeah, right. You kept me up half the night praying crazy shit. Said evil was here. You've lost your mind. You have a nightmare and no one gets any sleep."

The commode flushes. "Ohhh," Alex says, "bet that made your water cold."

"You bet what?" I say, not giving him the satisfaction of knowing I'm freezing.

"Never mind," he says.

When Ben commandeers the bathroom fifteen minutes later, I step into my closet in the hallway—the cubby of a closet in the bedroom I gladly bestowed the use of to Alex—and into a navy skirt, the hem of which I wish, today, extended a little more toward my knee.

I hear Alex asking where his clean underwear are, but I stay quietly sequestered in my closet, the best hideout in the house, and look out the window at the frost-covered backyard, glad that this may be the last day I have to wear tights. Spring whistles in next week carrying the possibilities of fresh starts, and I wonder if I will get mine.

The bowing pine trees remind me I should be on my knees, praying to never again see the macabre vision I did last night. I've read about Shirley MacLaine's out-of-body experiences, but didn't lend them any credence till now.

After morphing into an unfamiliar spiritual plane and playing the un-cordial hostess to a visitor from Hell, I've reconsidered the possibility that my spirit can detach from my body, and I hope that if the demon was real, it was just passing through and hasn't taken up residence in me.

The idea that I had been breathing in a body on the bed made of flesh and bones while simultaneously inhabiting an ethereal one consisting of swirls of energy defies any scientific explanation that I would understand—even if there is one. I saw myself from an aberrant prospective—one that I hope to never see again.

Twenty minutes later, I click out the door in my heels and am still tugging the truck door closed when Isaac says, "Ben won't let me borrow his BB gun. I *always* take care of his stuff. He says I *don't*. It's bull-crap, Mom!"

I guess a peaceful ride to church with my three musketeers is too much to expect. "Ben, what's the big deal about letting him borrow it?"

"Mom!" Ben says, "You know he lost my Mario game and a million other things. He loses *everything*. I'm sick of it! He can use his own BB gun."

"I didn't lose your stupid game, Ben!" Isaac pulls forward using my seat as leverage and peers around my shoulder. "Timmy's coming over today to shoot with me, and he doesn't have one."

Alex backs onto the main road, joining the chaotic chorus. "For criminy sakes, will you all just shut up?"

I wring out a laugh. "Perfect time for a mini-Bible lesson."

"Ah, man. Thanks, Isaac!" Ben says, raising his hands as if praying for divine intervention.

"You guys know who Solomon was?" I ask, turning to my young scholars.

"Yeah, Mom," is fired in unison.

"Let's hear it. What do you know about him?"

"He was a king," Isaac says.

I nod to Isaac and prompt Ben, whose silence announces his cluelessness. "He was king when two women claimed to be the mother of one baby."

"Oh, yeah," Ben says with a nod. "I remember. Solomon said he'd slice the baby in half, but he didn't have to 'cause the real mom said not to." He sticks an earbud in one ear as if the lesson were over.

I snap my fingers until his ear canal is clutter free. "Yep, he was wise enough to know the real mom would allow the other woman to take the baby so he wouldn't kill it. Maybe I'd be wise to lock all the BB guns in the closet so no one can use them." I maintain stare-down mode so they'll think I'm serious, but I'm not. I don't want them inside complaining they're bored. "Isaac, you can borrow the gun, but if anything happens to it, you're buying Ben a new one."

Ben flashes his baby blues at me in protest as Lady Gaga blasts through the car speakers about how she's on the edge of glory. I feel like I'm on the edge of insanity.

Squinting toward Alex who must have wanted to hear anyone except me, I punch the radio knob to stop the intrusion. I wish I had the nerve to punch Alex's nose instead. "Neither of you got exactly what you wanted. That's compromise. Since you two weren't compromising I played the role of Solomon. Guess that makes me wise."

I face forward, pleased with my dispersal of wisdom and wishing all my dilemmas were solved so easily.

Alex pipes up, "Sure, Savvy. If you're so smart, when you going to start making some real money?"

"Yeah, Mom," Ben says. "Make some money."

I pretend to ignore both of them, but I feel like my heart's been punctured like a hot dog on a roasting fork. Alex saying demeaning things to me is bad enough, but he's got the boys doing it. How can I explain to Ben that what he said was hurtful even though he's just repeating what his dad said? I've talked to both the boys before about this same issue and they've laughed it off with an, "Oh, Mom, Dad's just joking."

The boys don't understand that Alex's "jokes" are a comedy in his mind, but a tragedy in mine.

I scribble a check for double the usual amount for our church contribution, hoping God doesn't think I'm bribing Him even though I am. Bribing Him to forget all the compromises I make daily—like my values when I take a lover other than Alex—bribing Him to make me strong enough to stop compromising my self-esteem by permitting my husband to berate me like the only other woman he ever degraded, his mother.

The ten-minute pilgrimage to my mecca in MuddSock Heights seems to take an hour. The second the truck completely stops, the boys fling open the doors to freedom from my presence and the possibility of another lecture as if they're headed to prime seats at the Steelers' game. I follow behind my charges, feeling satisfied for the moral guidance I imparted and relieved to have a break from my duty as peacekeeper.

Once inside the church, my sore derriere meets the hard pew as I join the congregation in singing "I'll fly away" and wish I could. I'd fly up and perch on the neck of the hot guy in the peach shirt sitting two rows ahead. A dimpled boy licking a sucker climbs onto the man's lap. What am I thinking—he's someone's daddy for goodness sake. I tuck my hair behind my ear and my guilt into my gut.

I peel my eyes off of the yummy distraction that Satan himself must have told to sit smack dab in front of me, and force myself to stare into the eyes of Jesus who's painted with outstretched arms and wearing a red robe in the painting behind the pulpit. For the remainder of the song, I force myself to peer into the eyes of the imperial Savior. I wish church could provide a sanctuary wherein my mind was free from temptation, but I guess that's not the way the whole living-holy thing works. I'm going to be tempted just like Jesus was by Satan's proposal on the mountain when the outcast angel promised the Son of God the world, but I'd think the temptation to sin or think lustful thoughts should be less appealing when sitting in God's house.

For the next few verses of an unfamiliar contemporary tune, I study the depiction of my Lord, afraid to unlock my eyes from His even to look at the lyrics on the screen. I move my mouth as if I know the words while silently praying for God to patch the hole in my gut that's leaking decency like a sieve, and fill me with modesty. But maybe it isn't modesty I need as much as love.

As I look into the eyes of my Savior, I envision Him sitting at the well with the woman caught in the act of adultery, looking into her eyes with compassion and filling her with the love she was probably looking for just like I am. I keep staring at the painting, straining to extract love from the eyes of the Man who died for me, hoping that my desire to be filled with His love has a redeeming value that will guide me to just half of the peace the lady at the well received from her divine visit with the Master.

A nudge on my arm and the offering plate drifts past me like the barge floated by on the river. I feel like I'm the only living thing in an irrelevant world—an ant crawling across the glass of a framed still-life painting looking for answers to burst forth and connect me to other living beings—to all that I should know, but must have forgotten—like why God sent me here have this Earthly experience and how to be happy in the process.

I'm looking at the handsome face of Jesus, wondering how many women had tried to seduce Him and how many were successful, when I hear Pastor Todd praying to be led by the Spirit. "God gave us the grace to endure that which we are given—that which He has ordained will be our lot in life. Trials will come, but with God's grace, we will be victorious!"

His voice rises as if he can pierce my heart with the sword of the Spirit just by screaming. "Grace is preferential treatment from the King of Kings. It is not the treatment we deserve, but the treatment that His mercy avails us! Hallelujah!" His fist pounds the pulpit and rattles the attached lamp.

He's on a roll. Not in a holly-roller way like in the evangelical church I was raised in where people spoke in "tongues," yet more enthusiastically than late Grandma Lennie's Presbyterian sermons where I got more sleep than enlightenment.

The pastor's voice fades as my gaze strays from the pulpit and lights again on the man in peach a few rows ahead. I take a deep breath, imagining the scent of his cologne if I were to nuzzle against the nape of his neck and how his quad muscles would feel under my bare butt were I to straddle him right here on the wooden bench.

I pop a mint in my mouth and lay my hand on Alex's knee. If last night's brush with evil was any indication of my depraved condition, I should be daydreaming about devotions, not dicks. I pry my focus from the fantasy to the pastor, whose lips are moving even though I'm not hearing a word, and wonder if I'm the only person here who's conjuring up a sex scene rather than digesting the sermon.

As the altar call is ushered in with the congregation singing, "Would you be free from your passion and pride? There's power in the blood," my spirit moves toward the alter, but pride glues me to the pew. If I grovel to the sinner's bench, Mrs. Zavitch, the lead agent in the gossip ring at school, will come up to me after the service, coddle me in her bosom and assure me that she'll pray for me. She'll say, "Oh, dear, how bad can it be?" The prying little snitch.

No, I'll deal with my demons privately, the obscure, promiscuous ones and the one in my mirror.

The old hymn carries the memory of one other exposure I had to a demon during a Sunday-evening service when I was thirteen. A woman burst through the door of the evangelical church screaming and waving her arms wildly as she ran to the altar. Church members surrounded her and placed their hands on her back and shoulders, praying for God's peace to enter her. Her words were incoherent, and a putrid stench permeated the air when she burped. From several rows back, I smelled the burp, a foul meeting of rotted potatoes and sewer gas. If Satan wore cologne—that was it.

Someone announced that the stranger was possessed by a demon, which prompted parents to herd their young children to the social hall in the basement, mumbling about the possibility that the demon, or worse, legions of them, would jump into the little ones, the same way they'd jumped into swine in the Bible.

The exorcism continued as Preacher Bailey dipped his fingers in the anointing oil and deacons assumed positions closest to the possessed woman. While the deacons held her arms to her sides, the pastor swayed to the rhythm of her jerking body, waiting for the opportune moment to maneuver his oily thumb to touch her forehead. Finally, he succeeded and commanded the evil that plagued the woman's soul to leave, "In the name of Jesus Christ."

After several incantations and enough sweat to fill the Red Sea, a calm disposition replaced the crazed look on the delivered lady's face. Other than her bloodshot eyes and frazzled hair, she appeared normal. Shouts of "Hallelujah," rang out from the brothers and sisters in Christ.

The lady's peaceful demeanor after the prayers left no doubt in my teen mind that she had indeed been possessed and had been set free. But how am I supposed to know if a demon is really in me? I think I already look calm though my insides feel like a nest of wasps as I buzz from one thought to the other . . . from what's my life's purpose to what's for dinner and the ever present, lingering question—how can I continue to live with one foot on the stairway to Heaven and one chained to Satan's bed of fire.

I'm wondering what became of the lady, when I feel a hand on my shoulder and look up to see Alex frowning down at me. Great. He can tell I'm zoned out. I join the crowd that's already standing for the closing prayer, hoping Alex doesn't think something's wrong and interrogate me later.

There's so much wrong I wouldn't know where to begin. I wouldn't know how to tell my husband that I want to stay married, but that I can't unless I feel respected and loved, and he wouldn't grasp the urgency of it if I did. I wouldn't know the words to say that would permeate his being without threatening his ego and making him go off on me. I wouldn't know the words to say that would truly express my feelings of defeat at not being able to put a smile on his face unless cum's coming out his penis—words that would convey the depth of need I have to feel more than respected and loved. I want to feel admired—no—liked. That's it! I want him to simply like me and were I to tell him that, he would tell me I'm stupid—that if he didn't like me he wouldn't have married me.

After the closing prayer, Alex and the boys scurry through the line leading past the door where Pastor Todd is receiving sermon compliments. I imagine Pastor Todd's expression if I were to say, "Great sermon and by the way, any idea how I floated out of my body last night and saw a demon in my mirror. Oh, and do you think it could be a warning for me to stop screwing around?"

I'm up, hand extended, and the only word I can remember from his wisdom is "trials." "Enjoyed the uplifting word on trials," I say while the pastor pumps my hand like he's trying to coax water from a well.

"God is mighty good, Savannah, an all-consuming fire."

I smile, feeling like Dante's inferno is blazing inside me and ready to erupt any moment.

The pastor probably thinks my perky expression is due to his awesome sermon, but I'm still picturing his face were I to tell him that just last night a demon, straight from the lake of Hell-fire, revealed itself in my reflection.

Walking out of the church and into March's coldness, I glimpse the juicy guy whose peach-shirt I'd like to peel off. I tug on my skirt that's wrenched well above my knee and proceed toward my newest delicacy, even if he doesn't yet know he's on the menu. As my hand slides down the handrail, his eyes trail up my leg until they lock into mine.

I know those eyes—those hazel eyes.

The hunk's eyebrows shoot skyward, his right hand extending. "Savannah Templeton! I didn't know you come here."

My hand's just an elbow-bend away, but he withdraws the offer, opens his arms wide, and squeezes me to him for a hug so intense I feel like the string of sinners flowing out of church are conjuring up all sorts of adulterous stories about me for discussion at the dinner table. I pull away and glance at the chatty, hand-shaking crowd who is oblivious to my thoughts and realize it's my imagination that's stripped me naked, within view of the steeple-full of people.

Logan's more buff than last year when he was substitute teaching at Ridgeland High. "What're you doing here?" I say, realizing I sound like church is the last place I'd expect to see him. "I mean, we're all hoping to make it to the penthouse in the sky." I remove my hand that somehow got draped over his wrist. "I heard Kari's dad passed away last month."

Logan scratches his thick eyebrows. "Big fiasco at the church we were going to. It split. About like what happened to your mom's church when you were young, but . . ." He rolls his eyes. "Yeah, Kari's taking it hard. So unexpected. She's in Utah finishing the estate paperwork. She'll be back next week." Logan bends down and picks up the toddler who's pulling on his pants leg. "You still teaching?"

I trace a smile into the air a few inches from the real one shining on my face. "One more grading period till summer break." I tighten my sweater tighter around my middle. "Even if it is colder than a well-diggers ass, umm . . . butt out here." I raise my face, wishing the sunlight would warm my cheeks, and glance toward the car where my men are buckled up and probably arguing over something trivial like which brand of truck is more dependable or how good a football player Alex was in college.

"Restless, hungry men in the car," I say. "Nice surprise seeing you. We all need to get together. Do dinner or something."

"Sure do. Say bye to Savvy," Logan says, waving his boy's hand like it belongs to a puppet.

The little tyke turns and digs his forehead into his dad's broad chest that I'd like to lay mine on.

"He's adorable," I say, stepping off the curb. "You got on at MuddSock Middle, right?"

Logan says, "Yep. And after I complete one more class, I'll be ordained."

Clomping across the brick road, I turn, flashing a thumbs-up. "Congratulations!"

I know he preaches sometimes, but I also know that hug was a few seconds longer than a pastorally embrace hello.

Turning onto the main road through MuddSock Heights, Alex asks me if peach is my favorite color. Sure, Alex can tell I'm attracted to Logan, but I'm not trying to make Alex jealous. I just enjoy talking to someone who actually listens to me. Logan's looks are just a bonus. Alex would listen to me if he thought I had anything worthwhile to say.

My promise to Alex was "till death us do part," but the reality is that I don't know if I'm willing to let the real me die in order to keep it.

"We just talked about his wife. Did you know Kari's dad died a few weeks ago?"

Alex rolls his eyes. "Sure you did."

I *did* ask about her. Even though I could really care-a-less how she is since she fucked Alex. But Kari doesn't know I know about that. Oh, I could write a book about the things people don't know that I know.

"Well," I say, "did you know?"

"Know what?" Alex says.

"That Kari's dad died?"

"Oh, no," Alex says.

"You mean, Oh, no, as in how terrible or no, you didn't know he died?"

"Good God, Savvy! I just said I didn't know. For someone so smart sometimes you're such an airhead."

I look through the bug-covered windshield. The sky, the perfectly divine sky, looks speckled with dirt. All I want is for Alex to understand what I'm saying, but even with twelve years of teaching experience, I'm not able to help him decode the English I'm speaking any more than I can interpret for him the ineffable language of my soul.

Even though he may never understand a word I say, I have to make the effort to make him happy. I can't leave him knowing I had an ounce of effort left.

"Lunch is chicken, baked beans, mashed potatoes. Sound good?" There's silence, so I continue, trying to round up some enthusiasm for my efforts. "And chocolate pie."

Alex answers his phone, "Yeah?"

I hear a male voice on the other end. Sounds like Deputy Stranahan. He's the most veteran officer in Wooten County besides Alex and wouldn't call unless it's important.

"Mom, I'm starving," comes from one of the boys in the backseat.

I turn, finger to my lips with one hand and massaging my cell with the other, hoping Ryan enjoyed yesterday enough to text me.

"Which one called 911?" Alex says, glancing my way.

I watch him driving and talking, jaw clenched, as he maneuvers the car effortlessly past a sidewalk-full of people by the church on the corner. He is never off-duty. He can't just walk out of class when the bell rings like I do. But he chose his profession, just like I chose mine, and I think he wouldn't be satisfied with any career other than law enforcement.

For over two years I've sworn off other men and committed myself totally to Alex, hoping my faithfulness would draw us closer, but my devotion wasn't working even before yesterday when I called Ryan. I look at the phone in my hand. I'm not sure how I'd respond if Ryan did want to hook up again.

"Just let me know if I need to come out," Alex says, hanging up as he pulls into the garage.

"What happened?"

"Damn domestic at Patterson's. I told him last time that someone's getting arrested if I have to come out there again." Alex slams the truck door. "Idiot."

"All I have to do is nuke the potatoes and dinner's ready," I say, holding the side door to the house open for my entourage.

As I step into the kitchen, Isaac's already biting off a chunk of beef jerky and Ben's holding open the refrigerator door with one hand and guzzling chocolate milk from the jug with the other.

"I'm starving! What's for lunch?" Ben says between gulps.

I feel like I'm in a time vortex. Does anyone ever hear me?

Alex, whose fork is stuck deep into a pan of brownies, says, "Yeah, hon. What we having? I could eat my shoelaces."

Chocolate milk sprays out Ben's nostrils and splatters onto the shelves of the open refrigerator.

"Ewww, gross!" Isaac sputters, chunks of Doritos spewing from his mouth to the countertop while Alex coughs up the brownie he's wallowing in his mouth.

My jaws are tight enough to crack a walnut.

I wish I could spontaneously bust out in laughter with them, but if I do, I won't be prepared for that inevitable moment the laughter stops, and Alex is on a tangent again.

I don't want my aggravation at being unheard to ruin the light-heartedness of this moment for my jovial tribe so I swipe the counter with a rag, punch start on the microwave and say, "Fortunately, my dear, you won't have to."

Chapter Three
SURFING FOR SURVIVAL

Alex is scooping the last of the potatoes from his plate when Stranahan calls needing assistance. Stranahan's got the Patterson domestic covered, but he's got two other domestics pending and a toddler in ER with fractures from possible child abuse. There's only two other county officers in the sparsely populated Wooten County. Gilmore's got to cover night shift, and the rookie can't take a call independently yet, so Alex scurries to the basement for his uniform.

While Isaac coaxes Ben to the TV room for a PlayStation match, I sit alone at the table wondering if child abusers see demons in their mirrors. Surely, if sin attracts demons then child abusers would be at the top of hell's visitation schedule. Even considering my marriage vows, me having sex with another adult can't be as evil as breaking an innocent kid's arm or sticking a two year old in scalding bath water.

Suddenly, I hear water *splat* against the kitchen wall. I whip my head toward the direction of the noise. Water is dripping off the cabinets and part of the wall, but there's no water spraying now.

I quickly dry the kitchen and decide not to mention the water leak to Alex today. He's got enough to deal with right now getting called out on his day off to deal with the scum-bucket child abuser. Scum-buckets, as Alex calls them, aren't just criminals—they're pond scum, the most deviant of dirtballs, and it's his job to and to put them behind bars.

When Alex charges out in his blue stallion of a cruiser, I shuttle the boys to Tommy's house and glide off to Ridgeland's levy to form a plan for survival—how to either keep breathing in the same house with Alex or how to embark on a voyage of my own and employ the universe to resuscitate me.

My retreat that overlooks the Ohio River and offers a panoramic view of downtown MuddSock Heights is all but vacant today. Must be too cold for even the addicts to buy a fix from the maroon pharmacy-on-wheels.

I turn off my car knowing it won't stay off long—within a few minutes I'll be cranking the heater. I recline my seat to watch the teasing sun shine onto the river, melting the ice and creating a mist that float along with the current.

I hear children laughing as they sled-ride past me and down the small hill on the remnant carpeting of snow and it reminds me of my sister, Luce. Sled riding was the only time she didn't seem to mind actually wrapping her arms around me.

Back when the snows were deeper and the winters longer, Luce and I would round up the neighborhood kids and trounce off for what seemed like a mile hike to "Thomas's Mountain." The hill was actually only a block away, but it was our Alps complete with snow-covered chalets where neighbors from Harbor to Sycamore Streets gathered for the cider and the company as much as for the thrill of descent.

A spackling of brightly colored coats and toboggans against the backdrop of white gave the appearance that the slope was decorated with moving, dancing bulbs. Luce would sit huddled tight between my legs. The next in line behind us would give us a push and we were off—flying, tears streaming as the cool wind stung our eyes. On a tightly packed snow, the red sled with metal rails would transport us all the way to the edge of the road. We weren't always this lucky, but for one successful trip, we would try ten times.

Mom would be home reading, a meatloaf and cream pie in the oven. Even though she wasn't out frolicking in the snow with us, we knew she would be there, ready to listen to our gigglings of snowball fights and sled-tippings into the frosty bath of white.

A boy screaming, snaps me to the present. The windshield is fogged-over so I whip out of the car, searching toward the direction of the squeals. Standing on the river's edge is a boy who's leaning over so far he could fall in any second. Someone is flailing about fifteen feet out. There's no way he can reach that far.

I'm beside him without feeling my feet touch the ground.

"My sister!" he screams.

I look toward the spot where I just saw the girl, but she's gone. *Damn.* I'm kicking off my shoes and jumping into the icy cold before I process what I'm actually doing. I'm swimming as fast as Linda Blair's neck spins, my arms slicing through the water as I try to catch sight of the girl. *Where is she? God help me. I don't want to die out here.*

I see a dark shape bobbing barely above the surface and with one long stroke, grab a fistful of hair, yanking her to the surface and propping her head on my shoulder. She's not coughing—might not be breathing.

I've never been this cold. It's hard to think, but I remember playing the drowning victim for Alex when he practiced for his lifeguard license. He had grabbed me under the arms from behind—said it's less likely I'd pull him under, but it's all I can do to just hold onto her. No way can I get behind her.

I tuck her head to my chest and backstroke, slashing toward the shore.

Just when I think the current is winning, I feel my feet sink into the riverbed. I can touch! Her elbow hits my nose. She's fighting me, but at least she's alive. I dig my heels in, striving to gain leverage and get a wallop to the face again. One last heave lands me on my rear on the riverbank.

I'm numb. I can't feel the boy pulling his sister from my arms, but I see him. He shakes her frigid little body. The girl's young—five years old if that. She gurgles. Her coughing sounds like choirs of angels.

I try to cup my hands around the angel-girl's face, but my fingers won't budge. I have to get warm. "The car," I say as she slides her arm behind my back and presses her head into my abdomen.

We all stagger up the hill, the boy and I flanking the angel in the middle like we're her wings.

In the car, I try to turn the key in the ignition, but I can't grip them with frozen fingers so I have the boy do it.

Kneading the palm of my hand down my calf, I manage to remove my soaked socks, extend my toes to where the heat's blowing from under the dash and dial 911.

"What's your name?" I say, peering through the rear view mirror and into the backseat where the girl is laying against her brother's chest.

"Toby," he says, rubbing her arm.

The emergency dispatcher answers and I say, "Need an ambulance at the Ridgeland Levy. A girl almost drowned. I got her out . . . yes, in the parking lot at Ridgeland levy. No. No, parents here. Ok, hold on . . ." I ask the boy, "Toby, what your sister's name?"

Toby says, "Madi, well, Madison."

"Last name?" I say.

"Johnson."

I relay the names and hang up, reluctant to move my feet from the heat, but I need to check on the girl. I turn to the back seat. The girl is so pale it looks like she's a vampire in a Twilight series. Now that I'm getting a good look at them both, I'm certain I've not seen them before and I know most of the kids around here. "Hi, Madi. You're going to be okay. You hurt anywhere, honey?"

Madi doesn't move her head that's snug to Toby's chest.

"Where you live, Toby?"

"Pine Street," he says.

"Who with?" I ask vaguely, having learned to be tactful by dealing with the students I work with at school who are often living in dysfunctional homes.

"Mom and Grandma and Grandpa."

"Where'd you live before you moved here?" I ask, noting the sound of sirens echoing through the valley. Quick emergency response—one of the perks of living in a small town.

"Kentucky," Toby says.

"That where your dad still is?"

Toby nods as the squad squeals up beside us. A paramedic knocks on my window. I point to the back seat and tell Toby to open his door. No way am I getting out of this toasty car.

Toby and Madi are shuffled into the back of the squad and the paramedic asks me to join them—says I could have hypothermia and should go to the hospital as a precaution.

I'll probably get one hell of a cold, maybe even pneumonia, but I don't have it now, so I sign a waiver for treatment. I just want to get home.

As I push on the gas pedal, I realize I'm not wearing shoes, but I'm not going back for them. They can float down the river along with my sentiments of wanting to be buried in the deep. I want to live. I'm not sure whether I'll be living with or without Alex, but I believe I'm in this world for a reason. I just saved that little girl and feel amazing knowing she's alive because of me. I want to feel this helpful all the time. I just have to figure out how.

How could I even have a demon in me? If I did, I would think the demon would have prevented me from performing such an honorable deed. If I don't, maybe I've earned a degree of vindication from God for saving her.

At home, I walk into the kitchen where Alex is un-tucking his uniform shirt. He pulls a carrot stick out of his mouth and takes a gander at me. "What the hell?"

I trail across the tile floor toward him, dripping with each step and wrap my shivering arms around his waist, thick from the bulletproof vest that's still strapped on. I lay my head on his vest-covered chest, my drenched locks sticking to my face, and close my eyes, allowing the strength of the love I believe to be burning in his heart, to fortify me.

"You're soaked," Alex says, clasping my shoulders and prying me from his chest.

"I jumped in the river to get this girl," I say, wanting to stay pressed to him, but not sure how to tell him I just want held.

"You did what?" He leans back and looks down at me.

"At the levy."

"That was you?"

"You heard already?" I say, finagling the wet hoodie up my torso.

Alex's eyes soften into his wrinkled forehead making him look more like a pug than a pit bull. He seems to care that I'm safe, but I'd sure like to hear him actually say it. He plucks my hoodie off my arms as I stretch overhead.

"The ambulance got called to the levy when I was leaving the hospital. So, how far out you have to swim to get the girl?"

Rain No Evil

"Maybe ten feet," I say, my jeans sticking to my legs as I worm them off. "I don't know, just knew I had to get her. I'm wiped out. Going to get a bath."

Suds are up to my neck when Alex steps into the bathroom wearing only a white t-shirt that barely covers his belly. He squeezes behind the door to where the commode sits.

"There wasn't anyone else there to help her," I say, talking to Alex's back that's reflecting in the mirror above the sink. "Except her brother and he didn't jump in. Guess he couldn't swim. Or maybe he was too afraid."

I turn the faucet hoping there's more hot water. "When I grabbed her, I knew it was just like the premonitions I've had."

Alex's bug-eyed expression now reflects in the vanity mirror. "Premo what?"

"I keep having dreams—premonitions, about saving babies."

"Oh, bullshit! You really believe that crap, don't ya?"

Wish I'd have kept my mouth shut. Wish he'd just be proud of me for being brave, but I know better than to expect that. "Why were you at the hospital?" I ask, picturing his goofy face spiraling down the drain of his sink.

"You know I had a child abuse to check out there," he says, toothpaste dribbling off his chin. "What were you doing at the levy anyway? It's just a bunch of druggies."

I dunk my head into the warm bubbles and wonder where all the druggies were when the girl needed saving. They would have been numb already and not have felt the icy plunge—that is if they would have attempted to save her.

When I come up for air, Alex is facing me and flossing his teeth. Guess I will have to tell him why I was at the levy. "I just enjoy being near the water. It's beautiful and relaxing," I say, standing up. "Can you hand me a towel?"

Alex opens the cabinet door. "Maybe if you stayed home once in a while we'd have some clean towels," he says, tossing me a damp one from the hook on the back of the door. He raises his bushy eyebrows and chuckles. "Yeah, if you like water so much why don't you camp out in the laundry room and watch the clothes spin through the glass door of the washer."

I wrap the towel tight around my breasts, wondering what would happen to Alex if he were literally in my shoes that are probably floating downstream by now. A little concrete poured in them and I wouldn't have to decide whether to leave him or not. He would just be gone.

Car doors slam as I'm pulling on stretch pants. A few minutes later, I secure hugs from the Ben and Isaac—hugs that are a little tighter and longer than usual—and herd them to the living room couch. Their eyes shine as I describe my freezing river rescue of the girl..

I'm groggy and must have fallen asleep because the next thing I know, I'm waking up on the couch, my cheek stuck to a squashy pillow-full of drool. I remember the look of pride on the boys' faces as I told them of my brave rescue. I could tell they admired me. They both deserve to grow up in a stable family environment and I reckon, even with our shortcomings, Alex and I are more secure and nurturing than many families in Wooten County. I don't want to disappoint them—make them grow up in a divorced family like so many of the kids I work with at school. That seems worse than accepting Alex's disrespect.

The inspiration to connect to Alex pushes me off the couch and into redemption mode. I've got to make peace with Alex.

I sashay into the bedroom wearing a silky black negligee with pink hearts, not a smidgeon of pimple cream on my face, and flop into bed belly-first. Arching my back in cat pose, I drag myself next to Alex who is sprawled out watching TV in his best Fruit of the Looms, and nudge my crotch onto his thigh. "You tired?" I say, watching the flickering light from the television play across our intertwined legs.

Alex squeezes my shoulder. "Not really."

A picture of Alex's red face looming over the busted drywall this morning skitters across my mind, and lingers for the few moments his hand is on my shoulder. "Damn it, Savvy, Can't you do anything right?"

Releasing the images and sounds from the past, I join the more vulnerable Alex—the one that's in my bed—and focus on the one foolproof thing I know I *can* do right. It's the only common thread we seem to have, and I'm gripping it until it until the rope burn slices my hand.

If I have to swallow my disgust for Alex along with his semen in order to maintain the pretense that all is well with the Templetons—that's what I will do. Yes, indeed. If, by having sex with Alex, I can maintain a bond with him that will present the preponderance of a stable family unit for my two boys, then I will gladly spread my legs further than the wishing bone from a Thanksgiving turkey.

Inching closer to my hubby, I lower my cheek until it grazes his massive chest. He smells of Irish Spring. I close my eyes, teasing his belly button with my finger. "So, did the guy, uh, Patterson, put up a fight when you got there?"

Alex strokes my head. "Nope. He knew better. Didn't even use handcuffs—just threw him in the back of the cruiser."

I once suggested Alex cuff me—make me his prisoner and get dirty with me in the back of the cruiser, but he laughed and told me it was an "Improper use of county property," even though I know the dirt in his cruiser isn't just from the dirtballs he rolls into it. His cruiser seats have fondled more than one bare-assed woman even if he insists it's off-limits for such purposes.

I know I don't have a right to care, but it still hurts to know he screwed Kari and the others before her. Sex is the one thing I do to Alex's satisfaction, and knowing someone else can satisfy him too makes me feel that the one talent I can demonstrate to Alex that is exclusively mine, isn't good enough either.

Ryan would crank those metal conduits to masochism on in a heartbeat, but Alex can't be that playful with me. Alex and I have our sex mapped out in our heads before our lips even touch. To venture into a playfulness with Alex would be to expose my girly side—the sweet, silly, childlike side that giggles and cries and doesn't have all the answers—that frilly side of me I can only let other men see.

They can't hurt me like Alex can. I actually care what he thinks of me. I love him.

Suddenly, it occurs to me that if I'm seeking sex with other men, not for the sex, but for the satisfaction of feeling like I can accomplish something on my own—without Alex—without his knowing or ordering or smart-ass remarks, maybe he has sex with other women because he wants to experience a part of his life without me. Maybe he wants something he's missing that he can't find with me. If that's why he's messed around on me, I can accept his indiscretions, but I don't know if talking with him about it is a good idea. Talking seems to always create more problems than we already have.

My tongue slithers along Alex's abdomen, leaving a trail of moisture from his chest to his groin where I stay, gifting him with a generous tongue-lashing. His hands press on my shoulders, stopping me before he climaxes, his strong arms pulling me onto him. "You could make a living at that, babe."

I wish he'd remain my silent prisoner rather than attempting to say something nice. The idea of making money from securing someone's dick in my mouth makes me want to gag, but its Alex's idea of a compliment so I say, "Well, thank you, Sir." He always manages to butcher compliments until there's nothing left but minced bone.

"You probably already are," he says. "How much you charging?"

I spit his penis out of my mouth and it flops onto his stomach. If I charged, it would be toward him with a machete, not an invoice. I'm glad my bangs are hanging over my eyes, obscuring his crass face from view. The thought of looking into his eyes right now makes me feel sleazier than I feel pleasuring men I'm not married to. At least with Ryan, I expect he just wants me for sex, but Alex is supposed to enjoy my company so much he wants to rock into the golden years with me, or so he told me years ago.

I'm not answering his question. He won't believe me if I tell him I'm being faithful. I should tell him that I just want to feel appreciated. That I want to feel capable and successful when I'm with him, not like some peon he orders around, but I just climb on top of him and rare my head like the blonde-haired stallion that I am.

He clutches my face, licking up my neck until our lips meet. His tongue swirls inside my mouth, making me feel like I just got off the "Scrambler" at the carnival. I suck on his tongue, coaxing it into my mouth, but he withdraws it and tightens his lips. He never lets me control his tongue for more than a second, although he's obsessed with manipulating every word that rolls off mine.

I feel him inside me and imagine that he's a total stranger—he's never hurt me or loved me or held our newborn in his arms. He's just a man with a hard dick who can hoist me into oblivion with each jab into my delicate hole.

I'm a cowgirl tonight, riding this horse till it sweats—or at least until

I can buy it a beer. The country tune plays in my head until I climax to numbness . . . for a few trots, anyway. Cowgirl down.

Chapter Four

RAINING BABIES

A headache and Alex wishing me a "Happy Birthday, old woman," wakes me. "Older women are hot!" he says, rolling out of bed and smacking my rear that's buffered by the quilt.

"Just four months older," I say turning so his kiss will land on my cheek rather than my mouth that tastes like a frog just shit in it. I nuzzle my cheek against his stubbly chin and sigh. He remembered my birthday.

Alex flips on the overhead light and scavenges his drawer, probably in search of black knee highs with elastic that hasn't dry rotted. "I got to get new socks. Just like these," he says, displaying a pair he pulls from the drawer like a magician pulling a rabbit out of a hat. He sits on the edge of the bed, and slips on his find. "Where you want to eat tonight?"

"Eat?" I say.

"Cornerstone Quarry? Mexican?" He tugs at the second sock.

"Didn't know we were going out tonight, but the Quarry sounds good," I say, hopping out of bed. "Next weekend we're celebrating Luce's and mine together—one cake, less calories."

"I always take you out on your birthday, don't I? You get everything you want." Alex's soft brown eyes—the ones I fell in love with—seem to plead for reassurance that my heart's still in cadence with his.

He sinks his hands into the mattress and leans forward to get up, but I step between his legs until my cleavage is a breath away from his face.

My hand sculpts his prickly jaw-line. "Yes." I smile. "Yes, you do feed me well." I'd like to tell him that I have everything I've ever dreamed, but it's too early in the morning to finesse that lie. I wrap my hands around the back of his neck and pull his head toward my chest. "You've got yourself a date."

Alex tenderly kisses my breasts, and I hope the tranquilizing effect lingers with me all day.

After school, the boys squirrel away in the basement playroom with X-box and a snack while I flip through my closet in search of my favorite mint-colored sweater. I'm spraying perfume on my neck in anticipation of the romantic birthday dinner Alex promised me this morning, when my cell rings.

"Hey, I'm not gonna make it for dinner," Alex says. "Sorry, babe. Meant to call earlier. Balls to the wall all day. I'm starving. Haven't eaten since breakfast. Can you get me a few snacks together?"

He doesn't wait for an answer.

"I'll stop by in a few to pick 'em up. Got a possible murder—might be tied to the Mafia case. A body just washed up on the riverbank in Coraltown."

I slap peanut butter and jelly sandwiches together, throw the standard snack for such an occasion—protein bars and Rice Krispy treats—into a plastic Walmart bag, some bottled water and sweet tea into another. Alex isn't the lunchbox type of guy—carrying one for lunch would be considered gay, but bungee the same bright yellow lunchbox onto the back of an ATV or, four-wheeler, as referred to in these parts, and it's a redneck necessity.

The screaming siren beats Alex home. I slip on my shoes, making it outside just as the unmarked SUV careens into the driveway. Alex rolls down the window and plants a kiss on my cheek as I hand him the food and ask, "Know anything else?"

"Just some women walking along the floodwall path found a body—male and the crime scene team's already on its way. Stranahan's there and says there's a bulldog tattoo on the guy. Could be an informant of mine who was helping me build a drug case against the Mafia." Alex pops the cap off a sweet tea, the contents spraying his pants and the steering wheel. "Shit," he says. "Anyway, could be a Mafia hit. I'll call ya later."

I send a prayer with him as he squeals away and ask God to protect him and all those who guard the community with diligence. I'm proud of Alex, even though the intrusion on our private lives requires adaptation and patience, especially after the move from Ridgeland's rural countryside to Aspen Road, the main road leading to the county seat of Coraltown. The location, although heavily trafficked, can't really be considered town, not when a rooster can be heard crowing from the neighbors in the back and a goat bleats a few houses down.

I stand in the drive admiring my white, two-story house, porch wrapping around the side like a hug awaiting loved ones.

I just love this place.

This structure houses some of my dearest memories like the Christmas Alex sawed down the Chevy Chase tree that was so tall Ben, who was five, could sit under the lowest branch. And last summer when I talked Alex into foregoing the grass mowing to play badminton in the backyard and sit Indian-style with only a blanket between us and the ground just like when I was a kid. The graham crackers we dipped into plastic cups of applesauce that day left a taste of happy in my mouth that I couldn't get enough of. What I wouldn't give to mummify that unpretentious Alex!

I want to collect more of those types of memories, but the rusted bronze plaque that reads "Templetons Established 2002" hanging above the garage door makes me wonder if there will be an end date like a tombstone epitaph or if Alex will learn to embrace the simple side of me—the side that enjoys picnicking more than pretending to be perfect.

A few more police cars go screeching by, and I wave and watch the cars pull off the road to let them by. Movement is constant in front of the house, cargo trains clacking along on the railroad tracks across the road, barges heaped with coal putting along the river, cars and trucks zooming past in the fifty five mile per hour zone, even four-wheelers and golf carts bumping by on the side of the road.

Well, usually on the side. A few brazen souls maneuvering a form of transportation not road worthy, including riding lawn mowers, often veer into the middle lane after snapping their heads around and noting that "Taze Templeton" isn't perched on the porch. Alex earned the nickname because he doesn't utilize his taser—he doesn't have to; his reputation is his main weapon. If that isn't enough, his fists usually are.

More often than not, a vehicle ventures into our drive carrying a victim who hopes Taze is home to give advice or offer assistance for a wrong that needs to be righted. When he isn't available, I smile and take messages for everything from incorrigible children to where to find the best of this year's crop of wacky weed, but being in secretary mode at home and during my routine teaching day, on grocery runs and during kid's ballgames, requires a cordiality that I'm not always eager to disperse.

Members of the community may mistake my aloofness for conceit, especially when I struggle to identify the familiar face or name, but Alex knows everyone and I'm expected to as well.

My house serves as the community's lost and found drop-off with many items handed to me through a half-open screen door: a shotgun, a pack of pills, a random person's driver's license found in the woods.

I know exactly which window gives the best vantage point of the driveway while providing adequate concealment and which one for the side door or the front door, depending on where the do-gooder or drug dealer happens to head. At a glance, I ascertain if, during the exchange, I will be more comfortable outside or, on a rare occasion, extend an invitation inside.

This strategy works quite well for me, given the person isn't on foot, like the evening a knock at the unused side door transported in a barefoot lady, blood splattering her face and neck, stammering about how her husband was hurt, and she needed to use the phone to call the ambulance. While I turned to get the phone, wielding the standard interrogation—where did she live and how did her husband get hurt, the feeble stranger hobbled across the living room pointing north to indicate her place of residence and described hitting her dear hubby over the head with an ashtray.

Minutes later Alex, who had ran upstairs to put a pair of shorts over his undies, entered the room and admitted that getting a confession that quick was not too bad for a novice, especially since I didn't have to dunk the assailant's head into a commode to get it.

Alex's dedication to justice often trumps acceptable moral standards. Harboring the means to benefit the community at large seems to be an un-recited creed with the officers in Alex's command, and thanks to them, citizens in Wooten County leave their doors unlocked—at least in the daytime. Alex's methods may be rustic, even severe, but he's the good guy—the one a person wants on his side when his child's molested or his home's shot up and burglarized—or like tonight, when a murderer may be on the loose.

"Mom! Hey! Where's Dad going?" Ben says, crunching through the gravel drive toward me and clicking the channels of the portable scanner that's in his hand so often it seems to be an extra appendage.

I cock my head and smile. "What? You mean you don't already know?"

Ben scrunches his mouth. "Well, I heard a DOA. Is that it—he's out on a dead body?"

I drape my arm over his shoulder as we walk toward the house to the cadence of radio static. "You got it. A dead body on the riverbank in Coraltown. Might be a Mafia hit. That's all I know."

"Wow. Do we really have a Mafia? I thought those were just in big cities like New York." He stops clicking channels and lifts the radio to his ear.

The dispatcher repeats, "Control to CN1."

"CN1, go ahead." Alex says.

"CN1, CN5 wants you to public service him."

Alex gives a 10-4 while I follow Ben into the kitchen. "You know what public service means?" I say.

"Yeah, they want Dad to call on the phone. To call Stranahan—he's five."

"Right. Must be information too private for the radio." I stack plates from breakfast into the dishwasher and notice there's been no water spraying inside the house today.

"So," Ben says, opening a pack of peanut butter crackers and, seeing I've spaced-out adds, "What about the Mafia?"

"With all of Pawpaw Cal's old police stories, I'm surprised you haven't heard the Mafia ones," I say. "Been one around here for years."

"Cool, I'm asking Pawpaw as soon as I see him," Ben says.

"Asking pawpaw what?" Isaac says, running in and grabbing a bag from the snack drawer.

"Dad's out on a DOA," Ben says, "Man, Dad's job's awesome! I can't wait to be a cop."

"What's a DOA?" Isaac says, chouncing on a pretzel.

"Dead on Arrival," Ben says. "Duh!"

"You guys want to go out to eat with your mama for her birthday? Your dad was going to take me out, but someone had to go and get murdered."

Ben's jaw drops. "Oh, happy birthday, Mom."

I can tell Ben feels bad for not remembering, so I spread my arm, calling out, "Hugs from my babies—best gift a mom could ask for."

Ben squeezes me tight.

"Yeah, happy birthday. Where we going?" Isaac says, pulling open the door without grabbing his jacket

"Doesn't matter to me," I say, trailing behind my little men. Anything I don't have to prepare sounds divine.

Alex is still out when we return from our celebration so I send the boys to tackle their homework as I switch on *Sex and the City* and fantasize about being a cool, single Carey Bradshaw, writing by day, screwing by night, after a fabulous dinner at the trendiest of restaurants.

Bradshaw's comical search for true love gives me hope that I won't have to always settle for a hamburger and a quickie bent over the seat of a Harley. With Central Park in the background, Carrie tells Mr. Big, "I've done the merry-go-round. I've been through the revolving door. I feel like I met somebody I can stand still with for a minute and . . . don't you wanna stand still with me?"

I'm wondering if Alex and I will ever stand still and just enjoy being with me, when my cell buzzes. I ignore it, opting to participate in my on-screen life, but after numerous dings, I check out my texts, most of which are from nosey people I rarely hear from. Word about the body is out, and nothing makes friends, for me, faster than a possible murder.

None of the prying people even know it's my birthday, but they sure know my cell number when they want the latest scoop. There was no announcement at school today from a well-wishing co-worker making fun of my age—no cake in the teacher's lounge with my name on it. Oh, Joanne would have brought a cake if she'd have remembered, but her years of service to the kids of Ridgeland High have worn her down, and her memory isn't what it used to be.

A paralyzing thought grips me. I may be as unlikable to my co-workers as Alex is to me. If I seem that bossy or arrogant or obnoxious then no wonder I haven't had one cake presented to me at school in the grungy teachers' lounge during the twelve whole years I've worked there. But Mrs. Z gets cakes and even casseroles on her birthday, and no one's more snobby than she is so that shoots my theory.

I don't know why I care about what my co-workers think anyway. I'll buy my own damn cake and eat a sliver of it, not three slices then waddle down the hall, complaining about my rheumatism.

An alert flashes across the screen of the local cable channel. "Body washes up in Wooten County. More on this breaking story on tri-state news at eleven." I head to bed and indulge a few friends with texted tidbits I can share: the body is male, a few ladies walking on the floodwall path found it, and yes, the crime scene team was called out hours ago.

I fall asleep with the phone in my hand, and at 2:00 a.m. I'm vibrated awake by a call from Alex and put him on speaker.

"I'm pretty sure it's my informant, Hank. He was a Marine and the bulldog tattoo on the body has the letters "USMC.""

"What's that mean," I say, squinting and scrolling through my texts.

"United States Marine Corp," Alex says. "It's not going to be an easy one. Going to take a lot of resources. No leads yet, but I'll be out all night with CSI."

"Okay, love ya," I say, hanging up and clicking on a text from my love bear, Ryan. He wants me to come over tomorrow evening, but doesn't mention my birthday. I figure I'm tired and feeling overly sensitive, so I decide to wait till morning to respond to him.

I drift off to sleep where I'm ass-deep in a hammock at Hilton Head with a cocktail in my hand and a drizzle of afternoon sun kissing my skin through the palm tree I'm under. I'm swaying to the rhythm of reggae when a body washes onto shore, belly distended, and a stiff, cold hand reaches out and grabs my arm, pulling me under. I kick furiously trying to keep my head high enough to breathe, but I'm choking on the water filling my lungs and rain is falling on my head.

Suddenly, it's raining more than rain—it's raining babies. *Plop. Splat.* They're falling all around me as I gasp for air, wanting to save them, wanting to catch them, but . . . are they dead already? No, I hear them crying.

I awaken to the shrill sound of my own screams, in a sweat, panting, praying for babies I can't save. I grope the various bottles in my nightstand until I feel the grooved lid on the Excedrin and pop two in my mouth. I'm tired of dang baby dreams and headaches.

It's five a.m. and Alex's side of the bed is unoccupied. I rest my hand on his pillow, hoping he is safe and wondering how I would feel if he never came home. A moment of relief at the idea of being free from him, followed by guilt at such a thought, convinces me I damn well don't deserve a cake from anyone, not from co-workers who only pretend to like me, or from my hard-working husband who was supposed to take me out to dinner tonight.

In the morning, I wave to Isaac from the end of the driveway where he's climbing onto the school bus while Ben cranks up the heater in the car. Isaac prefers not to ride the bus to the elementary school. I'd drop him off if I didn't have to wake up fifteen minutes earlier to get him there.

Plunking into the driver's seat, I smile over at Ben. "Nice. Not one grinding sound."

Ben beams as I back out of the driveway. "How old were you when Pawpaw

Cal taught you to drive, Mom?"

"Nine, sweetie."

"Geez! I'm fourteen. I get to practice with him this summer, right?"

"Guess so."

"Dad's cruiser's not here. He been out all night?" Ben asks.

"Yep. He called in the middle of the night. The body might be an informant he was working with named Hank. Mum's the word, you know."

Ben dips his head to the obviously redundant remark.

As we pull onto campus, students are disembarking from the first fleet of busses in front of the junior high doors—not a moment too early, as usual.

"Mom, you still got those cookies in your room?

"Stocked up just for you," I say, pulling into my spot.

"Good. I'll be in at lunch with Cole and Andy," he says, hopping out and joining the stream of students heading through the doors to the illusion of enlightenment.

Grinning, I grab my tote bag and scurry to within a few steps of him. "Sure, bring 'em all. Convenient being at the same school with your ole mom, huh? And last year you thought it would be embarrassing."

"Just keep bribing me with food, ole woman," Ben says, his jaw opening wide.

I look at my oldest son, his face contorted like Jim Carrey's in *The Mask,* and I snort out an impromptu laugh, knowing this connection is what life's all about.

Ben holds the main door open until I walk through, dodges through the throng of kids and finds the bench by the office where his best bud, Cole, is waiting on him. It's the same routine every morning, but today an inexplicable joy fills me. I feel like royalty and I'm sure it's because Ben introduced a little humor into my rigid lungs.

When Ben gets married, I hope he treats his wife with respect and allows room for humor in his life. More than anything, I hope that Alex's behavior hasn't damaged either of the boys to the extent that it has me.

"Your anus has rings around it," a male voice says. I snap my head around in the direction of the comment.

Two seventh grade girls bump against me, jarring my lunch bag as they look over their shoulders and snicker at a boy about their age that must have made the remark. "Sorry, Mrs. Templeton," one of the girls says.

I glare at the boy and say, "Language alert." That's usually enough to cease inappropriate talk and keep me from having to write up every cuss word I hear in a day, but today, the smile on his face pisses me off, and my hand goes to my hip.

"Oh," he says. "That was a joke. Mr. Dingess told it in science. You know there's a planet called Uranus."

"Good ole Mr. Dingess," I say, shaking my head and remembering why I avoid the slaphappy seventh and eighth grade side of the building. Unless I'm taking a Tylenol to Ben or collecting make-up assignments for a sick student, I'm content with the high-schoolers who just skip class or fall asleep in it.

When I subbed at the Elementary level, I knew pandering to the younger audience wasn't for me. Teaching high-school has its advantages—no early morning duty with cute, little crusty-eyed people needing help opening milk cartons and ripping foil off plastic cereal bowls. All I have to do is lumber in as the bell rings, toss my lunch into my mini-frig, and stand in the hall listening to teachers and students gossip amidst the slam of lockers. If there are rumblings of a fight or a break-up or even a teacher firing for misconduct, this is the time to collect the tantalizing data.

I sign the attendance log in the copier room by the office and hurry along the corridor, reaching my room a few doors down just as Mrs. Zavitz is opening her classroom door across the hall. With a mangled mouthful of what appears to be her favorite breakfast—a sausage biscuit—she summons me over by tossing her head like she's fly-fishing. I trudge her way.

Mrs. Z gulps, diverting her bulging eyes toward the floor and covers her mouth as if she's calling plays for the Super Bowl. "I saw the news about the body last night. Do you know who it was?"

I glance down the hall. Mr. Feldman's holding a dingy Styrofoam coffee cup and talking with Tess, the custodian. Feldman's eye catches mine so I rest my bags at my feet and motion for him and Tess to join us. Huddled around like students buzzing about the latest suicide attempt, my peers lean in while I share slivers of inside information about the murder, making sure to omit the name "Hank," because no one's dropped it yet.

After repeating the same report all morning, I'm tempted to say that I know nothing, but I feel special knowing things other people don't—like which soccer mom is porking the preacher, which attorney has a fetish for getting defecated on, and which principal masturbates on the football bleachers when he thinks no one is watching.

I know I'm being manipulated because most of the people who talk to me like I'm their long lost friend when they want to know something, usually don't acknowledge I exist, but I can't resist the feeling of importance that providing information gives me.

After school, Isaac, who rides the bus from his elementary school to mine, clamors through my classroom door and zip-lines to the cookie cabinet. "I'm hungry," he says, plopping onto the counter where Ben's sitting and munching on a cookie.

Fortunate for me, tonight's "Two for Tuesday" at Pizza Bravo, buy one pizza and get one free—perfect for two hungry boys and one tired mom, so we drive off to the deal.

Ben is jabbering to Isaac in the backseat about how seventh grade classes are so much harder than Isaac's fourth grade ones and how Mr. Dingess's "Two whole pages of homework" is proof when Alex calls.

"Where are you?" Alex says.

Rain No Evil

"The boys and I are—" I say.

"Suppose it'd be too much to ask for you to cook dinner tonight." He laughs.

My heart shrivels up like a boiled pea. I remind myself that he's probably just tired from working all night. I wait for him to continue, holding the phone tightly to my ear so the boys won't hear their dad's sarcasm.

Alex continues, "I'm home. You going to the store? There's not a daggone thing here to eat."

I take a breath and try to sound cheerful. "Actually, I'm on my way to Pizza Bravo right now, you know every Tuesday—"

"I've ate like crap all day. I wanted—never mind."

My foot slips off the accelerator. I've disappointed him again, but how would I know what he's eaten today? I want to get something right—seems I could at least provide a suitable diner for my husband.

"The boys want pizza, but if you'd rather have a sandwich or spaghetti I can get that," I offer.

Isaac says, "Did you get one with just cheese and pepperoni?"

I tell Isaac that I did, and Alex says, "All right, get the ham sandwich."

"So, is the body Hank?" I ask, searching for an objective topic. "You get any sleep?"

Alex's voice softens. "A few hours. And yep, it's Hank. His sister identified him a few hours ago."

I relax my grip on the wheel. "You think he was murdered?"

"Holy cow, Savvy! You think a murder gets solved overnight?"

I'm not sure what just happened, but my head is ringing like its being gonged in a copper pan. "Okay, I just wondered," I say, feeling stupid. "Thought maybe you pulled a lil Sherlock out of your pocket."

"Sherlock? What're you talking about?"

"Nothing," I say, pulling into Pizza Bravo. "I gotta go."

I park the car, feeling as if I'm trying to run through water. The hopefulness I felt yesterday when Alex kissed my chest is gone, and frustration gurgles inside me, churning in my stomach like curdled milk.

Why does every conversation with the man I love have to be so excruciating?

Chapter Five

WATER SPRINGS ETERNAL

Alex is placing his gun on top of the refrigerator as we step inside the house. Before I can intercept the question that might set Alex off, Ben's asking him if the guy they found was murdered.

Alex punches Ben in the arm mock-Rocky style, "It's looking that way. The skull had a bullet hole—shot at close range. Should have the autopsy next week."

I gingerly place paper plates on the counter. I guess it's just me who's not allowed to ask about the murder.

"Hank was a damn good guy," Alex says, un-wrapping his hoagie. "We're gonna rattle some cages and see what kinda rodents come out."

I'm impressed with his use of "rodent" instead of the ordinary "rat." Not that he's stupid, he's just not into words the way I am.

I edited his essays in college and for a second, I'm back in that hard wooden chair punching the manual typewriter in Alex's dorm room that smelled of sweaty football cleats and piss. Alex is screaming at me because I ran out of typing paper. Next thing I know, he hurls a lamp toward me. I duck and call him an asshole, but still fetch another ream like a good little doggie does a bone.

"Mom, pass the pizza," Isaac says.

I swipe the tear that's escaped to my cheek and resolve to not think about the past. I can't change it anyway.

After dinner, the boys head upstairs and crank the volume on their televisions so high that I can tell what episode of *Full House* they're watching. I wiggle next to Alex on the leather couch that's toasty from the fireplace and stare at the TV that's playing the season finale of *Burn Notice*.

I squeeze Alex's leg, but he stares ahead like I'm invisible. I wonder what it would feel like to be a butt-kicking bitch like Fiona—independent and confident. What would she do if she was married to Alex? Would she waltz out the door and not look back?

Halfway through the show Ben bounds into the living room with his hand on his head. "Did you hear me, Mom?" he says. "Where the heck did it come from?"

"What come from?" I say, glancing back to my show in time to see Fiona spiral a kick to a thug's head.

"Water just dropped on my head."

"What?"

"In the hall," Ben says, motioning for me to get up. "Water dripped on my head."

I glance at Alex who's tuned out everyone's voice except those coming from his entertainment box.

"It's getting late, Ben," I say. "Did you get your homework done?"

Ben wrinkles his mouth, snags a cookie from the kitchen and runs upstairs.

Twenty minutes later, I'm building a virtual bomb with Fiona when Ben yells, "Mom!"

I snap back to the reality of a warm couch under my legs and a cold husband to my left. "Oh, yes, dear one."

"I got dripped on again!"

My Ben—always goofing off. I burst out in song. "Rain drops keep falling on my head, they keep falling . . ."

"Mom! I'm serious!"

Well, shit. I push myself out of the recliner and join Ben in the stairway where he's staring at the ceiling directly above him. I follow his gaze to a perfectly dry ceiling.

"Here," Ben says, pointing to a dark spot on the carpeted step by his foot.

I rub my finger over the damp carpet. "Did you have a drink in your hand?"

Ben shakes his head.

I stare at my oldest son like I do at the students who tell me their mom cleaned out their book-bag and threw their homework away.

Ben's eyes bulge. "Mom, I'm telling you something dripped on me."

"Heck, honey, I don't know," I say, heading down the stairs. "The ceiling's dry. Don't worry about it. Just finish your homework."

I'm enjoying the last scene of the show when Ben treks down and announces water dripped on him again. I swing my head toward Alex who appears to be under ass-kicking Fiona's spell.

I could kick some ass right now—Alex's—Ben's—Somebody's. I trudge across the floor to the stairway. Could the water that sprayed me in the kitchen yesterday somehow be leaking upstairs?

Ben's in the same spot as before, head tilted toward the ceiling. "Where's it coming from?" he says.

Just then, I see it—a single, solitary blob of water forming on the ceiling, ready to fall. "Alex," I yell, "we have a water leak!"

The recliner snaps closed. That moved him!

"You're kidding! I'm trying to chill here," he says, stomping up the steps.

Ben's mouth is hanging open, eyes fixed on the ceiling. "Told ya."

Alex scans the dry ceiling and sneers at me, "Well?"

"Water dripped from right there," I say, pointing to a spot smack dab in the center of the hallway ceiling.

"Looks dry to me. You got me up for this?" Alex rolls his eyes and backs down a step.

"Look Dad, the carpet's wet," Ben says, crouching and sinking his finger into the damp spot.

Alex rubs his puffed-out chest. "Since you're so bright, you tell me where it's coming from. There are no water lines above the second floor."

Ben's gaze returns to the ceiling.

The steps creak under Alex's 300 pounds as he returns to *Burn Notice* where no case goes unsolved just the way Alex likes his life.

I squeeze Ben's shoulder. "Your dad's just tired because he was out all night on the murder."

Ben wraps his arms around my waist and doesn't wipe off the kiss I plant on his forehead. "Mom, will you give me a brain drain."

"Ah, sure will." I say, following him to his room. "You haven't asked for me to rub your noggin in a month of Sundays—always did help you go to sleep."

"Yeah, you used to tell me rubbing it drains the brain of extra energy." Ben flops face-first into his bed.

"Think I need one, too," I say, rubbing his head and wishing mine would spin hard enough to make me drunk. "My brain feels like it's one of those science thingies that shake blood."

I don't have time to deal with a water leak. I have to figure out what to do about my marriage and how to keep sane and not see things that may not be real—like demons. I have to figure out what to do with my life—how to live everyday with purpose, and how to re-create the joy in living that bubbled inside me when I was as a child and laughed easily.

After I tuck Isaac in, I plop into my chair in the living room with my newest book, *Left To Tell*. Four pages later, what sounds like a dam burst in the hall. "That was no drip," I say, glancing at Alex who looks like a wide-mouth bass. I slam my book shut and run to the stairway where water's running down the inside of the front door.

As Alex and I stand in the foyer at the bottom of the stairway water forms pools on the hardwood floor. Two sets of eyes peer down the steps. I haven't seen the boys' eyes this big since the Christmas they each got a dirt bike.

"Wow!" Ben says, glancing at Isaac.

"What happened!" Isaac says.

"Good question," I say, wiggling my toes inside of my soaked socks and surveying the walls for the area that must have busted.

Alex's neck is exploding with veins. "You guys throwing water down here?"

"Not me!" Isaac says, twisting his pajama top around his finger.

"Me either! I was in bed," Ben says, pointing toward his room as if I don't know where it is.

I swipe my hand over the door panel and tap my wet fingers together, shaking my head in amazement. It really is water.

Alex and I climb the stairs, scanning the walls and ceiling for the source of the downpour. Water trails are running down both walls in the stairway and drops from the ceiling are falling on our heads, but there's no visible damage—no water gushing through a hole in the wall.

"Must be a slow leak somewhere." Alex squints, his eyes roving.

"Didn't sound very slow," I say, instructing the boys to grab towels from the upstairs bathroom and sop up the water on the second floor.

I nab towels from the half-bath by the kitchen and tackle the foyer area, drying the wall while water trickles from further up than I can reach.

"I'm going to bed," Alex says, passing by me. "Nothing we can do about it tonight. I got an interview about the murder with the news at nine in the morning. Got to debunk the rumor that the body was found headless. Crazy-ass people."

I cackle so hard my spit hits the wall, mingling with the liquid trails already on it. I hadn't heard that one at school. "Better hold off on defining 'crazy.' We're the ones standing in a drenched hallway where there aren't any busted water pipes," I say.

I turn, towel in hand, to meet Alex's mocking eyes.

He shakes his head. "Sometimes, you are so stupid, Sav. The other night you sat up in bed praying for evil to leave the house. *You* might have lost your mind, but I haven't," he says and heads upstairs.

I wasn't saying the water is evil. That would be crazy. I thought I was only stating the obvious, but my "obvious" is his "denial." Denial, I guess, that he can't explain everything and that I'm smart enough to admit I can't.

He must have just pretended to enjoy my quirky sense of humor when we dated. If he'd have revealed how he really felt about me back then, I'd have dumped him. Well, I'd like to think I would've dumped him because to think otherwise would mean I sabotaged my very existence—that I'm, not only, too weak to speak up for myself now, but I was too weak even before Alex told me I was. That would mean that my weakness is mine to own and not Alex's fault at all. Now how would I deal with that?

If, in order to maintain the façade of my marriage, I must create the illusion that I'm oblivious to Alex's put-downs, then I will play my part—both for my sake and for his. He doesn't want to believe he hurts me, and I don't want to believe he can, so I climb into bed and nudge Alex's arm.

"You know, I was crazy when you fell in love with me, but that didn't stop you from marrying me," I say, waiting for a gesture of re-assurance that he's not irritated with me anymore.

"Nite, crazy girl," he says, rolling over to face the river.

I take a deep breath. Tomorrow maybe I'll be better at making him happy, but probably not, not unless I morph into a puppy—a pet-able, non-talking canine without a desire to communicate an original thought.

The next morning, sun streams through the bathroom blinds, partially lighting the hallway as I canvas the walls, but they bear no signs of water.

Alex already hit the highway to work the murder, and I'm energized by the thought of his absence. Maybe I can think my way through this day without him around to argue with. I'm sure he'd rather be running down dirtballs than searching for a water leak anyway.

The boys and I advance to the kitchen for the five-minute breakfast scramble of microwaveable bacon and protein bars. As I spout off nutritional advice about how eating protein before sweets helps regulate sugar and build muscle, the sound of a power washer pummeling the front door interrupts my spiel.

The boys whiz through the kitchen toward the sound. I follow their lead, and we meet up in the foyer where water streams down the steep walls and drips from the ceiling. We stagger up the steps, one behind the other like drunks line dancing, exclaiming how "weird," and "amazing" this downpour is.

The walls are undamaged. No pipes peeking through—just water. It's as if an invisible water hose just sprayed the hallway.

I remember the demon's face that appeared in my mirror a few nights ago. A perfume of uneasiness settles on my skin, but I shake it off.

"Let's get going, boys. We're gonna be late. I'll call your dad and he'll have to deal with this." I grab the slippery handrail as a dollop of water hits my forehead and runs over my eyelid.

"Crap," I say, dabbing my face with my sleeve.

On the way out the door, I wrench my cell out of the pocket of my book-bag and call Alex. "Hey, honey, I know you're busy, but water just sprayed all over the hall again."

"Damn, Savvy, can't you take care of something by yourself for once? I'm working a mur—."

"I don't know what to do. There's water every—," I say.

"Got to go. In the middle of something," Alex says and hangs up.

"I love you too, dear," I say for my sake as much as for the boys who are listening. Alex isn't on the other end, but I can pretend he treats me with respect—create my own reality. It sure feels better than the raw truth.

Alex thinks I'm inept because I can't stop this water leak. My own husband can't stand talking to me, but I bet Ryan won't mind a little chat. I haven't responded to his last text asking to hook up, so before the first class charges in, I scroll to "Regina," Ryan's pseudo-name on my contact list. Regina is an old friend from college and I figure if Alex ever sees the number on the cell phone bill, I'm covered. That is, unless he uses his position to find out whose number it really is, but the precaution makes me feel safer than doing nothing.

I text him that I can meet him this evening, and he shoots back he's free. Brianna is staying at her mom's tonight.

When the 3:30 bell dings for school dismissal, I call Alex to see what he plans on doing to stop the water in the hall. He informs me he's going to be late and not even thought about it so I decide to entreat the aid of my handy father-in-law. If anyone can fix this leak, it's Keagan.

Moments after the boys and I pull in the garage, Keagan's red truck is in the drive behind us. Toolbox in hand, my seasoned plumber limps up the drive. He's not going to let a bum knee from years spent laying pipe buckle his pride.

The boys dash past me to hug their grandpa before running into the house. Keagan holds the door as I juggle through with a stack of papers.

I smile. "You can add 'door-holder' to your list of diverse talents."

His coco eyes twinkle like Alex's used to when he looked at me. "Just doing what I know to do. Men now-a-days don't respect women like they should."

I want to say, "Amen to that," but don't want to stir his curiosity as to how Alex and I are getting along. That would just backfire on me. Keagan would tell his sister, Klaire, who would not-so-subtly tell Alex that I'm causing contention in the family or being a "shit-stirrer" in Alex's lingo.

I stand a foot taller at the thought of Alex asking me what "contention" means. "Yep," Keagan says, setting his toolbox on the floor. "Whole world's gone to Hell. Reality TV and the daggone Internet just . . . there's no such thing as dignity anymore."

"Grandpa," Ben says, "can I help?"

Isaac breaks a Pop Tart in half. "Yeah, Grandpa! Can we?"

"Sure, kiddos, as soon as I know what I need to do. So, where's this leak that needs a fixin, sweetheart?" Keagan says, his hillbilly accent blending with his Irish brogue. He never lived in Ireland, but his parents immigrated to the States in the forties and brought their dialects with them.

Keagan's question is easier to answer by showing than telling so I motion him to follow me to the upstairs hall where we find water bubbles covering the entire ceiling. I point to the spot where the first drip on Ben's noggin fell from the ceiling and tell him how Alex said there aren't even water lines up there.

"Roof could be leakin," Keagan says. "I'll check out the attic."

At sixty years old, Keagan is agile enough to maneuver onto a stepladder, flashlight in hand and into the only access to the attic, a three-foot opening in Ben's closet ceiling. If the kids were up here they'd talk me into letting them explore the cobweb-polluted rafters, too, but I strategically placed Pillsbury's finest cinnamon rolls on the counter before coming upstairs.

Ten minutes later, an insulation-covered Keagan emerges from probing the cramped recess when a *splat* sounds in the hall. His furry eyebrows squiggle into a question. "Good golly, girlie. That what you been a hearin'?" he says, stepping off the last rung.

He follows me to the hall as the boys traipse up the stairs and join us in a staring showdown with the ceiling as if an unseen veil will lift and reveal the tangible origin of the water that's running down the walls.

With one hand on his hip and another combing his fingers through his silver streaked hair, Keagan says, "Attic is bone dry. Futile scavenger hunt up there. Never seen anything like this in all my years of repairin'." He points at the water dripping intermittently from the ceiling. "Could be condensation. Might be coming through the ductwork from the heat pump, I reckon . . . but how's it coming through the ceiling?"

For fourteen years, Keagan's been my knight with a knack for repair, and I thought he'd save me from this virtual tsunami.

"Keagan, if you're stumped, I think we're sunk," I say.

"Stumped indeed, Savvy." Keagan folds the ladder and hands it to Ben. "Put this back in the closet for your mom. Since there's nothing I can do here, you boys want to come out and help me put those windows in the tree house?"

I can't refuse the gleam in their eyes when they plead my way for approval.

The boys clamor out the door while I dry the walls and wash my sweaty ass. It'll just get sweaty again when I get to Ryan's, but that's fresh sweat and fresh isn't skanky.

I ring Ryan and he says he'll pick me up at the pharmacy in fifteen minutes. Hearing his voice on the other end, I imagine the hot whisperings he'll soon blow into my ear. He'll be saying, "Oh, babe, I missed your fine ass," but I'll be hearing, "Oh, babe I missed you."

I text Alex and tell him I'm running a few errands in Coraltown—just in case he spots me on the road. Alex thinks I'm stupid, incapable of solving a home repair that even Keagan can't fix, but I know I'm smart enough to reach out for the human connection I'm craving—even smart enough, I hope, to not get caught doing it.

Ryan and I rendezvous in the drug store parking lot. I hop into his black Ford Explorer, slink down into the leather seat and ride the few blocks to his house.

As the garage door eases down, I ease up and notice a single red toolbox sitting along the finished wall in the practically barren garage. Beside it sets two plastic totes, a push-mower, ladder, and pink ten-speed bicycle.

It would take a month to inventory the junk in my garage. If garages are a reflection of our lives, mine's overflowing, and I don't want to peck around in either. Both are filled with useless outdated trappings, some needing repair, some sentimental, and some only suitable for disposal.

Ryan grasps my knee and squeezes his way up my thigh until his hand lands on my crotch. My garage inspection is over. He rubs my clit like a wish will be awarded for doing so.

We trip up the steps into the house, giggling and groping each other.

Ryan presses his chest to mine, pushing me against the refrigerator door.

I push him off of me. "You're bad—making this church girl horny," I say, removing my clothes until I've not a stitch on except an orange thong and boots. Shivering from a draft on my bare butt cheeks that are more than peeking out, I bend over deep into the frig, knowing guys dig the whole naked with shoes on thing, and locate the chocolate syrup while Ryan pops open a beer and kicks off his jeans.

I squeeze some syrup into a bowl and prance around the island toward the microwave. With my hand just inches away from the handle, I see flames dancing inside.

I scream and in a flash Ryan is beside me.

"What?" he asks, prying the bowl from my hand as I stare into the empty microwave.

"What's wrong?" Ryan says, placing his free hand on my shoulder.

I blink. The microwave's not on fire. I can't tell Ryan I'm hallucinating. Stress must be playing tricks on me.

"Just joking around, love bear," I say, grabbing the bowl and placing it inside.

Ryan wraps his arms around me from behind, his chest on my bare back, and kisses the nape of my neck. "Damn you're crazy, girl!"

I don't tell him I may actually be just that.

Ryan's hand glides down my arm, and he twirls me like a ballerina to face him. His fingers dig into my butt cheeks, and he sticks his tongue into my ear. "Ass candy. My sassy ass candy, babe," he whispers.

Balancing the bowl of warm chocolate with Ryan pinching my nipples and nudging me backwards toward the bedroom is challenging, but I manage without spilling a drop.

"Mmm, yummy—chocolate dick," I say, drizzling the syrup over his erect penis. "Better than a DQ dilly bar."

Memories of mystical water melt like M&Ms on the hood of a sun-drenched car as I tease him with my tongue. Right before he climaxes, he growls, a deep gruff growl, but my mouth is full of his penis, and I'm not going to call him out for growling. I rather like it. At least I know I'm pleasing him. It's better than Alex's silent climaxes. Of all the times I'd like Alex's mouth shut, that's not one of them.

Ryan rolls off the bed, washes the sticky from his dick and walks into the kitchen while I lie on the bed wishing he would at least pour some chocolate on me and lick me to oblivion, but he is done and couldn't seem to care a less if I'm satisfied or not.

I hear my thoughts like I'm reading a book and realize that the hollow feeling inside me can't be filled by a dozen orgasms. What I really want is for him to hold me and talk to me, but I don't know how to tell him that I want to feel close to him. Ryan knows Alex and I have problems, but he doesn't know how close we are to divorcing and how much I'd like to know if he would be interested in more than this casual affair.

I march to the kitchen, scoop up my clothes and, while I dress, spout off about the sham of an educational system we have in Wooten County and how the problem extends beyond West Virginia. The checks and balances aren't working to educate the children, only to punish the teachers and create an endless supply of alternate routes for students to graduate even if they won't abide by school policies, can't read and don't attend school, but at least they aren't be counted as drop-outs which makes the school look like the failure.

Ryan digs into a bowl of ice cream and nods. I don't know if he heard a word I said, but at least he didn't interrupt me.

I return home feeling compelled to make up for screwing-under-the-pretense-of-shopping so I throw a load of jeans in the washer and scrub a few plates as if I can absolve my indiscretion through a few suds in the sink and freshly laundered clothes.

I head upstairs to shower the scent of sin from my skin and notice the hallway is dry.

The kitchen door bangs shut while I'm in the bedroom slipping into my PJs.

"Hey, Mom!" Isaac yells, pounding up the stairs.

"In here, sweetie, Grandpa drop you off?"

Isaac stands in the doorway. "Yeah. Can Tommy stay over Friday? His dad and mom are going on a date," Isaac says, snarling his nose like I just farted.

"You won't always think girls are disgusting, bud." I say, ruffling his wavy hair as I brush past him and into the bathroom. "Sure, he can stay. Grandma Lennie always said she didn't have to entertain your Aunt Luce and me as much when we had friends over."

Water slaps the hallway way, and I run into the hall, knocking Isaac into the wall with my momentum.

Ben is standing by his bedroom door, water plopping from the ceiling onto his crew cut and dripping off his chin.

"You've got to be kidding me!" I say, turning and addressing Isaac, "You were standing here. Did you see where it came from?"

"I think it came from there," he says, pointing to the middle of the ceiling.

For this much water to be dripping down the walls, a pipe must have burst, but if it did, where's the daggone hole in the wall? Unless . . . "Guys, I need to ask you something. Listen to what I have to say before you say anything." I look first to Ben then Isaac, maintaining eye contact until their gaze convinces me they are really listening. "If this is a joke, please—"

"But, Mom—" Ben says.

"Let me finish," I say, raising my chin, index finger pointing skyward. "Please tell me now before your dad and I go to a lot of effort and expense to fix something that's not broken." Water drops onto my head, trickling down my forehead and through my hair as if soaking me can shut me up. "If this is a joke, it's a good one—no harm done. But it's definitely enough. Time to stop."

I nod to Ben acknowledging his input is now welcome.

"You think *we're* throwing the water?" My oldest folds his arms across his chest and shakes his head. "Well, I'm not doing it. Isaac can tell you. I didn't even have water." His look anchors with his little brother. "Did I?"

"I didn't see any." Isaac points to the ceiling. "Just came from up there."

"You both swear?" I say. "If you come clean now I promise I won't tell your dad. You won't be punished either."

Ben's shaking his head and Isaac says, "Mom, if we lie, we go to Hell, and I'm not going to Hell over some stupid water."

Isaac's got a point. I don't want to go to Hell either, but I have more reason to go than he does. I think I'm in purgatory now, if there is such a place. This water leak doesn't make any sense, and I'm torn as discern what's real from what may be my imagination.

I know absolutely nothing, except that the love I feel at times, like when the boy's faces light up and wish me a happy birthday completely surpasses my expectation of joy, but when the look in Alex's eyes conveys an anger I can't decipher, I feel like a void, irrelevant being trying to wring an ounce of pleasure from barbed wire.

"Okay, I hope you're telling the truth," I say. "I just had to check—to give you the chance to tell me now before this gets out of hand. This is just ridiculous." I feel a few dirty towels from the laundry basket, toss one to Ben for his wet body, and wipe down my closet door with the other.

My cell rings, and I notice two unread texts from Alex. I answer and he says, "Hey. Gonna be late. Interviewing one of Hank's neighbors who may be a suspect. They had a big property dispute a month ago. You get my message?"

"I just saw two texts from you, but haven't read them because—"

"Of course not. Don't know why I bother sending them."

"But the water—" I say, waving the boys to their rooms as I step into mine and shut the door. "Will you just listen for a minute? This place—"

"I don't have time for your bitching about water," Alex says.

I swallow and let him continue. He won't hear anything I say right now.

"I just thought you'd like to know I'm going to be late, but there's always got to be an issue with you." He hesitates. "You there?"

"Yes," I say, looking out my window to the crows perched on the telephone lines feeling like I just ate one.

"Anyway, I left a message for you to call the plumber tomorrow. Dad called me and said you had him come to the house—like he's got time to keep up our house and his and Aunt Klaire's."

"He had time to help you hang the damn drywall in the garage!"

"Savvy, this is why I can't talk to you—you always have to be right."

I'm glad I don't have dinner on for his nasty ass. I'd tell him that, but he'd just keep talking and I don't want to hear any more.

"Who you interviewing?" I say, wondering if his "interview" is some cunt bent over a bedrail in the police barracks.

"I told you a suspect. Do you ever listen?"

"I heard you. Just thought you'd tell me the suspect's name. I might know them." I sit in Grandma Lennie's old chair and rock to a squeaky rhythm. "I'll call the plumbers tomorrow. Bye."

I press my lips firm. Not another word is coming out until I can say something nice—even if I never talk again.

I cradle my head in my hands and rock. I rocked my babies in this chair. I imagined them growing up, me protecting them from the ugliness of anger like I'm feeling right now—teaching them right from wrong, but I'm a farce so how can I teach them to live right and to speak the truth?

I insisted they tell me the truth about the water, but I lie to them and to Alex about my whereabouts when I'm off sleeping around with another man.

If Alex could speak to me respectfully and would stop getting angry for no reason, maybe I could get close to him again. I could understand him getting upset if he were to find out I'm screwing Ryan, but to get mad because I didn't see his texts is ridiculous.

I open my journal that glimmers in the moonlight as if it were bedazzled with sequins. I slide my hand over the hardback cover wondering if my eyes are playing tricks on me like when I saw the fire in the microwave and I write:

> Alex is a dick. Anger pours into me, filling me every time I talk to him just like water is pouring in my hall. I'm beginning to think my usually sharp faculties are searching for a new brain to inhabit. I'm trying to make good choices, but with flames in the microwave and an inexplicable water leak – hell, just one more conversation with Alex could put me over the edge.
>
> No wonder I gravitate to the excitement of being growled at... of being mauled just because I can.
>
> To be mauled or not to be mauled – that's a question to which I know the answer. Bell-ringer for class tomorrow – homonyms "Mall" and "Maul."

Finding irony in students benefitting from my warped sense of humor seems to drag me out of the ditches of despair.

I slide my prized diary beneath a magazine in my nightstand, wishing Alex would find it, read it and confront me so that I would have to deal with the reality of what I'm doing. Maybe if he read it he would see himself from my perspective or perhaps, if he caught me cheating, I'd be so scared he would divorce me that I'd stop.

I'm in the kitchen June-Cleavering some sandwiches together for the boys when Isaac pops in, a frown on his face, his eyes darting around the room.

"Mom, a witch just flew through my room."

I choke back a laugh. "A witch? Oh, honey, there's been so much going on here. You're tired." I look down at the slabs of meat. "You been watching vampire shows?"

"I just watched "Dukes of Hazzard," Isaac says, digging his chin into the neck of the t-shirt he's wearing. "Mom, I swear. It was on a broom."

I wrap the sandwiches in a paper towel and grab Isaac's hand that he doesn't jerk away. "Let's check it out," I say, trying to sound serious as we walk hand in hand on the hunt for a witch. I'm reminded Isaac is still just a kid and not growing up as fast as I think he is. I smile thinking it's not just any witch we're after, but one on a broom that's no doubt long gone.

After handing Ben his sandwich, I step into Isaac's room while the witch-seer huddles close to the wall in the hall with petrified eyes. Poor little guy. He must be stressed out from this water leak, too.

His lamp is on, television running. Nothing out of the ordinary.

I motion him to my room where I settle into the rocker, searching Isaac's face for a sign of a smile, but all I see is earnestness.

"Bud," I say. "You know, it's hard to believe a witch was in your room."

Isaac sits Indian-style on the floor beside me and says, "I can't believe it either, Mom. It came from my closet—zipped right by my bed."

"Honey the world's full of atoms and molecules in the air that I can't see, but I believe they are there. But a witch? I mean . . ." As I rock, the same squeak that accompanied grandma when she rocked me as a baby, seems to set an eerie tone to the witch subject.

"Well, I saw it," Isaac says, chewing the neckline on his shirt like a cow chewing cud. "I didn't 'spect to see it, either."

"Expect," I say, smiling, "and I'm sure you didn't. What did it look like?" Surely I can convince him that what he thinks he saw was just his imagination.

"Just like in movies. She had on a black dress. Riding a broom." Isaac says.

"What about a hat?"

"I don't remember. It was fast."

I'm familiar with my boys and students joking with me. They usually embellish the story so much that they giggle or look away, but Isaac is stoic.

He scoots onto his knees. "I'm scared. Can I sleep with Ben?"

He hugs my leg, and I realize that if he really believes he saw a witch maybe he's going crazy like me. After all, I saw flames in a microwave that wasn't even on.

I tell Isaac to wait in my room while I ease into Ben's to finagle the sleeping arrangement with talk of brotherly love and a promise of ten bucks.

A few hours later, Alex flips on the logging show in the bedroom. I'd rather be eaten by piranhas than hear all the yacking on reality TV, but I belly-dive onto the bed beside him.

Eyes focused on the show, Alex asks me to scratch his back. I'm curious about the interview with Hank's neighbor, but I won't give him the satisfaction of knowing he has information or anything else I want.

I slowly sweep my short nails across his freckled skin.

"Harder," Alex says.

I dig in, wondering who's been boring her claws into him recently.

There's a faint knock on the door and I yell, 'Come in!"

Ben steps through. "Mom," he huffs, bracing his hands on his hips. "Isaac won't scoot over. I can't sleep with his butt on me."

"Why is he sleeping with you anyway?" Alex says. "Just tell him to go back to his room."

"Wait, Ben," I say, sitting up. "Alex, I had it worked out. Isaac was having—" The sound of water spraying in the hall prompts Ben to duck into the room.

"Ah, man!" Ben says, but I keep talking.

"Isaac was having a hard time sleeping and Ben agreed he could sleep with him." No way am I mentioning a witch is behind the deal.

"Well, apparently it's not okay," Alex says, flipping off the TV. "Go on, Ben, get to bed. It's late. And somebody dry the damn hallway."

"Alex, why can't you just let me handle this?" I throw back the covers, traipsing through the wet hall and catch up with Ben who is already at the threshold of his bedroom. I reach with one hand and squeeze his shoulder, quietly asking him to just hear me out.

I promise him a sleepover of his own next weekend complete with a Nerf gun battle in the basement and iced brownies. He agrees with a roll of the eyes. I place a pillow between the two butts I bore, throw a towel on the floor and flop my exhausted butt back into my bed.

The light's off, but Alex is still awake—and there's enough fury in the air to generate heat for all of Alaska.

"You have to go against everything I say; don't you?" he says.

"I think *you* went against what *I* said. I'm the one who made the arrangement so everyone could actually sleep tonight. You really didn't have anything in it." I fluff my pillow and lay flat on my back staring into the darkness and wishing Alex would meet his demon in the mirror tonight. Maybe he would be a little nicer.

"You baby Isaac way too much. Even dad said so the other day. He's going to be a sissy. You didn't treat Ben that way." Alex heaves over to his side, his back to me.

I'm relieved that not even his foot is touching me. I don't want to breathe the same air he is, let alone have any part of him touch me. "I was trying to do what's best for everyone. That's a concept you apparently don't comprehend," I say, wiggling my toes and remembering the fresh coat of cherry polish on them.

I smile into the darkness—I'll retaliate against Alex before the polish wears off—nab me a someone to dig my nails into.

Chapter Six

HANDCUFF PARTY
AND A BARBER

The sound of bells ringing startles me awake. I grapple with the blankets, trying to figure out what's creating the racket and wondering if I'm late for class.

Alex groggily mutters, "Hello," and I realize the home phone is the culprit. I'm beginning to understand the old adage, "No rest for the wicked."

"Okay, I'll give him a call," Alex says and recites a number.

Sounds like this one's a domestic—man's threatening his daughter with a gun, his girlfriend's calling 911 from a neighbor's house. Alex hangs up and repeats, "3714. 3714" as he punches the illuminated numbers on the phone.

"It's 3741," I say.

"Just shut up," he says before answering the voice on the other end. "Hello, could I speak to Roger Collins?" He pauses. "Oh, sorry."

Alex slings his legs off the bed and sits up. "So. What's the number?"

I should feign amnesia. Then he'd have to call dispatch and get it. Boy, he'd be pissed!

"You gonna answer me?" he says.

I tell him the number and bunch the soft quilt under my chin, wondering where that whiff of Downy is when I need it.

"Hi, Mr. Collins?" Alex asks. "This is Sheriff Templeton, Wooten County Sherriff's Department. Can you tell me what's going on out there . . . I understand. I know you care about your daughter very much. She's probably frightened and my main concern is that she's okay. Is she okay?"

Alex is silent and I hear a man's gruff voice on the other end saying, "Damn girl—stole my meds. I need 'em. My back's killin me, Taze."

Alex won't have to go out for this one. Taze will talk him down from right here in bed. His reputation in the area has its advantages.

"We'll talk to her," Alex says. "Put the fear of God in her, but you have to put the gun away and let my deputy in to talk to you."

The gruff voice mumbles something and Alex says, "Yes, I know she shouldn't, Roger, but you don't really want to hurt her. Let her go to your neighbors. My deputies are on their way out to talk with you. We all just want to make sure the girl is safe . . . Now, Roger, you know me. I've helped you out many times and you've helped me. You need to help me again right now, okay?"

Alex stumbles into the bathroom and I hear his pee stream hitting the commode while he updates the 911 center.

I lay in bed snickering silently to think how often my bathroom has been a command post and wondering if I have the girl in class.

He crawls into bed a few minutes later. "Who's the girl?" I ask.

"Collins. Courtney Collins," Alex says.

I picture Courtney, long dark hair pulled back into a ponytail, wearing the grungy pink Aeropostale hoodie that seems to have melted to her skin—pretty girl, even with a limited and not often laundered wardrobe. Last year, she was on probation for stealing her mom's car so when her mom kicked her out, she moved in with her dad. Courtney proudly sported her home-confinement ankle bracelet and provided ample details behind its acquisition, explaining how she had taken off in the car in retaliation for her mom's cocaine-induced rage during which she piled Courtney's clothes in the middle of the bed and set them on fire.

"Courtney's in my class," I say. "No wonder she picks her arms till they bleed. Between the drugs Mrs. Z says she's taking and a gun-wielding dad, she doesn't have a chance."

Courtney's a little mouthy, but she doesn't usually give me a hard time. Perhaps she relates to my anecdotal high school stories such as setting fire to the toilet paper that was chained to the top of the stall in the restroom—my subtle way of revolting against the principal's decision to chain it there—and on a different day, prank-pulling the fire alarm. My students laugh when I tell them I got caught when a friend was with me so I went solo, setting students free from class with another fire alarm the next day.

I learned that if I wanted to be discrete, I had to operate on my own. I'm still motivated by the very nature of secrecy. I feel victorious when I get by with doing something I shouldn't, but my secrets could cause me to lose Alex, and who would I be without him?

He's popular and respected in the community. I am just a name on some juvenile's school schedule—just another class to endure, but I have skills I keep hidden. If my brain has rooms, I've dedicated the one in upper corner to the art of being who I need to be in any given moment, never letting the real me descend the stairs to enjoy the ball. This beautiful tapestried room holds my secrets.

In a small town like Ridgeland, secrets are challenging to keep. I squirm

Rain No Evil

my forehead deeper into my pillow knowing I have my share of tightly wrapped ones that could, at any moment, burst open and expose my inherent badness.

Streams of light puncture my eyes and I wonder if I'm up to another day on Earth's battlefield. I'm in the trenches with more than just Alex as an enemy now—there's a demon and a witch and water.

I roll over, cringing as my sore breast smashes against my arm. The image of Ryan on top of me, biting my nipple, sweat dripping off his chin, churns my stomach.

I felt better before I scrogged Ryan yesterday, and I realize that the enemy within may be the only one worth fighting, but I'm not sure I have the strength to stop searching for love behind every set of dreamy eyes. I don't know if the enemy within is just my dark side or an actual demon. I'm afraid if I search for my true self, I might see a demon in my mirror again, so rather than face it, I think I'll allow any would-be demon inside to lurk quietly in the expanding darkness of my soul.

I look at my clock and over to Alex, his smoothly shaven chest rising and falling. Morning—the only time he's vulnerable, peaceful.

I nuzzle up next to his back, so strong, and brush my cheek against his clammy skin that smells of morning sweat. I revel in this time alone with him, no talking—no arguments. Just being. Just breathing.

The sound of his breath is comforting, but with each exhalation my heart wrenches a little more, knowing this feeling won't last. It can't. He'll wake up.

I peel back the covers, stand and shake the sleepiness from my arms. Tiptoeing across the hall, my toes search for the feel of liquid, but only feel the shellacked wooden floor. Going to sleep in a drenched house and awakening to a dry one, adds an element of intrigue to my morning—almost as astonishing as me rising before my alarm serenades me.

I can't think of a better way to spend my gift of this quiet time than to write. I need to write more often—at least when I write, I can explain myself without Alex interrupting. I shower, throw on my robe and grab my purple notebook from the nightstand. Downstairs, I click on the fireplace and settle into my chair as warmth envelopes my bare legs. Blue flames from the fireplace lull me into a dreamy state.

Pen and good intentions in hand, I drift back into Ryan's arms, remembering how easy it felt to be unaccountable and irresponsible for a few hours, to have a man's undivided attention, and have him listen or, at least, pretend to.

Perhaps Ryan listens to my view of a dysfunctional public education system only because he enjoys screwing me. Even if so, I appreciate that he does so energetically. Alex's ears are numb unless I'm donning a pair of panties that beg for a spanking. His ears would perk right up for that message. Shouldn't someone who really loves me listen when I talk?

The floorboards upstairs creek and a door closes. Alex is up. A glimmer

61

on the mantle draws my eyes to our silver-framed wedding picture. Our smiles seem to cry out to be consumed by the flames illuminating the room. It is my face in the picture, but it feels like I was never really there. Were we happy then? I can't remember exactly, but his eyes were kinder. When he looked into mine I felt he cared—felt I was accepted and protected.

A tear plunks to my tablet, and I swipe the sleeve of my robe across the page and leave a wet streak.

I remember my arms on Alex's hard shoulder pads and around his sweaty neck after high school football games. Then later, faint mix of alcohol and Stetson in the air, a light flickering in the back of the gym illuminated shadows of couples making out on the bleachers. My eyes closed, lips on his neck still damp from showering, we twirled in circles to Madonna's *Crazy for You,* saving the backseat dance in his red Mustang for the finale. Desire filled his eyes under those Friday night bulbs. He did love me.

I sigh and write:

> Maybe it's not fair to blame Alex for the lack of intimacy in our relationship; familiarity and time has stomped the fire out of our romance, leaving warm embers. An occasional stoking creates heated arguments that add ashes to my pile of despair, rather than passionate exchanges I yearn for

"Mom, I need a towel!" Ben yells, snapping me out of the page.

"Okay." I say, rising. "I'll bring one up." That is, I will if there's a dry one in the whole damn house. I scamper down the stairs, across the cold concrete floor of the basement and onto the rug in the laundry room.

Finding the dryer empty, I sift through handfuls of damp towels until I find the driest one, spritz air freshener on it and deliver the freshest towel in the house to a grateful Ben. No harm done.

Knocking on Isaac's door, I call out, "Hope you're getting dressed, Bud." Not waiting for his response, I turn, open my closet door and hear the all too familiar *splat*!

Alex whizzes out the bedroom door, wearing only briefs and socks. "What the hell!" His jaw set firm, shoulders squared as if he was going to block for Peyton Manning, but he's not sure where his opponent is; so he stands, helpless—his only assailant the water dripping onto his back.

Ben steps from his room. "Dad, you know we got a leak. Why you so surprised?"

"I do *not* know!" Alex says as I slip into my closet and shut the door. "It's just ridiculous!" Alex yells, descending the creaky stairs. "Savvy, I hope you call the plumber today—if that's not too much to ask."

His demanding voice penetrates my closet door—my pounding head. I want to thump *him* in the head—unleash the fury from inside, but there's so much, if uncorked would spew like lava—probably burying me in the process.

I slide on my shoes and grip the closet doorknob, my knuckles turning white. Maybe if he'd just hit me—release the anger he's hoarding from old wounds—those probably caused by his own mother who couldn't, or wouldn't, hear him—he could heal.

I'd gladly be his punching bag if I thought for a minute, his love would rise like dough when smashed and kneaded. It might hurt less than the battering he's doing to my brain. If God doesn't give us more than we can bear, I guess I'm stronger than I thought.

I step into the hall, thankful Ben is in his room, sparing me the sight of his heartbroken little face.

I want to protect him from the hatefulness of Alex's words, from the discord in our family, but the only way to do that is to leave Alex. If I leave, that means I'm giving up and I don't want to be a quitter.

I shake my head as if I can dissolve the slightest notion of leaving, and I dry my closet door with a sweatshirt from the dirty clothes basket. Ben joins me in the hall with his damp towel, both of us swiping the walls like human windshield wipers.

"Wax on. Wax off," I say under my breath.

Ben recognizes the Karate Kid's mantra. "You're gonna be a pro with moves like that, but better work on your roundhouse, Mom. I've seen your kicks."

"Even though I'm out of practice, I can still kick your butt, little guy!"

Much needed laughter resounds in the stairway. I can't remember the last time Alex and I laughed together.

Tears fill my eyes, blurring the water trails on the wall.

I bark out marching orders, "Isaac, Ben, let's get a move on. We're gonna be late for school."

At school, I skip breakfast duty in the cafeteria, opting for my vacant classroom where I pop bacon in the microwave and slip a French vanilla cup into the Keurig before calling Tri-County Plumbing. They're the best in the area and pricey, but digits aren't important considering that my sanity and, quite possibly, my family's is at stake. Tri-County is booked for days in advance, a hopeful indicator that they'll have the expertise to get to the bottom of this leak. I schedule a house call for Monday, the soonest one available.

As I note the appointment, I realize my desk-sized calendar lacks the colorful mark-up I usually decorate it with this time of year. Like all good teachers, I usually highlight the monumental non-instructional holidays—the ones without students, but this year it's almost spring break and I haven't slashed through any of the dates.

I bite the eraser on the pencil in my hand. Summer means more time spent with Alex and more time means more arguments, and right now the thought of that makes me wish the water leak could actually wash my house away. We could start fresh in another house—free from the walls that have watched us close in on each other like barracudas—free from habits that are as ingrained in us as the tile is mortared to the floor.

Picturing our house sailing downstream, I remember Keagan mentioning the possibility that condensation from the heat pump could be creating the water leak, so I call the heating and cooling company who installed the heat pump when we moved in. I request a serviceman come to the house and emphasize that the water is "forceful" and "spraying" across the room.

"Excuse me?" the receptionist says. "Did you mean to call a plumber?"

"The plumbers can't come till Monday," I say. "My father-in-law thinks our heat pump could be causing condensation to form on the ceiling, but like I said, the water's spraying, not just dripping, but we don't know where it's coming from. I'd like to get a professional opinion from your company since you installed the heat pump."

"You mean you can't see the water line it's spraying from?"

"Yes," I say, trying to say something that will make sense. "I mean, we don't know if it's coming from a water line. Water just shoots across the room from nowhere."

"Could you hold please?"

"Sure," I say, knowing she must think I'm nuts.

After a few minutes the receptionist says, "I radioed a serviceman. He said condensation doesn't spray, but he'll call you."

I leave my number and figure the more professionals I have check out my house, the better, so I call the water company. Just getting this leak fixed will take some of the pressure off the whole family and maybe earn me a tad of Alex's respect.

After explaining my dilemma to the water company clerk, he explains that if the household's water usage is considerably larger than usual, a leak is indicated, and he schedules a worker to stop by after school to read the meter.

I feel like I'm making progress toward a resolution, and a rush of hope pulses through me as Terry bursts into my room.

"Where you been—sick?" I ask, sorting through a stack of essays.

He looks at his mud covered boots and stammers, "Mmm miss tah tah Templeton, my mom wah wah went nuts again. She said there were tah tah teeth in her bah bah bed trying to eat her."

I look up from my coffee—didn't know she went crazy before. Just thought she was a stoner. Terry delivering such a sensitive topic via his marked stutter makes me feel even more empathy for him than I usually would. "Oh, honey. Is she okay now?" I say, placing my hand over my heart.

Terry slides behind a desk, massaging the bill on his camouflage cap until it looks like it's going to crack right down the center. "Better. But she duh duh doesn't get to come home rah rah right now." He squints from under the fishing pole insignia. "They pah pah put her in that place in Huntington."

"There's a psychiatric facility in Huntington. I know the place. So what happened? Who took her away?"

The teary eyed junior relays how his mom had mixed alcohol and pain pills then started screaming at Terry and his younger brother one minute about how they were no-good, rotten whores and the next minute begging them to save her from the teeth that were biting her in bed. After flinging a few plates against the wall like they were Frisbees, she ripped pictures from the walls and slammed them to the ground. Terry shielded his brother from the shattering glass and got him out of the house. When he went back inside, his mom was standing on shards of glass, her bleeding, bare feet spotting the carpet beneath her as she yanked curtains off the rods.

"Every tah tah time I'd get close 'nuff to grab her, she'd hiss at me and make her fingers like this," Terry says, bending his fingers to look like claws. "She even ja ja jabbed a piece of glass at me, so I got the heck outta there and called the poe poe. The ambulance came. Took her away."

The bell rings and I haven't finished eating my bacon, but a little human tragedy is a hunger-squelcher anyway.

I smile at the poor soul in front of me. "Terry, I'm sorry about your mom. Sounds like she's in a good place to get help."

Students trickle into the classroom. "Terry," I say, "we're still reading Shakespeare. I'll get your makeup work ready and give it to you tomorrow. Just what you wanted to do on spring break, right?"

I want to keep him busy—distract him from his maniac mom issue. "Could you write the date on the board and maybe pass these out for me?" I say, handing him a stack of papers.

"Sure," he says, grinning from under the cap that he's not supposed to have on according to school policy, but I've got my own inappropriate crutches and I'm not taking his from him. Not today anyway.

As I turn to grab my textbook, a man with a shaved head and goatee I've never seen before steps through my door. "Sir, have you been to the office?" I ask, noticing he isn't wearing a visitor's badge. I walk toward the office call button on the wall a few feet from my desk, wondering if this is some nut job on a rampage or simply a lost parent.

He sticks his hands into his jean pockets and leans back on the heels of his biker boots. The students bust out laughing. One blurts out, "Mrs. Templeton, Matt's a student!"

Oh, great—seriously! Just what I need—a student who looks like he just got out of lock-up.

Matt glares at me, earlobes hanging from the weight of what looks like twenty gauge black spikes. "Where ya want me?"

Nowhere here, I'm thinking, but I stare him down silently so he knows I'm not putting up with any of the shit I'm sure he plans on aiming my way.

I climb onto my stool so I'll be at least as tall as he is. "Any empty desk for now. I'll assign a seat to you should I need to," I say, noticing a skull tattoo on his defined bicep. "So, Matt, right? Did you just move here?"

Matt high fives a few of the boys and plunks down in the farthest desk in the back, which is just fine by me. "No, just transferred from Beaumont High."

"Oh, what's your last name?"

"Boggs."

Matt Boggs. Sounds familiar, but I can't place it right now.

"All right, reunion's over, everyone. Get started on your bell-ringer." I explain our warm-up routine to Matt, pointing out the shelf of supplies by the door—loose-leaf paper and pencils.

No excuses for failure here. There's a levy in this county that pays for all the paper and pencils that students can consume—that is use, lose, or break. I tell Matt he doesn't have to do the "maul/mall" homonym review that's on the board. His bell-ringer today is to write a paragraph about where he sees himself in five years—should make an interesting read.

I slide into the chair at my desk and sit staring at the tropical island backdrop on my computer screen, wondering if I'll soon join Terry's mom in the lock-up ward. We could be bunk buddies, tearing up jack together, like Thelma and Louise. If water sprayed on me there I could just stand there, chin up, chest out, and allow it to soak me to the bone. I'd fit right in.

While I'm entering attendance on the computer, Matt walks up to my desk and pulls his pant leg up to where a black band wraps his ankle and announces, "I'm on probation."

If he's expecting to shock me, he's mistaken. "You are to be writing," I say.

Matt yanks his pant leg down. "There's no pencils."

Courtney smiles at me. "Someone's eating them again, Mrs. Templeton."

If Matt wasn't here I'd laugh, but he can't see the easy going side of me yet—has to respect me first.

"Courtney, I know I've joked about them being eaten, but," I say, surprised to see Courtney here after the domestic call from her dad last night, "seriously, class, I find pencils scattered all over this school—in the hallways, on the bathroom sinks, cafeteria tables—even stuck in potted plants in the office."

I snatch a pencil from my desk and hold it high realizing I'm more pissed at the indulgent educational system for providing the abundance of supplies than I am at the students' lackadaisical disposal of them. "Some students," I continue, "don't value things that are given to them—guess they think, 'Oh, it's just a pencil,' but people, taxpayers like your parents and grandparents are paying for all the broken pencils lining the lockers here."

Rain No Evil

Brandon yells out, "Hey, Matt, you on day report for the drug deal with Parker?" I'm curious so I give Matt the opportunity to answer before I scold Brandon. Matt, who is still standing a foot from me, grins, "Sure am. It was a badass bust." This dude is straight out of *The Outsiders*! I hand him the pencil, and in my most teacherly voice say, "That is quite enough entertainment, Mr. Boggs. Have a seat." I look directly into the eyes of this dirtball and point to his desk. "Now."

Matt complies and the rest of the class buries their heads into their books. They know when the line between casual and inappropriate is crossed with me. No need to call out Brandon now.

This new kid's permitted to attend school with an ankle bracelet—ridiculous. I'm supposed to entice this druggie criminal kid to want to learn English—impossible. Bet he has the most interesting resume of all the students though.

Five minutes later, the class and I join the fairies in my favorite scene of Shakespeare's *A Midsummer Night's Dream,* as Titania, the fairy Queen, announces her undying love for a man wearing a donkey's head who she believes to be an avatar. She has no idea that her husband's servant, Puck, has caused this delusion by placing magic flower powder in her eyes.

I pose a question for discussion, "Can peoples' perception of reality be altered by a spell?" Most students call hogwash and discuss the topic amongst themselves while I amuse myself, imagining a spell is creating the illusion I'm experiencing at home—that my own little Puck is camping out behind my headboard just waiting for my eyelids to close so he can dust them with his fairy potion, but I wonder what I would see because I already look at Alex and see an ass.

I actually laugh out loud and Courtney says, "What's funny?"

"Just imagining being put under a spell," I say, surprising myself with my honesty.

Brandon says, "I believe in spells. My aunt has a daggone witch book. She keeps dead cats under the floorboards of her trailer, and one time she brought one of them back to life. Creepy I'm telling ya." Brandon shudders and the bell dings ending yet another interesting period.

I call Courtney up to my desk. She shoves her notebook into a faded book-bag and sloughs up without her flip-flops completely lifting off the tile floor.

"I know about your dad pulling a gun on you last night," I say. "Where'd you end up staying?"

Her brown eyes, accentuated by the black circles underneath, tell me wherever it was, she didn't sleep much.

"I stayed with Nana. I'm staying there all week probably. Dad had to spend the night in jail—supposed to be out today. Our caseworker has to talk to us before I can go back home."

A ninth grader trudges in the door. I shoo him out and tell him to have everyone to wait in the hall.

I ask Courtney if she's taking the drugs she stole from her dad or if she's selling them. She says she gave them to her boyfriend and he sold them. He's a twenty-year-old dropout I had in class years ago. I ask if her mom knows about what happened, and Courtney says she hasn't spoken with her mom for over a year—ever since she took a job on a cruise ship.

For a second I wonder what it would feel like to just take off on an extravagant double-decker heading for the Virgin Islands—not stick it out in the trenches like the trooper I am. But thinking of leaving Alex creates the distinct sensation of my heart being wrung dry.

I walk toward the door with Courtney, the cell in my pocket vibrating, and encourage her to stop in my room at lunch if she wants to talk. I hand her a note so her next teacher won't mark her tardy, and a group of laughing freshman crash through the door as the tardy bell rings. I step into the niche between my door and the hall to see if I just missed a return call from heating and cooling guy, but I see it was Alex calling. Before I can slide the phone back into my pocket, he's calling again and I answer.

From across the hall, Mrs. Z raises her eyebrows my way, slides her belly against her doorframe and disappears into her room.

Alex asks if I noticed anything unusual about my car this morning. The only thing unusual I would have noticed is its absence from my garage. I allot no spare seconds in the morning to inspect a stationary piece of machinery.

"No, why?" I ask, holding the classroom door open and glaring the evil eye at a few boys inside who are pinching each other's boobs. "Alex, I have class. Is this important?"

"Important! Hell, I reckon it is if Bobbie Barber setting my cruiser on fire is considered important to you," Alex says.

"What? Oh my God," I say, turning away from my class.

Barber is an ex-con and an ever-evolving criminal, infamous throughout Wooten County. Once during a routine traffic stop, he jabbed a pair of handcuffs through a police officer's cheek. Barber was incarcerated for a few years for "battery on an officer," but was now out among the natives, scavenging the community resources once again.

When Alex first joined the force, Barber, who was a fugitive, wanted for breaking and entering, was scraping around the woods, hiding out in a makeshift cabin located just miles deep behind the home Alex and I built in the country. Scouring the area on a four-wheeler one rainy evening, Alex made out a figure at the cabin and hopped off his ride to come face to face with Barber. However, not having met him before, and only having seen a faxed image of him, Alex believed him when he claimed he was just a friend of the wanted Barber.

Alex handcuffed him as a precaution and left him standing outside in the rain while he searched the cabin. When Alex came back outside, ole Barber was gone, leaving a mud-covered, drenched, ATV tire-kicking Barney Fife to face his Mayberry—minus one pair of handcuffs.

Barber's escaping with Alex's handcuffs quickly penetrated the conversations of every policeman, firefighter and courthouse worker within a hundred miles, earning him a few sets of brand new plastic handcuffs. One pair of pink fuzzy ones donned a cake. Humor and sugar—always a good combination.

I'm not laughing now though as Alex tells me that this morning he noticed ashes scattering the concrete by his cruiser that was parked behind the house. Further inspection revealed scorched paint underneath the rear bumper. Maybe I *should* pay more attention to my surroundings in the morning, including the metal box I drive.

The tardy bell rang several minutes ago. I peer into the window of my classroom door where one boy is standing in the trash can. "Alex, hold on a minute—damn ninth graders."

I yank open the door and bark, "Bell-ringer. It's called a *Bell-ringer* because you work it when the bell rings. Do it. Now!"

I step back into the niche and peek around corner to see if Mr. Meyers, the principal, is parked at the end of the hall with his coffee cup, but he's not. He's probably walking the treadmill in his office or hiding out in the (PRO) Prevention Resource Officer's closet-sized office.

"I'm back," I say to Alex. "How do you know it was Barber?"

"I leaned on a few informants. They ratted him out. They won't sign statements, so I'll have to pin him with something else, but that won't be hard."

"Sure they won't sign, they're as afraid of Barber as they are of you. Why didn't you call me this morning?"

"I've been questioning people all morning," Alex says, "trying to find out who tried to set my cruiser on fire right beside my house—trying to keep my family safe and this is the thanks I get—you bitchin' cause I didn't tell you soon enough?"

"Alex, I wasn't bitching," I say softly, wishing I hadn't been so obnoxious. I know he must have had a hectic morning. He works so hard. Why can't I just be nice—appreciate that protecting us is his way of showing us he loves us? "Just would have liked to have known earlier," I say. "Hold on a sec." I prop open my door with a wedge and announce, "This is an emergency call. SSR. Ten minutes."

"You realize that if I'd have had a full tank of gas, the cruiser could've blown up near the boy's rooms? I almost stopped and filled up on the way home, but I was too tired."

"Alex, I know you want to protect us. I'm just shocked. This is a little unnerving."

We say good-by, and I step across the hall and ask Mrs. Z to check on my class that's supposed to be reading silently. I need a few minutes by myself to let this Barber threat sink in. I head for the restroom—about the only place a person can enjoy a bit of solitude in this rigid environment where a bell ringing determines your every move.

I'm tired of criminals interfering with my life. Alex must be tired, too—tired of working the twenty hours week overtime he gets paid for and the countless hours he doesn't. If he were an attorney, the volunteer time would be pro bono, considered philanthropy, but as a cop, his is expected. If he fails to pander to the public, offering advice and assistance at the place and time they deem appropriate, they call him a prick.

I think he's a prick, too—a hard working prick who squashes opposition rather than appreciates differences of opinion, but I feel sorry for him. He's in love with a job that has tainted his view of the world—where all he sees are the blooms of fostered ugliness.

I remember a different, more sensitive Alex. Before police-work—before hardened criminals hardened his core. He would kiss the kids' noses at bedtime and let them smear shaving cream on his face in the tub. I can see Alex spinning Ben around by his heels and both collapsing into giggling heaps on the floor while Isaac climbs onto his back.

What happened to that Alex? I want him back. I want that silly, playful, less masculine Alex back. I just don't know how to find him among the rubble of convoluted conversations and unrealistic expectations.

He has fallen and broken like Humpty Dumpty, and I don't know how to put him back together again. Only God with his special glue could do that, but it must not be enough for me to ask the Almighty to repair my husband or Alex would already be intact. Alex must have to ask for his own reconstruction.

A thought skitters through my mind as I clomp through the hallway. What if Alex *has* asked God to help him—to restore him to that joyful Alex I fell in love with? That would mean God must have turned a deaf ear, not only to my prayers, but to Alex's, too, leaving both of us hopeless and irrefutably broken; and since the God I'm praying to is supposed to be the embodiment of love, he couldn't ignore both of our pleas . . . I rub my belly trying to squelch the burning sensation that's the result of a gnawing, hopeless feeling . . . unless he doesn't exist.

Reaching the faculty restroom, I flip off the light and wrap myself tight with a hug as I stare into the darkness. This restroom is my favorite because there are no windows or light seeping in, except a sliver under the door. This is my hideout like my closet and the laundry room at home and the levy and the inside of any man's arms. When I stand here, I can be anywhere I want to be. My imagination can take flight, and right now I want to imagine there is a god. There has to be because the intricacies of the human body alone dictate so.

I take a step toward where I know the commode is and remember I didn't come here to pee. I escaped my classroom to process Barber setting Alex's cruiser on fire. Gazing into the beautiful darkness, I thank God for protecting my babies and Alex from Barber.

As I'm thanking God that Alex did not fill the gas tank, I see tiny flashes of lights. I blink, but they are still there like mini-sparklers. A red one in the corner, white ones toward the ceiling. I close my eyes and tell myself that I'm not going crazy—that it's just my eyes playing tricks on me, but I've been in this same restroom hundreds of times with the lights off and never seen them before.

Rain No Evil

I open my eyes, but the darkness still seems to be twinkling at me. The lights are tiny like ones a laser pointer would create. Suddenly, a blue one sparks right in front of me. I wonder if the lights are spirits or angels. God knows I sure could use more than one angel to keep me out of trouble. Whatever they are I hope they are harmless.

Then a terrifying thought hits me. If they are spirits, one of the lights could be my demon. I jerk open the door and jog back to class, actually relieved to see Mrs. Z's constipated-looking human face.

At lunch I return a missed call to the heating and cooling guy who agrees to meet me at the house tomorrow afternoon. Then in search of information on the Boggs kid, I cruise past the gym and around the corner into the teachers' lounge that smells of stale coffee and warmed-up sauerkraut.

The crossword section of the newspaper is under Mr. Feldman's pencil-smudged hand, and he holds a folded slice of school pizza in the other.

Mrs. Z., who is nuking her Lean Brand lasagna that doesn't lend the physical results the label implies, informs me that Matt was the student who was expelled last year for taking a gun to the neighboring Beaumont High. Wonderful—a student who may be packing more than cigarettes.

On the way home, I tell the boys they'll have to ride the bus home tomorrow afternoon because I took off to meet the heating and cooling tech. I'm waiting for traffic so I can turn into the driveway when a vehicle heading toward me in the oncoming lane snaps on the blinker. I don't readily recognize the new SUV Alex now drives. I scan Alex's face for a sign of recognition—for a smile, but he stoically motions me to pull in.

For a second, I focus on the imposing uniformed figure—on the siren bar sitting atop the vehicle like a beacon of light ready to sound justice through any dark night to save a damsel in distress. I'm comforted by how respected he appears, the authority he commands. It makes me feel important, too.

I'm important enough for him to love me so why do I feel like the damsel that needs saving, and is Alex the knight for the job? Maybe I need saved from myself—from the condemnation I fill myself with to the endless questioning of why I'm in this world and why I always feel inadequate.

Alex pulls in around back as the town's water department truck pulls in behind me. I jump out of the car in the garage quicker than even the boys do, scampering to reach Alex before he blasts the city worker with questions about why they're here.

Alex struts from his cruiser, hand resting on his gun belt. "What're they doing here?"

"I forgot to tell you," I say. "Sorry. It was a crazy day. Because of the leak, I figured it couldn't hurt to see if we're using more water than usual."

The city worker waves and Alex tosses his head in the air, turning to enter the kitchen door the boys left open.

71

I stroll through the front yard to where the city worker is hunched over the meter.

"Usage reads normal," he says. "Not consistent with that of a leak, unless it's a slow one." He scrunches his nose. "You say it's spraying? Like shooting across the room?"

I nod deeply and slowly as if I'm bestowing a sacred knowledge upon him.

"Sounds like a build-up of pressure that's releasing," he says so confidently, I tend to believe what he said it's possible.

"Better call the plumber." He turns and hoists himself into the driver's seat of his truck.

"They're scheduled for Monday. Thanks for coming," I say stepping toward the house and thinking that Monday's a long three days away.

All four of us sit at the dinner table, each boy vying for their dad's attention—Isaac recanting this morning's unwanted shower from our leak and asking if Alex is going to coach his biddy league football team this year and Ben inquiring into the murder investigation.

I want to ask Alex if Barber is still out roaming around, or if he's behind bars, or if he's at the bottom of the river in concrete boots, but I don't want the boys to know about Barber trying to blow up their dad's cruiser. Besides, it's refreshing to hear the boys engaged in a normal conversation with their dad. At least they're talking politely, taking turns rather than talking over each other. It's a civilized exchange that I imagine to be standard practice in most educated white-collar families.

With each comment, the boys' voices raise one octave higher while Alex crams spoonfuls of cornbread-sprinkled chili into his already full mouth. If anyone says anything funny right now I'm going to get a mouthful of the mess in Alex's mouth. I don't even eat beans, and I damn sure don't want his leftovers.

I'm just about to mention the newest addition to my class, the Boggs boy, when a splattering of water hits the overhead light, shattering the glass bulbs resting in their globes and sending shrapnel onto the couch and carpet just inches from my bare feet.

I'm not sure who hops up first—just know a slop of chili hits my cheek from Alex's mouth as if I'd have wished it true. Then Alex runs into the kitchen as if he can outrun our elemental enemy.

I must've thought we were being attacked—that maybe Barber had shot the windows out because when I regain my senses, I'm hunkering in the empty chair next to me, wielding a fork in my hand as a shield. I thought the boys' eyes were big when this water thing started, but now their eyes have taken over their whole face as they peer out from the safety of their armpits.

"Boys, don't move. I don't want you to get cut," I say, tiptoeing around bulb fragments. I suppose being calm in emergencies is a gift, but had I known I'd be in a war zone, I'd have worn my boots.

I retrieve the broom and dustpan from the closet while Alex moans about a piece of glass in his bleeding foot. I sweep up the biggest fragments and insist the boys stay seated while I vacuum over the area.

Glass is sneaky, bouncing into the most inconspicuous corners when broken just like the guilt tucked in various corners of me—guilt for being unfaithful—guilt for not being a wholesome mom whose love is intense enough to hold my family together.

Alex is ranting something about this damn water, but I've learned that when I add humming to the sound of the vacuum I can block the sound of his voice. I practice the technique in the lovely quiet of my mind until the floor is safe for little feet again.

Knowing I was diligent in protecting the boys from stepping on glass stirs a sensation of satisfaction. What I just did was enough—enough to matter. This is what being a good mom must feel like. It feels saintly and respectable, and I want to feel this way more often.

When I turn off the vacuum, I thumbs-up the boys, who've sopped up their second bowl of chili with butter-drenched cornbread. They pound toward the stairs, but I wave them back and tell them to get towels from the kitchen and dry the walls and couch.

"Plumbers Monday. Right?" Alex asks, hobbling toward the table and frowning over his cold bowl of chili.

"Yep," I say, joining him. "So, how can a water leak upstairs spray us down here?"

Alex stares at me, his cheeks full of cornbread and puckered out like a chipmunks. I glance over to the boys, who are toweling up the water, and hope Alex doesn't lambast me in front of them. He won't approve of the question. It's irrational, but so's the damn leak.

"Thank you, stinker-butts," I say as they run off.

"You know, Sav, for someone so smart, sometimes you ask the most ridiculous questions," Alex says.

I sink into the back of the hard chair, wishing I could disappear before his very eyes and wondering why I'm sitting here listening to his ignorant comments if I'm so fucking smart.

He used to think I was smart. He wouldn't have married stupid. Even though he *is* stupid. No, he's too smart for that.

"Obviously, there's more than one leak," he says. "Now, can we be serious? We've got more serious shit to talk about than a measly water leak. I found out from a snitch that just last week Barber flashed several pictures of you and the boys to his buddies—threatened to 'Put a good kinda hurtin' on the blonde.'"

I stare at my hubby's mouth that opens and closes like it's filled with molasses and wonder if that's what I deserve—to be humiliated—raped like the stupid whore I am.

"You hear me?" Alex gulps his sweet tea and sets his jaw. "He won't get the chance to get near you."

Leaning back against the chair, I stop chewing my salad and allow the joy from his caring words to cuddle my castrated ego.

"Tomorrow, I'm meeting with the BCI. They get involved when officers and their families are threatened."

"Is BCI like the FBI?" I manage to wring out.

Alex nods. "It's state. Bureau of Criminal Investigations."

"Where'd Barber get pics of us?"

"Right here—Ben and Isaac passing baseball and you carrying in groceries." Alex stares into space as if he's seeing another world before his eyes. "He won't be so brazen after I get ahold of him."

I collect the dishes and let the facts settle in. This is real. My family has been threatened. My boys—I'll do anything to protect them. If I can't protect them from the ugliness within these four walls, I can at least protect them from the lion roaring at the gate outside.

"Will you call me after you talk with BCI—or at least text me by lunch? Just keep me posted?"

Alex nods.

Progress. Now I just hope my bed is dry enough to crawl into.

Chapter Seven

One Amaretto Sour Short of Crazy

I have perfected my morning routine—honed it to a science. Two minutes too long in any department—the shower, shit, or shave and I'm late. If I'm late then Ben's late, and if Ben's late, the school's automated call-out system informs Alex by phone of the tardy, giving him something else to gripe about.

So, I'm not late—even if it means I apply mascara over the bathroom sink at school just like I did in high school when red heels with jeans was in and anything Madonna did was cool—especially smoking.

This morning is indeed a refined passing-off of the only full-bath in the house—a melody of ease from the moment our toes hit the dry floor until Isaac's butt's planted on the bus.

"I'm ready," Ben says, opening the side door as water squirts across the kitchen ceiling.

"Awww, man!" Ben says, grabbing a paper towel.

I dab my soaked shirt with a dishtowel and glance at Ben who's only been sprinkled. "You?" I say. "You're dry compared to me!" I toss him the towel. "I've got to change. Dry this up, please."

After changing my shirt, I gather my hodgepodge of a breakfast—hunk of dark chocolate, deli meat, and banana nut bread.

I can hear Grandma Lennie saying, "All things in moderation" after I scarfed down an entire strawberry-rhubarb pie one day and barfed all night.

But there's nothing moderate about getting drenched while standing in a perfectly sound house. It's as radical as Bill O'Reily and his "No-spin zone." I'm actually looking forward to absconding to work. At least with the little hoodlums I know what to expect—that is unless they walk in my room like my new ex-con student, Matt who looked around like he was casing the joint.

It's afternoon before I realize Alex didn't keep his promise about keeping me informed on the Barber/BCI project, but I'm not going to pester him.

The first ten minutes of fifth period every Thursday is allotted for "bullying prevention" at Ridgeland High. Just another prep I don't have time for—I'm already planning for five different classes, so rather than logging onto the website to display the prompt on the Smartboard, I read aloud the prompt for discussion. "Suppose you were to walk into the school restroom and see two students known to deal drugs push another student into the corner.

One of the bully's says, 'If you breathe a word of this to anyone, I'll cut your tongue out and flush it down there,' pointing to the commode. What would you do?"

I'm imagining the responses this will generate when Matt, who could be our antagonist in the scene and the poster child for the school's anti-bullying campaign, bursts out, "If they'd shoot his fucking ass they wouldn't have to cut his tongue out."

"Matt," I say, "detention for the language. The question isn't asking what the drug dealers should do, the question is what would you—"

"I don't do detention," Matt says, squaring his shoulders and leaning his seat onto its hind legs.

I point my pencil toward the little shithead and stare at him. "You need to leave. Report to IHS," I say.

"What's that?" Matt says with a shrug.

"In-house suspension. The room by the office."

"Bitch!" Matt yells, standing and heaving his desk toward the back wall where it crashes into the corner of the bookshelf. Piles of books collapse into the floor. The entire class is stone silent and staring at me.

I lock my gaze on the ex-con who I'm supposed to teach not only to analyze text and write persuasive essays, but to respect other students. "Leave!" I say in a gruff voice that would put Kathleen Turner to shame and push the office call button on the wall behind my desk.

When Matt slings his folder across the floor and stomps out the door, I don't bat an eyelash.

The secretary's voice booms from the intercom, "Yes, Mrs. Templeton."

"Matt Boggs is on his way to IHS," I say, projecting my answer loudly toward the speaker in the center of the ceiling. "Could you have Mr. Myers head this way and make sure he gets there?"

The shrill voice responds, "Will do."

The intercom beeps and the secretary announces an all-call, "Mr. Meyers you're needed in the office."

If he's in the building he's likely chatting with the football coach or tucked away with the school's PRO, Prevention Resource Officer, Bob, who's probably reviewing hallway video footage for possible culprits of the latest act of vandalism—rolls of toilet paper shoved into the commodes in the boys' locker-room and causing the new gym to flood.

Of course, he could be in one of various meetings—an IEP, Individualized Educational Plan; a SAT, Student Assistance Team; a PLC, Professional Learning Community, or an LSIC, Local School Improvement Committee. I often think I deserve another degree for just learning all the educational acronyms.

I scribble Matt's remarks onto the proper form and send it to the office with Terry who told me before class his mom's still in "the crazy house." Nixing my plans for Shakespeare this period, I manage to corral the discussion to our bully-in-the-bathroom dilemma for the remaining twenty-five minutes of the period.

Before I leave school early to meet the guy from the heating and cooling company, I slip into Ben's science class on the junior high side and navigate to the front where he stands by a sink wearing lab glasses.

"Make sure to ride the bus home," I whisper.

Ben nods without taking his eyes off the beaker in his hand.

I don't want to embarrass him especially since kids have been calling him "Big Bird," which I inadvertently promulgated at his birthday party last July when I showed his besties pictures of him as a toddler, squeezing his furry, yellow friend.

But isn't that what friends are for—to irritate and give us a false sense of acceptance? After all, Logan's wife, Kari, was a friend to me until she screwed Alex. Now, I just pretend she is.

It's easier that way. Sweet bug-eyed Kari. She hugged me when I confided in her that I was always afraid to make a mistake around Alex—that I wanted him to just be nice to me—to let me be human.

I felt Kari accepted my perception of Alex as I presented it to her—that she truly empathized with me; but, no doubt, her perception of my husband changed when she spread her legs.

I'm home at 2:00 p.m. with minutes to spare. I sit back in my chair in the living room, journal in hand, and a splash of water douses me, and suddenly, I'm even more in the mood to express myself even if it is only to a patch of paper. I write:

> This water has to stop. If I was an alcoholic, I'd be one Amaretto Sour short of dead. But sex is my crutch—an itch that I scratch like a patch of poison on my brain.
>
> Maybe I'm a sex-crazed version of Terry's mom, but at least sex puts a smile on my face and I'm not babbling about invisible teeth yet.
>
> Demon in the mirror and dicks in me, Oh, my mirror is special.
>
> Mirror Mirror in my room, Can I be saved and if so, by whom?

Teeth. That reminds me of the time a large woman in a smock walked up our front porch steps, head held high and with a toothless smile, asked for her false teeth. She had lost them in the back seat of the cruiser when Alex taxied her intoxicated butt home. After that, I teasingly referred to him as the "Official tooth warden."

Isaac, who was a toddler at the time, quizzed Alex, "Daddy, why you have that woman's teeth?"

One of a string of many odd questions and even odder people Alex had explained throughout the years.

Our boys are surely receiving an education not available in the public school system.

The sound of a vehicle's exhaust prompts me to part the living room curtains. A familiar red-haired fellow jumps out of a white van.

I slip on my flip-flops and mosey down the drive. "Hi." I say, extending my hand. "Gary, right?"

He squeezes my hand. "Good memory, girl," Gary says, sticking his fingers through his belt loops and yanking upward. "I gotta say, this is the first time a customer's asked me for a service call for a water problem."

I feel silly now that he is actually here. "I imagine it's an unusual request," I say. "We're running a dehumidifier, but there's so much moisture, it's not helping as you can see." I gesture toward the house where sunlight casts an eerie appearance on the steamy windows.

The center of Gary's forehead forms the shape of a "V." He slams the van door and follows me into the house empty-handed. Guess he's not sure what tools he'll need.

"The water sprays with so much force that it reaches the front door from clear up there." I say, ascending the stairs and pointing to the hall ceiling. "It shoots out like a hose on jet stream."

"No way!" Gary's eyebrows arch high and he shakes his head.

"Yes, way," I say, sounding like a teenager.

I follow behind him up the stairs, as he canvases the interior.

"Look, missy," Gary says. "I've done this a long time. Longer than you've been breathing, and if this was condensation, water wouldn't be spraying. It'd be dripping. You know, like it does from un-insulated pipes attached to air conditioning units."

I nod. "I didn't think it was condensation, but . . . any suggestions? We're kind of desperate."

Gary looks at the dry walls and floors then to the windows that are so steamy they look like they're crying, shakes his head and says, "Maybe a plumber?"

I walk outside with him wishing the house had provided a demonstration. Gary drives off and from the shade of a maple in the front yard, I stare at my house.

Even with the water leak, I love this old place.

Ceramic blue cherub wind chimes tinker a welcome to the warm weather while white rockers wearing red-striped cushions splash happiness about. Grandma Lennie would say the sound of chimes means a change is coming. Hope she's right. We can't live in these soaked quarters for long. Even if the house was dry, the atmosphere here is not conducive to my happiness, and I feel a change is imminent.

My gaze finds the moisture-speckled windows and for a moment the droplets of water form a face. I blink and it's gone. Suddenly, my face and arms tingle with goose bumps like I get when Ryan dances his tongue across my skin. A darkness takes root inside me as if I had just glimpsed an elusive demon like the one I saw in my mirror.

I step into the sunshine, telling myself I'm under a lot of stress and stress can make people see things. But what's the chances of seeing a face that's not really there just days after seeing flames in a microwave that isn't on fire?

A car crunches into the gravel driveway beside me. I'm surprised to see Alex pull in with Stranahan. He usually works alone. Wonder if he's caught Barber.

Alex rolls down the window and peers up at me from under his campaign hat. He looks delicious, like a tootsie roll ready to be unwrapped.

"What's the special occasion?" I ask.

"On our way to eat and Stranahan's car is at the country garage for new tires," Alex says.

Stranahan leans over from the passenger's side and goads me through a snuff-filled smirk. "Hear ya got a hot date with the repair guy. Alex just not doing it for ya?"

"Yep! And his most amazing tool was in his jeans," I say, playing along. Alex rolls his eyes. "You'd know."

"No, really." I say, not wanting to give him a reason to think I'm really messing around on him. "The heating guy didn't know what to say about—"

"Listen, Sav, we got to get going. I stopped—" Alex says.

"The heating guy, Mr. Robinson, didn't have a clue about what's causing the water leak," I say, raising my chin and looking past Alex to Stranahan for acknowledgement that my mouth is actually moving and words are coming out.

Alex's cohort spits tobacco into an empty coke bottle. "I'll have to check this water thing out for myself. Before I got on the force, I was contractor."

"I'll take you up on that," I say. "A deputy—a plumber—I don't care who stops the waterworks show."

Alex squeezes the steering wheel and locks his elbows. "I'm trying to tell you something. You need to pack up and take the kids to your dad's until we round up Barber."

I anchor my hand to my hip feeling like a scolded child. His rudeness burns my gut. I try to swallow, but my throat feels like I'm trying to cough up a camel. I'm madder at Alex for embarrassing me in front of Stranahan than I am curious about what he's saying.

"BCI will be here in an hour to install cameras," he continues. "I'll have Pete pull his cruiser around back. Make sure you get the boys outta here safe."

Alex motions to Stranahan who radios dispatch and requests Pete to public service him. This *must* be bad if Stranahan's not broadcasting it on the radio.

My legs are so rigid my kneecaps feel like they are going to explode. I pucker my lips, ready to refuse to be ran out of my own home by some tattooed Jesse James wannabe, when Alex's eyes deadlock mine. "Savvy, Barber's threats were verified as substantial enough to warrant the precautions."

Wow. Alex sounds so official. I grind my hand against my hip, wanting to bulk against the preponderance of being a victim.

"We have two boys to protect. This is not all about you," Alex says. "So, for once . . ." He sighs. "Can you just do what I'm asking you?"

I let my hand slide down my left leg and, with eyes toward the heavens, acquiesce. "All right, I just don't want this guy to think I'm scared of him. I'm not running scared from some tattooed dirtball."

Alex turns to Stranahan who nods like he's read his partner's mind and says, "He'd better hope I'm not the one to get my hands on him first. It'll be the last thing he feels—my hands wrapped around his slimy neck."

I know he means it. The judges in the county pay scanty attention to a defendant's depiction of officers who shock confessions from interviewees handcuffed to bed frames and who have, "Special black gloves that hurt like hell, but don't leave marks." There's no proof, of course, of this form of data extraction that, according to Alex, is "Necessary for the safety of all the good people in Wooten County."

Alex knows which officers he can entrust with his alternative interview protocol and which ones would tattle on his unorthodox behavior. He removes the "wussies," the "lazies," and the politically correct ones from his coveted list, leaving a handful that comprise a sacred guild of secrecy. Sharing illicit methods with his trusted crew seems to provide a relief to Alex. The camaraderie is his measure of normalcy, his guide for setting limits and for breaking them.

A cruiser turns into the neighbor's driveway leading to our three-car garage. Pete waves and positions his cruiser on the concrete pad where Alex's cruiser was parked when Barber set fire to it.

"Okay, I'll pack up," I lean into the open window and peck my man in green on the cheek, keeping my face close to his until he pecks me back.

It's us against the forces of evil. The danger is real and I prefer us united in peril than separated in love.

As Alex pulls off, I think of all the crazy criminal stories I could write about. If I added the wicked web of unity among lawmen and a demon in my mirror, I just might have a best seller.

Pete, the one city officer Alex would trust for this duty, walks toward me with his flirty smile as he turns down the volume of the radio clipped to his belt. "Hey, Savvy. Man, you all have quite the hopping place here."

"Yep, no rest for the wicked they say." I twist my hair and try to remember if it was Isaiah or Job that said that. I can't, but I know it's in the Bible somewhere, and I wonder how much I have to suffer before I find peace. "You going to catch Barber so I can come home soon?"

"Do my best," Pete says with a salute and a tip of his hat. Damn, he's cute—deep blue eyes straight from the Atlantic, rings of dark curls tight on his head. His department permits haircuts other than the buzz, and the lax standard makes Alex cringe.

"When the boys get back from school, they'll want to know why you're here. I'm just telling them that you're waiting on Alex for a special detail. They don't need to know about this Barber lunatic."

The man with the gold shield winds and says, "Gotcha."

I place my hand on the side door. Thinking of Pete snapping a pair of cuffs on me in his back seat gives me the sensation of a hive of honeybees buzzing in my belly, but it would send Alex over the edge. Screwing another officer is off limits more than an active crime scene, and that's not a line I want to cross. I need to get away from him before I say something flirty. "I have to pack. If you need anything just help yourself."

I rush upstairs, grabbing my journal from my chair in the living room on the way, my mind racing with the events of the last few days—inexplicable water leak, possible murder, disturbed students, my marriage sinking as Ryan anchors his hands to my ass, and now a dirtball threatening my family.

Tossing my journal into the duffle bag first, I scan my closet for an outfit, but in my hurry, my eyes won't stay focused. The colors and materials of all the clothes appear fuzzy so I sling in a few shirts and pants, not caring if they match, then pack ample clothes to last the boys a few days. I can always have Dad pick up more, but the boys will be home from school soon, and I'll need to have the car packed and ready to head straightaway to Dad's.

Dad! He doesn't know we're coming. I place the bags in the kitchen and dial him up. When I tell him the boys and I need to stay with him because of the water leak, he says, "Savvy" in such a way I know that he knows there's more to the story. His detective skills are as sharp as they were when he was on the force. I tell him I'll fill him in when I get there and that we might stay more than one night so I hope he's stocked up on food, especially Ben's coffee.

Compared to the caffeine-laden energy drinks Ben's buddies drink, the cacao bean seems a decent trade-off. I figure if I permit a few vices, he won't be a rebel like me.

Slinking into my recliner in the living room, I peer out back where Pete is parked and call Mandy, my best friend since before I needed to wear a bra. If I texted her everything I need to say, my fingers would be spastic like my brain feels.

Her move to a town hours away was tough on me, but our friendship isn't hampered by mere distance. The miles are elastic, stretching our friendship across the way when needed. Mandy enters a sacred space in my confidences, one that not many others are welcomed into.

"You're not going to believe this," I say when I hear her exuberant voice. "I'm not sure I even do."

I proceed to relate the cacophony of the past week to Mandy who says she's sure Alex will capture Barber and the water leak will be fixed soon. "But," Mandy says, "Alex will always be Alex and expect you to be his little wonder woman—to leap ladders and hold drywall in a single bound."

"You're probably right. He won't change. I just don't know how much more I can take. It's the worst it's ever been between us." I roll my foot from side to side on the footstool. "I even started seeing Ryan again. And I was doing sooo good."

"What? Girl, are you serious? Ryan!" Mandy says. "You know Alex will be pissed if he finds out. It almost broke your marriage up when you came clean last time. I saw Ryan on Facebook hugging a woman at the hospital fundraiser. She works there at the hospital with him."

I press the wrinkles out of my forehead. I don't want to think about another woman on Ryan's arm. "I know Alex would be mad. I do. It's just . . . Mandy, I can't stop myself. He . . . he makes me feel wanted, but it's just like when I used to go shopping to make myself happy." I picture my arms dripping with red bags embossed with the signature huge white star I love. "Full Macy's bags didn't my barren heart fill."

We both snort out a laugh.

"Hey, that's pretty good—journal-worthy for sure," I say.

"You writing again?"

"Yeah, it helps to put words to my feelings, but I can't keep living this way. I don't like myself anymore. At least Ryan listens to me. I mean, it's not like I'm in love with him, but I enjoy his company, you know?"

"Oh, Savvy, I know Alex has hurt you and you deserve to be happy. He's sure enjoyed his share of poontang." Mandy says.

I laugh. "I haven't heard that word in years. Whoever thought up that word anyway? 'Poontang.'" The sound of brakes hissing alerts me to arrival of the school bus. "Mandy, Got to go—boys are here."

Chapter Eight

BARNEY BADASS

The boys bound through the door and slap their books on the counter. Kitchen cabinets are yanked open like the munchkins haven't eaten since Halley's Comet streaked across the sky.

When I see my babies, a smile slides onto my face as easily as my foot into my well-worn Reeboks. Life for other children is much worse than these two have it—a roof over their heads, food in their bellies, and two imperfect parents who love them.

"Guys," I say, "guess what—well, there's no school tomorrow because of the special election, sooo we get to stay with Pawpaw Cal tonight. I've already packed your bags."

"Awesome! Really?" Ben says as he spots Pete's cruiser through the window. "Why's Pete here? What's going on?"

"Oh, waiting on your dad for a road detail or something," I say.

Oatmeal cookies in hand, they both bolt to the cruiser to talk with Pete while I place protein bars in my bag for my 2 a.m. baby-saving nightmare-induced feeding.

I'm glad I told Pete to keep the boys in the dark. They know too much already about their dad's necessary, but unscrupulous practices; they don't need to worry about Barber. I toss the duffel bags into the car trunk, and we're off to our hideout across the river. It's only a fifteen-minute drive from Dad's in MuddSock Heights to work, so even if we have to stay longer than the weekend, I won't have to wake up much earlier in the morning.

Crossing the bridge into Ohio, the boys chatter about which activity to get into first at Pawpaw's—fish in the pond, ride the horses, or shoot blackbirds. I nix the last option, telling them that killing anything they aren't eating is just plain evil. "I'm driving through DQ in a few minutes," I say. "Make sure you know what you want."

I know what I want—a table with a view overlooking the river at Cornerstone Quarry, raspberry martini on my breath, and oven-baked salmon against my palette. Never did get that birthday dinner. Maybe when things settle down Alex and I can have a romantic dinner—really tune into each other.

"Hey, Mom, how come Pawpaw lives in Muddy Socks?" Isaac asks.

I blurt out a sound something like, "Bah hah," and say, "Honey, Pawpaw Cal lives in MuddSock Heights, not Muddy Socks." I lean out the window and request two combo meals in the drive-thru. "Isaac, you know, maybe they should've called it Muddy Socks. The town got its name because of all the mud left over from a flood back in the 40s that made the roads impassable. People couldn't even travel on them with horses. The "sock" part means 'to sink.'"

Appropriate—I feel like I'm drowning in a cesspool of insanity. I'm seeing things that may not be real in a house that's sprung an invisible leak even as the boys and I sink into a safe haven to avoid a madman.

Order in hand, Isaac and Ben occupy their mouths while I occupy my mind with the mystery called God. The emerging beauty of pink dogwood blossoms and giant, hanging oaks along the brick stretch of road displays a tangible possibility of God's existence. Something divine had to make this spectacle of fluttering colors against the misty backdrop of sky blue. All this couldn't have just exploded into being—that is unless a divine eminence did the exploding.

I stop at the drycleaners and pick up Alex's uniforms that have been ready for weeks. When I click the hangers onto the hook beside Ben, I get a hunch and reach into the pants pocket. I feel nothing so I check the other pocket and pull out a gum wrapper. I've been wrong before, but I check the other pair anyway and retrieve a blue business card that says "Tutor's Textbooks." Stacey Chutney's contact information is printed on the bottom.

Why would Alex need to get in touch with a textbook company that my friend, Stacey, works for? Is Stacey playing bad girl/good cop with Alex? Even if Alex is screwing around, I have no right to be upset with him. I stick the find in my purse, and the idea of Alex's possible infidelity into the overflow drawer of my mental file.

Ben is rapping along with the radio and Isaac's hamburger is hanging out his mouth, and I know I have more important things to take care of than the likes of sleazy Stacey even if her cunt is accessed as easily as the World Wide Web.

Hearing the cadence of the brick road beneath the tires as we pass the only department store in MuddSock Heights, I'm nine-years-old again, pretending to be Nancy Drew, my bike bumping over waves of bricks as I scavenge the alleys looking for an elusive villain who invades my imagination.

Now I'm running from a real criminal—even running from my husband. Should run from men period. How did my life get this crazy? I never expected to be a harlot—a whore reaching for a halo.

Rain No Evil

If only the highway could hold me hostage, I'd drive like Forrest Gump runs—never be a man's pin cushion or lollipop again. His protrusions could go stick or lick some other sucker. Stand, I would, on my own.

The brick road meets gravel as I turn onto Cedar Lane where Japanese maples abound. A mile later, a honey pine log cabin snugged by lilac bushes comes into view. To the right a dock delves into the pond where a fishing boat patiently awaits company the boys will gladly provide.

I follow the curved drive planked by pine trees and pull up to the garage where Dad is watering the hyacinths and forsythia bush. His broad shoulders navigate the hose playfully near my car as the boys hop out, rushing to get a prized hug.

When he isn't fishing, he's planting. Plants breathed life into him after Mom's leaving knocked the wind out of him. Other than the bald head partially hidden by a baseball cap, he doesn't look sixty-five.

I shut the door. Dad's eyes meet mine over the spectacles that are riding the ridge of his nose. Just seeing the understanding in his face makes me feel like melting. I make my way to him on the cobblestone path and fall into his waiting arms.

He rubs my head. "Oh, punkin."

"Pawpaw, Can you tell us Barney Badass stories tonight?" Isaac says, picking up the fishing pole leaning against the rail.

"Who said you could say ass?" Dad says, laughing. "Didn't your mama teach you to not use such language?"

Ben says, "Oh, come on, Pawpaw. You say we're your legacy and that means we need to know your stories."

I wink at Dad. "I'm doing something right," I say. "Listen to that vocabulary—'legacy,' and look at these two gorgeous grandkids who're interested in an old man's stories and tell me I'm not a good mama."

The boys dodge Dad's rifle leaning against the porch rail, and fly to the barn for their tackle boxes.

Dad's been referred to as "Barney Badass" by his neighbors ever since he responded to the sound of glass breaking at old Mr. Fletcher's place next door and tackled Fletcher's thirty-five year old son who was busting the house windows with his bare and bleeding fists. The restrained "boy" who, unbeknownst to Dad, was off his bipolar meds huffed, "Get off me! You just think you are Barney Badass."

Dad and I gravitate to the kitchen where he hangs his cap on a hook by the back door and retrieves my dark chocolate from its special hiding spot behind the dusting cloths.

"Boys haven't found it yet." He chuckles through the toothpick teetering between his lips. "Coffee? Tea? Jack?"

"Jack in coffee," I say, getting a mug from the cabinet.

"Aw, honey. Must be bad. What's going on?"

"Some lunatic, well, you remember, Bobbie Barber, the criminal who took off with Alex's handcuffs that time?"

Dad nods slowly, his eyes trying to look through his forehead as he pushes "brew" on the Keurig.

"He's threatening me and the boys—even has pictures of us—so BCI is placing cameras at the house and staking it out in case he gets froggy and goes there. That's why we had to leave. I didn't want to tell you, but kind of hard not to when I had to come here to sleep."

Still nodding, Dad removes the toothpick and sucks on his teeth. He stares into space at a memory I can't see—maybe of the stalking case he worked ten years ago where the victim was so disfigured by her attacker, she drove herself right off the ramp of the unfinished bridge.

I know Dad's still pissed that he couldn't locate the guy who was suspected of using the lady's face as a carving board. He was a vagabond who moved through the area so quickly that not even his neighbors could describe what he looked like.

"I know, makes you want to come out of retirement. How long's it been now? Four years?"

"Six," he says pouring in a nip of whiskey before handing me the coffee.

Cradling my mug, I saunter off to the living room.

Dad chooses his leather recliner by the fireplace, worry reflecting from his eyes eager to know more. He commanded respect when he was an officer, but didn't have to browbeat his family into respecting him; we just did. He didn't just slip on a uniform and expect the fine folks of the world to lie prostrate and groveling at the bottom of his green pant leg like Alex seems to.

Flopping onto the couch, I give an edited version of life in the Templeton household for the past week—edited because I tell him about the mysterious water leak, saving the drowning girl, a possible mafia murder mystery, my new pupil fresh out of prison, and Barber's attempt to set fire to Alex's cruiser—everything except the demon I saw in the mirror. I know I can't help it that I saw it, but I feel guilty because it showed up as if it were condemning me for committing adultery. Even if I'm wrong about why it showed up, I'm not ready to present my reasoning on the topic to anyone, especially to Dad.

He peers over his coffee. "Good God, Savannah. You got to be making this shit up! You should have told me about all of this sooner—you're supposed to call the old, bald guy when you need help."

"I didn't want you to worry. There's nothing you can do to fix the water." I snarl. "Heck, we can't even find the leak that needs fixing. There's nothing you can do about any of it, but if you'd have been at the levy, I'd have gladly let you jump in and get that girl. It was freezing!"

"We'll figure out the water deal. Priority now is that you're out of that maniac's reach and that he's within Alex's. Remember me telling you about the creep who threatened to kidnap you when you were eight years old?" Dad's rests his hands fingertip to fingertip on his khaki vest. "When I caught wind of it, we had a little talk in his apartment. Pictures of you stepping into the school bus were on his kitchen table."

I nod and sink deeper into the plush seat, feeling safe with Dad to my right and warm coffee in my hand. I feel like I'm barricading myself into my own hemlock tree—like I'm burrowing into my own side of the mountain just like Sam in the novel I'm reading with my ninth graders. "What happened to the creep?" I say, feeling relieved to be able to open my mouth without being interrupted.

Dad shrugs, the corners of his mouth twisting into a downward grin, "The guy just up and moved. Darndest thing."

I grin. "No doubt. He have pictures of Luce, too?"

"No, your sister would have been five and home with . . ."

I draw a long slurp of coffee. *Mom.* He avoids saying her name, but he doesn't need to remind me of her. Her memory is always ready to rise when I come home—like the homemade cinnamon rolls she used to bake on Saturdays to tease our sleepy heads out of slumber.

Admission to memory lane can be pricey, and I'm spent for the day. "Dad," I say, "think I'll settle in and read a while. Can you check on the boys?"

I retreat to my old room where a pink shag rug still hugs the hardwood floor and lava swirls inside of a silver lamp. Sitting on the plump white cushion in the bay window to write, I find myself gazing out my second story window and watching Dad's two horses frolicking in the pasture.

Dad's already sitting beside the boys in their folding chairs—must've decided to not fool with the boat. Dad enjoys the boys as much as they do him. Mom's missing out—not being here to see her grandkids grow up, but why should I care when it's obvious she doesn't. She must be content to watch them grow up via the pictures Grandma Lennie, when she was still living would send in the mail.

Mom even missed my wedding. Her absence was felt more than her actual presence would've been. That's but a trinket in my collection of grudges I've carried over the years—guess she's not the only one who gets punished for her choice reneging on her promise to Dad. I'm so scared to emulate her that I stay with Alex despite the peril to my heart and mind.

But that's the penalty for leaving us—no invitation to participate in our most joyous moments. The word "joyous" lingers in my head along with the image of tears in Alex's eyes when he said, "I do." And I know he did. He may not anymore, but once he loved me.

We *were* happy and for that matter, Mom and Dad appeared to be. Dad told me that they received a proper "bell shower," as did every newlywed couple in the 60s. I imagine this very yard full of friends and family clanging their pots and pans, knowing Mom and Dad want to be alone on their wedding night, and waiting for the aggravated bride and groom to bring a gift of some sort—food, clothes, household item—out to the noisy crowd, bribing them to go away.

Mom's mom, Grandma Lennie, raised her. She didn't bow out of *her* responsibility. A thought enters my mind—one I don't want to entertain, but . . . maybe I won't let Alex see the real me, the sensitive, caring real me because I feel unworthy to be loved. My mom didn't love me enough to hang around and raise me. If a mom can't love me, who can?

God is supposed to love unconditionally, but I don't see the results of that either. He's certainly not helping my marriage get any better. Even when I was faithful, Alex still talked to me like I couldn't process information via the English language. He doesn't respect me and I don't know how to make him.

It may be too late for us to even have a chance at a mutually loving relationship—at least with each other. After all, I've allowed him to treat me like a harlot for years—a harlot with a ring on her finger that says to the world, "I need a man in order to be somebody because I'm so stupid."

I watch Isaac cast his pole in the pond and suddenly, I realize I'm enveloped in silence. A little spat between the boys or a hum of the washer I'd welcome right now, but the faint tinkle of wind chimes funneling from the terrace below is my only distraction. Grandma Lennie always said that with the clinking of wind chimes comes change. I smile up toward a cumulus pillow in the sky, imagining grandma blowing the wind to rattle the chime just for me—her way of beaming me hope from Heaven.

The strain of silence is too much, I reach to the dresser, releasing my former confidant from her jewelry box and watch her spin in a pool of satin to Tchaikovsky's "The Nutcracker." My precious ballerina. She's heard more of my dreams than I can remember—dreams of being saved from captivity like Queen Guinevere was by Sir Lancelot—dreams of being an extraterrestrial spy sent here to discreetly disseminate perspicacious truths to humans—or of solving neighborhood mysteries like a clever Nancy Drew. But the one I entertained the most was of being able to fly like the birds. I was jealous of them like Dorothy in the *Wizard of Oz* who questioned why blue birds could fly over the rainbow and she couldn't.

My ballerina twirls as I listen to the ballad and write in my journal:

> As a girl, I knew I had the power inside me to change the world. Now, as an educated adult, reformed by a practical society, I doubt my ability to change even my own life. My dreams consist solely of existing each day with the hope that one day I will again feel I married the man who was destined to be my knight—who charged forward to protect, not attack me.

Rain No Evil

I jaunt into the bathroom to brush my teeth and hear giggles from downstairs. I pause on the landing and listen to Dad tell how Barney Badass delivered dog poop in a pizza box to his irritating neighbors when they let their dogs do their business in his yard. A U-Haul was in their drive the following week.

"Pawpaw, you're so funny," Isaac says.

Ben says, "Cool."

And now I know why Freud said girls want to marry their daddies.

About seven in the morning a woodpecker at my bedroom window pecks me awake. I snap the covers off and, getting a whiff of coffee, realize I'm not in my house—no one there makes coffee except me. Holly Hobby is waving from my quilt, and I know Dad's in the kitchen flipping eggs.

Before Mom left us for the preacher, she'd griddle a golden breakfast and yell up, "Pancakes and Paddiwinks—get 'em while they're hot." Paddiwinks were colorful pancakes smiling with strategically placed M&M's below the strawberry eyes and blackberry nose.

Sometimes the berries would melt, making my breakfast cake look like it was crying red. Maybe that was an oracle on my plate—my warning that even if I bled in order to be the best Rachel Ray I could be, I'd never please my future husband in the kitchen.

I grab a tissue, blowing away my congested memory, and stomp off to the bathroom. Crying is for the weak—even Alex knows that—the one thing we agree on. My tears aren't red, but with the thoughts of Mom and Alex already swishing around in my head, I feel like I'm bleeding.

Breakfast and a cool jog later finds me running past the horses nibbling their morning hay, wishing I could outrun the memories lapping at my heels, but they're as relentless as the water I'm sure is still spraying inside my house.

A mile later, I round back to Dad's driveway where the boys are shooting BB guns at pop cans perched on a hay bale. Stepping through the front door, Dad says, "Savvy, Alex called. And coffee's made." I grab my cup of comfort and follow the sound of Dad's voice, finding him writing checks at his mahogany desk in the study that sits off from the living room.

I pry the black baseball cap from my sweaty head and slump down in the chair nearest the bookshelf housing the classics of Homer and Dostoevsky alongside new age by James Redfield and Edgar Cayce. "Still paying bills the old-fashioned way?" I ask, swiping the cotton sleeve of my hoodie along my forehead.

"I trust the mailman more than I do the cyber-thieves," he says, removing his glasses and placing them on the pile of bills illuminated by the desk lamp. "The police apprehended Barber."

I force myself to swallow. I'll have to go home. "Great!" I say as optimistically as I can. "Where'd they get him?"

"Damn dumbass was staying at his girlfriends a county over, been drinking and shot off a few rounds with his pistol. Neighbors heard and called the law. Alex was with BCI at your house when the call—"

"Oh, so that's why Barber's still breathing," I say, smacking the arm of the chair. "Another department got on scene first!"

"Yep, poor ole soul doesn't know how being an idiot spared him some misery." Dad rips an envelope open with a smooth metal object. "I wish Alex *had* gotten to him—put the fear of God in him or put him out of his misery altogether." Dad swirls his chair a notch, looking out the window to where Ben is aiming his Red Ryder at a pop can. "If so much as a fingernail on that precious hand of yours . . ."

"Dad, I can take care of myself, you know," I say, wondering if I'll ever take control of the reigns of destiny to my life. "You taught me well—shoot first and then call you to bury the body."

Dad tips back looking at me over his shoulder, a smile crossing his face. "My baby girl has her own babies."

A faint *ping* reaches us as the BB enters Ben's tin can.

Glancing out the window, Dad says, "Those are two fine shots right there. Those boys are going to make a career out of law enforcement or my name isn't Barney Badass!"

As I'm raising my coffee to a high-air cheers, the screen door slams and Ben yells, "Isaac fell in the pond!"

I don't remember running, don't remember jumping in, or the cold water engulfing me, but I do remember gripping my baby's chest, his flailing arms splashing water up my nostrils as I grab the rubber fishing pole handle Dad extends. I remember shoving Isaac toward Ben and Ben bending down from the dock, pulling Isaac out while Dad secured my arm.

I am aware my foot is sinking into the mushy bank, and I sprawl out beside Isaac who is coughing and trying to talk.

"Everything's okay, Buddy," Dad says, stroking Isaac's forehead and turning to Ben. "What happened?"

Ben says, "I just heard a splash and looked up and saw him in the pond."

Isaac stops hacking up water and whispers, "Mom, I can swim."

I want to say, "Too bad you weren't doing it then," but I don't. He just about drowned and I'm just glad he's okay.

Dad latches onto Isaac's triceps and pulls him to his feet, hobbling with him toward the house, Ben and I silently following.

We dry off and gather by the fireplace. "How'd you fall in?" I ask.

"I was reaching for a bobber, but I could have got out myself," Isaac says, jiggling his head like a bobblehead. You 'bout drownded me!" Isaac accepts the cup of hot chocolate Dad hands him and takes a snip.

Maybe he *was* swimming when I jumped in. I honestly don't remember how I reached the conclusion he was drowning.

Rain No Evil

"Maybe you over-reacted because of what happened with that girl in the river," Dad says, reading my mind and handing me a warm mug. Why don't you let the boys stay with me this evening, Savannah? You're exhausted and have enough to deal with at home. I'll make sure they stay away from the pond. The horses need ridden and brushed."

Taking a sip of the chocolate, I shoot a smile Dad's way—my drink's spiked with whiskey. "Okay then, you talked me into it. I'd stay too, but with that incessant water everywhere, Alex is probably going crazy," I say, picturing him in a straightjacket, helpless just like he makes me feel.

The boy's flip on *Sponge Bob* and Dad ascends the stairs, returning a minute later with my bag.

"I could've gotten that," I say.

"Makes an old man feel useful," he says, settling in his recliner.

I hug the boys and bend over Dad, draping my arm around his neck. "Dad, let's celebrate Luce's and my birthday next weekend. Not up to it tomorrow."

On my way home, I pick up a deli chicken at the market and scurry to the checkout lane where a delicious-looking guy with bronze skin is scanning a package of Ensure for the elderly lady in front of me. She's rooting in her change-purse for coins, so I press against the conveyor belt and read the cashier's name tag. *Joe.*

Joe smiles at her—sweet of him. Why do old people need to pay exactly the right amount?

I wish she'd just swipe a damn card and be done with it, but the old woman is still fumbling through her handbag.

Her wrinkled hand delicately places a penny into Joe's hand. Her veins are barely concealed by the transparent skin on her hand, skin so thin it reminds me of what mine looked like the night I saw the demon in the mirror except mine displayed swirls of energy instead of veins.

I run my fingers over the smooth skin of my left hand and notice my wedding ring. I feel important donning the two-karat. The size and clarity of the princess cut shows the world that I'm worthy of a man's love, but that satisfaction may not be worth the disdain I have for myself for not honoring the commitment it represents.

I know it's just a hand, the rock on it only a symbol, but it's a tangible reminder of Alex's love for me, even though it now represents a marriage that's on the rocks rather than the solid love and union it once did.

Reaching in my purse for my wallet, the business card I found in Alex's pants at the drycleaner's yesterday tumbles out and onto the floor. I pick it up, my heart pounding as I realize I must investigate the seemingly secretive connection between my friend, Stacey Chutney, and my husband.

I'm going to be old and wrinkly one day and don't want to regret squandering my youthful good looks and opportunities for pleasure. No siree! I'm not going to wait to go coin bobbing with wrinkled hands just to get a smile when I can have Joe's whole package now.

I dig a scrap piece of paper from my purse and scribble my cell number on the back.

The Samoan-looking clerk dismissively says hello as he rings up my chicken.

All right then—a challenge. Ole Joe's not ignoring me. He doesn't know what he's missing out on. When I hand him a twenty with my scribbled number on top, I fold my hand over his.

He cocks his head to the side, his naked eyes dazzling with intrigue.

I wink. "Just in case you'd like to get together."

His eyes dart toward the cash register as he fumbles for ones, rips my receipt off, and turns back to me. His hand hovers above mine as he stammers, "Thank you."

Oh, you will be thanking me, I think. I'm good at this game.

I'm pulling in the drive to the house and notice several vehicles I don't recognize parked around back by Alex's unmarked cruiser. Maybe Barber escaped. It wouldn't be the first time, but I can't believe he'd be stupid enough to come here. With Alex's reputation, Conan the Barbarian himself wouldn't tiptoe through Alex's tulips.

Hurrying in the kitchen door, I hear muffled voices coming from upstairs and Alex in the living room saying, "Needs castrated." His voice conveys no sense of urgency so Barber must not be loose.

I pass through the kitchen, eyes fixed on Pete who's facing me from his position on the couch. The navy uniform Pete's wearing complements his ocean blue eyes. My cheeks feel like they're in the slot of a toaster when he smiles at me. "So, what's going on?" I ask. "When I saw all the cars, I thought Barber had escaped already."

"Pete's uncle's trying to get to the bottom of this water thing," Alex says, smacking a fist into his palm.

Pete says, "Yeah, he's good. Done just about anything you can think of when it comes to build—"

"Where's the boys?" Alex asks.

It's not just me he interrupts—any thought that springs into his abyss of a head splurts out like steam from a teakettle.

"Dad's bringing them back tomorrow," I say, turning to Pete.

"Uncle Greg works for a construction company in Coraltown that builds houses from the ground up," Pete says. "If it's broke, he can fix it. Guaranteed. He brought some of his workers with him today."

"Thanks, Pete," I say, setting the rotisserie chicken on the bar. "God knows we need the help. How long the workers been here?"

"About fifteen minutes," Pete says.

I look at Alex. "I heard you say somebody needs castrated."

Alex nods, his eyes appearing to be stained glass as he relates an unsavory tale of a child abused to the umpteenth degree. The accused, a twenty-two-year-old high school drop-out, who I had in class five years ago, had explained in his statement to Alex that he'd used Vaseline to penetrate his eighteen-month-old daughter with his penis because he didn't want to hurt her—sick bastard.

Pete closes his eyes while I say a silent prayer for the poor baby and solemnly head outside to retrieve my overnight bag from the car.

I can tell Alex truly cares about the hurt child—about any child that's been abused in any way, but particularly the ones who are poked or prodded sexually. I wish he could show a fraction of that tenderness toward me. I can understand why he has to hide his emotions on the job. Being a hard-ass at work makes him a more effective officer and probably helps him feel immune—protected from the violence he sees first hand, but I wish he didn't need protected from me.

I remember Alex's first child abuse victim—how Alex teared-up as he laid pictures of a bruised and swollen two year old across the countertop in the kitchen, explaining that the little boy had been slammed against a wall and killed by his stoned father. I remember Alex jerking away when I placed my hand on his back and how he said, "Now you know what I deal with every day." I remember feeling inadequate, not knowing how to comfort him, but wanting to.

Alex knows I'll never really see the atrocities he does on a daily basis. But he doesn't know I have my own demon. It's only shown up once, but if I knew that committing adultery would prompt another visit, I'd swear off men for good. I hope that stoned father saw his demon and that it scared the wickedness right out of him.

The images of the disfigured toddler haunted me for days. I insisted he never bring gruesome pictures home again and was grateful he complied. His sharing the photo with me was his way of releasing his anger at the perpetrator of the atrocity, but I wasn't prepared for graphic descriptions of violence to infiltrate our daily dinner conversation as he figured out how to deal with the repulsive crimes and diabolical people he encountered on his job.

I'm glad Alex found a way to cope. He became the cue stick that knocks cue ball perverts into plush pockets at the federal prison even though the scum-bags deserve to be lowered into one six feet down. I just wish Alex didn't have to shield his heart around me.

Having retrieved my groceries, I reach for the doorknob and the door opens toward me, knocking me off-balance.

A man I've never seen before is standing in the doorway. He apologizes and steps back inside, allowing me to enter.

A familiar voice says, "Good to know I'm not the only one who's stumped."

"Keagan, I didn't know you were here, too!" I say, sliding my bags onto the counter and scoping out the short, stocky guy who introduces himself as Pete's Uncle Greg.

Keagan's picking his fingers and leaning against the bar where two other men I've never seen before are planted.

"If I'd have known we were having a party," I say, "I'd have baked a cake. So you're all stumped?"

"I've never seen anything like it, ma'am," Uncle Greg says. "Me and my guys just inspected every square inch of this place and can't find a leak. Searched the attic—not one ounce of water. The chimney isn't leaking either and even with the faucets all turned on, there is no water visibly leaking from anywhere."

"Did you get to see it spray?" I ask.

"Yes, well, we heard it spray from somewhere in the bedroom," Greg says, brushing flakes of insulation from his rotund midsection, "and saw water running down the walls. We didn't actually *see* it spray though. Damndest thing I ever experienced in my whole convoluted life."

"I know," I say. "I was beginning to think I was imagining the sprays. Any suggestions?"

"Unless a pipe bursts or something—well, I just don't know what to tell you." Greg shakes his head. "A dehumidifier might not be a bad idea. It's so damp this whole place feels like a catacomb."

"A cat what?" Alex says from the living room.

Greg replies, "Damp in here like a catacomb."

"Oh," Alex says.

No doubt I'll be defining for him later.

As I head upstairs and over the creaky stairs that I wish I'd have asked Uncle Greg make stop creaking, Pete and Alex speculate about suspects in the rash of burglaries at the local gambling establishments.

In my room, I peruse the stack of books I'm reading and choose the one that discusses the esoteric significance of *The Wizard of Oz*. I'm reading how the yellow brick road symbolizes our journey to spiritual enlightenment and the ruby slippers, our innate ability to maintain our passion for life, when Alex yell's up that he has to run to the office to complete his weekly report that's due tomorrow.

"Okay, honey," I yell back, betting his paperwork likes slapped on the ass.

A few hours later, I'm tucking jeans and shirts into my closet when Alex closes in from behind, sliding his arm around my waist and nibbling on my neck—his silent apology for being a jerk over the drywall deal, I guess, or maybe he's just glad I'm safe from Barber. The nibbling morphs into sucking, the sucking into rubbing and with a fuzzy line of consciousness, Alex's fingers become Ryan's. His fingers slip into me, but I still feel empty.

I imagine Stacey Chutney watching Alex make love to me—watching forlornly as Alex ignores her and ravishes me. I was making him happy long before he even knew her name.

I want to connect with Alex, even if it's just by molding our physical frames into one body. We spin through the hall and into the bedroom, Alex's sturdy hand spreading wide, grasping the back of my head. My chin extends as he yanks on a handful of hair and smooches hungrily up my neck. We fall back onto the bed, our eyes meeting with mutual desire.

Rain No Evil

I wriggle my backside across the mattress, adjusting my hips as his legs straddle mine. The expansion and contraction of Alex's chest towering above me is his only visible movement as he enters me. He lowers his face to my ear, framing my face with his hands, and whispers, "I love you, Sav."

His words sweep over me, enveloping me in a cocoon of safety. He wants me. He loves me. This is how I want to feel every day.

Our bodies smash against each other, yearning for a closer contact than is possible. We smolder with a still desire until, barely moving, we orgasm simultaneously.

Alex rolls off me and I lie still, hoping the harmonious union we just experienced means we're destined to be together and that all we need to do to stay together is to carry this compatibility into our lives outside the bedroom.

Chapter Nine

CREAMSICLE CHAKRA

I'm up early and curl up in front of the TV. With the husky voice of Joyce Meyer droning on the show in the background, I wonder if it's possible for Alex and I be as in-sync in matters of the mind as we are in sensual intelligence gathering on each other's naked bodies.

Suddenly, the lady preacher from the TV belts out, "Speak what you want as if it already exists." My hand goes limp around my pen as I listen. "God spoke the world into existence. Words are powerful. Creating our world using words is an integral part of displaying faith."

Speak what I want into existence—can I actually do that? If what I learned as an Apostolic teen is true, God created the world by speaking it into being, but I didn't know I could create my whole world by doing that too.

I grab my journal and write, my fingers sliding, scribbling to catch up with my racing mind.

> Last year I heard the talk-show host say people can speak their desires into existence and she recommended her audience read *The Secret*, a book on the power of positive thinking and the law of attraction. When I Googled it, the search produced a plethora of Christian articles deeming her a heretic and a witch—said she was into new age spiritualism and that creating your own reality is not only incompatible with Christianity—that the concept is demonic, so I decided not to read it for fear of being sucked into the occult.

But Christians believe that God dwells in humans who accept Him—that He is the "I Am" inside of us. Doesn't that make "Us" the "I Am" too? God appeared to Moses as a burning bush and referred to Himself as "I Am." If "I Am" created the whole world and "I Am" is in me then maybe I can create my world, too—that is—if I believe that I can. But right now, if I thought I could create a full day of joy, I'd consider myself a bigger miracle worker than Anne Sullivan who taught Helen Keller to communicate.

My synopsis: Stoning the messenger doesn't change the message—truth told in many forms from different perspectives is still truth. Like beauty—truth is in the eyes of the beholder. What the secular world calls the "Law of attraction," Christians call, "Speaking with faith." This "New age spiritualism" may be a synonym for "Truth." Regardless what I call this truth-seeking spirit inside me, faith is the key to everything. I have to remember that and not give up on my marriage just yet.

As I close my journal, vowing to read *The Secret* and take my chances on it turning me to the dark side, a flash of light illuminates the cover of my journal for a moment. I lift the book toward the natural light coming in the window and try to replicate the flash, but I can't make it happen. I don't know if what I'm seeing is real or imagined. All I know is I want whatever is going on to stop, or, at the very least, to understand it.

I'm scrambling eggs as a naked Alex trudges into the kitchen and swipes a piece of bacon from the platter.

"Why'd you get up so early?" he asks, frowning.

I look at the grandfather clock standing erect in the corner of the living room. I'm an hour into my day and already he's finding fault. "Didn't realize it's only eight. Just thought I'd make breakfast," I say, attempting to foster the intention of a copasetic marriage. I hoist my glass of orange juice above my head and grin. "I worked up an appetite last night."

"You'd know what time it is if you'd turn the chimes on on that thing," he says, glancing at the clock and rubbing his broad chest, his fuzzy balls swaying like the pendulum that should be ticking out time. "It'd help if you set the damn thing, too. It's an hour later than it shows. Clocks were supposed to be set forward today for daylight savings."

"Well, shit," I say. "I won't be ready in time to get to church." I scrape eggs onto a plate and hand it to my husband whose dick is tick-tocking away. His private parts would be much more useful for keeping time than to keeping me tethered to this farce of a life.

"Clock chimes drive me crazy, but I like wind chimes," I say, wondering if the change that Grandma Lennie said accompanies the sound of wind chimes also applies to clock chimes, and, if so, maybe it'd be worth replacing the batteries so they would dong every hour.

Sundays at grandmas were different than they are here. I felt like the cherry nestled inside a piece of fine chocolate rather than a slab of rotted cheese. A game of croquet often followed a candied yams and meatloaf dinner. I can hear the garage door scraping open and Luce and me arguing, the taste of butter still on our lips from the homemade rolls as we bickered over who got to be red, the coveted color.

Grandpa "Happy," as everyone called him even though his name was a rather bland, "Dave" would prop open lawn chairs as I lugged the rickety croquet cart across the pavement behind little Luce and me, stepping over the cracks in the concrete along the way. To step on a crack was to "break your mother's back" or so it was said. Mom was still around then, and I didn't want to take any chances on causing her pain.

Often a few neighbors would stroll across the brick street, joining grandma and grandpa in the webbed chairs for a glass of ice tea as they shared the neighborhood watch report, which always contained gossip gleaned from grandma's latest beauty shop visit. I preferred sprawling in the grass to sitting in the chairs anyway—the webbing was unraveling on them and the fibers would itch my bare legs.

Croquet balls would clink into each other in the hole-ridden side yard that grandma and grandpa had, years before, conceded ownership of to the moles. When I'd smack the mallet too hard, the balls would crack into each other with such force they sounded like they'd broken. To my amazement, they never did.

Maybe Alex and I won't break either, I think, sliding into a chair beside him at the table.

"I thought you'd stay in bed a while this morning," Alex says, setting his plate of eggs on the table. "Thought we'd . . . never mind."

But I do mind. What he means by "lay in bed" is that he'd hoped I'd give him head this morning, but I pretend I don't get the innuendo. Can't he just appreciate that last night was nice—a good start to build from. "I was in the mood to write."

"Just be nice if you'd ever be in the mood to spend time with me," Alex says.

I'd like nothing more than to believe my husband isn't the tin man—that he truly wants to spend a leisurely morning in bed with me in his arms and not just his dick in my mouth. Maybe if he could apologize for the times his words have crushed me like an aluminum can beneath his feet, I could accept that the softer side of him still exists. Then I could believe that he really wanted to lounge around in bed this morning playing footsies and tickling me.

I push my half-eaten plate of eggs to the center of the table—the thought of anything in my mouth makes me want to gag—and I force myself to talk. "The plumbers will be here at 3:30 tomorrow afternoon so I'll just cut out as soon as the bell rings."

Alex soaks his toast in a busted egg yolk. "How much that going to be?"

"Seventy-five dollars for the service call."

"Gee. They better find out what's—"

As if summoned, water shoots across the kitchen ceiling, splashing me then dripping like it's tap dancing on my head.

I'd pay *one hundred* and seventy five dollars for relief from this drenching, but I stay quiet and squeeze-dry my hair with a napkin. Not much pretense left in my frazzled head.

We sit in silence. Alex takes his last few bites of breakfast and traipses out the side door without saying a word. Maybe he thinks that if he ignores the water it will go away—maybe that's what he thinks about me.

About noon a car door slams and the rugrats scuttle into the house.

"We went to church with Pawpaw and he's taking us to Dairy Queen," Ben says. "Wanna go?"

What a question! I plant a kiss on Ben's cheek, flop my arm around Isaac's shoulders and say, "Don't say anything to your dad about falling in the pond. I didn't tell him."

Dad must have bribed the boys with D.Q. to get them inside his church doors where the long evangelical services almost always include a miracle healing, demon removal, or prophesy in tongues—all included free of charge. The last time he took them was last summer, and they both said they wouldn't go back.

I hop in the front seat of Dad's Silverado and he says, "Hey, baby girl."

I grin up at my daddy. "Expanding the boys' view on religion, huh?"

Dad clamps his jaws on a toothpick. "You betcha."

As we back out, I wave to Alex who's raking the gravel driveway.

He throws up a hand.

I'd ask him to join us, but he wouldn't anyway. He seems to prefer work to my company any given day, but I'm going to create my world—my marriage—and it's going to be a nice one. I'll bring Alex a milkshake. He'll like that.

I reach toward the back seat and snap my fingers. "How'd you guys like the service today?"

"People there raised their hands," Ben says, "and ran around the church talking Spanish or something."

I choke down a laugh.

"There was like 'tricity in the air!" Isaac says.

"You mean electricity?" I say, looking at Dad who's staring in the rear view mirror like he's anticipating Jesus himself to appear between Ben and Isaac and shock them into reverence.

Isaac says, "Yeah. It was electric. My arms were all tingly like when they fall asleep."

Hell, maybe I should have gone. I thought Ryan was the only one who could make my arms tingle.

"Arms couldn't even sleep there. Too loud," Ben says, covering his ears.

"Pawpaw Cal's church believes that when a person accepts Jesus as their Savior, God enters their body in spirit form called the Holy Ghost, and they pray in a new language," I say. "It's called the gift of tongues. The disciples knew they had it when fire appeared over their heads."

I tell them how my rite of passage into the land of salvation occurred when I was seven. I remember fearing I would enter the fiery gates of Hell if the gift of tongues didn't blow my way like it blew into the upper room on the day of Pentecost, so I prayed harder and faster until, by golly, I felt a draft. Words rolled off my tongue as if an ancient Egyptian was channeling through me.

"Wow. You got a fire spirit inside you, Mom?" Isaac says.

I twist over the console. Isaac's mouth is open so far that with a little more effort I could see his tonsils.

Dad's laughing and crying, his face contorted like he's going to sneeze a grapefruit out his nose. Gravel crunches under the tires and he eases his Silverado back on the road.

Ben's gaze floats from Isaac to me as I smile and decide how I can best explain the intangible, unseen Holy Spirit that just last week I declared may not exist—well, at least the God that sent it may not.

I smack Dad's arm and Ben says, "Mom, really. Was there fire on your head when you got the Holy Ghost?"

"She's a fireball all right. Always has been," Dad says still laughing as he pulls into the ice cream shop.

I wallop him on the arm again and say, "Ah, I hadn't thought about it quite like that, bud, but yep—guess that makes me one hot mama!"

"Mom!" Ben says.

"No, honey, there was no fire on my head, but I do believe God's spirit is in me," I say, thankful the boys' doors are open and they're ready to disembark. I don't want to have to validate my salvation status right now.

I order a sherbet—orange for my sacral chakra—at least that's the color one of the books I'm reading says my base chakra is. I've never seen a chakra so I'll have to take the author's word for it.

Meditating on the color corresponding to one of the seven chakras, or "wheels of energy," while imagining energy coursing from the base of my spine to deep inside the earth is supposed to "ground" me.

Alex would laugh his butt off if he knew I'm practicing visualization techniques to stay calm and balanced, but for me, desperate times call for spiritual measures, and I'm beginning to feel that "spiritual," isn't necessarily synonymous with "religious."

Our favorite booth by the only TV in the building is available, so we make ourselves at home and lick into our mounds of creamy sugar. I spoon a mouthful of dreamy coldness in and picture the cold hue of orange sliding down my throat, melting me into the ground right here below my table. What a tasty way to touch base with Mother Earth.

While I attach an invisible line from my ass to the ground, Ben babbles on about an older gentleman at church who recommitted his life to God. Ben says he "re-caught," the Holy Ghost as if it were a cold he caught.

Isaac perks up. "This other lady got the ghost this morning at Pawpaw's church. She kept saying, 'Ah Banana, Ah Banana,' and doing this." He flings his hands into the air precariously close to the ice cream piled in Ben's cone, and makes an "S" shape like he's doing the wave at a concert.

Dad snorts himself into a coughing fit, tears dripping from his chin into his onion rings. He pops the plastic lid off his cup of water, chugging and coughing until he can talk. "That's . . . that's God's language for bah . . . banana split."

I giggle, my invisible orange chakra anchoring me in this moment of what will one day be the good ole days—the days when Dad laughed himself into a tizzy over Isaac's imitation of a convert who recited her fruit order in tongues.

I'm glad Dad's not a stodgy religious fanatic, just a bald-headed, God-searching guru with a sense of humor as deep as the chocolate shake he's slurping.

On the way home, Dad says, "I called Luce and filled her in on your crazy week. She wondered why she hadn't heard from you. She figured you were busy, but holy moly, neither one of us knew you're living a Barnum and Bailey circus act."

I tell him that yesterday a houseful of men couldn't figure out where the water's coming from, and Dad offers to check it out even though his expertise in criminal investigations exceeds that of his carpentry skills. I assure him he'll get the chance to inspect every crevice if the plumbers come up dry-handed tomorrow.

At home, I'm squeezing soap under the faucet in the kitchen when Alex bursts through the door. "Damn truck's got a flat tire! So, what the hell else can happen around here?"

I'm leery of addressing that question out loud. I pretending the woozy sensation in my head is a sugar rush from the sherbet and nod toward his treat sitting on the counter. "Got you a milkshake."

"Did you hear what I said, woman? My tire's flat and you're talking about ice cream?" Alex takes a deep breath, his lips welding together as if to say no air will be coming out that way. He stomps his 300 pounds across the kitchen looking like a locomotive about to expel steam.

My hands ache for something to hold onto. I plump the dry towel lying on the counter, wringing the plush cotton over and over and manage to swallow.

"I heard you," I say focusing on the bubbles in the dishwater—some are popping and some are climbing onto the existing ones like they're striving to reach the summit of their existence and I realize that's what I want to be—a bubble and reach my full potential before I pop. "I can't fix the tire. Just thought you'd like a treat." I tip my head in an attempt to look worthy of affection like the abused babies I know he cares about.

I barely have "treat" out when his pointed finger seems to stab me from across the room. "Of course, *you* can't fix it. Have *you* ever fixed anything in your whole life?"

Wow. So that's what he thinks of me—I'm not just stupid; I'm inept and lazy. With everything I do here—bills, laundry, grocery shopping, housework, ballgames, birthday parties, and oh yeah, that thing on the side called "teaching," and none of it qualifies me as a hard worker—none of it's enough for him.

I watch my hand scrubbing hash browns that are dried to a plate. It's as if the hand belongs to someone else. I feel detached from my body—guess the chakra grounding didn't work. And to think he actually wondered why I didn't hang out in bed with him. He really doesn't understand why I don't enjoy being around him. Pathetic.

"Why you have to be so mean?" I say, almost pleading for an apology, for pity and I know it, but I don't care. I just want to feel better.

Alex jerks my purse from the counter and swims his hand around inside. "Mean? You think I'm mean—you should live with the assholes out there—no-good bums, never worked a day in their lives." He smacks my purse back onto the counter. "Where the hell are your keys? I come home every night, don't go out drinking and partying like other guys do, buy you anything you want, take you on vacation, and you're still not happy." He grips the checkbook.

I can just imagine the hole he's boring through the back of my head with his eyes.

I can't conjure up the energy to explain what I want. Not again. He doesn't understand my love language and probably never will. He is right though—about the stability he offers me. I could do worse than an egotistical, money-making asshole.

He's also right about me being unhappy even though I have a million reasons to be happy. I'm healthy and have two boys who I love more than Frosty loves snow. I have a career that allows me to be off in the summer with them, but if I've got it made, why do I feel so alone and misunderstood and empty?

I turn to face the stranger I've been married to for fourteen years, my palms swiveling toward the ceiling like I'm offering them to be pierced for crucifixion. "I *am* happy," I say, but I hear the lie. "I just . . . just wish you'd stop screaming at me."

I catch a movement out of my peripheral. Ben's standing in the doorway to the living room. Arguing shouldn't be a spectator sport, especially a kid's, so I smile at him to take the edge off the tense vibe in the air, knowing it's too late.

"I wasn't screaming!" Alex roars, his voice echoing off the walls, his eyes darting madly about until they settle on Ben. "Well, I wasn't—but I am now." Alex looks at me. "You make me so mad!" He opens the side door and hesitates. "You gonna give me the keys to your car or not?"

"They're in the ignition," I say.

The door slams. No lecture on proper protocol on car theft prevention. Lucky me.

Ben must feel as terrible as I do after hearing Alex. It's my job to smooth this over—cheer him up. I dangle a bag of ready-to-bake cookies his way. "Your dad's just mad because the truck has a flat tire." I place a few rounds of dough on the baking stone and look up.

Ben's staring at the tile floor in a daze. "There's a nail in the tire," he says like he's amazed to be saying it.

Forget the cookies. I stare at Ben. "What? How'd you know that?"

"I just know it." The frown on Ben's face tells me he's as confused as I am.

"Honey, I don't understand. Did you see a nail in the tire?"

Ben nods slowly. "Dad'll have to back the truck up to see the nail. It's in the tire. The part you can't see that's on the ground."

"I don't understand. How'd you see it if it's under the tire?"

"I didn't *really* see it," Ben says, staring as if he's looking through me. "I just saw it in my head."

I don't want Ben to freak out, even though I am, so, as casually as I can, I tell him I'll have his dad look under the tire when he gets back from wherever he went—probably the auto parts store.

Twenty minutes later, I hear my car pull in, and I approach Alex in the back garage where he's inspecting the truck tire. "Did you check under the tire—like where you can't see? Maybe something's in it."

I don't dare mention a nail. He'll know I'm not that lucky of a guesser and will wonder how I know it was there. Besides, there may not be one in it anyway. Ben could be wrong.

His mouth gapes open and eyes roll back in his meager head making me feel like I'm the most retarded person he knows, but it's better than hearing him yell. He continues caressing the tire and squinting. Guess my question must have been so stupid that it didn't warrant a verbal response.

I rest my hand on the fender. "Why don't you just humor me, back the truck up a little and look? It is possible, you know."

Alex tosses the keys to me. "If you want to look so bad, move the damn truck yourself."

I hop in the cab, start it and let it roll back.

In the rearview mirror I see Alex waving his arms so I park and get out.

"I'll be damned," he says, pulling out a nail, the look on his face saying, "Wow, and little, ole you knew that?"

He grabs the newly purchased can of fix-a-flat. "Where in the hell did you run over a nail?"

It's been weeks since I've even driven his truck, but of course, it had to be me—*he* couldn't possibly have run over a nail. "I'm just glad you found it," I say, strolling toward the house and straight to Ben's room where he's gluing a wing onto his model airplane.

"Honey, you were right. A nail was right where you said," I say, wondering if there's a connection between the hallucinations I've been having and Ben's newly discovered talent. If there is, what's the common thread and does it have anything to do with the demon I saw? Maybe we've opened a portal like I've seen in horror movies.

Ben looks up from his desk. "I told you I saw it. Did I have a vision, Mom?"

I tell Ben I guess that's a good word for it and not to say anything to his dad about his vision. If Alex knew about Ben's uncanny ability, he'd accuse Ben of being nuts like me.

After dinner I'm scraping turtle cookies from the pan when Alex gives a war whoop for the Cardinals' win over the Cubs in the season opener and says to the boys, "You two wanna help stack some firewood for a campfire?"

Isaac squeals, "Heck, yeah!"

My little fire-starters run to the closet and bound past me, wiggling into their jackets, and bang out the side door.

Alex nudges up behind me, and I feel his lips smooch the nape of my neck that's peeking out from either side of my ponytail. His breath on my neck tickles and I jerk away.

I want to rest in his arms, but the just the thought of it feels needy as if I'm admitting I deserve his disrespect—and I don't. He owes me so many apologies that I've lost tally. The silent kisses he offers are meager collateral for such an outstanding debt.

He pinches my nipples and heads outside.

I finish the dishes and stagger down the hillside wearing a yellow hoodie and a purple toboggan toward the blazing fire, a bag full of the makings for s'mores in my hand.

Isaac's first to spot me. "Mom, you look like a dork!"

I *could* easily pass as a hobo and I just don't care.

With a chill in the April air, the heat from the magnetic fire pulls me closer. Joining three of the most important men in my life, I skim the area for a chair and notice one lying on the ground by Alex. I feel like pouting. He would open it for any other woman who was here with him.

"This dork has treats," I say, handing the bag to Isaac. "Better not call me names anymore or no s'mores for you."

I bend toward the chair, but Alex picks it up, unfolds it and places it beside his.

"Thanks," I say, feeling sorry for assuming he wouldn't be gentlemanly.

Maybe my expectations do manifest like *The Secret* describes, but what just happened was the opposite. I expected him to *not* open the chair for me, but he *did* so how am I creating my own reality? I really want to grasp this idea of manifesting my desires, but I have to understand all the principals of it if I'm going to make it work.

I push two marshmallows onto my roasting stick while Isaac animates his version of SpongeBob's latest skit, sparking laughter from all our glowing faces.

Sitting in the faint light of a crescent moon, I'm not sure if the fire, the celestial view, or simply my attitude is responsible for the warmth soothing my insides, but whatever's responsible, I know I want this feeling to last.

Alex pokes Ben with a branch, "So, how's the 'not girlfriend?'"

Ben reins in a grin and kicks a stone into place that's jutting out of the homemade circle surrounding the blaze.

"How many times she call you today? Two? Three?" Alex says, swirling his finger in the air until it points toward me. "You know, your mom was always calling and chasing me, too." My husband's eyes twinkle in the firelight.

I pucker my lips and peddle my elbows in the air like I'm running for Olympic gold.

"She caught me. Man—should have ran faster." Alex's robust laughter splits my eardrum. He laughs as hard as he yells.

The awesome feeling of cozy contentment I had just moments ago is gone. I feel like crying, but I tilt my head demurely in Alex's direction and smile like I totally believe he is joking, but I know he wishes he hadn't been "caught," trapped like a tiger in a snare. The boys don't seem to notice the cruelness crashing through the comment, and I won't be pointing it out.

I smash a marshmallow between graham crackers. "How'd the interview with Hank's neighbor go the other day—he a suspect?"

"That was nuthin. Just rumors," Alex says, biting off a square of a Hershey bar. "The neighbor's an orthodontist that just moved in beside Hank and had the property lines surveyed before he bought the place. There was no dispute."

"Oh, gee, you mean that huge house finally sold? That took forever. People 'round here just don't have that kind of money."

"Yep, sold for 400 grand," Alex says, glancing at each of the boys. "Hope neither of you need braces. I don't want to help pay for someone's half a million dollar home."

"Dad," Ben says. "Mom said there's a mafia here—that they might've killed Hank."

"She did?" Alex says, resting his hand on mine. "Yesterday we did question two mafia-linked drug dealers who Hank was helping us build a case against. Hank was making buys from them. If they found out Hank was helping us, they would've had a reason to kill him, but I couldn't get either of them to cooperate."

Alex's hand is heavy on mine. I feel handcuffed to the chair and I don't like it. He says something crass, then he's nice—I never know what to expect. Well, I do know one thing—I know the cycle well.

Looking over my shoulder to Alex, I ease my hand out from under his. "They wouldn't talk? You losing your touch?"

"Yeah, right. Those scum-buckets lawyered up—couldn't touch 'em." Alex blows on his blazing marshmallow. "At least the autopsy's back."

"What's a "top see" Dad?" Isaac asks.

Ben beams Isaac with a jumbo marshmallow. "Goober!" he says, "Ah-top-see. That's what the police do when they're not sure how a person died. Well, it's what the M.E does, but, Dad, what's M.E. stand for?"

"Medical examiner," Alex says.

"So, the medical examiner," Ben says, "cuts the body open and checks for wounds and traumas. Can the M.E. tell what kind of gun killed Hank?"

Alex says, "Yep. A single gunshot from a 30 gauge shot from close range killed him. Bullet passed straight thru his head. Blew his brains out the back."

"Wow—that what trauma is?" Isaac says, squeezing a gooey marshmallow between his fingers like it's Playdooh.

"Duh," Ben says, through a mouthful of goo. Ben looks at his dad. "So he probably knew the person who shot him cuz it was a close shot?"

"You're going to make a heck of an officer one day, Ben. Also, Hank's back and shoulders had lacerations—that's cuts—like he'd been dragged over a rough surface." Alex pops a toasted marshmallow in his mouth and leans over, pretending to kiss me as it dangles from his teeth.

"Ewww," Isaac says and wrinkles his nose at Ben.

I lean in and kiss my temperamental hubby, part of my lips on the warm marshmallow and part on his cold, puckered lip.

Alex says, "'Bout time to wrap up this shindig, boys. Got school tom—"

Isaac screams and Ben and I duck as an entire flock of bats screech through. For a second it looks like every bat in town is rallying at our campfire.

"Whoa!" Ben yells, as they dart off and into the night as quickly as they flew in. "That was crazy!"

Alex leans back and laughs. "Scared ya, didn't it? Wait till you're an officer and you gotta walk into a pitch black house not knowing where some asshole's gonna be hiding."

"When was you the scaredest, Dad?" Isaac says, looking into the darkness behind me.

"A lady hiding with a gun in her living room scared the living hell out of me. We went to her house looking for her boy who had just robbed one of the neighbors. The electric had been turned off so Gilmore and I had to search the whole house by flashlight. We made one swoop through and found nothing. So, we're walking back through the living room and hear a thud, and there's this fifty-year-old woman holding a gun on us. It was by the grace of God I didn't drop her right there. She was wedged between a box and the wall. We'd missed her." Alex rubs the heart side of his chest. "Something that simple can get ya killed."

"Hey, the bats reminded me," Ben says, scanning our partly shadowed faces. "Did you hear about what happened at old man Robinson's place after he died? His grandson, Caleb, said his grandpa took over the body of his parrot."

"What!" Isaac says, peering around like he's expecting the bats to reconvene and take over his. "How'd he do that?"

Alex rolls his eyes and says, "Yeah, and I saw Big Foot in the backyard."

Ben digs his boots into the ground. "Seriously, Dad. Caleb, his mom, and sister moved in his grandpa's house before he died. They bought a parrot and it started saying stuff like, 'I need to finish the roof on the front porch,' just like his grandpa would say. The parrot talked about all the house repairs his grandpa had told Caleb and his mom that he wanted to make even though his grandpa died before they bought the parrot. Weird, huh?"

"Baloney," Alex says.

"Spirits in the Bible could transfer from one being to another, Alex," I say. "Don't you believe the Bible?"

"Of course, I believe the Bible, but that kinda stuff's not in there—ghosts taking over birds—bullshit." Alex clicks open a picture on his cell and hands it to Isaac. "Look at those muscles on that dude."

Isaac passes the phone to Ben, and I figure I might as well deviate from the spirit topic. Alex would rather look at something he can master like muscles than at the identity called "spirit" that he can't actually see. He says he believes in God and I believe he does, but he always changes the subject anytime spirit or ghosts or scriptures comes up.

I've only seen a demon in my mirror once, but just because I can't see it all the time, doesn't mean it's not there all the time. Maybe the demon I saw is influencing my thoughts and actions even if it's not inside me. Maybe it's making me perceive Alex's comments out of context, skewing my view of him and making me want to screw other guys. Ultimately, maybe I'm as much at fault for our failing marriage as Alex is.

"I got a new student a few days ago," I say, trying to distract myself from my own thoughts. "He walked into class and I swear I thought he was a parent. He looked like he was at least twenty-five. Anyway, I asked him if he had a visitor's pass and the students, who all knew him of course, say, 'Mrs. Templeton, he's student!' His name's Matt—"

"Savvy, good grief. Is there a reason you're telling me this?" Alex pops open a Dr. Pepper."

My tongue toils inside my mouth until I can form enough spit to swallow. "Yes, Alex. His name's Matt Boggs and guess why he was expelled from Beaumont High School."

Alex stabs a prong through a hot dog and dangles it over the fire. "I don't wanna guess. Just tell me."

"He's the student that took a gun to school last year."

"Now you know what I deal with every day," Alex says.

I fold up my chair. If only Alex could see what *I* deal with every day just trying to communicate with him.

Chapter Ten

THE COMMODE GEYSER

I tuck the boys in bed and am closing the drapes in my bedroom when I hear Alex's cell phone vibrating on his nightstand. He usually takes it into the bathroom with him which I figure is his way of preventing me from reading his messages.

He's still in the shower—I can hear it running. I rush over to the table, snatch the phone and punch in his pass-code that he doesn't know I know.

A message from someone named Raven reads, "Hey sexy-last night was amazing! I can't wait to see you again. Next time longer."

I feel like the Earth just collided with another planet—like every hope I had of hot-wiring my relationship with Alex was jerked out from under me—like I'm a crystal candelabra left teetering after the magician yanks the tablecloth away. I have no right to feel hurt by his betrayal, but I do.

I lean against the table to steady my shaky stance and read the text again, the words wringing the last of the campfire joy from my heart. Who's Raven? I thought if he was seeing anyone, it was Stacey Chutney. Maybe he's screwing them both.

The shower water is silent. I click the phone to lock, place it on the table and gain two steps before Alex struts in clasping a towel around his wet waist. He hasn't even bothered to dry off. His eyes search the table, then my face.

Does he know I've been sneaking peeks at his messages? No, he can't. A sense of pride spirals up my spine. He doesn't even know I have the pass code—probably thinks I'm too inept to discretely watch him enter it.

I could call him out now. So what if he knows I was a snoop and read his text. He's the bad guy here—not me.

Alex snatches up his cell, checks it, and swivels toward the door. Drops of water dot his tanned shoulders and funnel into the crease in his spine.

I step close to him and reach out, my fingertips touching the towel. I want to rub the soft cotton across his back and have his moist arms hold me. I want him to hold me like I'm special, not just some chick he's been slamming, but he jumps like my fingers are poisonous fangs.

"What's wrong?" I ask, my hand still outstretched.

"You always have to do something better than me?" Alex says. "Think I can't even dry myself off?"

"What?" I say, my eyes pleading with his for a semblance of understanding. "That doesn't make any sense. I wasn't . . ."

But he's already thrown on a pair of shorts and is walking down the steps. I'm not sure why he said I always do something better than him. Hell, he always tells me how I'm doing something *wrong*. Now he's saying I'm always doing something *better* than him. I wish he could hear himself and how confusing his statements are. I could tape him, but he wouldn't listen to himself any more attentively than he does to me, and he'd be pissed at the mere suggestion that he needed to.

Maybe he's mad because he suspects I've snooped a look on his phone. Maybe he's mad because I was right about there being a nail in the tire. I could spend the rest of my life trying to figure out what triggers that man, and I'd still clueless.

Damn him. I just find out he's cheating on me and somehow I still feel like the one at fault.

What if Alex is in love with this "Raven" and leaves me for her? My legs buckle and I collapse into a heap on the floor. I'd be nobody. I'd be 'Templeton's ex' in the community, his throw-away, and that might be worse than staying married to him and knowing I'll never live up to his expectations.

I'll never be enough. I'll never be good enough at cooking or cleaning or communicating to please Alex, and now I'm not even tantalizing enough in bed to keep him from wandering about. But maybe he's looking for more than sex too. After all, I'm getting it from other guys even though he sexually pleases me.

Isaac comes panting into the room, and I jump off the floor like a jack-in-the box. The intensity pouring from his eyes draws me into the hall where he points toward his room.

"What now?" I say, trailing behind him as he forges past Ben's room.

Isaac cups his hand over his mouth so I lean close—so close I get a whiff of smoke lingering in his hair from the jocular campfire that seems locked in a cave far-away. "Mom," he whispers. "A hand came through my wall."

I pull back and look into his eyes for the slightest insincerity, but there's not so much as a smirk. Maybe my crazy is contagious like lice and my youngest has caught it.

"A hand? "I say. "In your wall?" I glance around the room like a hand's really going to reach out from behind the camouflage curtains and choke me.

"Yeah. Right there," he says, scooting in close to me and pointing to the exterior wall with a window that looks out over the backyard.

The stairs creak. Alex must be heading our way. I definitely don't want him to catch this latest bizarre story so I pull the door shut, my line of vision trailing Isaac's finger to the olive-colored wall.

All I see is the framed plaid cross that's made with the excess material from Grandpa Happy's hemmed pants. After grandpa died, quilting the scraps into a symbol of Christ's physical death and spiritual ascension seemed an appropriate way to display the concept of Grandpa's spirit merging into eternal oneness with God.

"There's nothing there now, sweetie. Were you watching something scary on TV when you saw it?"

"You always ask me that. *The Cosby Show* isn't scary. Mom, please," Isaac says, pleading for me to listen to him like he's asking me to buy him a dirt bike for his birthday. "I swear. I was on my bed. I rolled over and a hand was in the wall."

"Honey, I really don't know what to tell you. Maybe you were dreaming." As soon as the words are out of my mouth, I realize I sound like Alex when he tries to convince me that I am wrong about spirits in the Bible—or about anything, and I'm sorry for making Isaac feel like his truth must be a lie.

Isaac folds his arms. "No, I wasn't."

Even if he did see it, I don't know what I can do about it. This is a more elaborate problem than I've encountered as a parent, and wasn't addressed in my high school parenting class where all I had to do was carry egg with me for a few days and prevent it from getting broken—a difficult task at the time, but right now I could prop Humpty Dumpty on my shoulders and march him through the Macy's Day Parade!

The more chaotic my life becomes, the more determined I am to outsmart whoever dumped the contents of Pandora's box down my chimney. After all, I've survived living with Alex's arrogance ass and his infidelity for years. I've educated the young vandals and bullies at school that Alex arrests when they graduate to criminals and now I'm dealing with these weird, possibly paranormal, events on my own because Alex is too chicken-shit. Underneath his strapping muscles is a squeamish boy who runs when confronted with the unknown. I'm thankful I was raised in an evangelical church where I was exposed to not only concepts about spirits, but given the opportunity to witness the principles in action.

"So, was it on the wall like this?" I ask, pressing my hands onto the wall.

Isaac jumps knees first onto the bed and places the backs of his hands on the wall, palms facing us. "No, like this."

Could a ghost in the wall have tried to press its way out? I don't know what's going on, but something is definitely strange around here, and it all started about the time I saw that damn demon in my mirror.

Michele Savaunah Zirkle Marcum

I usher Isaac into Ben's room and instruct Isaac to keep the hands a secret from his dad because Alex won't understand—not that I do either, but unlike Alex, I'm willing to accept the fact that I don't know everything.

Isaac scooches into bed beside Ben, who rolls facing away from his dear brother, mumbling about how Isaac's a baby. In my room, Alex is snoring, the sound of which annoys me. I know he can't help it that he has sleep apnea, but the sound is just one more way Alex intrudes on my peace, and knowing he's been flying high with Raven makes me want to pinch his nose shut and listen to him gasp for breath. I want him to feel like I do just once—to feel like he may be taking his last breath any moment and come panting alive and realize he wants to live the magic in every moment—maybe even realize that he wants to enjoy that magic with me.

I fall asleep dreaming about carrying eggs. They explode and ghostly, white hands reach through the jagged, broken shell.

Over a protein drink Monday morning, I'm still swallowing the images of delight on Raven and Alex's faces as they soar together—Alex cocking his hips to just the right angle, pushing hard until the dear Raven squawks, her claws digging Alex close for as long as possible.

By fourth period, the images of their naked bodies appear on the page obscuring the words I'm trying to see as freshmen take turns reading "My Side of the Mountain" aloud. Imagination kidnaps my comprehension making me feel like a student again—not really listening to the words being read—just hearing a hum of chatter as I create scenes in my head.

I don't know anyone named Raven. Could she be someone Alex is in contact with during the day—possibly an attorney's secretary or a courthouse employee? If the business card I found in Alex's uniform is an indication he's having an affair with textbook Stacey, he could have dubbed her, as "Raven," using a pseudo name like I do for Ryan, but at least that would mean he's seeing only one other woman instead of two.

I wonder how many others I don't know about and if Alex is as empty as he makes me feel. That would mean he doesn't have any love to give, and maybe he never will no matter how much I pray, or pout, or cry, or yell, or fuck other men. Alex may *never* be capable of giving me the love I need.

The bell rings for class dismissal without me asking an "exit" question like all good teachers do to reinforce comprehension of the fresh material. I don't even know where the last reader left off in the chapter. Last thing I remember, Sam, our main character, burnt out a hemlock tree to live in. I'm not so desperate to escape my family that I'd abscond to the woods and live in a tree—yet. A tent's sounding pretty comfy though—a waterproof one.

A colorful poster on the bulletin board in the back of my room catches my eye. I've read it to students numerous times, but today the words take on new meaning. "Attitude. A small thing that makes a big difference," it reads, and I realize that my attitude is one of jealousy—that just thinking of Raven getting her hands on my man makes me feel desperate and determined to keep him. After all, I have agency here—the house—the history—and most importantly, the kids.

But my jealously is binding me to a situation that is not enhancing my life. I feel like a meadow full of seedlings ready to burst through the soil to full bloom, yet I want remain safely tucked in the earth for fear of flood or wind or of the scorching sun. If I ever hope to sprout into a joyous daisy, I need to spread my roots and dig into the fear—the fear of failure—the fear of being alone.

I've been jealous for long enough—guilty for long enough. My guilt about fornicating is thick like a layer of wax compared to Alex's spackle of pledge. He can't feel as badly as I do.

Enticing men to touch me may be unscrupulous, but that's better than being marooned on an island of despair or worse, being a floating corpse. I can't allow that to happen. I can't allow myself to feel so desperate for Alex's love that I kill myself.

By half-way through lunch period, I come to the conclusion that the only time I feel I have any self-worth is when I'm spending time with another man, but it's all I've got. So, if I must contend with a demon because I choose to cheat, then I'll plead for God's mercy, swearing I made the best decision I could. Besides, He's had ample opportunity to extend his mighty, helping hand onto our marriage and hasn't.

I scroll through my phone contacts looking for an old flame that would be a sure-fire bet to want to reignite. There's Kent. It's been years since I've slept with him, but when I ran into him at the post office last week I could tell he wanted me—biting his bottom lip like he already had my nipple clamped between his teeth. His eyes traced the length of my body from my toes to my new boobs. If Kent's like Alex, he's probably tired of having "married" sex with his wife, so it's a safe bet he'll be up for a romp. It's a few minutes past noon, but if I'm lucky, I can catch Kent at his office before he heads to lunch.

On the phone, I tell his secretary that I need an accountant to file my taxes this year—that I'm opening a writing business. Maybe I really will. Tax write-offs alone would be worth the paperwork and could inspire me to manifest the invisible novel scripting itself in my head.

Before transferring my call, she asks how I've been and if I'm still teaching, how the boys are doing, blah, blah.

When I worked in town at the library, she and I would do lunch at Cornerstone Quarry. She's just being friendly, but I just want her to patch me through to Kent, hoping he's as receptive as his screener.

Kent must know his secretary is nosey because he answers professionally, giving his full name and title even though he knows it's me calling. I hear excitement hidden beneath his formal tone and find it reassuring, so I dive right in and admit I don't need an accountant, I need a lay and wonder if he is interested in providing it. Cold and direct maybe, but straight's the only way he understands—there's no romantic mush with Kent.

"Sounds good, Mrs. Templeton," Kent says.

"Mrs. Templeton, huh?" I say. "Nice touch. You can call me, 'Oh, God,' later."

I know he can't say much with his eavesdropper near, so I ask questions that only require a "yes" or "no" response until we have our rendezvous set for early in the morning at his accounting firm—not my favorite time of day for sex, but I can work it in before school.

Getting him to agree to meet was too easy to create much of an endorphin rush, but I hang up, my arms tingly in anticipation of the skin mingling to come. Even though the intimacy will be generic, it'll make me feel wanted and that's something I desperately need to feel. Without that I *will* be that floating corpse without hope of resurrection.

Just as I'm finishing my fish and veggies, the school secretary broadcasts a request on the intercom for me to report to the office. Not knowing which parent this is, I grab a notebook and pen. I just hope this is quick. I only have five minutes to pee and get back to my room to greet the young education-starved minds even though my own mind feels void of wisdom.

I hopscotch over the legs of students who are reclining in the hallway and peer into the office where a line of parents are signing in and signing out students, some toting gym bags no doubt forgotten by their child on the morning rush to school. I jerk open the door, scanning the room. The secretary points to a man in a navy sports jacket sitting by the copier.

Standing, he shakes my hand. This is definitely not a parent. Most of the parents in Ridgeland that I meet with don't wear sports coats or initiate a handshake—they are good flannel-shirt-wearing folks who, if I'm lucky, remove their ball caps and spit their tobacco out before they entered the school.

"Hello," the stranger says, sounding very formal, but his bourbon eyes say, "Hi, babe. Looking mighty fine."

"My name is Marcus," he says, rubbing his palms like he's trying to start a fire. "I'm the new rep. for Tudor's Textbooks, the adapted series you've ordered in the past, and I'd like to show you the new titles available in class sets."

Tudor's Textbooks. That's where Stacey works.

"You know Stacey Chutney?" I ask before I realize the words are out of my mouth.

"Oh, sure. Stacey. She's got the southern region," Marcus says, his gaze exploring the cleavage in my barely school-appropriate blouse before snapping up to meet mine.

"Marcus, nice to meet you." I curl my tongue over my front teeth, hoping I don't have broccoli stuck between them.

Marcus squeezes the leather binder under his arm like it's a football and crinkles his forehead into a puzzle.

I know that look.

Rain No Evil

My hand brushes against my breast as I adjust the tiny, pink belt hitting right below my sternum and try to avert my eyes from the hard legs bulging beneath Marcus's khakis.

I clear my throat and click the pen against my thigh, thinking if God sent this man to tempt me, God must have one helluva sense of humor. "I only have a few minutes till lunch is over, but my planning is last period. Could you come back then?"

"Absolutely," he says, his eyes twinkling. "I'll grab a bite to eat and give a shout-out to the elementary schools up this way." Marcus flings a backpack over his shoulder. "So, about 2:45, right?"

"Yep. Perfect," I say, stepping into the hall through the door he's holding open. I click past a giggling group of senior girls wondering if they're as intrigued by Marcus's exotic looks as this teacher is. I feel Marcus's gaze pulling up my yellow skirt, his hands massaging my rear and think maybe it is time to purchase a new series of books for my class. Yes, indeed.

But could I be misinterpreting his mating signal? Maybe he's just a flirty salesman. Ted's already on my agenda anyway and one indiscretion is enough.

One's actually too many. I can't keep living this lifestyle. It's not flagrant, but I'm bound to get caught. Gossip circulates throughout Ridgeland's beauty shops and grocery stores like sperm in a moist vagina, just searching for a place to land and germinate. The fastest flourishing word-of-mouth news is always who's doing who—and Alex with his other women and me with my other men, have made our share of headlines in that category.

I have to stop blaming Alex for my decisions and blaming myself for his. I can't make him treat me with respect any more than he can prevent me from cheating because of the lack of it. If I keep cheating, I have to own up to the fact that it's my decision to do so and no matter how cruel Alex is to me, he's not in control of my body and what I do with it—I am.

I can stay under Alex's radar for a while, but he's bound to catch me cheating. Maybe I want him to catch me. Then maybe he'd leave me, and I wouldn't have to make the decision whether or not to leave him.

I'm afraid of being caught, but I'm even more intensely tired of feeling guilty. I want to feel like I did last year when Alex and I came clean with each other. We promised to be faithful, or at the very least, to be honest with each other if we were going to screw around. We started fresh with the intention of cultivating honesty and respect. I loved that feeling—the restfulness of being at peace with myself. It was as if a salty ocean breeze blew over me in a cleansing baptism, making me whole.

What happened to that feeling of righteousness? Oh, I know what happened— Ryan happened, but did I have to run into the arms of another man just because Alex wanted me to hold up some damn drywall?

Promptly at 2:45, the office buzzes my room and tells me my visitor is back. As

I escort Marcus through the hallway crowded with student's changing classes he tells me he moved here from Florida a few months ago to be with his ailing father and luckily got this rep job right away.

I tell him it's sweet of him to help his dad and I notice Mrs. Z. practically at attention by her door. Her head is facing the office, but her eyes are on me and my exotic visitor. I direct Marcus to a table in the corner of my room by the bookcase, excuse myself and strop over to squelch the rumor that's already gurgling in Mrs. Z's throat.

"New guy from textbook company," I say crossing my arms and mimicking the Veteran hallway monitor extraordinaire. "Yeah, like I don't have anything else to do during planning."

"Oh, I can tell he's new all right," Mrs. Z. says, as I stare down two boys who are lollygagging by the restroom until they mosey down the hall. "The seasoned guys don't make appointments—they just stick a flyer in our boxes," she says. The bell rings and she snaps her head toward her class. "He'll eat up all your planning," she says, cocking her chin upward, her eyes half-shut. "Wouldn't that be a shame?"

I fake a laugh and strum across the corridor saying, "He's only getting a few minutes. Then he's outta here. Lesson plans due tomorrow."

I slip into a hard plastic chair across the table from Marcus, half-listening to his sales speech and half- visualizing him smacking me on the ass with one of the books he's piled on the table.

I pick one up, the latest version of Shakespeare's *The Taming of the Shrew*, and within minutes, I tell him I'll complete a requisition for a set. As I help him pick up the demo books, his tan hand brushes mine.

"Oh, sorry," he says, resting his hand on the pile.

I place my hand on top of his so that it looks like I'm pledging an oath. "It's okay," I say withdrawing my hand and pressing my palms together prayer-style as if doing so will help me find my way back to that righteous feeling I crave. But it's too late for morality to soak into me right now—Marcus's whiskey-colored eyes have drawn me in like the aroma of French vanilla coffee pulls me into a café.

Marcus leans over the table and plants his lips on mine. Okay, that was fast. I can't believe this guy is being this forward. He doesn't know anything about me except that I'm friends with Stacey. The word "easy," must be scrawled across the wrinkles in my forehead.

Marcus edges around the table not releasing his grip on my bottom lip.

I don't want to do this.

Marcus's fingertips trace my cheek and my entire face tingles.

Oh, man. I got to stop this now. I peel myself from his grasp and tuck my hair behind my ear. "Why'd you think it was ok to do that?"

He wipes my drool from his mouth. "You look lonely. I can see it in your eyes."

I stare into his eyes. He's right. I am lonely, but I didn't know it was so obvious.

"I felt a connection to you," Marcus says. "Wanted to make you feel better."

I do want to feel better and that kiss felt really nice. Besides, Alex is screwing around, too. Images from the past week stampede through my head—Stacey's card in Alex's pocket, the sex text from Raven, the anger on Alex's face as he screams, "Can't you do anything right!" and the ecstasy on it as he comes inside of God-knows-who in the back of his cruiser.

I *can* do something right. I can make myself happy for a while.

"Got to lock the door," I say, jogging toward it.

My newest distraction wraps his arms around me, and I free-fall into them as if they are a safety net. Men are my nets and I have several of them. If one breaks, there's another just waiting with pleasure to come to the rescue. At least if God fails me, fails to change Alex, maybe I won't have to be alone.

I loosen the belt on my shirt while Marcus loosens his on his trousers. He kisses my neck, his fingers fumbling with my shirt buttons. I pop the last one free and his lips dive onto my chest, licking my nipple till I'm ready to scream. The dismissal bell could ring any moment, but I don't care.

Fiercely, Marcus caresses my abdomen then lays me ever so gently on the cold tile floor, pulls up my skirt and sucks on my clit like he's tapping out Morris code. My ass is cold and his lips are warm and . . . the bell rings just as he enters me.

I sigh and grab his shirt from the floor, roll it up and tuck it in under my lower back. I don't need a bruise that I'd have to explain to Alex. I eye the poster again, "Attitude is a little thing that makes a big difference." I arch my back. My attitude is getting better with every stroke.

A door shuts down the hall. Dang janitor usually comes in to clean my room early since he knows I have planning last period. If he happens to unlock my door, hopefully I can make a run and get my shirt on behind the bookcase. Or I could grab the folder on my desk, stick a pen in my hand, bellow out some education lingo and be having the most exciting parent-teacher conference this school has seen since Barbara Eden hit Harper Valley's PTA.

While Marcus gyrates me to paradise, I imagine the flames of hell engulfing me—licking at my clit like Marcus just did, except this burning sensation is not one I want to continue teasing me. This fire is the wrath of an almighty God who's punishing me for the fornication I just can't seem to avoid no matter how much I try—no matter how much I pray or how earnestly I listen to the man behind the pulpit on Sundays.

"Oh, babe," Marcus says, half snorting. "You're hot."

He has no idea how hot I feel right now—how I feel like I'm on the edge of hell itself, my feet dangling above the highest reaching flame, ready to devour me should I loosen my grip of the one thing that keeps me suspended over, rather than falling into, the pit of no return—the hope that one day, I'll be strong enough to withdraw from all that tempts me and maintain integrity with myself—for myself. The hope that one day I will like myself again.

For now, I push the image of prayers and pulpits into the crevices of my body—squishing them into my toes, folding them behind organs and dissolving them into corpuscles. I'll deal with the regrets later.

My favorite salesman grabs my hair, lifts me up and bends me over a desk, pumping me the way a train glides down the tracks, smoothly for a bit, then a jerk, a screech, then smooth again. I'll pay dearly for this ride, but for now, I'm bowing to the will of the conductor.

Five minutes and one orgasm later, I pull down my skirt, usher Marcus-what's-his-face to the office to sign out and am squirting the secretary's hand sanitizer into my palm when I see Isaac, fresh off the elementary school bus, bobbing through the hall on his way to my room.

A wave of disgust washes over me. What kind of mom does what I just did? Isaac and Ben deserve to have a mom with morals. I clear my throat that feels like it hasn't felt liquid since Christ was on the cross and manage to say thanks to Marcus who is walking out the door.

As I scurry to my room to touch base with Isaac, I feel unconnected to my own body—like I'm only an observer and not in control of myself at all. My feet are carrying my body through the hall out of rote memory.

Last year when Alex and I resolved to be faithful to each other, I planned on living up to my end of the agreement, and I did, for almost a whole year, but I've broken the promise twice now within a few days. I wonder if Alex's intention was as robust as mine, and if it was, why are we both screwing around? All I know is I feel incapable of changing. I can't change him either, and maybe it's irrational of me to expect God to change either one of us.

Isaac's in my room at a desk with a brownie in one hand and the computer mouse in the other. Ben's probably playing basketball in the gym. I gather papers I should have copied last period and ruffle Isaac's hair on my way back to the office.

When I was a girl, I never thought I'd be a whore when I got big. I was going to be Betty fucking Crocker, cranking out a *New York Times* bestseller while the casserole baked. My husband would come home from his executive job, untie my apron and spank me till I said I'd be a good girl. It was my fifty shades of fantasy before the beans were spilled on how good it feels to be bad—or at least, pretend to be.

Sometimes in a fantasy, I was Isis and twirled myself into a captivating siren that no one could hurt—like Mom hurt me when she left—not the God of thunder or the likes of men like Alex. I'd pretend that I captured everyone under my spell. Women and men alike loved me. They had no choice but to, for I was Isis, Goddess of love and healing.

I vacillated between fantasies, but never did they consist of me being a whore. The daydreams began when Mom left dad for another man. I was eleven and I knew I didn't want to be like her. Maybe I've stayed with Alex because leaving him would prove me more like her than I want to admit. Maybe it's me and not Alex who isn't capable of true love.

Rain No Evil

Whatever the case, I'm not a Goddess with the power to make people really love me—not Mom or Alex. I'm only human with the womanly wiles to physically seduce a man, not the charming Isis that can endear myself to his heart.

I'm making copies in the mailroom by the office when Mr. Meyers calls to me from behind the counter. He's manning the front desk—probably so the secretary can pee. "Savannah, did Diane's mom get a hold of you?"

"Yes," I say, motioning him into the mailroom so the group of students decorating the bulletin board won't hear the conversation. "You know, Diane's not even in my class anymore."

Mr. Meyers swipes his ever-sweating forehead with a hanky. "Well, what the heck did her mom call you for then?"

"She said she was concerned over Diane's grade in science—you know, feigning the concerned parent," I say, sliding a stack of papers out of my mailbox. "She's just trying to stay in my good graces so I won't call Children's Services again. I figure she might know Alex is investigating her, but let me check with him to see if he's close to pressing any charges and then I'll fill you in."

Mr. Meyers thanks me and heads off to play secretary, one of his many roles as the mayor of our establishment that's more like a mini-city than a school. Other than not having bunks for everyone, the building is equipped with enough food, medicine, and entertainment that staff and students could survive for weeks without leaving campus.

Our rural school is certainly cleaner and has more food in the fridge than many of our poverty-stricken students have at home. Some students like Diane, have told me that they'd prefer living at school to living in their own homes.

I've had a soft spot for Diane ever since she confided in me about being molested by her dad who's now in prison for burning down his trailer to collect the insurance money. Her mom says she loves Diane and wants to help her, but Diane's told me stories of drug parties with men coming and going at all hours of the night, and how, on occasion, one of the drunken slobs will offer her money to sleep with him. That's bad enough, but her mom encourages her to take the offer, and a few times she has given into her mom's demands.

About four months ago I called Child Protective Services regarding Diane because the heat in her mom's house was turned off. Now, mom's afraid the court will declare she's unfit and take custody of Diane, which means she'll lose the social security income Diane receives for being a student with a learning disability.

Alex's snitch is supposed to make buys from Diane's mom so he can pin her with distributing and get Diane out of the environment permanently. Drug enforcement is usually handed over to the undercover drug agent, but in this case, Alex is involved as a personal favor to me.

My phone reminder dings. It's 3:30 and the plumbers are supposed to be at the house! I forgot. I bolt home. The plumbers haven't arrived yet, so I dial Luce even though I can't remember what time her school dismisses.

It's been forever since I've called her at work, but her wedding is just a few weeks away, and I've been neglecting my duties as Matron of Honor.

The fact that we both chose teaching as a career is surprising because we're so different. I'm always juggling more of life's fireball's than my little sister, even now as she's finishing her degree to be a principal, preparing for a June wedding, and typing her fiancé, Jack's, assignments he brings home from the police academy on the weekends. Teaching and police work runs in this family's veins.

As I slump into my living room chair, Luce answers and I tell her about my house that seems to have a mind of its own—about the water leak and how Isaac saw a hand in his wall and Ben had a vision.

Luce says she can't wait to come over Sunday for our birthday celebrations, not so much for the cake as to see the phenomena here for herself. Every time I mention the wedding, she diverts the topic back to the weird stuff going on at my house.

I miss our visits. Before she met Jack, we'd spend hours on the porch chatting about everything from the latest music and fashion trends to anecdotal stories of student mayhem.

When we were girls, I tried to make Luce be more like me—dressed her like me—had her practice talking fast and loud like me. Now, I'm not so sure *I* want to be me. Maybe I should be more like her. More responsible—less obnoxious. More demure—less risqué.

We're deciding on what kind of cake to have Sunday when a van pulls in the drive. I greet the two plumbers from Carter's Plumbing. A middle-aged man shakes my hand and introduces himself as the "Chief plumber of sorts." A young man about twenty years his junior stands holding a toolbox. I'm impressed that they're wearing uniforms and hope competency is indicated by their appearance.

We walk through the office next to the kitchen, past pictures wrapped in plastic and leaning against the walls, past family pictures displayed in pewter frames and store-bought prints framed in cherry veneer. I lead them upstairs pointing at the completely dry area on the ceiling where the water first dripped and explain my quandary—how the first night it happened a single drop of water fell from the ceiling right here, and before the night was over, water was shooting across the hall and down the stairs.

I admit finding the leak will be tricky because no one in the house has seen it actually spray from the ceiling or a wall. We just hear a *splat* and see a soaked room. I feel like I'm giving a persuasive presentation on the existence of aliens to the two faces staring at me, wrinkled with doubt.

John turns on the faucet in the shower and both bathroom sinks as his partner steps into the bathroom with him.

I silently replay the hand-through-the wall conversation I had with Isaac last night. I wish I could see what he saw. Maybe I could understand it better if I saw it myself.

After a few minutes of listening to the running water, John turns it off and peers speechless into the hall where I stand speechless, too. Nothing. Not a drop.

John yanks his pants up by the empty belt loops and says, "Are you sure it's water. I mean are you taking any medications that . . ." He looks at his partner like they are reading each others' minds.

They don't even believe me. If they think I'm hallucinating from drugs, they aren't going to help me. I wish Alex were here to corroborate my story. The boys could, but they're just kids and I told them to hit the basement playroom.

"What would you do if this were your house?" I say as we all clomp down the stairs.

"Well, dear," he says, "I'd check the—"

Splat. Water smacks the wall. The most pleasant sound to my ears. John's head jolts toward the living room. Now my "Chief plumber" and his buddy will know I'm not crazy—at least not the crazy that gets locked-up.

They rush into the living room, cocking their heads like dogs listening for a rabbit. I stick my hands in my jean pockets and grin while they scour the structure, squinting at the dripping wet walls and ceiling as if their vision is off kilter.

John's cohort swipes his hand across a wet section of wall and sniffs the liquid on his fingers. "John, there's no smell. Appears to be water. You ever seen anything like this before?"

John's head is telescoping in slow motion. "Nope, I sure haven't. Not in all my twenty-four years of doing this job." He trucks into the kitchen, hunching and scoping every inch of the living room like he's expecting another wallop at any moment. "There are no water lines above the living room . . . no visible pipes in here either. Damned if I know."

John walks toward the door, his partner a few steps behind, and says, "Going to check the meter,"

I slip on my jacket and meet up with them in the front yard.

"The city worker already checked it and said our usage is normal for a household of four," I say.

"Yep. Usage is average," John says, "but you could have a slow leak. That might not show on the meter."

Doesn't seem slow when it's whizzing across the room, but I'm tired of describing the indescribable. The only sound that trundles from my lips is a popping noise like I peeled a suction cup from a window, and the only two words that I can form are, "Thank you."

The two plumbers pile in their van as I tip all 110 pounds of me back to my heels and wave the guys onto their next job that I'm sure won't be nearly as interesting a house call as mine.

I stand in the yard and strain to see the river through the space between the boxcars on a passing train. I'd hoped the plumbers would fix the leak so we could have a normal dinner full of the standard mix of the day's stories and trivial arguments, but now, I'm sure Alex's aggravation with the unresolved situation will dominate dinner.

I'm surveying the contents of the freezer when I hear tapping on the door glass. Dad's juggling a drill and Subway bags.

Dad may not ever host his own home improvement show—home repairs for him are changing the furnace filter once every six months and slapping a new color of paint on a bedroom wall—but he heralds a broad scope of problem solving abilities, and I need a fresh perspective.

"Aw, baby girl!" he says, a toothpick teetering between his teeth.

Before he has a chance to unload his arms, I hug him. Closing my eyes, I inhale the familiar Polo fragrance. The same hug that told me I was worthy company when a boy stood me up at the Sadie Hawkins dance is now conveying the message that somehow everything is going to be okay.

"How'd you know I wanted dinner?" I say, unlatching myself from the one person who wraps me with hope with every hug he gives me.

Dad's eyes are wild. His whole face appears sucked backwards like he's traveling at the speed of light. "I didn't. I always carry food and tools!"

I yell, "Boys, Pawpaw's here!"

The sound of feet pounding up the steps precedes Ben's surprised face. He runs full-force tackling Dad, and knocking him back into the counter.

"What you doing here, Pawpaw?" Ben says, spotting the yellow slogan on the bag. "Awesome!"

Isaac rounds the corner. "Mom, I just got sprayed upstairs."

"Oh," I say, shrugging toward Dad. "Ben, get paper plates, please." I point to the pantry. "Boys, the plumbers couldn't find the leak so Pawpaw's going to take a look. You can help him after you eat."

Isaac snatches the bags dangling from Dad's arms and Dad says, "Wasn't sure what to get. Just wanted to give your mommy a break. Pizza subs for you hammerheads and chicken for me and *my* baby."

"Oh, cookies. Awesome!" Ben says, elbow deep into the bag.

I slide a mug under the coffee maker. "Dad, French vanilla or hazelnut?"

Dad nabs one of the three cookies stacked in Ben's hand. "French vanilla's perfect."

"Thanks for the food, Dad. Have you eaten?"

"Am now," Dad says, taking a huge bite of a cookie and waving the rest of it in the air. He sucks his lips around his gums and talks like he's toothless. "Pawpaw like cookie."

Ben gasps, inhaling his cookie and embarking on a coughing fit.

Isaac snickers. "Pawpaw, you're crazy."

Dad clears his throat. "Mine's in the bag. Yours too, Savannah. Chicken salad with all the veggies I know the boys won't touch." He points at the boys like he caught them stealing money from the church's offering plate.

"Veggies. Yuck," Isaac says, cheese stringing from the bun he's inspecting.

The aroma of teriyaki chicken makes my stomach gurgle for a bite, but I can wait. I motion for Dad to follow me. "Want to show you upstairs before Alex gets home."

Dad and I walk upstairs to find water running down the walls and trickling over the white chair rail.

I point to a spot directly in the middle of the hallway. "Haven't seen it actually come from there, but that's where it first dropped on Ben."

Dad lays the drill on the bookcase in the hall. "We could drill a hole there and see if it's wet." He rubs his chin as if he's grasping for more possibilities. "Roof or chimney could be leaking. The chimney runs up this wall," he says, pointing to the hall wall that also serves as one of the walls of Ben's room.

"Yeah, but wouldn't the attic be wet?" I say. "Like I told you, Keagan and Pete's uncle have already checked the attic and it's dry."

"Probably, unless the subfloor's holding water. I'll get a ladder from the garage."

Dad returns grasping the top end of the ladder, the boys hoisting the legs.

Dad mounts the ladder in the hall and angles the drill bit toward the ceiling. "Here?"

"A little more to your left . . . yeah, there," I say. I can't believe I'm letting him drill a hole in my ceiling.

As drywall dust floats through the air, Ben glances behind him to Isaac and exclaims, "Wow, Dad's gonna be mad."

Ben's probably right, but I can't worry about Alex right now. Dad's long shot is my only hope.

"At least we're trying to figure out where this leak is," I say. "Your dad's too busy to care." Instantly, I'm sorry I said that. It's not fair for me to say that—he's out keeping the world safe. But my world is the one I want him protecting right now. I want him to be here even if he can't fix the damn leak—just be here with me so we can go crazy together.

"Your dad's just too busy right now and Pawpaw's willing to help. I'm sure your dad will appreciate us trying." Even as I hear the words, I know they're a lie—he'll be pissed and say Dad's stupid, and I'm loony as a blackbird eating fermented berries.

Dad drills a hole and sticks his finger in. "Dry as can be," he says, descending the ladder.

Ben and Isaac help dad navigate the ladder through the house and back to the garage while I sweep the drywall from the carpet. Maybe Alex won't be quite so mad if there's only a hole and no mess.

Over coffee, Dad suggests I make a claim with our home insurance company. Even though we don't have water damage yet, Dad reminds me that we may if this continues and says insurance companies often arrange outside contractors to help with special repairs.

Ours is special all right. We don't even know what needs repaired.

Dad heads home and a few minutes later, Ben comes screaming into the kitchen where I'm stacking clean glasses. "What the heck was that? Mom! What the heck!"

"What now?" I say, shutting the dishwasher.

"The water from inside the commode just shot up and hit the ceiling!" Ben says, both thumbs pointing skyward.

I can't comprehend. His words aren't making sense. I stare at him, feeling woozy.

Ben points to the half bath and walks off.

"What—how?" I ask, but I'm already a half trot behind him before he has a chance to answer. In the half-bath, water is dripping from a huge spot right above the commode.

As I shove down on the handle, I'm thinking there's no way water from the commode hit the ceiling.

I flush. No gusher. I look at Isaac who's now joined us.

"Mom, I *swear* it shot straight up there!" Ben's eyes are earnest as he looks at the wet ceiling.

"Wow!" Isaac says.

I flush again. Still nothing except a normal flush. "Oh, Ben," I say," I can't take much more of this insanity. You've got to be joking."

Ben hangs his head. "No, Mom, I swear, it just hit the ceiling when I flushed it."

"Ok," I say. "*You* flush it then."

When Ben pushes the lever, the commode water forms a funnel and shoots to the ceiling.

"Holy shit!" I say. This can't be really happening. It's impossible to have this many weird-ass problems at once. Pretty soon I'm going to be licking lithium from a salt block.

I spread my arms for a group hug. That's all I know to do—show my boys I am here even if this damn house tries to drown us. I'm here and we're going down together.

After the embrace, I send the boys to their rooms with a handful of snacks and orders to not come out. I'll have to tell Alex the news and he is *not* going to be a happy daddy.

Ten minutes later, Alex bursts through the door. "Where you been? I've been calling you for hours!"

The plate I'm setting in the cabinet teeters on my hand. Must I have to start every sentence with an apology?

"Oh, sorry, I don't even know where my cell is," I say, pulling my sub out of the bag and realizing Dad's sub is still inside. "Here's your sub, Alex," I say, heading to the living room and wondering if Dad purposely left the extra sandwich. "What'd you need?"

"Nothing now! I wanted to see what the plumber said." Alex slides his gun out of the holster and onto the fridge.

I scoop my cell from the seat of the recliner. "I must have forgotten to turn my ringer on after school. I see one missed call from you," I say, scrolling. I have a text from a number I don't recognize—could be from Ryan or Kent, but I'll read it later—family first. "Did you call more than that?"

"It wouldn't matter if I called a million times. You never answer your phone," Alex says.

His words smack. I have to focus on a mundane task that I could perform in a coma. I plump the couch cushions and a few large pieces of lint from the rug in the living room. "Plumbers came. They didn't have a clue. They turned—"

"Just what I figured, so we paid them for nothing." Alex unbuckles his belt and opens the basement door.

I continue, "*turned* all the water faucets on and still couldn't find where it's coming from, but at least they did get to experience it. It sprayed across the room and—"

"This is ridiculous! How hard can this be—like we are the only people in the world to have a water leak."

Every time he breaks in I feel like breaking down. I don't want to try to communicate anymore. I'm tired, but this is important.

"Alex," I plead, "just calm down a second and listen."

"I am listening, damn it! What do you think I'm standing here doing? Sticking my finger up my ass?"

Now that I'd like to see—his finger inside his own butthole—him humiliated like he likes to make me feel.

He unbuttons his stiff shirt and opens his eyes toward me. "Well? I said I'm listening."

"Just a second, Alex, I don't remember what I was saying." I sit on the stool, resting my elbows on the bar. It's difficult having two conversations going on—the rational one in my head and the nonsensical one with Alex.

"The plumbers were shocked shitless when the water sprayed right past them. They had no suggestions. Anyway, we have another little problem." If I talk faster and breathe less maybe he won't get a chance to interrupt me again. "Something's wrong with the commode in there." My gaze lights on the door to the half-bath. "Ben flushed the commode and water from it shot up and hit the ceiling."

"What you mean hit the ceiling?" Alex says, unsnapping the keepers on his gun-belt.

"It actually hit the ceiling. Ben came and got me the first time it happened. The ceiling was soaked when I walked in and I had him—"

"Boy, you'd fall for anything wouldn't you? He's just messing with you. Dealing with kids at school, I'd think you wouldn't be so gullible." Alex descends into the basement, hangs his overworked uniform on the hall-tree, yells for Ben and stomps into the half-bath.

"The commode flushes just fine," Alex announces as Ben saunters in and leans against the doorframe.

"A bunch of nonsense, Ben," Alex says, "you flush."

We watch the water spiral down the drain like it's supposed to, Ben looking at me for help.

I shrug, fishing to pull Alex's eyes to mine. "It did hit the ceiling before. I saw it."

"Shit, Savvy. You'd see pigs fly if someone else did!" Alex jabs his finger toward the window. "You've got to stop talking about stupid, crazy shit. You're going to have the boys as looney as you are."

I'm shaking my head. "There's no way you can blame me for seeing what I see just because you don't." I fold my arms and bow my head like a genie, wishing I had the power to make Alex disappear. My luck I'd vanish too and still be stuck with him.

"If anyone . . ." I say slowly and deliberately, the words climbing from my gut, "is making me crazy, it's you."

Alex orders Ben to bed and I collapse into mine.

Chapter Eleven

BLEEDING GREEN

I wake to the phone ringing and Alex saying, "What? I'm on my way!"
He's out of bed and down the stairs before I even sit up—this is bad. Jerking back the covers, I fly down the stairs, my hand gliding down the wooden rail.

Alex is in uniform when I reach the kitchen squinty-eyed.

"Pete's shot. Grab my gun." Alex snaps the keepers shut on his gun-belt."

Reaching on top of the fridge, I grip the handle of the Smith and Wesson 45.

Alex's lips land on my forehead as he takes the gun out of my hand, sticks it in his holster, and bolts out the door.

Pete. Some asshole shot Pete. Damn-it. I hope Alex peels his fingernails off—no decapitates him.

An "officer down" call is rare here in Wooten County, and even though the agencies bicker amongst themselves, when a uniform is down it doesn't matter what color it is. The bond between cops is a woven tapestry of practical jokes played on each other, wacky criminal behavior, calls and clusters of fuck-ups, and beat-downs that aren't reported.

Their backs aren't against the wall—they're against each other's.

I stand in the kitchen door watching him peel out of the driveway, spraying gravel into the yard, the siren's blare polluting the somber darkness. Red and blue flashes illuminate the bedrooms of our slumbering neighbors as Alex's cruiser hums along the route that may carry him to his death.

A stranger has penetrated our lives once again.

For a moment a fear of losing him grips me, and I'm grateful for the stranger who has unknowingly reminded me how much I love my man in green. A knot in my throat hardens. I want to pull Alex close—not push him away. I make an intention to siphon this sentiment tomorrow when he's angry and unreasonable and when I'm wishing he'd disappear.

I'm not usually scared for Alex's safety. Growing up with a dad for a cop prepared me for this lifestyle long before I knew I'd be living it as an adult.

Dad's stories were dinner entertainment for Luce and me. Like how he piled seven men into the back of his cruiser after a cue stick was jabbed into his lip after breaking up a bar fight and how he lobbed tear gas into a bar then rolled across the floor in complete darkness to get a guy who was holding a gun on his wife, only to find the man had shot himself and killed his wife who was still holding their crying baby.

We knew Dad's job was dangerous, but he always said he was happiest when he was whizzing across the county to assist a victim. And tonight as Alex whizzes to find the thug who shot Pete, I have no doubt he feels the same way.

I trundle to bed, remembering I'm supposed to meet Ted in the morning and wishing I hadn't set up the morning rendezvous. I hug Alex's pillow close like it's actually Alex I'm embracing and fall asleep on my pillow, soggy with tears.

Convenient that Alex is still out on Pete's shooting when I pass the kid's rooms at 6:30 a.m. With such an uncustomary early departure, if Alex had been home, I'd have had to lie about needing to get chips from the store for a potluck at school or something.

Getting up an hour early to have intercourse with a married man, or any man for that matter, feels so raw in the wee hours, especially after seeing Alex heading toward such danger on last night's call, but I can't just call it off with Kent. I'm the one who arranged this get-together and the least I can do is follow through. Being a tease is worse than being a whore.

The stairs creak as I amble down, hesitating for a moment, reconsidering my decision to meet Kent. I squeeze the handrail and hang my head wishing someone would tell me I don't have to do this—don't have to prostitute myself to be loved. But the someone I need to listen to is me, and I'm not strong enough to stop myself.

The "open," sign is on as I pass the bakery on the otherwise vacant main street in MuddSock Heights. I park in the library lot next to the post office. If anyone recognizes my car and word gets back to Alex I was over here this early, I'll tell him I was returning a book in the drop box. Poor excuse, but better than none.

I scan the street to make sure no cars are coming before scurrying to the front door of the renowned accountant's office. In an hour many of my acquaintances will be humming around, none the wiser to my special appointment.

I twist the doorknob hoping it's locked, but it's not. I slither up the stairs and peer into Kent's office where he's sitting behind his desk.

He comes toward me, arms outstretched, and offers a coffee-breath kiss with his embrace, mumbling that I get hotter, not older. Kent's not only a friend of Dad's, but he's old enough to *be* my dad.

I tell him that he's as handsome as ever—and he is. His wavy gray hair and glasses add refinement to his horny eyes. He takes my hair in his left hand, smells it and slides it away as he nibbles on my neck. He doesn't know the neck is my favorite foreplay spot; he's never even asked what turns me on. Guess he figures he already knows, but he'd be wrong. Not once have I had an orgasm out of the dozens of times in the past that we've had sex.

Kent unbuttons his shirt and leaves it hanging off his narrow shoulders, brushes my cheek with his thumb, and gazes into my eyes. There it is. That look I crave. He may not love me, but he certainly is looking at me like he does.

I grab his jaw, press my lips to his and suck on his tongue that keeps trying to pull back into his mouth. So, I allow him to play with mine like a kitten with a bowl of milk.

Pushing me backwards into the narrow hall between his office and the restroom, his fingers reach up my skirt and graze my mound briefly with one hand, his other hand cupping a breast. I feel like a dashboard, all lit up and ready for takeoff, but the pilot is struggling to navigate, still gathering coordinates.

I yank on his belt, unthreading it from the buckle. It snaps free from the pin, and I drop to my knees, taking his cock into my mouth that still tastes of mint toothpaste.

It feels like someone's watching, encouraging me to perform. I wrap the base of his dick with my hand and peer around the corner into the main corridor. No one is there, but I'm not surprised since my imagination seems to be on overdrive.

Licking long strokes on his penis I ponder the power of the kneeling position. Kneeling when praying demonstrates a humbleness—a subservience that is disciplined and confident. If I stop giving this man head right now, his desire to climax would overwhelm him. I'm in a more powerful position than he is even though he probably doesn't perceive it that way.

A few moments later he's saying his version of a prayer, crying out and rubbing my head. "Oh, Savvy! Oh, God!"

Yes, I think, even though I'm the one kneeling, I'm the one with the power here. I am your god. I wish I could find my God, but I don't think I'm going to find Him here.

I wouldn't mind that Kent came already if he would complete my takeoff, but he's already landed and I'm stranded on the ground. I feel like the office cleaning lady, just performing a service—except she gets paid, and I can't even get an orgasm from the deal.

I get up, press my lips together so the cum won't run out and prance to the restroom to spit into the sink. No monies were exchanged—only body fluids, but the blood inside me feels black, like death. I wish I could spit it out, too. I couldn't feel cheaper if he *had* paid me.

Kent gushes as he brushes past me toward his pants that are lying on the floor. "Wow! Been too long, Babe. You know you're the best at that!"

"Thanks," I say, knowing I have to be good at something that matters more than a head job does.

Kent buttons his shirt. "I got Luce's wedding invitation. Guess I'll see you there," he says, brushing my bare shoulder.

I don't even want to think about facing him and his wife at my sister's wedding. I want to shower away this grimy feeling from my skin. I glance at the clock behind his desk and announce that I have to get the boys to school.

Back home, I suds up with lavender, diffusing the scent of Kent's musky cologne and wake the boys who are still snoozing. I'd left a note on my bed saying, "Ran to the store," in case they woke up before I got back or Alex made it home before I did.

While the boys dress, I microwave sausage egg biscuits. My domestic duties like breakfast are my lifeboat, keeping me afloat in this bog of deceit.

After I return a text from Dad who wants to know who got shot because the news just said, "An officer in Wooten County," the boys join me at the counter where their breakfast sits. I tell them, between sips of coffee, that Pete was shot last night and their dad's still out.

"Is Pete dead?" Ben says.

"I don't know, bud. All I know is he was shot."

"Will daddy be home to take me four-wheeling? He said he would after school," Isaac says, chomping on his biscuit.

I haven't heard from Alex since he sped into the night to apprehend the villain, God help him, who was responsible for injuring Pete, but I don't want the boys to worry about their dad's safety.

"I imagine he'll be very tired, but he might," I say praying Alex is safe and comes home to me—to us. Suddenly, a stream of water shatters across the kitchen ceiling from the direction of the living room.

Ben doesn't miss a chew, but Isaac's mouth is open so wide that you'd think he'd just seen a witch fly through the room again.

I dry the countertop and floor with a dishtowel, and a few minutes later, Isaac's climbing onto the school bus, and Ben and I are racing to the car.

At school, Mr. Feldman knocks on my door and calls me out for a pow-wow in the hall with Mrs. Zavitz before I can even get the bell-ringer on the board. Feldman wants to know how Pete is doing, but I have no inside scoop. Feldman knows more from the news report than I do. I haven't even seen the news. I was too busy on my knees at Kent's and sopping up water.

Word through the school hotline, of whom Mrs. Z is president, is that Pete was shot by a sniper, but I don't know why a sniper would want to shoot him.

After first period I return a missed call from Alex who tells me that the man who shot Pete had called 911 after beating his wife—then planked with his rifle, trudged in the woods behind his house and waited on officers to arrive to begin his sordid target practice.

Pete was the first officer on the scene. Fortunately, the shooter was inebriated and the bullet hit Pete's leg rather than his heart. He's stable at the hospital, but his right leg is shattered, and he may never walk right again.

The fugitive is still out in the woods—K-9 team is tracking him. By the time school is out Alex hopes to be home and in bed, wants me to keep the boys quiet so he can sleep.

During the next class change, I step across the hall to Mrs. Z. who is chewing out two boys for having their cell phones out, and motion to Mr. Feldman to join us. As I dish out the latest developments on Pete's shooting, the tardy bell rings. This bell is as sacred to Mrs. Z. as a church bell announcing that service is to begin, but she doesn't budge and neither does Mr. Feldman who never gives a shit about tardies anyway.

Last period during planning, I'm passing through the cafeteria when Mr. Meyers steps from the kitchen with his coffee mug, and I remember that I still need to ask Alex about the pending drug sting on Diane's mom, but in the meantime, I can at least check in with Diane—see how things are at home.

I swing by the office for Diane's schedule and her transcript, find her class and summon her to the door. As she steps into the hall, Diane pulls her phone from her hoodie pocket and clicks it, claiming she's, "checking the time."

I ignore the texting. I have more important things to discuss with her than her disregard for the school's cellphone policy.

I dip my chin and try to make eye contact with her through the bangs draped across her forehead. "Just checking on you. Haven't seen you for weeks. You been absent?"

Diane flings the hair away from her face. "A couple times."

"I miss having you in class, but I know Mrs. Z. enjoys having you in hers," I say, lying. Mrs. Z. hasn't even mentioned Diane to me once, and I haven't mentioned Diane to her either. I don't want the scuttlebutt quizzing me about Diane's mom's activities and Alex's involvement with the situation. "You don't come see me at lunch anymore. Everything all right at home?" I say, leaning against the wall.

"Well, Mom's still a whore. Got men there every night." Diane digs her palms into her hoodie sleeves, stretching them enough she fits both arms inside.

I put my arm on her shoulder. "I'm sorry. I know it's been rough on you living there." I remove my hand, wishing I could tell her Alex is supposed to be working on a sting that could land her Mom in jail, but I can't because that could put her in danger and create an additional problem for her to worry about—who would she live with if her mom's locked up?

"Diane, you need to come to school," I say, handing her the transcript. "If you pass science you'll have enough credits to graduate next year."

Diane unwinds her tangled arms from the hoodie. "You know I'm supposed to be graduating this year, but I got behind when I got sent to alternative school."

"I know, hon." I say. "Your mom called the other day to check on your science grade—said she wants you to pass and to be happy." I look into her eyes. We both know what her mom really wants—for Diane to stay in school so the checks keep coming from the feds.

I wonder if Diane will ever be happy or if she will still be searching for happiness well into her thirties like I am.

Diane bites her bottom lip that's red with gloss and says, "Sometimes I stay with Matt."

"Matt your boyfriend?"

She smiles. "Yeah, He already has a job promise. Going to drive a truck. Truck drivers make lots of money."

"What's his last name?"

"Boggs."

"Matt Boggs?" I say, forming the image of the tattooed thug and newest addition to my class, my heart aching for Diane who is so desperate for love that she'd date the likes of him. I married and had kids with my high school sweetheart, too, but even with Alex on the correct side of the law, it feels like our marriage is being held together with Elmer's glue.

"Hey, Mrs. Templeton," echoes down the hall. I turn to see Terry piggybacking Brandon who is collecting a Monster drink from the top of the lockers.

I salute from afar. What the hell does it matter the energy drink is contraband—I wouldn't mind a taboo drink right now either.

"Yep." Diane pulls the cuffs of her sleeve until they partially cover her palm that's been scribbled on so much it could be a notepad. "He'll make a good daddy," she says.

"What? Are you . . ."

"No. I'm not pregnant—I mean someday." She giggles. "I told Matt you're the coolest teacher here."

"Sure am," I say, knowing Matt wouldn't agree with her opinion of me.

I usher her into class knowing her most important lessons are presenting themselves in the real world—a world of drugs, neglect, and dirty old men.

Diane will have to carve her own path over the terrain of her life. I can't make her decisions for her. I'm having a hard enough time making my own.

School dismisses and Isaac bursts through my classroom. "The kids asked me if Dad was the one who got shot."

I turn from the board where I'm listing character traits for the fairy queen, Titania, from "A Midsummer Night's Dream."

"That's what Darrell's dad told him and Darrell told Mrs. Murphy. Mom, Mrs. Murphy ran up and hugged me. She was like, 'Isaac, what on earth are you doing here!' I told her I like school and then she asked me wasn't my dad shot." Isaac's, big brown eyes glaze over.

"Oh, honey," I say, flipping the marker into the dry eraser tray and rounding my desk toward my baby. "I bet that scared you."

Isaac nods. "I thought maybe he got shot after Pete did."

"Can mom have a hug?" I say, opening my arms. "I think I need one more than you do. When something tragic happens people often get the facts messed up."

I squiggles loose. "Timmy said he bets Dad beats the crap out of the guy who shot Pete."

"What'd you say?"

"Just that he probably wants to, but he's not allowed to do that," Isaac says, tearing open a pudding pack.

"Good answer, bud. The public needs to trust the police," I say, wondering if I'll ever be able to trust my officer husband again.

I write on the board "Theme: Be careful who you trust."

Titania trusted her fairy king, Oberon, and he made her fall in love with a donkey—I trusted Alex then married the ass.

Alex's cruiser is parked around back by the garage when the kids and I pull in. Inside, I remind the boys their daddy is asleep as they sling bags and books onto the counter. Isaac doesn't mention the four-wheeler ride his dad had promised and heads to the basement with Ben.

I turn smooth jazz on and am sprinkling thyme on tilapia when Ben flushes the commode and lets out a war whoop that cuts through Boney James's serenade. I totally forgot we have a commode gusher!

I step toward the bathroom door with my finger over my lips as Ben steps out of the half-bath.

"Shhh. Your dad's asleep," I say. As I lay towels around the commode to absorb the water dripping from above, I listen for the creaky steps, hoping Ben's scream didn't wake Alex even though I wish he could see what this commode is doing.

I locate the video camera that's tucked in the closet and summon Ben from the basement. "I'm going to video this so your dad can see it," I say, clicking the record button. "Flush it."

He flushes and water shoots up like a fountain, hitting the ceiling.

"Whoa!" I say in my deepest whisper. "Ben that was crazy!"

"You're telling me!" Ben says, stepping back from the dripping ceiling.

I push the replay button on the camcorder, Ben huddling in beside me to watch. The image is clear for the first few seconds, but as soon as Ben flushes it goes black.

I video the geyser again, but this time while we are viewing the recording, a bright light shines through the window obscuring the commode completely.

"What the heck?" I say. "Just perfect. Something's wrong with the dang camera now. Ben, you dry it up this time."

I walk back into the kitchen and zap lasagna into the oven. The only thing keeping me from losing my mind is the littlest bit of normalcy I find preparing food.

Bedtime creeps in without a peep from Alex. I'm brushing my teeth when Isaac calls me into his room.

"Mom, there's bright spots all over the room."

"Isaac, I am so tired I'm seeing spots, too," I say, flipping on his Power Ranger's nightlight. "Please just go to sleep."

Isaac walks up to me and wraps his arms around my waist, head on my belly. "I'm scared. What are they?"

Hell if I know, I'm thinking as I squeeze him. "Maybe from the cars going by, shining in your windows?" I look at the curtains and blinds that are pulled tight. There's no way light's coming through there. "Describe the lights."

"They look like one of those tiny pens. And they're different colors. Blue. Red. White."

"Sounds like the American flag." I look to Isaac's upturned face to see if my smile is being returned.

It's not.

"You mean like the laser pens?" I say, remembering the light display I saw in the restroom at school.

He nods.

"You can leave your TV on and if that doesn't work, just sneak into Ben's room. I'm worn out. Okay?" I tuck the quilt up around his neck, but not before planting a kiss on it and getting him to giggle.

I lay in my bed and a feeling of déjà vu comes over me. I remember looking into the darkness when I was a little girl and seeing lights. They were deep in the pockets of air around me, some sparkly, some dim, but all of them forming a virtual constellation.

I wonder if they are still there in the dark just waiting for me to look for them again—for me to be open to the possibility of an active world within my three-dimensional one.

I'd thought the lights I saw the other day at school were just a fluke, but maybe they are present all the time.

I stare into the dark—looking for lights—looking for confirmation that the dimensions I believe could exist around me are real. Then, just maybe, I can accept that all the weird things going on here are real.

Closing my eyes, I breathe in thinking about how the molecules I'm inhaling—the ones I can't see—are sustaining me. A flash suddenly illuminates the darkness of my eyelids.

I pop my eyes open. Speckles of lights flicker to the upper right of where I'm lying. I can hardly believe it. I'm not just imagining them. They are really here. How had I forgotten to see them?

A red pinprick lights up in the left of my peripheral vision. The entire room of pitch black has become a pattern like a chain-link fence made of sparklers—an enchanted world I have totally blocked from my vision for years.

I close my eyes and still see the same pattern, the same lights as I do with my eyes open and wonder how this is possible. I somehow know what I'm seeing is a sign that the invisible world hears my thoughts and wants to promote my faith in them—whoever *they* are.

I fall asleep viewing the light show, and a few hours later, in the middle of a nightmare, I wake with a jerk. My head is throbbing. I'm opening my nightstand to get an aspirin when I notice my journal seems to be sprinkled with lights like I saw before I fell asleep. Maybe whoever *they* are in the other world, want me to write in it, but I'm too exhausted right now.

I love babies, but dreams of dropping them, forgetting to feed them or, worse than anything, losing them alone, is interfering with my sleep more and more often. This time it was a little boy left by the road. Just sitting there, bloody, in a stroller. I unsnapped him, pulled him close to my chest and flew him through the air to a nursery, leaving him in the protective arms of a nurse.

I'm re-living the feeling of him in my arms, when a thought occurs to me—maybe I save babies because I can't save myself.

Chapter Twelve

The Honorable Monster

I skip the college day assembly the next morning at school and search Alex's cell-phone records online. I didn't write down Raven's number the night I saw it so I can't check his contact with her, but I know Textbook Stacey's number. Current usage shows 27 calls and 83 texts in the past three weeks between my friend Stacey and my husband.

Scrolling back through the previous months, I find they've been in almost daily contact since last summer. Late night calls and six a.m. texts constitute a relationship that amounts to more than a one-night stand. The list of numbers and texts are a blur through my tears, but I'm no better than Alex. I have no right to cry.

I blow my nose and print the pages. I may need them for leverage if this comes to divorce. I darn sure don't want a nasty one like Mom and Dad's was.

I'm justified for screwing Kent, but that doesn't squelch the guilt that's gutting me. I know the affairs are wrong and useless. Not one of the men I've had sex with made me feel loved or accepted for who I am, yet I keep shooting up with semen, knowing it's just a quick fix.

I should just leave Alex—for his sake as much as mine. We should cut our losses. We're both thirty-four and that's young enough to begin a new life with someone else—young enough to fall in love with life again.

I imagine my life without Alex. Without him I wouldn't have someone to argue over dinner with—wouldn't have someone to sleep beside me and protect me. But the person I most need protected from isn't the criminals he's arresting, it's from the monster that Alex has become from dealing with them.

He used to be the teddy bear I wrapped my arms around to feel safe, not the ogre I want to run from, screaming with my hands over my ears, but he's my monster—mine till death us do part—mine to tame, to feed, to play with. I'm locked in this cage with him, and no matter how much I plead or snap the whip is taming the monster that I love.

I stay in my room during the entire school assembly and call our homeowners insurance company to ask if they can recommend a contractor who can help us fix the leak.

The feminine voice on the line says, "We have professionals who specialize in water leaks."

I file a claim and schedule the team to come to the house, but then she says, "The water and electric must be turned off to the structure before the crew can enter."

"I don't think you understand," I say. "We need the utilities on. We're still living in the house."

"Oh, you are?" the lady says. "I figured the structure was uninhabitable the way you described it. How are you living there, dear, with all that water?"

"We just dry it up with towels." It sounds so simple, I laugh.

"So there's no standing water that they will have to wade through?" she says.

"Oh, no, it's not like that. The sprays are rather sporadic," I say. I'm willing to turn off the power and live by candlelight, if I have to in order to get the team of experts here, but I'd rather not.

"Okay then," the lady says. "Our guys will be there tomorrow at four o'clock and the utilities can remain on."

I hang up and notice the text from an unknown number I saw last night, but forgot to read. It says, "Hi there! It's Joe. How u doin?"

Who the hell is Joe?

"Hi right back!" I text. "Refresh my muddled memory plz."

"The guy you handed your number to on the back of your grocery list. lol"

Oh yeah, him—Mr. Adonis—Mr. I'm going to ignore you.

I sit back smugly in my leather chair, my thumbs hovering, frozen over my cell. I can still smell Kent's coffee laden kiss from yesterday morning, and the thought of his breath on my neck turns my stomach. Barely a day's gone by and I'm already tempted to repeat the same scenario.

I can practically smell Joe's sweaty sheets that have likely not been laundered since his last poke into an unknown orifice and remember another promise to myself—no more skanky sheets.

I have to respond to Joe, but I don't know what I want to do. I dangled my number wanting to see if he would bite—if my bait looked tasty enough to entice him. Now that it has, I'm not sure I want to reel in my catch.

This is too complicated. Maybe tossing the whole damn pole in the river would be easier.

I don't have to do anything I don't want to do, but my head is spinning, and I know I have to postpone any decision about this Joe.

Rain No Evil

I text, "Joe, nice to hear from you. I'd like to talk, but real busy here. Text you later."

Joe, "Sounds good. I'd like that!"

Just thinking about someone touching me makes me want to hurl. I yank open my desk drawer, fumbling for Excedrin when my hand bumps into a tattered burgundy Bible. Figuring it can't hurt to read a few lines, I pull it out and thumb to Psalms. They're a quick read and students could stampede in from the assembly any minute.

My finger lands on number 23. I skim to "He maketh me to lie down in green pastures. He leadeth me beside still waters." I want serenity and the idea of water that's not moving sounds wonderful.

Standing, I look out the window across the field of daisies, watching the crows land, form a V-shape, nibble, lift off and fly a few feet away—all done in unison while maintaining the V-shape. I watch them repeat the pattern and wonder how they learned to eat in such synchronicity and how they do so elegantly.

The verse floats through my head about God watching the sparrows and how they don't worry about what they will eat. I want to fly away and not worry about water, or unexplainable flickering lights, or illusions of demons and microwaves on fire, or about trying to live with Alex, or about being alone.

I bow my head and sob. Just sucking in air is laborious. Endless water, reams of arguments with Alex, storage bins full of sex and distortions of truth, and visions of unattainable serenity whirl inside my head.

As I lean against the bookcase by the window, goose bumps pop out all over my arms and the sides of my face. From the sunshine streaming through the window, I feel warm and safe like I'm being hugged all over—held together by the strands of lights surrounding me.

"God," I say, petitioning the Almighty who promises to lead me beside still water. "This water leak is driving me crazy and I know I have no right to ask for help, but I've done everything I can to fix it. What else can I do?"

Immediately, I hear an unmistakable voice. "There is nothing you can do. You are not in control." I know that no one is in my room, but I look around anyway searching for the person who just spoke to me.

The pressure on my head feels like a giant iron's pressing on my skull, and I grab the bookshelf, steadying myself. Somehow an imprint of divine knowledge has been stamped in my mind. I have a spirit in my house.

As if blinded by the light of knowledge like Saul on the way to Damascus, I grope my way to my chair and sit down. I have a spirit in my house! God actually just spoke to me! I can't believe God just spoke to me. I can't believe I was still long enough to hear Him. I can't believe I have a spirit in my house.

Everything that's been happening from the demon to the water to Ben's premonitions and Isaac's laser show really is more than a battle of the senses—

more than a battle for my sanity or for my marriage. It's a spiritual war, and I am in no way equipped with the arsenal I need to win that.

Everything makes a confusing sort of sense now as snippets of the past week pervade my mind—my demonic face in the mirror; Isaac's spooked-out voice calling for me to explain the witch, the hand in his wall and twinkles in the dark; Ben's visions and water spraying inside my house.

I slap my hands to my head. Now I know my prayers aren't just heard by the empty air. There is a God. I just heard him.

The water that sprays my walls and trickles down my forehead is being hurled by an evil spirit. Wonder why it's slinging water rather than knives that could actually kill us. Could it be that God chose water because I was in the shower when I dared him to prove He exists?

Or perhaps He's letting the demon try to drown me—or drown all of us because I challenged him. But God is supposed to be loving and merciful and surely He can't blame me for wanting to know He is real.

Wonder if He sent the demon or just removed his protection like He did Job in the Bible?

God let the devil destroy Job's health, kill his entire family, and steal his material wealth, but Job refused to curse God. To reward Job's faithfulness, God provided him with a new family and twice as much property as he had before.

I wonder what my reward will be if I pass my test.

In the Bible, water was good and bad. It was the source of floods and the symbol of salvation as John baptized Jesus. Maybe that's it—God's trying to baptize me and letting me experience evil so He can lead me to goodness—to the still waters where He will restore my soul.

The bell rings after lunch, and Terry rushes in jabbering about this afternoon's assembly and how he's signing out—no spring concert bullshit for him. Seems most of the class must feel the same way about this afternoon's concert—only three kids report to class for roll.

I have an awesome excuse to skip it, too. How many employees can say that they need relieved from their duties because they have to figure out how to get a spirit out of their house—not that I would actually go to the daggone concert if I had no excuse. Heck, I'd skip it for no reason. No one ever comes looking for me anyway.

Mr. Meyer's voice blares across the intercom, dismissing the seventh graders first as they are the youngest group. I smile at my tenth graders and order, "Get outta here," to which they gladly comply.

Sitting in my vacant room, I wonder if I can re-claim my house if I plead the blood of Jesus over it when I get home. The preacher at the evangelical church I grew up in was always pleading the blood over some problem or some person like the night the possessed woman crashed our evening service. I guess pleading the blood at my house is worth a try.

Rain No Evil

Alex is going to really think I've gone bonkers when I tell him of my revelation, but I have to tell him, and I definitely can't explain this to him over the phone. I'd like him to reassure me that everything's going to okay—our house, our family, our marriage—but I doubt he'll reassure me of anything.

I pick up the phone and call him anyway. I just want to hear his voice.

I soak in his strength as I listen to him relate how Stranahan located Pete's shooter in a cave and quickly notified Taze who gave permission for the "V.I.P treatment." The criminal was dragged through the woods, over brush and rocks, earning several cuts and bruises. Of course, the official report will document his rough appearance is a result of trying to "escape through such perilous terrain."

Alex says, "He shoulda got the R.I.P. version, but I was in a good mood."

I tell him I agree even though I really don't, but I don't think Alex would actually kill someone. When I ask him if he will be home for dinner because I need to talk with him, he insists on knowing what I want to talk about. Maybe he thinks I'm going to ask for a divorce or corner him about Raven's text. I wish he could be patient, but he keeps saying, "Sav, just tell me."

He may wield his shield and get all the scumbuckets singing, but he's not going to interrogate me like a criminal. I tell him I can't hear him—that there's a bad connection and I'll have to talk with him tonight then hang up mad at him for making me lie.

I really need to talk to someone about my revelation so I text Mandy, "God just told me that a spirit is throwing the water in my house!"

The aroma of roast sifting from the crock-pot greets me when I get home. I feed the boys and send them to the basement so I can promenade through the house, praying aloud without frightening them.

Rummaging through the bottom drawer of the nightstand I feel the soft knobby leather of the worn Bible I was given as a baptismal gift when I was seven years old.

Whipping out the King James and shoving it high above my head as if extracting power from the Omnipotent, I say, "In the name of Jesus Christ, I command any evil demon, entity or spirit in this house to leave. By the blood of my Lord and Savior, Jesus Christ, you must leave this house and never return!"

Hoping I sound more authorative than I feel, I proceed through the house, repeating the same mantra.

When my prayer parade of one enters the kitchen I hear the telltale buzz of interference on the police scanner sitting in the windowsill. Alex is home. Ben has it programmed with the local police and emergency channels including those across the Ohio River in MuddSock Heights.

Alex's voice streams live across the air, announcing off duty at residence in radio lingo. "CR1 to control. 10-7-10-42."

I will have to skip the basement for now. The boys are down there, and I can't chance Alex catching me mid-chant, so I tuck my Bible inside the end table.

145

Alex steps through the door. "So, what'd you want to talk about?"

"Well, first, how's Pete doing?" I say, slicing a tomato.

"In recovery right now. Had surgery to remove the bullet," Alex says, placing his gun on top of the fridge. "Now will you tell me what's going on?"

"I called our homeowners' insurance," I say, "and Dad was right about them having teams that specialize in what the secretary called 'hazardous settings.' Their team is coming at 4:00 tomorrow—oh, and it's free."

Stripping, Alex heads to the basement. "That's all you wanted? Why couldn't you tell me that on the phone?"

I flip on the garbage disposal, pretending I didn't hear his comment. He doesn't know that my story has only begun—we have a demon in our house, and that's not typical Templeton dinner conversation.

My cell beeps and a text pops onscreen from textbook Stacey wanting to see what I've been up to—wants to go shopping and have a girls' day. I'd rather grow horns on my demon head than shop with her.

I don't respond. I ladle the roast and potatoes onto plates, and with the evening news broadcasting on TV, sit at the counter by Alex. The dinner table is covered with a plastic tarp, sheltering the various valuables I've stacked underneath.

"Dad's coming by tomorrow to insulate the attic," Alex says. "He thinks we could have inadequate ventilation and that could be causing the water." He bites into the tender beef. "You should fix this more often."

I observe the juice on his lip and my pride swells into a grin. Since my enlightenment today, I know the ventilation theory is hogwash, but I just nod. This light-heartedness feels nice and I hesitate to delve into the supernatural topic, but I have to tell him about my revelation.

Even if pleading the blood of Jesus just now made it stop, I want to share the amazing message I got from God today. If my prayers didn't do the trick, I'll have to employ the help of a professional, and it'd be nice to have Alex's support.

"Alex, I need to tell you—"

"So, who you scrogging now?" Alex says, stabbing his fork into another slice of beef.

"Yeah, right," I say, smacking his arm that's wrapped around his plate like he's eating in prison. He's just fishing to see what kind of response he gets from me, hoping I act concerned. "This isn't about sex, Alex. It's about this water. I was praying at school today about how to fix this leak and—"

"You actually pray about that kind of stuff?" He shakes his head. "Like God cares about your house repairs."

Sometimes his pure ignorance amazes me. He goes to church and says he believes in the Bible, yet he doesn't believe God cares about our daily needs. I have my own doubt about what God's plans are for me, but at least now I know He's real. I heard His voice today.

"Yes," I say. "God cares about what the sparrow eats, and I think He enjoys helping us in all aspects of our lives no matter how mundane."

Rain No Evil

Alex swishes a swig of tea in his mouth like its Listerine. "I think He's got more important things to help people with—like people dying in the hospital. I can understand praying if you had cancer."

"I believe God doesn't have a limit on how many miracles He dishes out. Alex, I know this is really going to be hard to believe, but God spoke to me today." I hesitate and look at Alex, whose has stopped chewing. "He told me we have a spirit in the house."

Alex's puffy cheeks turn red as he chokes, beef juice oozing from the corners of his mouth. He looks like a slobbering gargoyle.

"Really, Alex," I say, taking advantage of the extra few moments he can't talk. "I know it sounds crazy, but God spoke to people in the Bible. Why do you think it's so funny he spoke to me?"

"A spirit! Good God, woman, have you lost your mind?" He gets up from the table. "Do you know how loony you sound? I could have you committed."

"Just listen for a min—"

"Listen to what? How a ghost is in our house?" Alex pounds off to the kitchen and points toward the corner of the room. "Oh look, it's Casper with a bucket of water."

Alex shovels two pieces of pie onto his plate that's speckled with leftover carrots. "You know, Sav, you were normal when we got married. What happened to you? You talk about weird shit like spirits talking in parrots and God speaking to you.

He raises his arms, fingers wiggling and eyes bulging like he's the victim of a hold-up. "There's no ghost here and I don't want to hear your wacky ideas any more, and the boys don't want to either."

He's not acknowledged once how weird the water coming from nowhere is. It's as if the fact that I got a divine revelation makes less sense to Alex than the water does. I glare at him. I knew he wouldn't believe me, but does he have to be so vicious?

"The boys?" I say. "I didn't tell the boys there's a spirit—"

"I'm sure you will be," Alex says through a mouth-full of blackberry pie. "You're going to make them crazy, too. Is that what you want—their friends making fun of them and calling this a haunted house?"

I've got to convince him. "Alex, I haven't told you this, but before all this water started, I saw a demon in my mirror." I hesitate, expecting Alex to interrupt me, but his mouth is motionless and open as wide as his eyes.

I continue, "Remember the night I woke you and told you evil was in the house?"

His mouth contorts until words come out. "You actually believe that, don't you? You *have* lost your mind. You even think your crazy-ass dreams are real. You didn't walk out of your body and see a demon."

"If you know so much then why can't you fix the leak?" I say, getting up. I've had enough of the insults.

Alex is saying, "I fix everything around here," when water slaps across the ceiling and drizzles onto his crew cut head.

I couldn't have planned the timing of that *splat* better—it's as if the demon that threw the water was telling Alex to shut the hell up like I want to. If I weren't so leery at siding with evil, I'd smile at the invisible creature in appreciation.

Alex throws a dishtowel on his head and says, "I could fix it if I had time, damn-it—if I wasn't working all the damn time—little things like murders and child rape cases, but hey, Savannah has some water in her house, and I'm supposed to stop the world for Casper whose throwing it! Bull-shit!" He slams the dishwasher door shut. "Guess I'll take off work and take care of some of the shit around here so you don't go off the deep end. That's all I need going 'round—Tazes's wife's in the loony bin!"

Alex storms off to the weight-room in the garage and I stand staring out the front window, dazed. He doesn't understand that I don't *think* a spirit is responsible—I *know* there is.

I don't care if the whole damn community thinks I'm crazy—they aren't the ones this is happening to, and they sure as hell don't live with Alex who would cause anyone to lose their marbles. I know what I know and I just can't un-know it!

The only way Alex will believe anything is to see it for himself. Maybe if I could prove the commode water is hitting the ceiling—capture it on camera—maybe he'd believe it then.

I grab the camcorder and video the passing cars to see if it's recording them without malfunctioning. When I play it back, the images show up perfectly, so I recruit Ben to flush the commode.

Ben flushes and water shoots onto the ceiling, but when we watch the replay, a bright light shines through the window blinding the image on the screen.

"Mom," Ben says, stepping back from the dripping water, "why didn't it hit the ceiling yesterday when Dad watched me?"

I wondered that yesterday, but at the time I didn't know a spirit was in my house. Maybe the spirit didn't torpedo the commode water for Alex because he isn't open to the possibility of something paranormal being the cause, but if that's the case, why is he able to see the water spraying out all over the house?

I set the camcorder for one more try. "I don't know, Ben. Let's try one more time."

An attempt from a different angle is blacked out like the first time I tried it yesterday, so I release Ben from flushing duty. This spirit is camera shy.

I head upstairs and flop onto my bed and see Mandy has texted me back. "A spirit!! Holy shit girl! I've got to see this. Will be in a week from Monday to visit Mom and Dad."

I text back, "There's way more than water too. Way too much to text. I can't wait to see you!"

Mandy says, "I know you're busy and have to be stressed to the max. God I wish I could do something to help you!"

"You are! Just you listening makes me feel better☺"

I grab a pen and write in my journal:

> *I thought the Camcorder was malfunctioning when I videoed Ben flushing the commode, but now that I know a spirit is responsible for the water leak, all the strange events that we've been experiencing make sense—even the digital interference.*

Alex doesn't believe God actually told me that a spirit is in our house. The more I know, the less I understand, but acknowledging my ignorance puts me miles past Alex. Actually, I think we are running two entirely different marathons—his feet are pounding the ground and I'm flapping my arms for lift-off.

I want to see the unseen and understand the inexplicable while Alex seems to immerse himself in the physical world that no longer seems real to me. I slide my journal into my nightstand as water shoots across the ceiling directly above the middle of the bed.

I've had enough of this wet and wild ride for one night. I pack a bag and tell the boys to gather their things for an overnight at Pawpaw Cal's.

Downstairs, I tell Alex that I'm heading to Dads. I'm too exhausted to care if he's ticked because I'm leaving him to sop up the water himself.

I collect my school bag, listening to a barrage of accusations from Alex about how I'm making the situation worse by uprooting the boys on a school night and how he doesn't know why we are even married since we never have sex.

"Never?" I say, slamming my car keys onto the granite countertop. "A few nights ago was never?"

I'm ready for this confrontation. No more cowering for me. It's time he knows I know he's not innocent—then he can get off his high horse. "I'm sure *Raven* won't mind helping you out."

Alex's lips seep air like he's blowing out a candle, his eyes peering away from their corners. "Who's Raven? Why'd you say that?"

He's scared. Good. I want to scare him; he deserves it. I brace my hands on my hips. "I don't know who she is, but you obviously do. I saw your text from her the other day—said she enjoyed her evening with you—called you sexy."

"I'm telling you, Sav, I don't know a Raven." Alex gets up from the sofa and saunters to the kitchen. "I think you're the one screwing around—maybe with that Logan guy from church. I saw the way you looked at him."

I pry my frozen lips apart. "Diverting the conversation to me isn't going to work for you, dear. I saw the text so you can deny it till the cows come home, but

I can't go on like this. The only way we have a chance is if you're honest with me. I'm not going to leave you because you are seeing her, but I will if you lie to me. If you don't tell me the truth, I won't be able to move past it and ever trust you again."

I turn my gaze to the backyard where Alex's cruiser is, wondering how often Raven's came in his backseat.

Isaac walks in lugging a duffel bag, and Alex says, "Hey, bud, your mom and I need to talk about something here. Go on upstairs till she's ready."

Isaac sets his bag on the floor, grabs a handful of cookies, and heads upstairs.

"Look Sav, Raven is a day report officer." Alex rubs his chest, like just talking about this makes him actually sore. "I only met with her once. It was quick and didn't mean anything."

Picturing Raven spread eagle in the barracks, and Alex bragging later about the dick thrashing he gave her makes me feel like I'm viewing my life from the top of the Eifel Tower, swaying with the dizzying reality that I'm on the edge and may have no control over falling.

I brace my foot on the bottom ledge of the barstool and ask if any of the other officers knew he had the weed monkey bent over the police bunk bed.

Picking a weed monkey is as common with men in uniform as picking marijuana plants during harvest season is with the stoners. I've never asked why cops refer to their whores as weed monkeys—guess it's because, for drugs, the women munch on their banana dicks that are hard on the outside, mushy when peeled back—just like many of their owners' egos.

"How many of your buddies know you did her?"

"Sav, I didn't tell anyone—like I want that information getting out."

I'm tempted to omit Stacey from this conversation—I just don't know how much more truth I can handle in one day, but maybe the scary truth is just what I need to hear in order to decide how I'm going to spend the rest of my life.

"You seeing anyone else, like say, Stacey Chutney?" I ask, scraping my foot along the base of the stool.

Alex wrinkles his nose and cocks his head. "Stacey? Hell, Sav, she's a friend of yours. Why'd you ask that?"

I don't tell him I'm asking because I know how other women are—I *am* the other woman.

I picture myself standing here with Alex like it's not really me, but someone else. I can pretend for a while, until the hurt subsides. Alex's not going to admit anything about Stacey unless I mention I've seen the phone records, and I don't have the gumption to embark on that journey tonight. So, having banked one confession, I yell upstairs for the boys to get in the car.

On the way to Dad's I critique my performance—not bad for a rookie on the fly. I didn't break down and cry—didn't show my weakness.

I insisted he tell the truth, but I haven't told mine. I want to. I just don't think he would really listen and try to understand if I did.

Rain No Evil

As I turn into Dad's drive, I realize he's probably already locked up for the night. I didn't even call and tell him we were coming, but there's no need to knock—his security system's no doubt already alerted him that a car's entered his drive.

The porch light snaps on as I pull up to the garage. Dad's at the door with his hand in the pocket of his flannel robe that no doubt bears a revolver.

The boys and I pile out and Dad waves us onto the porch. "What's wrong, baby girl?" he asks, his arms extended as far as the door is open. He hugs me, the hand holding the Smith and Wesson wrapping around my back.

"Just too wet at the house for me tonight." I remain folded in the plush warmth of his robe. "Sorry, I was too aggravated to call first," I say, my head heavy on his chest.

"Open invitation here. You know that." He pushes his glasses onto the bridge of his nose.

Isaac runs past us and into the house yelling, "What you got to eat, Pawpaw?"

"You hammerheads are always hungry," Dad says, releasing me. "You both must have a hollow leg."

Ben says, "Ayyy," with a thumbs-up like Fonzie on *Happy Days*."

"My leg's not yellow, Paw Paw," Isaac says.

Ben slaps Isaac on the back of the head, and Isaac punches Ben's arm.

"Not yellow—hollow," I say, sliding past Dad with my bag. "It means empty. Like your leg's empty and that's where all the food goes instead of into your belly."

"I'll wrangle up a surprise," Dad says. "Round-up in the kitchen cowboys." He winks at me. "You go settle in, baby girl."

I take my bag upstairs while Dad does kitchen duty.

God, I love it here. I'm not holding my breath, waiting for an upset student to console or an explosive husband to diffuse. All I have to do is be—be alive, not be the buffer in this pinball game of a life.

I change into my jammies and wash my face. When I reach the kitchen, popcorn's in a bowl and Dad's layering ham and cheese into sandwiches.

I won't tell Dad about Alex's infidelity or about my prayer in the shower that I think instigated the water plague. That's just too personal for me to share with Dad. I don't want him to worry about my marriage, but the topic of spirits will be welcomed here.

The boys scramble off to watch Nickelodeon with their feast. I retrieve my bar of dark chocolate from the cabinet while Dad sits and opens his oatmeal cookie.

Breaking off a chocolate square, I join Dad at the table. "Dad, I've had a revelation. It's going to sound unreal, but bear with me. I was praying at school yesterday and God told me we have a spirit in our house. That's where the water's coming from—a demon."

He looks up over his glasses that have slid to their usual resting place.

"I know it sounds bizarre, but I absolutely know it's true." I move my legs, sitting cross-legged. "Now I just have to figure out how to get rid of it."

Dad's nodding his head, not interrupting.

I feel like what I'm saying is actually important to him. "I pled the blood of Jesus through the whole house yesterday afternoon and water's still spraying."

"Did you tell Alex?" Dad says.

"Yeah, at dinner and I'm sure you can imagine his reaction, First he laughed and called it Casper. Then he got mad and said I was crazy."

Dad walks to the sink that looks out over the sprawling lawn toward the pond where an oak tree looms that he helped me plant when I was in kindergarten.

"Savvy, I raised you girls to be open-minded—to question the obvious and have faith in the abstruse. If you say there's a spirit in your house then, by golly, there's a spirit there, and it better be saying its nighty-nighty prayers." He jams a rolled-up slice of ham into his mouth and smiles with part of the meat hanging over his chin.

I laugh. "And that's why all my girlfriends always had to sleepover at *my* house—you're too damn funny!"

An hour ago, I wouldn't have believed I would be eating chocolate and laughing right now—and I wouldn't be if I had stayed with Alex tonight. Makes me wonder if I could be this relaxed every night without him.

"Oh, and the insurance company does have a team of specialists. They're coming to check out the house tomorrow," I say, hugging my knees to my chest, "but you know as well as I do, no physical remedy is going to defeat a spiritual enemy. They'll leave shaking their heads like everyone else has, but Alex would be furious if I cancelled them because of . . . as Alex says, Casper."

"You need a preacher that speaks tongues to roll through there and evict ole Cass," Dad says.

"I hadn't thought about calling Pastor Todd. He doesn't speak in tongues though," I say, nestling the chocolate back into its hiding spot. "But he may have dealt with this type of thing before."

"Probably hasn't broadcasted it if he has." Dad laughs. "It's not like there's a subsection in the yellow pages under preacher called 'Ghostbusters.'"

"I'll check with Todd tomorrow—see if he can pray it gone. Cause I sure can't."

I debate whether to tell Dad about the demon in my mirror and the paranormal experiences the boys are having, but I do. I share it all while Dad sits breathing so shallow I can barely see his chest rise for air.

"Sav," Dad says. "I didn't think much about this at the time, but something happened here with water, too." He opens the cabinet beneath the sink, slides the dishwashing liquid to the side and pulls out a bottle of Jack Daniels. "Similar to what's happening at your house," he says, sitting and pouring the alcohol into a glass with a splash of Coke.

"And you didn't tell me! Was it scary?" I say, pouring myself one with more of the Coke than the Jack.

"Not scary, just weird. But I really didn't connect it with your situation until now. Last fall, I woke up and heard water dripping. I thought it was one of the bathroom faucets so I checked, but both the sink and the shower faucets were tight and dry. I listened for a minute, didn't hear it so I went back to bed. As soon as I laid down, I'll be damned if I didn't hear it again. I moved my feet to get out of bed and felt a wet spot. I flipped the light on. Water was dripping from the ceiling. Just like it started at your house."

My hand covers my mouth. "Oh, my gosh, Dad. Why didn't you tell me before?"

"There was no reason to. It only happened that night. I just thought it was a fluke of nature—never thought of it being a spirit. I did think it was strange because there are no water pipes in my attic and it hadn't rained for days. Next day I climbed into the attic and it was dry, so I knew the roof wasn't leaking. Never happened again."

"Ok. But that was last year and what would that have to do with my house now? If yours was a spirit, too, what made it leave?"

Dad shakes the last drop of elixir onto his tongue. "Honey, I could write a book about what I don't know."

I believe I will write about this when it's over—even if I can't explain everything that's going on.

"Dad, have you read a lot about the supernatural? I saw the book in your study by Cayce."

"Yep, It's called *The Power of Your Mind*. Talks about the metaphysical realm and the God-consciousness within all of us."

"So if God's within me, why didn't my prayers make the spirit leave?"

Dad shrugs.

While Dad rattles on about how he could come plead the blood at my house, I sit wondering why it didn't work for me. Maybe I had no true authority over it because I'm sinning by cheating on Alex. In the past, I've asked forgiveness from God for adultery, but I haven't asked forgiveness for Ryan or Kent because I figure God's got my number and is tired of hearing me make promises he knows I'm not going to keep.

I tune back into Dad who's saying, "Cayce believes our minds work with God's to create solutions to our problems, and I do believe you will find the solution to yours."

I finish off my nightcap as Isaac strolls in with an empty plate. "Tell your brother bedtime." He swivels and scurries out before I insist they go immediately. He knows he can squeeze another ten minutes out of me.

I turn to Dad. "So what's metaphysical mean exactly?"

"Basically any concept that the mainstream science community deems not observable and measurable."

That would seem to be the sort of science that would explain my out-of-body experience when I saw the demon in the mirror. "Like the study of an alternate reality," I say. "One that we don't necessarily see with human eyes, but could see if the conditions were right?"

"Exactly," Dad says, taking a plate from Ben who lumbers in.

"What can't you see with your eyes, Mom?" Ben asks.

I haven't told the boys about the spirit in the house, but Alex is right. I will tell them—just not tonight. "I can't see where the water is coming from," I say. "Hug Pawpaw night and hit the hay, you old horse. You got some learning to do tomorrow. School. Yeehaw!"

I hug Dad. "Thanks for listening, Dad. I'm beat."

Snuggled under my pink Holly Hobbie quilt, I remember laying here as a girl, words whirling through my head, dreaming of writing a novel—not about any certain subject—just for posterity—for the whole notion of leaving a legacy when I'm dead.

Now, my life is actually writing the book for me, and I'm the main character. How cool is that?

Chapter Thirteen

Dangling Diane

When I pull in the school parking lot Thursday morning, groups of students are holding each other and crying. A few girls dabbing their face with tissues stagger into the building. The sidewalks are lined with counselors and administrators, forming a perimeter to the school's entrance. This is bad.

"Mom, what's going on?" Ben asks.

I scoop up my lunch bag. "I don't know, but it can't be good."

I shut my car door as Mr. Feldman, who's parked beside me, gets out of his and says, "Know what happened?"

I shrug and jog through the parking lot toward the school, passing Ben who's already hooked up with Cole and Andy.

Mr. Meyers is standing by the front doors near Joanne who has her arms wrapped around a girl racked with sobs. Joanne nods me over. She rubs the girls back and steps to the side.

"Savvy, it's Diane." She takes my hand into hers. "She was found this morning in her backyard. She hung herself."

Not Diane. This can't be. I just talked to her. She didn't tell me she needed help . . . or *did* she say something and I missed it . . . a word or gesture for help that I didn't notice?

Joanne hugs me and rubs my shoulders. I can't move my arms to hug her back. I want to cry, to scream, "No! It's not fair!" but I can't fall apart in front of the students.

A heavy-set boy trotting up the walk screams what I'm thinking, "No! No! Where is she?"

155

Joanne intercepts him before he reaches the door, stepping in front of him and opening her arms as he buries his head in her chest, knocking her back a step.

"Michael," Joanne says. "I'm so sorry."

Michael's an eighth-grader, Diane's half-brother, but he doesn't live with her and must've just found out about her death.

In a daze I meander from student to student, their tear-stained faces a blur, hugging anyone who opens their arms and whisper, "I know," even though I don't know a damn thing anymore.

Memories of Diane flash through my mind like a PowerPoint. Last year she'd pop in my room at lunch and chat; sometimes I'd bring her a cupcake from home—vanilla—her favorite. She'd bring me sketches from art class of her rendition of O'Keeffe's flowers. The magnet one with a lily on it is hanging on my fridge at home –holding up a worthless schedule of some sort. What good's a schedule—Diane's dead.

Maybe I could've prevented her from killing herself, but how? Oh, who am I kidding—I'm too absorbed in my own crumbling, scrambled mess of a life to help anyone. Wasn't too long ago I was daydreaming about drowning my own cares in the Ohio.

I segue inside with the crowd of mourners to the commons, where teachers, a counselor from the elementary school, and a few ministers from local churches sit around tables talking with grief-stricken students, some of whom have gathered around a senior who's strumming his guitar to a country song.

I scan the room for Joanne and Michael, but don't see them. Joanne probably has him in her office.

From the crowded hall, Ben's eyes meet mine. He makes his way to me and hugs me.

"Sorry, Mom," he says.

All I can do is nod. Since he is years younger than Diane, he didn't know her very well, but I am proud to have raised such a caring son.

My cell vibrates. Alex is calling. Alex! I never even asked him about the drug sting on Diane's mom. I'll feel worse if I find out her death had anything to do with drugs. Stepping into the faculty restroom, I answer the call.

"Savvy," he says, a rare tenderness in his tone. "I'm sure you've heard by now—about Diane."

"Yes," I say, leaning against the wall, grungy with mildew. "Joanne said she hung herself. You have details?"

"A neighbor boy found her," Alex says, his voice rising over the garbled police radio traffic. "He was cutting through Diane's backyard to catch the school bus and noticed that more than a limb was hanging from the tree. He went running back home and told his mom. She called 911. Gilmore was the first on scene."

I close my eyes. "I just talked to Diane yesterday and she seemed fine. I just want to know what changed overnight that would want to make her kill herself."

Rain No Evil

I sit on the commode seat still wearing my pants. I just have to get off my feet. "I forgot to ask you about the investigation you were doing on her mom."

"Hank, our dead body, was the snitch set up to buy from her mom so, yep, that didn't happen."

I tell him to let me know as he gets more info about Diane's death, and I rejoin the grief counseling in the commons where parents cascade through, looking for their teenagers—for their own babies to hug.

Throughout the morning, students roam from the cafeteria where snacks are set out, to the commons, to the auditorium, to classrooms, just wherever they can find an open ear or soft shoulder to land next to.

In the afternoon, Joanne and I reminisce about various students who've died over the years—an elementary student who was smashed under the weight of an unsecured swing set last year. The girl was only in second grade and didn't choose to die, but grief is the feeling of loss, no matter the circumstances. Then there's the two students killed in a head-on with a semi on their way to school, the drunk country boy who crashed his four-wheeler and died, the pregnant teenage girl who was crushed under a filing cabinet.

Alex calls again and I take his call right at the cafeteria table. "Savvy, thought you'd want to know Diane's mom is in the hospital. Had to have her stomach pumped clean of Oxys. When Gilmore got to the house, he found Diane's mom face down in a pool of vomit on the couch and Diane hanging from a tree in the backyard wearing all black. Gilmore said it looked freaky cuz she had a pink scarf around her belly."

I can just picture Diane draped in black garments, her body dripping from the branch, a pink sash around her waist waving in the wind as if to say goodbye.

I stammer a goodbye to Alex and a silent goodbye to the girl hanging from a bough who I couldn't save from pulling the final curtain.

Tears flood my face. I wish I could've saved her like I do the babies in my dreams, but I feel more helpless in my waking hours than I do in my sleep. I can't seem to regain control of my life that's torpedoing toward the unknown at an unsustainable rate. Eventually, I have to crash.

When the bell rings, I bolt out the school doors like a rodeo bull through an open gate. I step into the house, ready to let the demon shower me—It'll remind me that I still have problems, and that I'm still living. I have to believe there's a reason I'm still here—that there's a reason I didn't run my car into the river with as much determination as Diane wrapped that rope around a tree.

I listen to the boys arguing over which video game to play. I just want to breathe and observe my imperfect world just as it is.

I drop my lunch bag onto the counter and imagine what it would feel like to stand here in total silence, no pounding of feet down the basement steps, no bickering boys—just silence. My days would be unbearable for there would be no one to nurture, except myself, and there'd be no reason to be here in this dense world.

I enjoy guiding my boys to make wise decisions—to choose right over wrong even as I struggle to distinguish between the two perceptions myself. I'm not the best parent in the world, but even shitty parents can love their kids. If Diane's mom can stay sober long enough, she'll probably miss Diane just like I'd miss my boys if they weren't here.

But compared to Diane, Ben and Isaac live royal lives. They have two parents who aren't dope-heads—who love them, and love each other—even if that love is skewed by misunderstanding. Granted, Alex and I are both screwing around and living a lie, but they don't know that. At least, I hope they don't.

Rumors of Templeton adultery have floated about for years, but till now I've never considered that one of my boys could get wind of the scandalous information, and I pray they never do. The older they get the more aware they are to circulating rumors and the more apt they are to catch one that involves Alex or me scrogging someone on the side.

I watch them tearing into their snacks and goading each other like brothers do, and I know one mission of mine is certain. I have to pioneer into the unknown territory of independence so that I can help them become independent, too.

"Isaac, Ben," I say, motioning them near. "I want you to know I love you both dearly. I can't explain everything that's going on here, but I'm going to figure it out. I have faith that there is a reason for it all."

Isaac's eyeing the cookie jar so I tip his chin up and draw his gaze to mine. "You understand? I have faith that everything happens for a reason, and as long as we love each another everything's going to be all right."

As the doorbell rings, I coerce a few hugs and shoo the snack-laden lads to the basement.

A few days ago I'd have believed the insurance company's specialists to be the cavalry, but now I know their efforts will be a waste of time.

I answer the door with a smile. The first to enter is a six-foot tall hulk of a guy wearing rubberized overalls who introduces himself as "Greg, the Specialist." Two men donning waterproof boots and jackets stream in behind him, following me upstairs with clipboards and scribbling notes as I relate the sequence of events leading to their arrival.

Greg lugs on the bag on his shoulder, his stone-hard chest prominently displayed within the snug-fitting overall. Pulling a wand from the bag, he extends the telescoping pole and taps the ceiling. "Seems solid," Greg says. "You say that's where it seems to be coming from? Are you sure there aren't any water pipes up there?"

"I'm sure," I say. "My father-in-law and a whole crew already checked it out."

"Can we go into the attic?" Greg asks.

I nod. "Knock yourself out."

"Jeff," Greg says to his co-worker, "grab a ladder."

Greg follows me to Ben's room.

"Attic entrance is in here," I say, opening the closet door and transferring suitcases to the bed to make room for the ladder.

"It's really humid in here," says the third guy who's tagging along.

"If you think it's humid in here you ought to see the living room," I say. "It's been spraying down there a lot."

"Downstairs?" Greg says.

"Yep," I say as Jeff struts in and scales the ladder.

"You mean water is leaking downstairs, too?" Jeff says with his head in the attic.

"That's what she said," Greg says. "Jeff, you check out the attic and we'll check out downstairs."

Greg and his buddy follow me to the living room where I rub my hand across the wall, water trails still visible from previous splatters. "Water shoots across the ceiling," I say, bending my arm and slinging it forward as if I were casting a fishing pole.

I know I'm futilely describing the ineffable, but I continue. "That's why all my pictures are under there." I point to the dining room table, where pictures of smiling family members peer through the droplets of moisture that have clustered on the clear plastic tarp. My cherished Van Gogh knock-off of *Starry Night* is cowering behind the billowing cloud of plastic.

"Greg, you ever seen anything like this in your life?" his co-worker asks.

Greg skims his fingers over the steamy windows. "No, man, I haven't."

Jeff huffs in. "No pipes up there and it's dry," he says as he spots the object of our attention—the frosty windows. "Man, it *is* damp in here. Greg, let's see what it registers."

Greg rummages through his satchel like Mary Poppins searching for the ideal item for the occasion and pulls out a square electronic device. He places it on the damp living room wall, pushes a button, winces and removes it.

Jeff and me and guy number three exchange glances, having a silent conversation of skepticism between us while the "specialist" shakes the object and remounts it on the wall.

Greg, still holding the device snug to the wall, turns to us. "Look at this."

We take turns peering over his shoulder. A zero is displayed on the monitor.

"No way," Jeff says, smacking guy number three who's massaging his jaw.

"What's zero mean—that there's no moisture?" I say.

Greg clears his throat. "Exactly. That there are absolutely no water molecules in this structure—in this specific room and well, that's impossible." Greg slings his bag over his shoulder. "There must be something paranormal going on here. It's obviously damp in this place."

I can't believe he actually just said "paranormal."

Jeff and his buddy are holding their silent conversation again. Their gaze roves from Greg to me like they aren't sure how I will react to such an oddball statement.

"You really think so?" I say to my mesmerized audience.

"If you believe that kind of stuff," Greg says.

Michele Savaunah Zirkle Marcum

"I do," I say. "I'm just surprised to hear you say it. Have you experienced supernatural events before?"

"I lived in a house where the last public hanging took place in West Virginia," Greg says, looking at his speechless co-workers who must not know this either. "Lots of freaky things happened there—knocks in the walls—crashes like the daggone roof caved in. I was in the kitchen one afternoon and forks from the counter flew across the room. That's when I decided to move."

"Wow." I say, laughing. "Think I'd move, too."

As we walk through the kitchen, Greg says, "I'm sorry I couldn't help."

"Oh, you helped," I say, smiling. "I know I'm not insane."

As soon as they leave I grab my purse and yell down to the boys that chili's in the crock-pot and I'm going to the store. I forgot to pick up Alex's blood pressure medicine, and I promised him I would.

I'm in line at the grocery store's pharmacy when I feel a tap on my shoulder and turn to a curly haired woman in her fifties.

Her voice is low and raspy, "Do you still have a ghost in your house?"

"Excuse me?" I say, "Do I know—"

"Oh, my. I'm sorry," she says, clasping her hand over mine. "Ruthanne Sayre. Friends with your Aunt Klaire."

Oh geez. Alex must have told his aunt about my revelation. Our house ghost will be the hottest topic in Ridgeland. I can hear it now, "Casper's taken up residence at the Templeton's."

I step closer to contain the story. "Oh, Alex's Aunt Klaire. So she told you about the spirit?"

Ruthanne lowers her double chin to her blossoming bosom and announces, "Yes, dear. My dad's a preacher who has rid many a place of evil spirits."

Preacher. Shit. I forgot to call mine—with Diane dying and all and . . . well, I don't need her dad's help. I don't trust just any preacher. The sound of decaying truth still fills my ears—lies from a preacher gone rogue are too fresh even twenty-two years after the hypocritical pastor absconded away with Mom.

I lean in so close to Ruthanne that I can smell the butterscotch candy on her breath and ask, "So you think it could be evil?"

"Honey," she says, pulling a hanky from her purse. "Only something evil is going to try to drive you crazy. You haven't got a ghost. You got yourself a demon."

My gaze darts down the aisle to the preoccupied group in line while I debate whether I should share my demon-in-the-mirror experience with my newfound friend. Anything I confide in her will be pumped straight into Klaire's auditory canal. I don't want the community thinking I'm crazy either—my kids have to grow up with these people. But if Aunt Klaire already knows that I told Alex there's a spirit in the house, my chances for maintaining the illusion that I'm sane, is that of Frosty's surviving the greenhouse.

I dive in close to the smell of butterscotch and relate my out-of-body experience.

Ruthanne's mouth gapes open, her floppy chin jiggling as she squeezes my forearm. "Last year I had a very real dream about helping someone I knew because they had a demon living in their dresser mirror. Is there a bathroom on the other side of your mirror?"

There's no way Ruthanne could know that unless what she's telling me is true. I hadn't mentioned that the mirror was my dresser and she's never even been in my house so she couldn't know the bathroom is right behind my mirror.

"Yes," I say. "So, Klaire didn't tell you about me seeing the demon in my mirror? I figured Alex filled her in about that too."

"Goodness, no, child." Ruthanne clears her throat. "If I'd have known, I'd have definitely asked you for the details. You know, God's got a message in all of this for you. Do you have any idea why this is happening to you?"

"No," I stammer, noticing the pharmacy clerk is strumming her fingers. I advance to the counter and ask for Alex's prescription then turn to Ruthanne who's so close I step on her foot.

"Sorry," I say.

"No, dear," Ruthanne says. "I'm the one who's sorry. I know it was you in that dream I had, and I remember the demon was very powerful. You had to put up an aggressive fight to make it leave." She lays her hand on my arm. "But it did leave. So don't give up. If you need me, just let me know."

"If I need a preacher, I'll get in touch," I say. "Thanks for your support."

Ruthanne's rotund body swallows me in an embrace. "I'll be praying for you, dear . . . oh, and for that officer that was shot. Pete, was it? How's he doing?"

"Yes, Pete," I say, sliding my debit card through the payment device. "His leg's tore up, but he was lucky. From what I understand the shooter was drunk and his aim was off."

"Bet you worry about Alex a lot with him being an officer," she says.

I grab my bag and walk off. "Nope. God blessed me. I didn't get the worry gene. Growing up with Dad—"

"Oh, that's right. Of course, Cal was *very* respected," Ruthanne says, waving.

As I'm passing the store's furniture display, Alex calls wanting to know what the insurance guys said. I tell him that they didn't find the leak, omitting their final verdict of paranormal activity. Alex says the guys must be worthless and before hanging up, tells me his Aunt Klaire wants me to call her.

I collapse into a lawn chair on display. Good grief. I don't have time for a lengthy conversation with Klaire right now, but I know better than to ask him why Klaire can't call me. Keagan's younger sister wants *me* to call *her*—she has to be in control.

Klaire answers with a refined, "Hello, Savannah," informing me I need to call an old friend of hers who's a priest in MuddSock Heights. He has experience with this "Sort of issue" and the ghost needs removed expediently so that Alex can have some peace and quiet.

Really? I'm thinking. What about my peace and quiet? But I say, "Oh, yes, we could all use some peace and quiet—especially Alex. I'll call the priest. What's his number?"

I scribble down the number and tell her I have to go—that I'm in the checkout line even though I'm already sticking the key in my car ignition. I'm not sure if I'll call the priest, but I'm not telling her that.

On the way home, I stop at the beauty shop to pick up my glam shampoo. My stylist, Sarah, stops mid-cut on her customer's hair when she spots me. Ten bucks says she knows about my "ghost." If one wants to know the gossip in a small town like Ridgeland, either the totally fabricated kind, or the tale that has splinters of truth running through it, the beauty shop or barber chair is the place to perch.

Sarah skips over. "Is it true? Your house is haunted?" She seems enthralled by the idea like a newborn is with his toes.

I grin and shrug. "Yep." I'm already tired of talking about it.

Sarah plops her elbows onto the counter and looks at me intently. "I know a lady about an hour north of here who cleans houses—not like a maid. She clears houses of unwanted energies and spirits." Sarah writes on a paper on the desk, rips it off and hands it to me.

Great. A house-cleaner whose disinfectant strips away a whole lot more than germs—just what I need.

Sarah must see the bewilderment on my face. "Don't worry. She's a good Christian lady."

I thank Sarah and stick the paper into my purse. I'm collecting numbers for priests and mediums now rather than adding to my special collection of men—the nipple-munchers and the tingly-touchers.

I just want to think—to be by myself and process the possible solutions presenting themselves. I'm driving to the riverfront levy with a warm caramel latte before I realize I forgot the dang shampoo I went to the beauty shop for, but I'm not going back. I'll just wash my hair with the generic brand I buy the boys. Shiny hair's not going to matter if that demon gets inside me—it'll be disheveled like the possessed woman's at church.

I park and watch the glistening water glide by, wishing it would carry me downstream. South to Mississippi maybe—with Tom Sawyer, the trickster with an ornery edge, like me. I could float on a raft and fish all day. It'd be cool to hang with Tom, who always finagled himself into and out of a mess just as aptly as I do.

I've had three people suggest various remedies to get rid of the spirit in my house. I've got to try something, and I'm not involving Aunt Klaire's priest friend, so I head across the river to see Pastor Todd.

I stroll into the church office where Tina, the secretary is folding bulletins for the Sunday service I probably won't attend.

Tina notices my quivering hands. "Hi, Savvy. Are you . . . is something wrong?"

"Just need some help." I smile and smooth my hand over my stray hairs. "Is Todd here? I really need to talk to him."

Rain No Evil

"He's on his way out of town. Has to preside over a funeral."

I hesitate to divulge the supernatural topic to Tina, but I'm desperate and Tina's been a friend of the family for years. Besides, this is church. Church—where people believe in spirits.

As matter-of-factly as possible, I say, "I need Todd to get a spirit out of my house."

Tina slowly looks up from the church bulletin. "You need Todd to get a spirit—did you say spirit—out of your house?"

"Yep. I sure did," I say, tugging at my shirt. "I know it's probably not a common request, but I need Todd's help. Water is spraying inside our house from nowhere. I prayed and God told me there's a demon in the house."

"Oh," Tina says, clicking the end of her pen again and again, and staring at me like she's been asked to write a note in Russian.

"Could you just ask Todd to call me, please?" I fake a laugh. "I can explain it to him on the phone easier than you can on paper."

"Sure. Sure, dear." Tina's face relaxes. "I will . . . I will definitely tell him you need help."

I bet she will.

She takes down my cell number. "Is that all?"

That's all? All? I have an evil spirit in my house and the one person I thought might just be able to help me is out of town—no, that's not all—I want somewhere to cry, to pray for deliverance from this feeling of surreal desperation.

I scurry to my car and drive across the brick streets, into alleys—turning corners until I find myself in front of the church in downtown MuddSock Heights where Dad and Mom fertilized my early indoctrinated years—the church where she fell in love with the man behind the pulpit. Maybe not a practical refuge, but I'm here and maybe this is where God wants me to be—back where my doubt in Him began when Mom ran off with the anointed dick.

Grabbing my purse and my latte that's no longer warm, I climb the steps to the ordinary brick building where weeds straddle the *For Sale* sign in the front yard. Several ministers have attempted to lead a successful congregation here since Mom left with the preacher, but the site must be jinxed—no more doling out salvation or threats of damnation here—just an empty building full of memories. Memories of times when I kneeled with reverence and stood with the hope of a final resurrection that would whisk me to a heaven I couldn't see.

My mind goes bobbing down memory lane, squinting for a glimpse of that lifeboat of hope—of that wholesome Holy Spirit that used to infuse me with victory. I want to feel that kind of faith again.

I sit on the cold concrete floor of the covered porch. I can almost hear the old songs rolling out the windows, "Victory in Jesus," "Power in the Blood," as I reflect on the hundreds of sermons I've heard behind these doors. Sermons of victory. Sermons of power. Where's the power behind my words now? Why can't I make the demon in my house leave?

Am I so evil that evil doesn't have to obey me? A demon was removed from a lady inside this building, and maybe there's one in me. I un-wrinkle the paper Sarah gave me and call her version of The Ghost Whisperer.

As I describe my quandary, the lady asks the name and age of the person the water first dripped on. I tell her it was my son, Ben, who is twelve.

"Puberty," she says, "creates a hormonal imbalance that attracts the spirit world." She goes on to tell me that Ben's a Cancer, which is a water sign and maybe that's why the spirit chose water as the antagonist.

I didn't know spirits get to choose the medium they use to provoke humans, but I hadn't really thought about it before. I'm not telling this house-cleaner lady that another reason could be that I was in the shower when I accused God of not being real. I may need her help, and if she's a Christian she may take offense to my anger at God and refuse to help me.

She offers to clear my house for one hundred dollars.

I ask her to explain the clearing process, and she says she calls on good spirits while burning sage to purify the space. Having a stranger inviting more unidentified spirits into my house seems as harrowing as knowing a demon is already there. I'm not sure about this sage-burning ceremony—seems a tad like voodoo.

I tell her I'll talk to my husband about it and get back with her even though I have no intention of mentioning our conversation to Alex. I'd be beside Terry's mom, being spoon-fed my dinner for sure.

I'm not comfortable with the sage-wielding exterminator and who knows when Pastor Todd will call me, but am I desperate enough to call Klaire's priest?

Staring a hole through the door to the church, I picture my twelve-year-old self in the sanctuary, hands folded, eyes closed, thanking God for giving me the victory the conniving preacher had so convincingly taught me I had.

If I really had victory then, I can get it again, and just because the preacher who reached me with the sermon eloped with my mom and broke Dad's heart, doesn't mean that the premise of his teachings were invalid, or that all preachers are adulterous pricks.

Sitting in the pew as a girl, I never expected to be here as an adult calling a priest to exorcise my home, but I never expected to be someone's verbal punching bag either—never expected to be angry with the God who created me—never expected to spread my legs to feel worthy and to close them feeling worthless.

The priest's answering machine kicks on and I leave a vague message saying Aunt Klaire believes he can help me with something. I've barely swallowed the last drop of liquid caffeine when he returns my call.

"Hello, Mrs. Templeton," he says. "It's Father Nick. I was upstairs and the ole knees aren't cooperating this morning. How can I help you?"

Words trickle out as I attempt to find a casual, yet accurate, way to describe my odd predicament to this man on the phone I've never even met. I ask him if he's ever prayed a spirit out of a house. "A demon has been spraying water inside my house for a week now and I'm calling because plumbers and repairmen can't help us."

Father Nick cautions me to not jump to conclusions about demons—often it's simply a restless spirit that needs to be directed toward the light. Then he says, "A few years ago, a young couple who had just moved into an old house kept hearing a baby cry inside the walls. I blessed the house and directed the baby's soul to move toward the light. They never heard the crying again. We should bless your house. How do you feel about that?"

"Anything you want to do is fine with me. You're the expert."

"Ok," he says. "I have a wedding tomorrow and a full Sunday, but Monday I can come. No, that's Parish council meeting out of town. Okay, how's Tuesday?"

I agree. Next week is perfect because we're out of school for a mini-break, although I would meet him this moment with no makeup and even less sleep, if he could come right now.

As I head home, I call Dad with the news.

"I'll be there, honey. A few more prayers to remove Casper surely can't hurt," Dad says.

I can almost hear Alex referencing the cartoon ghost—hear him mocking my belief that a spirit is residing with us.

I know Dad's trying to make me laugh, but the memory of Alex's derision is too raw for hindsight humor. I can't let Dad to know how stupid Alex makes me feel so I say, "Damn straight, and neither could a few dozen donuts!"

Maybe Shakespeare was right. Maybe everyone is an actor on the world's stage. We just let others see the us we want them to see, not the real us—the demon us—with charcoaled scars that are too ugly for our fragile egos to acknowledge.

Chapter Fourteen

LETTER LINK TO MURDER

A few minutes after getting home, I'm washing dishes when static on the police radio announces Alex's arrival. Hearing the door click shut, I say hello without turning around from the sink. I feel someone's breath on the back of my neck.

Alex is behind me. His lips smooch my ear as water runs over the bowl I'm holding under the faucet.

Nice. Unexpected and nice.

I want to relax into his touch, but I can't trust this moment. These kinds of moments are over faster than a breadcrumb lasts on Dad's duck deluged pond. My shoulders stiffen.

Alex's walls may be down at this moment, but the drawbridge to my heart is damaged and may never fully open again.

I'm still frozen when Alex descends to the basement. If he could accept me, just love me for who I am, maybe I could let him see the vulnerable me—the me beneath the bitch he sees, but until I feel safe doing that, he'll have to live with the moat of emotions I've corralled to protect me. I love him, but I don't love how I feel when I'm around him.

Alex strides through the kitchen in boxers and black knee-high socks. "Dad's coming shortly," he says. "Insulating the attic. He thinks more holes in the soffits will prevent moisture from forming, so we're gonna do that, too."

"More holes?" I ask, noticing there're only a handful of crackers by the crock-pot and hoping there's more in the cabinet. Alex has to have crackers with his chili.

"Just drill holes. Add to the ones already there," Alex says, munching on a carrot stick. "You get a hold of Aunt Klaire?"

"Yes, and I called him," I say, hunkering in the cabinet searching for the Saltines. "Called who?"

I peer around at Alex. "The priest."

Alex stops chewing and scrunches his face.

"To come get this spirit—"

"What!" Alex shouts, pointing the carrot at me. "You called a priest to come here?" He snaps the carrot stick in half. "That's it! I've had it."

And there it goes—that bit of tranquility I had when he kissed my neck. It didn't last any longer than a fresh-baked cookie at a packed Panera.

Alex is going to drill holes in our soffits to prevent water from spraying inside our house—and he thinks I'm the crazy one.

I nod and water *splats* right down the center of the kitchen ceiling.

"Yes," I say, wondering if it's just a coincidence that when we argue the water sprays. "Your Aunt Klaire suggested it and *you're* the one who told me to call her."

Alex's face flushes red, and he jabs the broken carrot in the air like he's Sir Lancelot wielding his sword for battle. "I did want you to call *her*—not a priest!"

He can't comprehend the enemy isn't me—it's the principalities and powers of darkness.

"You know I would never agree to have a priest come here for a water leak!" Alex says. "Good Lord! Everyone's going to think you're a freak! You're getting stranger every day, Sav. I don't know how much longer I can stay with your crazy ass." Alex slams the cabinet door. "Well, I won't be here when Father whoever comes! You guys can shower in holy water for all I care!"

I nestle my trembling hands under the dishtowel. "Didn't Klaire tell you that she thought we should call Father Nick?"

"Hell no! Good God, woman! I come home thinking we'll have a peaceful night and you pull this shit! Damn, you just got to ruin everything!" He opens the fridge. "I don't suppose you have dinner ready."

The crock of chili on the stove looks fuzzy as my eyes fill, but I point toward it and slip unceremoniously to my room—to hibernate with my thoughts and my journal.

> I'm teetering on the brink—straddling the ever-closing gap between seen and unseen worlds. What happens if the two worlds collide—Will I die? I'm living in a physical realm and feeling like I'm actually somewhere that's beyond time and space

I sit in the corner, pull my legs in tight and close my eyes. Maybe Diane's

Rain No Evil

in a better place than me. Maybe I'd be better off hanging, neck broken like my spirit feels. Maybe Alex would feel guilty and maybe he wouldn't. I doubt he would. In his mind, he is always right and has nothing to be sorry for.

I can't change Alex—can't change how he makes me feel, but I can enjoy my life anyway. To hell with my hotheaded husband. I'm going to live a little—have fun with or without him.

I click on the first name in my phone's contact list, Adonis, and text: "Hey Joe, wanna hook up?"

Romance and roses I neither need nor want from him. Those fluffs only mean something to a gal if she knows a guy cares about her when she's fully clothed.

Joe texts, "I'm up for it! I can kick my roomie out of the apartment tomorrow night."

I text, "Now's better! Want to get my hands on you ☺."

Joe says, "Well, since you put it like that. Ha Drive those hands on over doll."

Make-up covers the tear trails on my cheeks, and a fresh set of purple polka dotted panties stir empowerment from within my belly.

As I'm backing out the drive, Keagan is securing a ladder that's propped against the front of the house and Alex is shimmying up, drill in hand.

I open the car window and yell up at Alex. "I'm running over to Dad's. Be back in a bit."

He raises the drill in acknowledgement.

A delivery truck sits in the road, its blinker on, waiting for me to move. It's full of insulation that the Michael Holmes wannabees are blowing into the attic for extra insulation.

I feel sorry for Alex. He just doesn't want to admit that there are some things he can't control, but he can't control me.

If invisible spirits can laugh, the one at my house is chuckling its see-through ass off. The entertainment around here is better than *Big Bang Theory*.

I drive across the bridge to MuddSock Heights, but Dad's is not my destination. I've got a date with a store clerk who's gonna ring my bell, not my bill, tonight.

Cruising through Joe's neighborhood, I notice Mr. Feldman from school grilling on his deck a few houses from the apartment complex I'm seeking.

I forgot he lives in this part of town. I jerk my head back to the road hoping he didn't see me as I pull my sedan beside a huge metal trash bin behind the building. I remember feeling like trash when I left the hotel where I met Ryan, and I hope I'll feel more highly of myself today when I leave here.

I know Alex isn't going to change. I'm going to have to leave him or live this way. I just can't keep sliding into rooms in shades to feel the only kind of love that's not evasive.

Sunglasses and a ball cap in place, I shuffle through the side door that my new conquest is propping open with one hand and snuggling an apple martini in the other.

169

His spread is more like a dorm room than an apartment. Posters of roller derby girls in bikinis and a movie ad for "Hangover" line the hallway, and a beer pong table leans against the kitchen wall.

I accept the fruity drink he offers hoping it will help me relax so I can actually enjoy this. I sink into a slouchy chair in the living room opposite him while he spouts off names of baseball players I know nothing about, but at least, he's not pressuring me into initiating the sex we both know I'm there for.

I smile and nod and sip from the bottle in my hand wondering how I've gotten myself into this situation again and wondering why I need a man to make me feel good about myself. But I'm here and I'm going to pretend Alex doesn't exist. I'm going to pretend that me sleeping with this Joe is as insignificant in the universal scheme of things as is an ant drowning in a drop of water. I'm going to pretend that there's no God to punish me or demon to spray me. The whole world is just me and this moment.

Declining the second shot of courage, I replace the bottle in his hand with my breast. Joe sucks on my lower lip, gently at first then winds his tongue into my mouth and sucks harder. As he slides his tongue across my teeth, tickling the inside of my upper lip, I'm intrigued—never had anyone do that before.

His kiss has me drawing up toward him like a calf to a nipple. I unbutton my shirt, allowing my size Cs a breath of fresh air. Joe pulls his Old Navy t-shirt over his head and looks down at me—my cue to rub his chest or unbutton his jeans. I squeeze his pecs and hard kiss his nipples. My tongue trails up his neck and pauses below his earlobe to smell the damp skin of this man—a distinct blend of cologne and sweat.

I hear a door in the hall creak open, and I look around toward the sound. "Your roommate's gone, right?"

Joe's hands move from my hips to the buttons of my blouse, exposing my purple bra and goose-bumped chest. "Yep," he says.

"Did you hear that?" I say, pointing to the bedroom door. "Sounded like the door opened."

"No one's here, doll, just the martini talking." Joe's fingers slide under my bra straps, his lips kneading my neck. I'm on automatic, suppressing the feeling that I'm being watched.

I blindly jerk his belt to loosen its hold on the prize, and crawl my fingers inside the back of his jeans, digging my nails into his tight glutes. I feel as if someone is watching me from the direction that I heard the door open. I peer down the short hall. "You sure we're alone?" I say.

"Take a look for yourself," Joe says, squeezing my shoulder. "I'll wait."

I drop to one knee. Maybe I'm hearing things. With the stress I'm under, just a snip of alcohol could affect me. I fold his Hanes over his hard dick, and with one last glance at my victim, I go for the goods and it's a prize all right—huge—a good ten inches. Biggest penis I've seen that wasn't on a porn flick—and it's all mine.

170

Rain No Evil

My hand doesn't quite wrap around the base. After a few long tongue strokes I allow my throat to form a cavern and welcome the intruder. A few minutes later I stop. Joe won't last much longer with me flicking my tongue like this.

Joe growls and grabs my thighs, lifting me high enough I can wrap my legs around his waist. I guess growling must be the newest expression from sex-crazed males.

My nipple pops out as he bites on it, and I'm pretty sure I will have to explain a bruised boob to Alex later. *Oh, that's right there is no Alex.*

Joe falls forward, pinning me against the itchy couch and slams his penis that's befitting a god, inside me. My glistening Adonis grinds my back into the scratchy, sweaty polyester cushions until a tonic of pleasure-filled spasms practically squeezes the life out of me.

Joe lies back against the couch arm, his dangling dick leaking onto the couch.

I roll over and onto the floor, gathering my clothes and dressing so quickly my shirt may be on inside out, but I'm not taking the time to check.

Focusing on the stained gray rug beneath my feet, I mumble how I've got to get going. I tell the man who just ejaculated into me, to keep in touch even though I don't want him to ever touch me again.

I run to my car in the rain, wishing the drops from Heaven could rinse all the bad off me and into the storm drain I'm stepping over. But the storm brewing inside me has no easy wind or peaceful flake.

Rain pounds my windshield on my dazed drive back across the bridge. The joyous feeling of revenge I felt before the interlude seems to have flowed downriver.

An unknown number showing on my cell turns out to be Pastor Todd who says he's calling from a hotel out of town where he's performing the funeral for an old friend who lost his wife to breast cancer. Todd says he's never encountered an evil spirit, let alone had to remove one from someone's house. He suggests that I contact Father Nick.

I thank him and don't mention that I already have a date with the dear Father.

Returning home, I hesitate to enter, my hand on the side doorknob. Alex is probably on the last mile of his insulation blowing expedition in the attic.

Waves of energy from within the house reverberate throughout my body as if the knob is an electrical conductor of the emotions from inside the house. I step in and hear angry voices resounding from upstairs and something being dragged across the floor.

I barrel up the stairs taking two at a time. Alex is saying, "Isaac, turn that vacuum on and sweep this mess up."

Rounding the corner into Ben's room, I see Isaac pulling the sweeper from the closet and Alex stepping from the attic entrance looking like he's the star of a parody of a home improvement show. One strap on his faded bib overalls is all that's holding them up and a blob of insulation is holding onto a nipple for dear life. The paint and oil stains on his attire blend in with the yellow pieces of insulation covering his entire body.

171

I flop onto Ben's bed and burst into laughter.

Alex brushes some of the yellow flecks from his eyes as he gags out, "Than . . . thanks a lot! Where the hell were you?"

His anger can't stop my cackling. I'm hysterical, tears flowing onto my knees that are curled in front of me as I laugh at the man who I had promised, "For better or for worse." Damn shame I normally feel better when he feels worse.

Isaac turns on the shop vac and begins sweeping as Alex whisks the insulation off with an old shirt and stomps off toward the bathroom.

Ben is staring at me. "Couldn't you help Dad once in a while? Isaac and I have to."

My comic relief isn't worth the distressed look in Ben's eyes. From Ben's perspective, I'm sure my laughing at his dad, is simply not nice. Sure, he's twelve and can't relate to the intricate relationship of marriage, but he's twelve. He isn't supposed to understand.

Ben doesn't know that his dad's labor is a total waste of time. I haven't told the boys a spirit is responsible for the water. I don't want to scare them, but they're going to be here when Father comes, so I might as well tell them now.

I stand up and feel Joe's cum run into my panties. I want to wash up, but I owe Ben an explanation even if it is a lie.

"If I hadn't been at Pawpaw Cal's, I could've helped," I say, projecting my voice above the hum of the vacuum and feeling shitty for lying about where I was. I pluck a piece of insulation from Ben's head. "This," I say, holding the piece up in front of him. "This stuff isn't going to stop the leak. You see, babe, a priest will be here next week to pray with us about what's going on here. This water is not normal."

"Yeah, Dad said you think there's a ghost throwing the water." Ben rolls his eyes. "He thinks you've lost it."

"I haven't lost it. God told me a spirit's throwing the water. You know how God gave you a vision about the nail in the tire," I say, folding the ladder and handing it to Ben. "That's kind of like how I know."

"Okay," Ben says, "but I'm sick of Isaac sleeping with me every night. He's not sleeping in here tonight. I don't care if there is a ghost in the house!"

I motion him to the hallway so I don't have to keep shouting over the vacuum. "Ben, weird things keep happening here. I think we're all on each other's' nerves. I told Isaac he can keep his TV on and maybe that'll help him sleep." Alex slips downstairs without a word, and I hear the television kick on. Silence can indeed be golden.

After I shower, I take graham crackers, marshmallows and Hershey bars to the boys' rooms, allowing them to melt s'mores over candlelight, a practice usually reserved for power outages, and I tell Isaac I'll give him ten bucks if he'll just stay put in his own bed for one night.

I'm sound asleep when I hear Isaac to my left asking me to come with him and Alex to my right shouting for Isaac to get his ass to bed.

Holy shit! Does this ever end? I grope for my nightstand and squint to read the time 10:30 a.m.

Isaac's clammy hand wraps around my wrist as he leads me through the dark hallway. Stumbling into his room, I peer behind his door where he's pointing. A circle about ten inches in diameter is glowing on the wall under his trophy shelf. I blink and it's still there.

"What is it, Mom?" Isaac whispers. "Is it the ghost?"

"I'm not sure," I say trying to sound nonchalant.

I have to touch this orb—show Isaac I'm not afraid, so I pray silently, *God, please protect me.* As I flatten my right palm squarely on the circle, I half expect my hand to sink into the wall and disappear, but the wall doesn't suck me in. The surface is solid. I stare at it a moment and the light fades until it's gone completely.

"I'm not sleeping in here, and I don't care what you say." Isaac opens his door and steps into the hall.

I tiptoe behind him into his brother's room, but Ben's onto us and is already saying, "Oh, no!"

Alex yells from our bedroom, "Shut-up and go to bed!"

After ten minutes of explaining that the priest is coming Tuesday and Isaac should be able to sleep in his own room, my Ben throws back the covers, plants a pillow in the middle of the bed and says, "Stay on your side, you big baby."

I'm sure Isaac couldn't care less what names he's called as long as he isn't sleeping by himself in his room that seems to be more haunted than any other room in the house, and I can't blame him.

Back in my own bed, a loud huff and rollover is my kiss goodnight.

I lay listening for the sound of spraying water, but the water seems to sleep soundly with the family. It's as if the demon knows we're sleeping and figures it will let us rest up so it can torture us tomorrow.

I'm on the ebb of consciousness when I see a vision directly in front of me. A large, black spider is crawling out of Alex's mouth, and I know he is lying. He is having an affair with Stacey.

Friday morning I get our mail from the mailbox located across the main road. I'm crossing back over while sorting through the stack of correspondence when my gaze fixates on a grimy, white envelope bearing handwritten words, "Policeman Templeton." No address. No postage stamp. A Bud Light can is the usual message pitched out the window toward Taze's mailbox, not a personalized envelope. I have no doubt that some Cretan wants to snitch a secret to Alex.

I imagine a dingy maroon sedan with a rusted quarter panel, black garbage bag secured by duct tape over the passenger side window, creeping by our house. A needle-marked arm juts out the window and flings the envelope into our mailbox—the envelope I'm holding in my hand.

Linking this letter to that car may be a stretch since Alpine road is a common carrier of such a vehicle, but the maroon one is the most notorious for nefarious activity.

Alex, even though well- respected, has acquired several enemies in his thirteen years on the force so the contents of this letter could be dangerous—could be anthrax powder sprinkled inside—although the idea that someone would go to all that trouble to kill Taze seems extreme, even for my marbled imagination.

I pinch my fingers around the envelope. Whatever is in it, it's flat like paper. I crunch up the drive and place the intriguing item on the countertop. Wonder if I've got time to take a peek inside.

Alex will be up soon for his overtime detail. I could steam it and slide a butter knife under the flap, satisfying my curiosity within a few moments, but then I'd have to glue it back so Alex wouldn't know I opened it.

Before I decide, a beep from my cell displays a text from Ryan.

"Hey, busy later tonight?"

I figured love bear's been pawing someone else since I haven't heard from him all week. Ever since Mandy said he's got a girlfriend who works at the hospital, I've forced myself not to think about him.

I stare into the neighbor's backyard where their hound, Lazy, is basking in the early rays. lucky Lazy—no decisions to make other than when to yawn, but if I only had to wonder about who was going to scratch my belly next, I'd be as insane as Alex thinks I am.

"Can you stop by the bank for me today?"

I turn to see Alex opening the fridge door. I must be slipping—didn't even hear the stairs creak.

While Alex scours for something on the top shelf, I slip my cell into my pocket and point to the mysterious message. "That was in our mailbox."

Alex glimpses at the envelope. "Oh, this is going to be good." He shoves his square hands into Ziploc bags, wearing them like gloves, rips open the envelope and pulls out a folded sheet of ruled notebook paper.

"Interesting," I say, peeking around his shoulder and reading aloud, "Big John killed Hank Schooner. The gun's in Mud Run Lake."

Alex is quiet.

"What are you thinking?" I say.

"Could be real," he says, scrolling on his cell. "So much for an easy overtime detail today. State police will have to be called in for this. Oh, and you touched the envelope didn't you? Damn-it!"

"Duh!" I say. "I didn't know what it was until I sorted the mail."

While he informs the state police sergeant of the clue, I get the cooler out of the pantry.

"I'll be out with the dive team at the lake. No checkpoint today," he says, clicking off the phone and placing the letter and envelope into a quart-sized baggie. "This better be a good lead. I'll have to get your fingerprints too because yours will be on the envelope. Deal with that later. I gotta get going. Can you . . ." He notices me tucking crackers into a bag. "Thanks," he says and stomps off to the basement.

A few minutes later, he re-emerges with a gun belt draped over one shoulder, and a cell phone squeezed to the other. He orders someone on the other end to meet him at Mud Run Lake ASAP.

Suddenly, I feel sorry for this man who promised to protect and serve. He doesn't have much time to relax. There's a weariness in his eyes I haven't noticed before. Spikes of his hair are gray, his bushy eyebrows are, in places, standing to attention on either side of a furrow that's permanently present. His career has taken its toll—not just on our marriage, but on him.

Maybe I should excuse his extra-curricular jaunt into the skies of ecstasy with the dear, squawking Raven. If he would treat me with respect, I think at this moment, I would forgive him, no questions asked.

He slides the gun-belt off his shoulder and onto the kitchen counter where I'm making sandwiches to add to his stash. He's talking on the phone and tucking his shirt into his pants when an immense, stabbing pain sears my foot.

I scream and grab my foot, squeezing it as tightly as I can, trying to squeeze it hard enough to stop the indescribable pain.

A gun lies on the floor. Alex's gun broke my foot!

I look at Alex who's waving his hand in the air and shushing me.

Maybe it was my contorted face that got his attention—maybe it was my shrieks that could have raised Lazarus from the grave, but without saying a word to the person on the other end, Alex sets the phone on the bar and rushes over to where I'm bent over my bashed foot.

He scoops up the gun. "Man, I bet it's scratched."

The pain isn't subsiding. I feel tears running down my cheeks and look up, hoping Alex will see them, too. Surely, he will be nice to me now.

Alex is caressing his gun. "How'd you knock it off?"

I want to yell, "What the hell difference does it make—it hurts, dumbass! How is this my fault? You've got to be kidding me." But I say, "It slid."

"Well, I don't see how," he says, placing the gun on the counter. "Sorry, but you shouldn't have . . . you okay? Let me see."

I uncover my swollen right foot, revealing a gigantic turnip-colored bump on the fleshy side of my.

"Ice it. That's all you can do."

I nod, hoping he's going to get some ice, but his hand is already holding his phone, not an ice bag.

"Will you be here at two o'clock today?" Alex says. "Got some guys coming to replace the septic system and dig a new leach bed to stop this commode spraying. They say pressure is building up. I was planning on leaving the checkpoint for an hour and meeting them here, but there's so much shit going on. And now this letter about a gun in the lake."

"Sure. I'll be home," I say, opening the freezer and pulling out an icepack.

Alex snaps his keepers shut, plants a kiss on my forehead, grabs his bagged letter and his cooler before going lights and sirens south—toward Coraltown to hunt for a murder weapon.

I sit in my recliner and prop my foot on ice. Alex really thinks a bigger septic tank is going to stop the commode from being a bidet. He won't even consider that a spirit could possibly be causing the chaos here.

I return Ryan's text, "Haven't heard from you. Been busy?

Ryan: "Natalie was in the hospital with the flu."

Me: "Oh, hope she's ok."

Ryan: "Yep, she's out. I just got back from a pharmaceutical conference yesterday. Thought you might come over tonight."

I can't believe I'm even contemplating meeting him. I just played this game yesterday with Joe and felt horrible, but I've known Ryan for years and he *does* care about me. If I ever leave Alex, I have a shot with Ryan.

Me: "Sure! I'm ready to get rough. Feel like a caged animal here!"

Ryan: "Really? Bad girl! Picnic table rough enuf for u"

Me: "No splinters tho, babe, just a rod up my ass!"

Ryan: "Damn I have missed u!"

Me: "See u at 7. I'll just drive into ur garage."

Ryan: "ok"

Five minutes of ice on my foot seems like thirty. I hobble upstairs, slip on camo undies with pink trim, dab Channel behind my ear, and squiggle into a mini-skirt. I wrap a bandage around the ever-growing knot on my foot and snag a pair of flip-flops that I can slide my foot into. The tight bandage relieves the pain enough that I think I can manage to push the gas pedal in the car.

I rouse the boys and drop them at Keagan's to put finishing touches on their playhouse. Alex had asked me to go to the bank, but between the mysterious letter and the gun mishap, he forgot to tell me what transaction to make so I pass the bank and head toward Ryan's.

As I near downtown Coraltown, a blockade of flashing lights is blocking the road ahead. Traffic is deadlocked. The barricaded main street is buzzing with reporters and camera crews, each waiting inside the cordoned area of yellow tape where several paramedics stand behind ambulances.

Seems like every police officer and emergency vehicle in Wooten County is surrounding the only hotel in town. The officers don't have their guns drawn. They're just milling around, glancing toward a window in an upper story of the hotel. From my position in the long line of traffic, I'm not close enough to read the unit numbers on the cruisers so I'm not sure if Alex is here, but my bet is yes. He's always in the middle of the action and usually the first one through any barricaded door.

I'm wondering if the activity here is related to the letter this morning—maybe they found the gun and have a suspect quarantined—when shots ring out. I don't know which direction they came from, but I'm guessing from inside the hotel as badges and barrels gleaming in synchronicity with the swirling lights, point toward the historic building. Within minutes a SWAT team member beckons the paramedics to the hotel's front door. The scene must be secured. Two paramedics strike out, grasping either side of the stretcher as it jostles over the brick road.

I say a quick prayer for whoever just got shot, and for whoever did the shooting, before backing into the nearest driveway and worming my way around town. I don't want to be late to Ryan's. My foot throbs as I accelerate, reminding me of my injury, but thoughts of a Ryan-style picnic carry me through back roads and alleys until I reach his subdivision.

Careening into the area, I barely miss a parked car and realize I have to be more careful. If I have a wreck, I would have to explain to Alex what I'm doing here.

Pulling into his garage, I smooth on lip-gloss and limp up the steps to his kitchen. Ryan removes the sunglasses from my face and cradles my head in his hands, kissing me.

He pulls me close, knowing I relish a nice long hug and that he'll be paid back with a nice long tongue-lashing. He swings me around until my head is swirling right along with my body. I forget my foot is hurt until he sets me back on the floor.

I tell him how Alex placed his gun-belt on the counter.

"That's a dumbass thing to do," Ryan says.

"Almost as stupid as jumping off the bridge." I say, grabbing his hand and leading him out to the backyard.

Ryan grips the sides of my waist and leans into me, my hips grinding into the edge of the picnic table. "I offered to show you how to jump off safely," he whispers, his minty breath revitalizing me.

"And I told you . . . if I jump, safe will be the last thing on my mind," I say, raising my puckered lips and standing on tiptoes to kiss his collarbone.

"I love your wild side," Ryan says, dropping his shorts and raising my skirt over my hips.

Could he really love me I wonder as my love bear bends me face down over the wooden table and growls in my ear.

The fragrance of his amber cologne and freshly cut grass are intoxicating. From here it's like driving down a familiar road, not noticing the scenery, but somehow, miraculously ending up at my destination—the pinnacle of the pleasure of orgasm where nothing—absolutely nothing matters except coming.

This is truly what heaven must be like.

The first thing the kids will want to know when they scramble into the car at Keagan's is what's for dinner so as I pull out of Ryan's garage, I order a pizza.

Our first pizza delivery to the house on Alpine Road was a monumental moment of liberation from the isolation of country living. With a warm box delivered right to my front door, the world seemed to be at my fingertips.

The first such delivery was on a snowy December night eight years ago when we moved into the house that solidified a new beginning for Alex and me—a fresh wholesome beginning infused with love and tenderness. I sat on the side of Alpine Road in my car stacked with boxes and watched through tears of happiness as family and friends unloaded furniture from the U-Haul.

I believed the traditional stick-built house would support not only its own walls, but would dissolve the walls that separated Alex and me, but that didn't happen and now I'm speeding away from my lover's toward an uncertain future.

As I'm pulling up the lane to Keagan's, Alex calls. He's processing paperwork on a "Piece of shit" he just apprehended at the hotel.

"So what happened?" I say. "I saw the barricade."

"You mean you haven't heard?" Alex says. "It's been all over the news. Damn sleaze-ball robbed Go Mart and holed up in the hotel. What were you doing in Coraltown?"

"Oh, just had to return a library book," I say, glad he doesn't pay any more attention to my books than he does to my feelings. "So how'd you get him out?"

Alex chuckles. "Offered the dumbass a cigarette and when he reached for it, I grabbed the gun from his hand, but not before he squeezed off a few rounds."

"Oh, wow," I say. "Glad you're okay. How's Pete doing?"

"He's being transferred to Columbus. Got to have reconstructive surgery and intense therapy. Hey, I got to go. See you this evening," Alex says, as the boys pile in the car. "And, Sav, I love you."

"Love you," I say, pointing to Isaac's unfastened seatbelt.

The boys talk over each other, telling me of the new windows they helped Keagan install and how hooking up the electric is next on the list.

My mind drifts from their chatter. Alex is oozing charm today. Maybe he saw his demon in the mirror during his morning shave. If there is one inside me, then Alex must have one, too. The vision of the black insect full of lies crawling out of his mouth is still crystal clear. I lie, too, but at least I screw strangers, not his friends.

Maybe it was his brush with a madman's gun that's got him all sentimental. Whatever the reason he said it—he said it, and damn it, I almost wish he hadn't—makes me feel even guiltier. Alex says "love" like a dog licks a wound—quickly, to get it over with. And Ryan used the word casually like it's insignificant. I know that just because Ryan says he loves my wild side doesn't mean he loves me, but I feel more at ease with him than I do with Alex, and Alex does say he loves me.

I feel like a mermaid luring my husband into a false sense of security—acting like things between us are sublime when actually death is waiting in the waves—the death of "us."

But I have to maintain the pretense that I'm fine even though I'm not. With each notch in my tarnished bedpost or picnic table or wherever I just numbed myself, I feel like I parcel off bits of my soul—like the incomprehensibly tiny cells that make me who I am are suspended in midair, out of my reach, and I must function with bare bones and a smile.

At home, I smack a twenty on the counter, instructing Ben to listen for the pizza delivery.

I limp upstairs, my injured foot throbbing, and after showering away some shame, expel some of what remains into my journal:

> *Feeling violated felt satisfying. Bad girls need to be held in their place. Today that place was bent over a wooden table, bare butt high in the air twisting side to side, banging back and forth. I wasn't supposed to be there. That was the mental satisfaction no physical gratification can quench.*

Ben yells up that the workers are here about the septic tank so I run downstairs and give them the go-ahead to do whatever it is they need to do. They can dig up the whole damn yard for all I care. Unless they're the ghostbusters, their efforts will amount to the shit they are pumping from the tank.

I'm swiping the duster along the shelf in Isaac's room, light on the touch between miniature motorcycles and t-ball trophies, when I notice a shattered glass globe resting in Mickey Mouse's arms. The souvenir from Disney stands about six inches tall, the famous mouse cradling the snow globe that now looks like cracked glass.

Smashing my hand to my gaping mouth, I stand staring at the globe that, although shattered to pieces, remains intact. The surrounding knick-knacks are undisturbed, and no shards litter the shelf or the floor. There's no way that what I'm seeing is possible. If Isaac had dropped it or broken it, glass would be everywhere.

I wonder if this could have just happened, or if it's been broken and I haven't noticed. With several items perched on the shelf, it would be easy to overlook.

My eyes traverse the room as I wonder if the demon is the culprit. Could it show up and entertain me—possibly repair the globe right in front of me, or surprise me and explode the television?

Hobbling on my sore foot to the top of the stairs, I yell for Isaac, but there's no answer.

I find him on the side porch dangling a doggie snack above Lazy's head and pleading with him to roll over.

I plop onto the concrete step beside Isaac and notice Ben standing in the yard watching the workers hooking a contraption of some sort into the ground.

"Lazy's got *you* begging," I say, ruffling Isaac's hair. "Thought it was supposed to be the other way around."

"Yeah, right." Isaac rolls his eyes. "Your foot better?"

"Yep. I'm gonna live." I smile as Isaac waves the treat again. "Think he's gonna do it?" I ask just as Lazy jumps and nabs the snack.

"Awesome!" Isaac says, scrounging in the bag for another bone. "You see that, Mom?"

"I did," I say, reaching over Isaac's knee and scratching Lazy's auburn coat. "I must be good luck . . . Uh, honey, can you come inside a sec? Need to show you something."

Isaac follows me to his bedroom where I point to the glass anomaly.

"Any idea how that happened?" I say.

Isaac's mouth falls open. He looks at me and back toward the shelf, stepping closer to the globe. "Who broke it?"

"That's what I'm asking you."

"I haven't even been upstairs," he says, obviously still mesmerized by the sight of it. "How's it staying together?"

"I don't know that either," I say. "So you never noticed it was broken?"

The tears in his eyes look like they'll spill over any minute. I don't want him to be upset, but it's not just a broken piece of glass to him, it's a keepsake from our vacation to Disney a few years ago. Alex helped him pick it out when we went to Animal Kingdom, and Isaac's shaken it before bed every night and made a wish.

I hug his shoulder into my belly. "The only thing we can do is just pitch it. I know it was special to you, but we can get another one." I snap a few pictures with my phone just in case it falls apart before Alex gets home to see it. "Just leave it like that for now and I'll get it cleaned up. I don't want you getting cut."

"Okay, Mom," Isaac says, hanging his head.

When Alex pulls in at three thirty, the old septic tank is being loaded into a truck. I hug Alex and kiss him on the cheek. "So, busy day for you, huh? You even have time to look for the gun?"

"I didn't, but Gilmore stayed with the dive team," Alex says, laying his gun on the microwave.

Steady, I tell myself. Alex doesn't know how I spent my afternoon. The demon in the mirror may, but Alex doesn't know that while he was wrestling a guy with a gun, I was scrogging the daredevil who led emergency crews on a wild goose chase for two days when he jumped off the bridge in the dead of night last summer. While Alex and other officers, along with the coast guard dredged the river, Ryan was watching and laughing over a beer from the veranda at the golf course. Alex didn't see the humor in the prank—said Ryan should have to repay the county for the emergency workers' overtime.

"The one link Hank had with the mafia," Alex says, "is conveniently out of town."

"You know where he might be?" I ask, placing cold pizza onto a plate.

"He's got family in Kentucky. Stranahan's on it. Oh and Barber's out already. Made bail."

"Will I need to go stay at Dad's again since he's out?"

Alex rubs my back and kisses me on the forehead. "No, he knows if he so much as breathes in your direction, he's a dead man."

I feel dirty, lower than even the dirtball he just arrested at the hotel, possibly can. Just because Alex is screwing around doesn't give me the right to.

"How many pieces you want?" I ask.

"Honey, I'm taking you out." Alex brushes his thumb across my cheek. "I still owe you that birthday dinner."

The ice is broken between us. Now if I can just keep it thawed.

Chapter Fifteen

MUMMIFIED LOVE

Before Alex gets his uniform off, a worker comes to the kitchen door with Ben and reports that the commode should flush normally now. The old tank was entirely too small for a family of four and could definitely have caused the commode to back up.

Both workers tromp into the half-bath behind Alex, Ben and me to test the theory. When the commode flushes normally, I'm shocked. "Ben, you try it," I say.

Alex shoots me an eye-roll. "Like it matters who flushes it," he says.

Ben flushes it and water hits the ceiling, sending the workers scattering and Alex dripping wet and speechless.

We have $2,000 less in our checking account than we did this morning and still have an unwanted bidet. Knowledge is priceless. If Alex would just listen to me we'd be less poor—even a new septic system can't flush a spirit.

Since Alex is taking me out to eat I decide to hold off on showing him the broken globe. I don't want to explain that I feel the demon is responsible for that, too. That would spoil dinner before we even get there.

I call Timmy's mom and she tells me to send the boys over. She'll watch them till Alex and I get back.

At Cornerstone Quarry, Alex asks for the riverside table by the fireplace that he knows is my favorite. He pulls my chair out for me more gracefully than usual, orders the fried calamari he knows I savor, and asks how I'm handling Diane's death.

As I'm telling him Diane's mom is not having a service for her, I mention that she was dating Matt Boggs. Then it dawns on me—what if she didn't actually hang herself—what if he killed her? "Alex, are you sure Diane killed herself?

She was dating that punk that I just got suspended for a week for insubordination. Matt Boggs. You don't suppose—"

"No, Savannah. No signs of homicide. She definitely killed herself," Alex says, checking his text. "Dive team at Mud Run wrapping it up for tonight. Going to dredge for the gun again tomorrow."

While Taze texts various other officers, I notice an older couple sitting in a booth across from each other. They're talking, not laughing, not smiling or touching, but communicating, and I realize Alex and I will be that couple in twenty or thirty years. We'll be discussing and discoursing, not enjoying each other's company—just tolerating the choice we made so many years before. That year is right now—this very moment—and the importance of each second suddenly takes my breath away.

"Kentucky police picked up our suspect in Hank's death—the mafia dude Hank was buying from," Alex says. "Stranahan's heading back to our office to interview him. I'll probably go out and help him tonight."

I sip the bit of chardonnay that's left in my glass and listen to Taze Templeton ramble on about work even though I'd rather he were holding my hand and looking deep into my eyes without saying a word. I thought the drink and the view would work magic between us, but I feel alone, and I know that I need something more substantial than ambiance, no matter how elegant it might be.

We're both avoiding the subject of spirits and water leaks as if neither exists. Alex and I just don't connect any longer, and watching the mummification of the couple across from me—knowing I'm staring at my future—scares the fear of being alone right out of me and onto the barge that's puffing down the river.

We pick up the boys from Timmy's and minutes after we get home, Alex breezes through the basement door carrying his campaign hat and announces he's going to the office to help Stranahan interview the "sleezeball."

I melt into my bed pillow and prop my swollen foot on ice, resuming a book I haven't picked up for weeks, *Left to Tell*. For a whole hour I read about an eighteen-year-old girl, Immaculee, who recounts an out of body experience she had while surreptitiously cramming into the bathroom of a preacher's house with eight other women for almost three months during the Rwanda genocide in 1991. Members from an opposing tribe, the Hutus, were in the bedroom adjacent to the bathroom, brandishing machetes and yelling, "Immaculee, we will find you!"

Immaculee says her spirit body floated to the ceiling, hovering over her physical body and those of the others hiding with her. She saw a glowing cross covering the entire length and width of the room and knew they were safe.

I'm engrossed in Immaculee's miraculous escape, when I hear Isaac yelling, "Momm."

I jump out of bed onto my sore foot and limp into his room. He's sitting upright and staring past me into the hallway. "How'd you do that, Mom?"

"Do what, sweetie pie?" I say just as I hear water spraying in the hallway.

"You just . . . you just walked through that guy," he says.

"Oh, Isaac," I say. "What on Earth did you see now?"

"A guy in a black robe outside your door. A tall guy—almost as tall as your door—and you walked right through him."

I peer into the empty hall, lit only by moonlight that's streaming through the bathroom window, and turn back to Isaac who's still staring and gripping his camo comforter around his neck.

Now we have a boogieman in black to add to our list of characters attending the party we seem to be hosting.

"Honey, I didn't see anyone outside my door. Could you see his face?" I ask, hoping he didn't. The poor kid may never sleep again.

"No. He had a hood on," he said.

Hell, sounds like the Grim Reaper. "Then how do you know it was a man and not a woman?"

"I just know."

"Honey, spirits messed with people in the Bible, too, but God took care of them and protected them." I hug my baby.

"Are eyeballs spirits, too?" Isaac says, scrunching tighter to my chest.

I glance around the dimly lit room, wondering if there's a pair staring at me now. "What do you mean eyeballs? Why are you asking that?"

"I saw one," he says.

"Just one?" I ask, wondering if that's scarier than seeing the whole daggone being.

"Where did you see an eyeball?" I say, noticing the shattered globe is still on the shelf.

Isaac points to the foot of his bed. "Right there."

"When?"

Isaac sits frozen in place. "Right before I yelled for you. Then you came out of your room and ran through the guy in black. And, Mom, I want out of here."

Amid his speculation of my membranes passing through a dark permeable creature, I'd forgotten to ask Isaac why he'd yelled for me in the first place. He seems less concerned about the floating eyeball than he was about the dude in the hallway.

I might as well keep my sense of humor. I know God certainly must be laughing His ass off. I can hear him saying, "Wanna question me again, woman?"

"So, why one eyeball, not two?" I say, attempting to lighten the mood.

Isaac jumps out of bed. "Mom! I really saw it."

"I believe you, bud. I do. I just have more questions than answers," I say, stepping into the hall. Isaac's already following me out the door, knowing he will get to sleep with his big brother again tonight.

"Aw, man!" I say, stepping into a puddle on the hall floor.

Isaac steps to my left and into another wet spot. He removes his socks and hands them to me then invades Ben's room as I traipse back into Isaac's and scoop the globe that's still intact, yet shattered atop Mickey's hands, into the trash can. I'm not showing Alex. I think it best to keep our future conversations as spirit-free as possible.

I snuggle back into my own bed and look into the night, tiny flickers of white lights and flashes of blue, dancing in the darkness. Bedtime in my house brings out more sprites than All-Hallows Eve.

I'm wondering if Alex, too, could see this light show if he prayed earnestly enough when I hear knocking coming from behind my dresser. I walk over and press my ear to the wall and hear it again, but I am not asking whose there. I may not like the answer.

Isaac must be scared to death. I'm not seeing half the weird shit he is, and I'm freaked out. I say a thank you to God for allowing me to experience the spirit world even though it's unnerving and ask Him to make my family more enlightened from this whole ordeal.

As I drift off to sleep in my bed alone, I try to imagine how I would feel if I knew Alex wasn't coming back to my bed—ever. Not that I want something terrible to happen to him, but what if I got the chance to go to sleep every night alone with my thoughts—no one complaining to me about work or the boys or how something wasn't done right.

It'd be more peaceful, even though there's more thoughts floating around in my head than there are spirits and water in my house.

Seems a curse that I can't sleep in when I'm able to. It's church day and I don't have to get up until eight, but I'm awake at seven with a sex hangover from the binge of the last few days that's left me wanting more just like alcohol did when I drank.

I consider nuzzling my head against Alex's chest and sucking on his penis like it's the beer that equalizes my sugar after a drunken night, but he's off work today and won't appreciate being woken up so early, not even if my head's spinning on him like a top.

I stretch, my hips dipping into the mattress, my feet spreading till one touches Alex's leg.

Alex jerks, rolling his back toward me. "Damn, your feet are like ice!" he says, yanking the quilt high into the air, ripping embroidery from the stitches as he tugs it from under my torso. "Woke me up."

Nice, I think. Might as well get up.

"What time you get in?" I say, scooting off the bed.

"Eleven," Alex says.

After eating breakfast and showering, an unusual quiet prompts me to walk into the hall and peer into the bedroom. Alex is still in bed.

"You not going to church?" I ask.

His muffled voice carries from deep within the pillow. "I'm tired."

"Oh, okay," my eyes linger on his muscular back, so strong, so rugged, so ready for a fight.

"Worked my ass off yesterday—like you care."

My chin falls toward my chest, but I press on to Ben's room carrying my makeup bag and chirping, "Rise and shine, honey bunch. Bathroom's yours first, Ben. I'm going to put my make-up on in here. Your dad's still asleep in our room."

I peer into Ben's dresser mirror, mascara in hand, when the whites of my eyeballs turn black like cracked glass. I blink and they are white again. My eyes can't get any bigger as I look into the mirror and inspect my eyeballs to see if the cracks show up again.

"What's wrong?" Ben says, pulling a t-shirt from his drawer.

"Nothing," I say. "Just had something in my eye."

No need to frighten him. Sure he knows I think there's a spirit in the house, but he doesn't know I saw a demon in my mirror last week.

Ben staggers to the shower while Isaac smashes a pillow to his head and I flip the wand over my lashes.

If Ben knew I just saw funky eyeballs in his mirror, he might just think I'm nuts or he might refuse to sleep in his room. Then where would he and Isaac sleep? Even worse, what would happen if both the boys refused to stay here at the house?

Wish Alex would see something, anything, creepy in his damn mirror. Then he'd believe or go crazy and jump off the bridge—and probably not as smoothly as Ryan did.

I wiggle into the navy linen skirt that hugs my hips like I do my coffee cup. I scan the shoeboxes that line the walls of my closet, my finger skipping over the labels of each box that encapsulates a unique mode of travel. The range of possible characters is endless—alluring vixen, cute curmudgeon, carefree silly-head—whoever I'm in the mood to pretend to be today. I snag the taupe pumps; they'll tone the snug fit of the skirt to that of a refined desperate housewife.

From the closet I hear beeps throbbing from Alex's alarm. Picturing his groggy expression and saggy morning balls swaying to the beat of the alarm as he staggers to his nightstand makes me grin.

The humorous image gets me to giggling as I balance on one foot and attempt to slide a pump onto the other. I topple over, smashing my arm onto a shelf and breaking the fall. A nasty red mark creases my forearm. Serves me right, I guess.

As Ben lumbers out of the bathroom, I scramble in and dry my hair. Ten minutes and counting. I beat Isaac to the steps, and we race down the steps to the kitchen.

"Grab me a protein bar," I yell to Isaac as I lean over Ben who's crouched among a mangle of shoes in the cloak closet and yank my purse from its hook.

Ben huffs, "Can't find my other shoe."

My hand scoops through my purse for car keys. "I know they're in here, dang it."

Ben tosses one shoe after the other into the corner of the closet. "I know it is, but I can't find it."

"Oh, I mean my keys," I say, flinging a few pairs of shoes into the pile he started and high salute with the one he's seeking. "Ah, the missing mate to your sneaker, Matey!"

Isaac hands me a breakfast bar and asks, "Where's Dad?"

"He's sleeping in today." I open the door and usher their disgruntled faces through. "Yes, we are still going."

"Man, why we gotta go?" Isaac whines.

Ben adds, "Yeah, that's not fair."

I walk to the car thinking this might be my last trip to church anyway. If Pastor Todd doesn't know how to deal with a bad spirit, how can he be my catalyst for the good spirit I want to foster? He's not an expert just because he's behind a pulpit. Todd preaches about fruits of the spirit like kindness and generosity, but if these positive qualities are derived from God then our negative qualities must be, too.

As I back out of the garage, the car suddenly drops to the right. The kids and I hop out looking behind the car to see what I hit. Air is hissing out of my right rear tire.

"Perfect," I say bending down and searching the tire and the ground for what I could've run over. "I don't see anything." I look at Ben, wondering if he sees a vision of what busted my tire, but he just shrugs.

I leave the car parked half-way out the garage door and route the boys to Alex's truck. It's church or bust.

During what may be my last church service, I pull off my sweater in the stuffy sanctuary and scour the congregation. Missing faces from the crowd bob in and out of view in my mind's eye.

There's Barbara Stimson typing lust-filled letters to the internet romance she now lives with in Nebraska, leaving her ex-husband, Emmitt, to raise their two girls; there's Mike and Sharon Whittaker holding hands by their new beachside cottage on Florida's coast where they moved—Sharon's stipulation for staying together when she found out Mike was screwing the county clerk; and there's Bo Jones holding a huge lottery-sized check, grinning from ear-to-bank-account after embezzling a few grand from the youth football league.

Have these sinners seen their demons in a mirror, too? If they did, did they tell anyone? Have their eyeballs looked cracked? Were their houses possessed as a result of their sins, and were their cries for liberation from evil unheeded?

I'm so engrossed in remembering all the members who have marched through these doors and crawled out, that I don't hear the sermon, but I do scan the crowd for Logan and don't see his fine ass anywhere.

The organ pipes croon as the choir sings, "He's calling oh, sinner, come home. Come home. Come hō-ō-ō-ō-me . . ."

A breeze of grace seems to blow my way, and I imagine there is hope for me yet. I close my eyes and petition God to not give up on me, reminding Him—like He needs reminding—that He said He is my light and my salvation and that I can trust in Him.

Rain No Evil

A white light flickers in the darkness of my eyelids. *Cool!* Surely, it's not a bad spirit, assuming it is a spirit at all. Could this is my angel reminding me it's here? White is supposed to be pure.

I keep my eyes closed and think how everyone probably thinks I'm praying really hard. As I watch the flashes I feel I should be pressing the button like I do to identify the lights during my annual eye exam.

I want to keep praying and take advantage of all this holiness I'm feeling, but everything's gotten quiet. Looking up, I see the alter call is over and not one person glided down the highway to heaven to kneel. Damn it. Aren't there any sinners who need saving today?

Doesn't matter. If God hasn't already heard my hearts desires, He isn't ever going to. I step into the aisle behind Ben and exit past Pastor Todd who shakes my hand slowly and speaking with a matching rhythm says, "I'm so sorry that I couldn't help you with that *matter*. Let me know how it turns out."

I say, "Thank you. I could use a few extra prayers," and release his hand knowing I won't ever be back here. The fulfillment I'm seeking is not to be found here, and Todd can't help me to find it.

I'm on my way to the car when I hear, "Savannah, wait up."

Mrs. Zavitz is clutching the purse on her wrist as she scurries ahead of her husband and toward me.

"Aw, can I go to the car, Mom?" Isaac says.

"Yeah," I say, to Isaac, and handing the keys to Ben, whisper, "Run."

"Why didn't you tell me you had a spirit in your house?" Mrs. Z. says. "I had to find out from Tina. She said you came to the church office the other morning looking for Todd. My word, Savannah, is it still there? Is that why you've been . . . well, preoccupied lately."

I've held my breath during her entire diatribe so I suck as much air into my lungs as I can before I answer. "Yes, there's a spirit throwing water around in my house, and so, yes, I've been very busy. I've only told the people that I thought could help. Alex doesn't want everyone to think—"

"To think your crazy?" Mrs. Z. says. "I can imagine. And then that poor Alex. Grabbing the gun from that thug at the hotel. Boy, you have had a rough week."

If she only knew.

"I've got to get going," I say, giving her a quick hug. "I really appreciate your concern. See you . . . let's see, Wednesday's our next day back to school, right?"

"Yes, maybe you can get some rest," Mrs. Z. says, walking toward her hubby who was wise enough to dawdle by the flagpole with his grandson.

Back home, Dad's on the porch giving the rocking chair a workout. A box wrapped in pink paper sits beside him on a table with a vase of spunky red daisies.

"Grandpa's here!" the boys screech, scrambling to unbuckle their seatbelts and be the first to get the hug, and just maybe, the five bucks for showing ambition. It's "Healthy competition," according to Dad.

I trot across the walkway bordered by dwarf Alberta spruce and azalea bushes. I make it to Dad and open my arms wide. "Dad, you didn't have to sit out here. Alex is home, isn't he?"

"I didn't knock. Just rocked and enjoyed the view." Dad's arms fold around my shoulders and he rubs my back. "Aw, my baby. Happy Birthday—again."

My hugs are longer than the boys' who are experts at the wrap and run. I snug into Dad's soft shirt, warm against my cheek and smelling of Polo. All is right with the world.

A car honks for attention. I throw a hand in the air, not sure to whom I'm waving, and not really caring. My grip on Dad tightens, the feeling of acceptance in his embrace indelibly attaches to my memory for retraction later when I may need it.

Dad nods toward Luce's car that's pulling around back. "And there's my other baby," Dad says, his polished loafers already landing on the step. "Let's grab the KFC. It's in my car."

Luce is trailing up the walkway from around back as Dad passes a few KFC bags to me. "We still on for Tuesday with Father . . . Father what's his name?"

"Nick," I say. "Yes, and I hope it works."

"What works?" Luce asks, grappling with a balloon bouquet that's bopping her in the face.

"A priest is blessing the house tomorrow morning," I say. "Hope our goblin leaves."

"Hi, Dad," Luce spreads the balloons and pecks him on the cheek. "Well, the demon's departure would be a better birthday gift than I got you. You get a re-gift from me." She laughs. "A re-gift from Christmas no less. Wedding's got me broke," she says, her brown eyes sparkling.

Luce favors Grandma Lennie with her prominent cheekbones. Grandma loved parties. Wish she was still alive. She'd be saying, "Savvy, I hope I have enough candles. They are the flame that wishes are made of." It didn't matter how many candles were required or how big the cake had to be in order to accommodate them—she insisted there was a candle for each year. And nothing doing with the candles shaped like numbers—that was cheating.

"*You're* broke! I've been broke since you were in diapers," Dad says, as we all three walk to the porch with arms loaded. "Shoulda kept the tire business. It was a gold mine."

"Dad, I can't imagine you being happy wearing any other uniform than that of a police officer," I say, sticking a spoon into the tub of coleslaw on the side-porch table. The front door slams and before I can pop the lid off the baked beans, Isaac's armpit deep into the bucket of chicken—digging for a drumstick no doubt.

"Luce, did Jack have to stay at the academy this weekend?" I ask.

"Yeah," Luce says, "but since he graduates Friday, how about a celebration dinner at Bob Evans that evening? Quick and easy."

I nod as Alex struts out the front door. He slaps mashed potatoes onto a heaping plate before sitting in the swing. "You outdid yourself, Savvy."

"Hey," I say, smiling. "It's my birthday celebration. I shouldn't have to cook."

"Savvy," my baby sister says, motioning me inside. "Girl talk."

I slink into the living room behind her as she glances into each corner of the room and whispers, "Where's the water thing?"

"Ah," I say, smiling, "it has a mind of its own. Never know when it will spray you."

"Damn," Luce says, stomping her foot and heading toward the door. "Thought it'd be cool to see, but it *would* be a little creepy."

We join the rest of the clan on the porch. As Luce babbles on about her Jamaican honeymoon plans, the boys eat and laugh at Dad who's pretending to pull a chicken wing from his ear. I could sit here forever basking in the humor and easiness, but I might as well get this over with.

"Alex, I had to drive your truck this morning. My car has a flat tire." I put a chicken breast on my plate knowing he's going to blame me for the flat, and I'm not going to feel like eating it.

Alex pops his jaw to the side, his chest expanding for a possible eruption. "Gosh dang-it! Do you have an idea how much tires cost? What'd you run over now?"

"Nothing. Just backed out this morning and noticed it," I say, sitting in a chair by Dad who winks at me.

"You *had* to run over something. Crap, Sav. I have so much to do." Alex pushes off in the swing and hurls toward us. "Cal, you can have her back—causes me too much work and way too much money."

With Dad present, Alex will usually only throw soft jabs at me, saving the spirit amputations for later, but today he's holding nothing back.

Dad pats my knee. "Well, honey. Daggone. You guys have had a string of bad luck."

Bad luck? Is that what they call demons and spirits and asshole husbands nowadays?

Alex takes a call from Gilmore while Luce passes paper plates piled with cake and ice cream to the boys who've pulled chairs up, forming a circle around Dad. He's sucked them into a back-in-the-day story about a poor family who was given a new house, but didn't know how to set the thermostat for the furnace because they'd never had one so they built a fire in the middle of the living room, burning furniture as fuel and burnt the damn house down.

Ben snorts in cake and Isaac's spoonful of ice cream is searching for his mouth. Luce and I look at each other with a gleams of acknowledgement that we've heard the story a few hundred times—and it's funnier every time.

"No more jokes at the table for you guys. I swear you're going to choke to death one day," I say, biting into a flower of yellow icing.

I'm hearing bits of Alex's conversation. "Great," he says. "Doubt there's fingerprints."

They must have found the gun in the lake.

Luce instructs Isaac to smile his "Shittiest smile." She's the only one who can get him to smile in a picture and cussing is the only way she can get him to do it. "Sav, the bridal shop can do our final fitting this week. What day's good—"

"Divers retrieved the gun," Alex bursts out, "but chances of it having a complete fingerprint are about as good as Savvy having a normal brain wave." He erupts in laughter, his body swaying back and forth in the swing like an elephant teetering on a hammock.

Amazing—he knows we have brain waves. To hell with pretending everything is ok and that I'm cool with his malicious remarks. I'm going to say what I want to say. He's going to make fun of me regardless if my brain waves are vibrating faster than his, or not.

Cherry nut ice cream melts down my throat too quickly and I cough, grabbing the arm of the chair, and turn to face my opponent—the source of my love and of my misery.

"How can you believe there are waves in our brains since you can't see them?" I say.

Alex pushes higher, the swing so close it's almost hitting my knee. "Duh, there's EKGs and MRIs that show brain waves."

"True," I say, "but I trust people more than machines and many people—prophets, saints, and scientists, alike believe in spirits. I also trust myself, and I know God told me there's a spirit in this house. Just because you are too closed-minded and dense to believe it doesn't make it untrue. Maybe *your* brainwaves aren't functioning at full capacity!"

Alex's mouth is open as wide as his arms are spreading, grasping the chains on either side of the swing. He looks like Fred Flintstone with one side of his red face drawn up as he laughs. He must be surprised I'm calling him out in front of Dad who's picking his teeth intently and grinning.

"Mom got you!" Isaac says, through a mouth-full of cake.

"Good one!" Ben says, looking at me like he's never seen me before in his life, and then looking at Alex. "Did you say someone found a gun?"

Alex continues chewing so I fill them in. "There was an unsigned letter in our mailbox yesterday saying that the gun that killed Hank was in Mud Run Lake. Sounds like they just found it."

I hesitate to ask how the interview went last night, but curiosity gets the better of me. "Alex, did the Mafia link pan out?"

Alex looks past me to Dad like he's the one that asked the question. "The guy's brother in Kentucky is giving him an alibi the night of the murder. So, we're deadlocked for now."

Dad says, "So you think the Mafia's involved in Hank's death?"

"Yeah," Alex says. "Hank was an informant. He was buying from a member of the local Mafia, and if they had somehow figured that out, they could have wacked him."

Rain No Evil

"Pawpaw, Mom says you had a Mafia when you worked," Ben says.

Dad laughs. "Well, I didn't exactly *have* one, but there was an active cell in MuddSock in the late seventies that was selling guns illegally. When the feds busted it, they found hundreds of thousands of dollars in water-tight barrels at the bottom of Butterfly Lake."

"Cool, Pawpaw." Ben says, looking up from his phone. "Hey, guys, I Googled about how to lift fingerprints from items in water. Was the gun metal?"

Alex nods, legs still flapping within inches of mine with each swoop of the swing, each upswing his head precariously close to the ceiling. Maybe his hard head would soften, should he bang it.

Ben gives his oral Google report. 'Thirty-four fingerprints were lifted on metal handguns re . . . um, retrieved from freshwater. That's out of seventy-two."

"Sounds like there's about a fifty percent chance of getting some prints from this one," Dad says.

Ben squints. "Oh, yeah, because thirty-four is almost half of seventy."

"Back in the eighties," Dad says, "the MuddSock Heights Police Department retrieved a .38 Special from the bottom of the same lake that the Mafia money was found in. The gun had been used in a bank robbery that didn't have anything to do with the Mafia.

"So you *did* learn something at school. I thought you just went for the girls," Alex says, disregarding Dad's comment and jabbing Ben with his toe on the upswing.

Ben rolls his eyes.

"So, Dad," I say, "how did you know the gun was in Butterfly Lake—you get an anonymous letter like we did?" I say, finishing off my cake that's soggy from the melted ice cream.

"No, the robber had actually told his friend where he had tossed it. Several months after the murder, the friend was busted for trafficking and ratted out his robber buddy for a lighter sentence."

Isaac's gaze is riveted on Dad. "Did they lec-tro-kite him?"

Dad laughs. "Electrocute. No, buddy. He was sentenced to fifteen years, no probation, but only served two before he was stabbed to death during a fight with an inmate." Dad wrangles a strip of chicken from the thigh he's holding. "Yep, the universe provided justice."

"That's what should happen to all these dang stupid asses. We should just let them kill each other off," Alex says.

"How to accomplish world peace—Taze style," I say, wondering if he realizes what a stupid ass *he* is.

The chimes tinkering to the left of Alex's head catches my attention, and I hope the change that's coming, comes soon. I silently ask Grandma Lennie to blow those winds of change faster than a polar jet stream so they reach me before my cells are so fragmented that I know longer recognize myself.

Quickly, I turn to Luce, "Oh, Luce, about the dresses. How's Wednesday

193

after school? It's been so hectic here, I feel like I've neglected the prized Matron of Honor status. It's hard to believe the wedding is less than a month away.

"Perfect," Luce says. "I'll stop and get you."

"What's Jack training for this weekend?" Dad asks, tossing his plate in the trash.

"Breaking down doors or something." Luce twists a long curl around her finger. "No, wait, it's called tactile entry. I'm learning the lingo just like the good teacher I am."

As a police officer's wife, Luce is going to learn more than lingo. Jack's more docile than Alex, but that may change once he's on the force a while—Alex didn't used to be an ogre either. She may learn how to defend herself from her husband who has vowed to protect and serve the public while forgetting the vow to love and cherish her.

Chapter Sixteen

MAN IN THE MOONLIGHT

As the sun casts an orange glow on the river's horizon, Alex and I take a walk to Blue Goose Pond.

Alex waves to his honking, adoring public with practically every step. "You get to see your favorite color peach this morning?"

"Color?" I say, knowing that he's referring to Logan who wasn't even at church. I should tell Alex I'm certain his text-book bunny, Stacey, is giving him more than the reading material she sells, but I don't want to explain that the reason I know is because I had a vision of an insect crawling out his mouth.

"Peach," he says, arms peddling to stay one stride ahead of me.

"Funny. Nope, didn't see Logan," I say, feeling an odd sensation that something is wrong. The hair on my arms is sticking up like the needles on a cactus. Something is very wrong.

We're about a quarter mile away from the house when my cell rings. Ben's on the line screaming, "Mom! A guy's out here—out back! Hurry!"

I swivel and run toward the house, yelling back to Alex who's just standing in the middle of Alpine Road. "Someone's at the house! Hurry!"

Even with my bruised foot, Alex barely beats me back. I hear Alex shouting from inside before I reach the door. "I told you to stay inside!"

Just as I'm about to pull the storm door open, the trio bursts out and past me, barreling toward the garage where my car is jacked up, still only partially inside of the garage.

Ben's jammies drag the ground as he shuffles over beside the left rear tire. "He was right here."

Barefoot Isaac chimes in, "Yeah, Dad, there was this splo-zun."

"Explosion," corrects Ben. "Then I looked out the door and yelled, and the guy took off."

"So you're telling me that a man—some guy dressed in black—came here and slashed this tire as soon as your mother and I left? Bullshit!" Alex shouts, bending to within inches of the tire that has a visible gash.

"Yes," Ben says and walks around the corner of the garage, leaving Isaac nodding.

Following Ben, I find him staring toward the neighbors blacktop driveway that winds past the rear of our garage and veers to the left of a patch of woods.

"What you looking at, honey?" I say.

"He lives back there," Ben says, staring into the distance.

"Who?" I ask. "The guy who did this?"

"Yeah," Ben says.

I glance around the corner of the garage to see if Alex is coming. "How you know he where he lives. Do you know who it was?"

"I don't know *who* it was, but somehow I know he lives back in those woods."

"You think it was a real man?"

Ben locks his eyes on mine. "Looked like a burglar, Mom, not a ghost."

"We should tell your dad," I say, hearing a shuffle behind me.

"Tell me what?" Alex commands.

"Ben says the guy was dressed like a burglar," I say.

Looks like lava could splurt from Alex's eyes any moment. "This is ridiculous! All of it! There's no guy. No one would dare come to *my* house and slash a tire right outside *my* door."

Ben steps away from Alex and stands beside me, looking at his slippers.

My head feels like the ball in this verbal tennis match. I have to be the mediator and try to get Alex to at least acknowledge the possibility that Ben is telling the truth. "Ben has no reason to lie, Alex," I say, turning to Ben. "Besides, wasn't Isaac with you when you saw this guy?"

"Yeah," Ben says, "we were both in the living room, heard this *boom* and ran to the side door."

Alex slaps his feet onto the concrete to within inches of Ben's face. "You had to have done it, Ben. Just admit it—you slashed it!"

Alex is acting like Ben's just slashed someone's throat. Even if he had slashed the tire, Ben deserves to be treated better than this. He's just a kid— and a good one at that. But even good kids can go crazy when a madman's in their face.

Ben's head seems to rise in slow motion, his words precise and clear. "I did not do it and I will *not* say that I did."

Nudging myself between the two, I turn my back to Alex, my hand cradling Ben's jaw as I look softly into his eyes.

"Sure. Baby him, mamma!" the madman says. And with that Alex tromps off, back to the house and no doubt, to his TV remote that he can control.

Isaac tugs on my sleeve and points toward Alpine Road. "Just a minute, bud," I say turning back to Ben.

"You believe me, Mom?" Ben asks.

Isaac yanks on my shirt again whispering, "It's him," and pointing.

My vision follows Isaac's gaze toward Alpine road, where the only forms I can make out in the twilight are our trash cans waiting for pickup day tomorrow.

"He just jumped like this." Isaac hunches to all fours and leaps forward like a tiger. Have we all plunged into the pool of insanity?

Ben starts toward the road, Isaac and I trailing behind.

Two trash cans sit undisturbed at the edge of the gravel driveway.

"Right here, Mom." Isaac squats to the ground and leaps, knocking the can with the missing lid over—bags, napkins and water bottles trickling out.

Ben yells, "That's great, Isaac! Cause more work."

"It's okay, Isaac," I say, bending over and picking up a cereal box. "We're all on edge and fighting isn't going to alleviate any of our troubles."

Isaac tosses a bag in the can Ben has sat erect.

Holding an armful of trash, I smile and drag the boys' gaze to mine. "And Ben, I do believe you. I know you didn't slash the tire."

"Dad doesn't," he says, tossing a pizza box into the can.

I dump the load in my arms into the trash. "I really think he knows you wouldn't do it. He just doesn't want to believe that someone would be brave enough to vandalize a car on his own property. To your dad, it's easier to blame you, rather than admit he is vulnerable."

I lay a hand on each boy's shoulder. "And I think it's important that you both keep in mind that God did speak to me, and I do believe what He said—there's an evil spirit here. I'm not saying it's responsible for the tire, but I wouldn't rule it out either."

The white of Isaac's have overtaken his face, and Ben's eyes are rolling back in his head. I want my boys to be open-minded, not hardheaded like Alex. I squeeze their shoulders. "I'm not crazy and I'm not trying to scare you. I just want you to understand that sometimes we *can't* understand things that happen, and it's okay to admit that you just don't know everything."

"Well, Cole's coming over to lift with me since there's no school tomorrow," Ben says.

Isaac scrunches up the sleeve on his t-shirt and rubs his flexed bicep. "Me too."

Ben protests, "Mom, does Isaac have to . . ."

"Ben, we just talked about getting along," I say.

The boys head to the garage weight-room while I enter the house to brave the storm raging inside.

Alex is eating leftovers so I slip upstairs to write an entry in my journal:

> Made it through another day as peacekeeper. I continue to pacify the starving animal called family. This animal is my favorite pet, but the beast part of it is lurking, always ready to pounce on my only fire of protection—protection from the pain always bubbling beneath my skin. We now have some dark creature or boogieman pouncing around outside—and he busted our tire. Both boys saw him. I hate to admit Alex is right about one thing—no human is brave enough to tramp on Taze's property, slashing tires in broad daylight—not unless he has a death wish.

Minutes later, I'm trying to skirt through the kitchen and into the basement without Alex hearing me from his spot on the couch, when a shrill scream penetrates the room. It seems to come from outside.

I open the side door and see Ben, broom raised over his head, racing out of the weight-room and rounding the corner of the garage. He's heading in the direction of the driveway that connects us to our neighbors up the hill—the same direction he indicated that the man who busted the tire lives.

I hobble behind him, watching his silhouette gallop up the driveway in the dusk until I can no longer make it out. I stop. He's way too fast for me. Moments later, I hear a crash and Ben appears in the shadows facing me.

"What is it?" I huff.

"He was here, Mom," Ben says, his voice closing in on me. "The guy who slashed the tire. I was setting up for a deadlift and I just *knew* he was out by the bushes. I grabbed the broom and oh, my God, Mom, he's tall—taller than the bushes and fast! I couldn't even come close to catching him."

I'm taking short sips of air even though I wasn't in full throttle. I look behind me expecting Alex to be behind us. He must have heard the scream, too, but all I see is headlights from cars and, in the background, a light from a barge shining on the river. "Did you have a vision of him out here like with the nail in the truck tire?"

"No, I just *knew*. It was like I felt him. He had on all black—like a bugler in a cartoon—even had on a black face mask." Ben extends the broom handle. "Sorry. I broke it. I tried to hit him with the broom and it hit the pavement."

Something rustles behind me and I jerk around. Isaac is shuffling along in the grass.

"Did you see the guy in black?" I ask.

Isaac presses in close to me. "No. You mean the guy came back? I just saw hear Ben yell and thought he was messing with Cole."

"Is Cole here?" I ask.

"Not yet," Ben says, "but he's supposed to be any minute."

Isaac's might be comforted to know about his brother's newfound set of skills.

"Ben, tell Isaac how you knew the guy was back," I say.

"No, you can," Ben says, twirling the broom handle like a baton.

Isaac looks up at me.

"Your brother just knew. He has a gift of intuition. It's kind of like the gift you have of seeing lights that not everyone can see."

"You mean Isaac sees lights—that why he always has to sleep with me?" Ben says.

"That's cool we both got gifts, Ben," Isaac says, stepping so close to me his shoe is touching mine.

A car pulls in as the boys and I reach the carport. Cole jumps out of the passenger side and his mom waves me to the car.

"Savannah," she says, "it's been crazy here from what Cole's told me. Anything I can do to help?"

"No, just letting Cole keep Ben company under the circumstances is gracious of you." I say, stepping to the open window of the driver's side door. "I don't know what all Cole's told you, but a lot of people wouldn't let their kid stay in a haunted house." I fake a laugh.

"Cole told me you have a spirit in your house that's throwing water around inside. It's like the house is crying," she says, snarling. "But he's not scared. He actually thinks it's pretty cool."

"That's the only kind of ghost I would let in—a cool one," I say as she backs down the drive. I turn to head inside knowing that not just any spirit is throwing the water—it's a demon.

A movement in the neighbor's backyard by Lazy's doghouse catches my attention—a tall figure bending down toward the hound. I glance into the garage where Isaac is curling a dumbbell. That means it's either Alex or our burglar. I punch Ben's shoulder and point to the backyard.

Ben takes a step, but I grab Ben's arm and shake my head.

Cole is holding his gym bag and gawking at the mysterious figure only 500 feet from us.

The figure stands erect for a second then takes off running up the hill.

I attempt to tighten my grip on Ben, but he's already slipped out of my grasp and is dashing past Lazy in hot pursuit. *Dear lord!*

I run inside yelling, "Alex! The guy's back. Ben just took off after him!"

"What?" Alex says, hopping off the couch. He grabs his cruiser keys and gun from the frige top and heads out the door. "Which way?"

I point toward the neighbors, "Up the hill!"

Alex hops in his cruiser activating the mega-bright spotlight, and pulls up the neighbor's drive. The roving light pans across the houses bordering the hillside and illuminates the trees and castes shadows across the lawns.

Cole is still standing, holding his bag like the Statue of Liberty holding the torch as Isaac huffs in from the garage.

"Is Dad out looking for him? Awesome," Isaac says, making a mad dash toward the action.

"Isaac, get back over here. Now!" I say, and turn to Cole. "You saw that guy, right?"

"Yeah, I sure did. He was tall!" Cole says. "My old house in Coraltown had a ghost. It knocked things off my dresser and threw things at me. One time the music on my radio stopped playing and a voice growled, 'Get out.' I slept in my brother's room until we moved three months later."

"It growled at you?" I say, wondering if the spirit that's infesting my house could follow me, say, when I'm at Ryan's or Joe's. If so, maybe the growling I've been hearing has been coming from the demon!

"Yes," Cole says, setting his bag on the ground.

"Did it growl just that one time?" I ask, picturing a twisted evil grin on the creature that could have followed me to my lovers. It probably watched us having sex. The thought makes my skin feel like I'm taking a bath in red ants.

"Well, no. Actually I would hear growls like if I was just doing homework or playing X-box, but I just thought I was hearing things."

"How do you know it wasn't your imagination?" I ask.

"When we moved," he says. "I stopped hearing it."

Isaac steps into the yard and watches Alex's searchlights sweep the area behind our house.

"Gosh, and I thought it was crazy here. It threw stuff at your Mom, too?"

"At my whole family. Once it threw a salt shaker. It hit the wall. Mom was glad it was empty. She never put salt in it again."

"I bet. Maybe she should've made a circle with the salt."

"Why's that?" Cole says, turning to watch the cruiser creep past us and onto the main road, the bright light leading the way, telescoping through the subdivisions to the north of our house like a beacon in the night sky.

"Ole wives' tale that salt protects against evil. Hey, that's what I need—a ton of salt. I could encircle this whole property!"

Ben comes panting from around the garage. "Man, that guy is fast! I chased him all the way to the church," he says, eyes tracing the light panning across the sky. "That Dad's spotlight?"

I nod and Isaac joins our circle.

"He'll never find him. He's living in the woods," Ben says.

"When you say living there, do you mean like camping there?" I say.

"All I know is he's living there. He's there all the time. I don't know how I know this stuff, but I do. It's weird," Ben says, studying Cole's face like he's expecting him to be freaked out, but Cole's face is as placid as the still before a storm.

A wave of light floats over the front yard and up the drive. Alex is home.

He jumps out of the cruiser in unlaced tennis shoes and plaid boxers, and the boys all snicker.

"You wore that! In your cruiser?" Isaac says.

If Alex had made an arrest in that get-up the neighbors would have been talking about the crazy Templetons. We'd be as iconic for being oddballs as the Addams family.

Alex slams the cruiser door, stomps into our circle and points a key at each kid as if to emphasis he wants to hear individual reports. "Did you all see this guy? What'd he look like?"

"I did," Cole says. "He was tall and had on all black. I couldn't tell much else cause it was dark."

"He was too fast for me, Dad. He ran like the bionic man." Ben smacks his hands together, skimming them, one across the other.

Alex pokes a key toward Isaac. "What about you?"

"Yeah. When he was in front by the trash cans," Isaac says.

"Trash cans?" Alex glances toward the road.

"Yeah, Dad. He jumped like a cat," Isaac says, demonstrating.

"Bull-crap," Alex says.

About thirty minutes later, I'm in my room praying for an end to this trial that must be the trial by fire—or, in our case, a trial by water—when Isaac yells from the bathroom.

I find him staring towards the wall from a tubful of bubbles.

"What?" I ask, but he says nothing. "Isaac, what's wrong?"

"How'd she do that?" he responds as if in a trance.

I scan the empty room. "Who?"

"That girl with blonde hair," Isaac says, turning toward the window.

"What girl, honey?"

He shakes his head saying, "She ran right out the wall."

I'm not sure whether to keep asking him questions or tell him to finish his bath. If we keep talking about this spooky stuff, none of us are going to get any sleep, but I'm curious about our newest visitor and probably too much has already happened to get any sleep anyway.

"Did she scare you?"

"No," he answers, still staring into thin air. "But how did she run with no legs?"

"She didn't have any legs?" I say, leaning against the sink top.

"No, she had, like a tail," he replies, swooping his hand like a roller coaster rolls. "It was swirled up."

I keep probing. "Was she touching the floor?"

Michele Savaunah Zirkle Marcum

"Nope."

I picture a mermaid. They go with the whole water theme we have going on at our indoor waterworks show. "So, she kind of floated?" I ask.

Isaac snaps his head my way like a turtle. "Yeah, Mom! That's it! Floated."

Isaac's words are like a puzzle I'm trying to decode. "How did you know she had blonde hair if you could see through her?"

"It was blonde on the top," he says, touching his straightened hand to his ear, "and the bottom part I could see through." He gets a faraway look in his eyes. "I could see through the whole rest of her body."

"How old do you think she was? Was she a little girl or older than mommy?"

"Not as old as you. She was older than Ben, like twenty."

"The priest is coming next week to make all this stop," I say, hoping he can.

I'm on my hands and knees reaching for the totes of summer clothes under my bed when a splatter rips across the ceiling straight above the center of the bed as if to cut it in two. I scoop up my journal and descend to the only room in the house more private than my closet—the laundry room—where no one except me ever darkens the door because if anyone with balls enters, they are never heard from again.

With the exception of the hum of the dryer, it's quiet—a shrine of peace.

Sitting Indian style on a pile of dirty jeans, I pour words onto the paper— words I'd like to let flow into Alex's ears, but his are corked tighter than a bottle of Henri Jayer.

> Add mermaid to ghostly sightings in the house. A blonde one floated through the bathroom tonight while Isaac bathed. Is she responsible for soaking my bed, too?
>
> The spray wasn't random tonight. The spray on the ceiling separated Alex's side from mine and I wonder if that is an omen showing me that Alex and I are supposed to split.
>
> God must be laughing so hard He's shaking the angels' wings loose.

202

Chapter Seventeen

A Huckleberry Kind of Breeze

Downstairs, I crack the eggs and put the bacon on to fry. I enjoy cooking in the morning—barefoot, with bad breath and all, although Alex would never believe it, but I don't care what he believes.

Today's a new day and I'm determined to enjoy my day—my cooking—my life!

The stairs creek as I butter the toast. He's up.

"Hey, can you go to the store?" Alex says, strolling into the kitchen.

"Good Morning to you, too," I say, smiling. "Mandy's coming in this afternoon. I'll be so—"

"I need some oil for your car. Hope the kids can help me change it after I mow the grass."

"Oh, crap!" I say, rushing over to the stove. "I forgot to stir the eggs."

"That's not my fault!" Alex says, slapping a spoonful of grape jelly onto toast.

I stir silently. I didn't think it was—I'm the one with my head in the clouds or in the underbelly of Hell at any given moment.

Alex couldn't give a rat's ass if Mandy's coming in or not so I don't know why I was bothering to tell him. I search his face hoping to feel a trickle of that gooey teenage love I used to, but all I feel is hopeless for seeking something that's more evasive than the slippery sucker spraying my house.

I try to draw Alex's gaze up to mine, but he is too busy inspecting the floor.

"I don't know why the kids have to leave their daggone shoes right behind the door all the time!" He picks up two pair of sneakers and slings them into the cloak closet. "Gets old."

I'm not throwing in the towel this early. "The day's all up from here, dear!" I say, my finger pointing toward the sky. "Sure, I'll pick up the oil," I say, approaching him and looking into his eyes for a few seconds—the seconds I used to live for.

Maybe he's looking for that gooey teenage love, too. Maybe he's as unhappy as I am and that's why he acts so nasty—he's afraid to admit he's unhappy and has failed at love. God knows he doesn't know what to do with fear except unleash full-scale war.

I take Alex in my arms brushing my cheek against his, wanting a kiss, but the peck he places on my forehead will have to suffice.

"I took off today since you all are off. Hope I can get some work out of the boys," he says.

"Breakfast is done," I say, removing the eggs. "And Joanne, the school counselor called me. She saw the news this morning. It showed you on the scene at Mud Run Lake.

"So—" Alex says.

"Let me finish," I say. "Hank is Zoey Clemens' grandpa. Zoey's in tenth grade. Joanne reminded me that Zoey moved in with Hank when her mom and dad were killed in that bad wreck on Dead Man's curve a few years ago. I figure you already know her since she was living with him. Anyway, because Zoey's a druggie Joanne wondered if there could be a connection to Hank's death."

I step into the living room where Alex has switched the TV on and me off. "Did you hear what I said?"

"I know her."

"Oh, so you did hear me. Why didn't you answer me?"

"When's breakfast gonna be ready?"

I place a plate full of eggs and bacon on the end table. "Orange juice?" I say, stepping in front of him, blocking his view of *Two and A Half Men* and thinking Charlie Harper is the male version of Carey Bradshaw, and a show with them both would be cool.

"What?" he looks at me like I'm a commercial for tampons during the Super Bowl.

Rain No Evil

"Nothing." I sit and shove some eggs in my mouth. I'm sick of feeling like an intrusion on the man who is supposed to want to share his life with me, but I get nauseous just thinking about the life I would have without him. At least with Alex, I know what to expect—arguments, infidelity, plenty of food in the fridge and on a good day, an 'I love you.'" My life could have been worse, I suppose, like he could be a deadbeat, not work, not provide for his family. We could live in a roach-infested apartment or in another country with no safe drinking water.

Alex looks at the plate in front of him. "I didn't know it was ready. Why didn't you tell me?"

My gaze remains fixed on the boob tube. There's more chance of Charlie Sheen hearing me from his Malibu terrace than Alex from a foot away.

By the time I get the dishwasher loaded, Alex is straddling the riding mower donning his bib overalls and floppy hat with Mickey Mouse square on the front. Not his usual attire, but Disney World was hot the day he bought the hat, and he made an exception to his just-grin and-bear-it attitude. Now, he can't mow grass without it. For this family, the Mickey hat is a symbol of grass-cutting season.

The smell of freshly mowed grass reminds me of bending over Ryan's picnic table—his desire for me so consuming. I want to preserve the feeling of being desired and open it when needed.

I close my eyes. Lord, please help me find enough self-respect to look for that feeling somewhere besides the arms of another man. Until then I'll ignore any urge to repeat my destructive patterns with men. I don't need a man anyway. God graciously gave me two hands.

I finish the silent petition just in time—round two of breakfast is descending the stairs. I plop bread in the toaster and Ryan out of my mind.

"Morning stinker-butt, eggs in the pan," I say, tickling the back of Ben's neck. "Is Isaac up? Your dad wants some help changing the oil in the car later."

"Yeah, but I doubt he will help," Ben says.

Alex slings the door open, "I need some help out here. You ready, Ben?"

Ben holds his plate out for the toast I'm buttering. "I'm eating. Mom said you need help later."

"Everything's always later around here," Alex rips off a dozen paper

205

towels and swipes his sweaty head. "I need help with the mower. The gear's sticking."

"Hope Isaac can help cause Cole and I are just chilling today, " Ben says, pouring orange juice in a glass.

"When do *I* get to chill?" Alex grabs the door handle. "Every time I need something, everyone's too busy! I gotta get a new tire on the car, too. Dang fix-a flat didn't work."

Ben presses his lips together and puffs out his cheeks, maybe hoping that by doing so, he won't say something to make his dad madder. Adding a bite of bacon to his mouth seems to do the trick, and Alex whips out the door and onto the mower.

"Ben, just check with me later to see if he still needs help," I say, heading upstairs, "and I'll get Isaac motivated to help, too, ok?"

I knock on Ben's door and twist the brass knob. "Daggone thing always sticks!" I mutter, jiggling it till the door opens.

Isaac pulls the blue comforter over his head when I flip on the light.

"Hey, Bud, can you help your dad change the oil here in about an hour? He's mowing grass. I have to run to Walmart to get the oil first so you have time to get your belly full first. Sound good?"

"Uh, I guess," he mumbles and rolls over.

"Ok then. Great. Thanks!" *Check!*

I slap some foundation on my face, a ponytail and ball-cap on my head, and I'm out the door. I grab the oil at Walmart and step up behind a woman with a skirt to her ankles and hair piled on her head that hasn't been cut or styled in a month of Sundays. She must be a holiness nut like Mom.

I want to be holy, but I don't want to look like some hag to do it. Surely, there's a place in the middle of the extremes where God exists. God created beauty in nature—the skies and the flowers. He must love beautiful people as much as the ones who make their features bland like they are ashamed to be attractive.

I glance to the front of the line and stop inhaling the oxygen I need—Joe is at the register. *Crap.* I can't stay in his line and take the chance he will propose another hook-up. I don't want to be rude, but I don't think he's spotted me so I slide into the longer line to my left and scurry out the door without looking back at my Adonis who's packing plastic bags.

When I get home, I hear Alex's booming voice trailing from behind the garage. "All I asked is for you to help me for a minute."

I slow my stride, wanting to know which kid he's talking to when Isaac shoots around the corner of the garage, eyes full of tears. "You told me an hour right, Mom? Dad's yelling at me because I wasn't out here soon enough!"

I try to talk and realize I'm holding my breath. I don't know why I keep holding it unless I think that if I don't breathe then I'm not really here.

"Yes, honey, I did say an hour." I wrap my arms around my baby's rigid shoulders. "Sorry. I'll talk to your dad. Just go on in the house and calm down."

I shuffle to the garage where my car is jacked up.

Dingy white tennis shoes with paint and oil stains are protruding from under the Buick. Alex slides out in faded bibs, his dark eyes oozing disgust that penetrates my resolve to be collected. "Your boy! He's not worth a nickel!" he says.

My wits swim for a peaceful response. "Ok. Listen. I told him you needed help in about an hour because you had to finish mowing and I had go to—"

"I couldn't get the mower working so I couldn't finish the damn grass, Sav!" Alex's cell rings, and he swipes his screen. "Damn it. It's Stranahan."

I sit the bags of oil on the concrete. Guess part of my life's mission is to be the peacekeeper—to be smack dab in the middle where I always am—in the damn middle.

When Alex slides his cells back into his pocket, I say, "I'm sorry the mower's broken, but how was I supposed to know that? It's not Isaac's fault and it's definitely not mine. You don't need to take it out on us. Do you still need help?"

"Never mind. Easier to do it myself," he says disappearing with a push of his foot.

I'm shaking as I wander toward the house. Why can't Alex just be reasonable? I know this whole situation isn't my fault, but I feel like I've done something wrong. I try to understand everyone's point of view and why they feel how they feel. Sometimes I wield the finesse to convince the boys and Alex to consider others' feelings, but today my efforts failed.

My cell vibrates with a call from Ryan, but I ignore it and walk inside to find Isaac. My boys must take precedence over my booty call.

Isaac is on the couch watching his favorite cartoon, "Ed, Edd 'n Eddy." I tiptoe across the hardwood floor to my recliner. "Your dad's aggravated because the mower broke. He just gets like that sometimes, you know." Isaac's face is red. He's been crying. "I know you like to help and you're a hard worker. You can wash my car this week and I'll pay you, ok?"

"Sure, Mom, I'll wash it. Dad just makes me so mad!"

"I don't understand him sometimes, either, babe, but he loves you." The boys are in their critical years of learning what it means to be a man in this world—what it means to be a father—and I don't want them treating the women in their lives like Alex does me. I get my journal and, hoping to smooth away this morning's roughness, scoot in beside my Isaac. As I keep silent company with him, I write about our guy in black.

I hide my journal under the phone book and head to the laundry room—the perfect hideout to call Ryan covertly. I throw towels into the dryer for the noise. "Hey, what you into?" I ask, doubting he's been dealing with the crap I have.

"I'm at Natalie's soccer game. She wants to switch days with her mom so that means that I'll have her tonight, but tomorrow night I'm free. You want to hook up then?"

"I, uh, have a work thing," I say, leaning against the warm dryer not believing I'm actually declining. "Maybe later in the week."

"Hope so. I wanna push your nasty button. You're sooo good nasty."

He's probably squeezing his hard-on right now. I'm disappointed— seems he's all about the sex, but I've never told him I want more.

"I'll take that as a compliment," I say with a smile in my voice and a knot in my throat.

"Way to go! Natalie just got a goal! Talk to you later, Babe."

I slump onto a pile of laundry and into a ball. I stopped seeing Ryan over a year ago when his texts became brief with no feelings of urgency to see me, but now that I've re-gained his attention, I realize I'm jealous of the girlfriend that he's parading around in public. I'm just his whore with a hole.

A commotion bids me to the kitchen. Ben is high-fiving Cole who says he's ready to max out on the bench today. As they rush out to pump iron, I tell Isaac, who's still brooding on the couch, to round up a neighbor boy and find a tree to climb.

The porch draws me outside like a hummingbird drawn to the red sugary drink that dangles from it. Seems I'm usually sweeping the porch rather than sitting on it, but today I plop in the Adirondack, guilt from my last romp with Ryan swelling inside me, begging to be released. I gorge on memories of Ryan's touch, the roughness of the picnic table scratching my hands as I look behind me, glimpsing the pleasure on the love bear's face between strokes.

I'd like to scrub my mind to wash away the innocuous mixture of sensations, desires and deceit, but the misery in this pleasure is a paradigm I can't seem to part with.

A horn honks me back to the moment. Mandy pulls in the drive, and with arms open wide, runs full throttle toward me, teetering on her heels through the grass, her pink blouse flapping.

"Oh girlfriend!" she says, hugging me. She pulls back, and braces both my arms like she's propping up a bowling pin. "Dear Lord, you look tired, Sav. Have you been sleeping?" With a wink, she glances around the porch. "Other than with Ryan."

"Don't worry—Alex is piddling in the garage. God, it's good to see you," I say, nodding toward a chair. It'll be nice to confide in the one friend I have who, I'm pretty darn sure, hasn't slept with my husband.

"Mandy, I swear, weird things are going on here. God not only told me a demon's throwing the water in my house, Ben's acquired this uncanny ability to perceive things impossible to know, Isaac saw a damn mermaid and floating eyeballs and last night someone, or something, dressed in black slashed my car tire. Oh, almost forgot—I also saw a demon in my mirror. That's what really kick started this party."

"What? Oh my word," she says in her best squeaky soprano. "I need a drink already." She hops up and tosses her handbag over her shoulder. "Let's go have our Poseidon Adventure, girl!"

"Yep," I say, pushing out of the chair, "you got here just in time. A day later and you might have missed it. The priest is coming tomorrow and hopefully giving it the boot."

I follow her inside as she oohs and ahhs on a self-guided tour through the living room past the foggy windows, plastic-covered dining table and water-stained walls, bare of the usual paintings.

I move a basket of fresh towels from the bar to the floor and sit a basket of chocolates in its place. "Coffee'll have to do. I don't keep alcohol," I say, shaking a dash of cinnamon into my mug. "Man, I feel old—we used to drink 70 proof, not medium roast."

Mandy recounts the story of her favorite outing when I got drunk at a club, puked on the table, and looking up from my drunken stupor, announced to the waiter who threatened to call the cops for my disorderly conduct, "We *are* the fucking police."

Classic. But I'm not the tabletop girl anymore—not dancing on them—not puking on them. Bending over one maybe, but I'm working on stopping that, too. Not one splinter today.

As I'm filling her in on my haunted house and how I had to leave it last week to avoid Barber, Ben bounds into the kitchen wearing a red t-shirt with the sleeves cut out and grabs a protein drink. "Hey, Mandy," he says, flexing his bicep our way. "I'm benching two hundred."

"You're gonna be a hulk just like your daddy." Mandy pops her biceps back at him and says, "I can still take ya."

Isaac and Timmy, bearing BB guns, zip past Ben and out the door, not even noticing we have a guest. Ben, the little flirt, strikes a bodybuilder pose with his chest puffed out, belly sunk in and backs toward the door before blowing a kiss to Mandy.

As soon as he pulls the door shut, water shoots from the ceiling above the refrigerator to where Mandy and I are sitting.

Mandy grabs the table. "What the hell?"

I take a sip of my coffee while water drips on my head.

"Savvy, good God almighty! If I hadn't been here to see this for myself, I wouldn't have believed it!" Mandy throws a towel from the basket onto the floor and stomps on it with her foot while I napkin off my forehead. "Sav, I mean, I would have believed you—you know I would. It . . . it just seems impossible. I'm actually scared. I mean, that had some power behind it. Maybe it *is* Poseidon!"

"Yep, it's more surreal than Salvador Dali's depiction of time melting, but no one's been hurt though."

There's a knock at the door, and Mandy cowers like she's going to get sprayed.

I laugh and clasp her hand as I head to the door. "You are spooked, aren't you?"

Joanne's peering through the glass and I open the door. She just called me this morning about Hank's relation to Zoey. What could she possibly want?

Joanne spots Mandy and says, "Oh, I'm sorry. Didn't know you had company."

"Come on in," I say. "You know Mandy. She's in visiting her folks. Would you like some coffee?"

"Oh, of course, Mandy. Hello. No thanks on the coffee. I won't stay long," Joanne says, stepping inside.

"What's up?" I say.

"I'm sure you know everyone's talking about your ghost. I just thought I'd stop and—"

"Oh, well, Mandy's here for a tour, too, so you're right on time. We haven't been upstairs yet," I say with a wave of my hand. "Follow me, my pretties."

As soon as Joanne's foot lands on the second floor water literally forms in mid-air—from a place invisible to the human eye, and beats across the hallway ceiling to the bathroom door.

"Oh!" Joanne screams, and leans against the wall, both hands crossed over her collarbone.

I stop dead in my tracks. I saw where it came from—the air!

I cast a look at Mandy who looks like Lot's wife who was turned into salt. I look back toward the space where I just saw the water form, and I stare as if just focusing will make it manifest again.

"You guys see that?" I say, holding my gaze.

"Oh my, Savannah," Joanne says, "Sure did. How—"

"Fuck if I know!" Mandy says, swooping her arms through the air until her hands meet then extending them toward the ceiling. "It was like an invisible water balloon crashed into the ceiling."

I strum my fingers on my head, trying to convince myself I'm actually conscious. "That's the first time I actually saw where it's coming from," I say. We thought it was coming from the ceiling. Hell, it's coming from the air—the air!"

Joanne mumbles something about needing to get going and gropes the handrail on her quick descent that leads her to the kitchen and out the door in what seemed like one long stride.

With Joanne gone, Mandy and I plop on the couch. "Savvy," Mandy says, "if the priest gig doesn't work, there's a lady I know who might be able to help you. I've been going to her for a few months for energy work, but I just found out yesterday that she clears houses, too."

"What do you mean energy work?" I ask.

"She's a spiritual healer. She lays her hands on me and balances my chakras. Chakras are—"

"I know this one—wheels of energy. I've been reading about them," I say, realizing I just interrupted her like Alex does me. "Sorry for interrupting. Go ahead."

"Her name is Jenn and she's sort of a spiritual counselor."

"What's she counseling you about?" I search my dear friend's face for signs I've intruded with the question, but she doesn't hesitate to answer.

"Jenn's helping me to heal from the abuse Frank dealt out. She's teaching me to speak up and live my truth without fear."

Mandy's ex-husband would lock her in the master bath all night for not having his shirts pressed to his satisfaction and smack her around during his drunken rages, but it took a tumble down the stairs and the resulting miscarriage for her to have the courage to leave him. I hope I don't need that degree of encouragement to leave Alex—that is *if* I leave.

"Sounds like I need to see her even if Father *can* get this spirit to leave. Maybe this Jenn can help me with my relationship with Alex," I say. "Where's her office?"

"Jenn's about an hour away in Bloomingdale, and she can help you with just about anything. Check out her website," Mandy says clicking away on her cell. "I'm texting you her name and website. Let me know what your holy man says tomorrow," Mandy says, heading to the door.

I hug Mandy good-bye and settle into my living room chair, watching Timmy and Isaac in the backyard pinging the cardboard target with each shot of the BB gun.

"Sav," Alex says, the scent of cologne trailing behind him as he walks through the living room. "I'm going to the office to finish up some paperwork. "Probably be about an hour."

"Okay," I say, wondering who he's going to bang.

The refrigerator door opens and shuts, and he is gone, leaving me alone with my thoughts—thoughts of how I can expand my world to include the love I want.

Mandy says Jenn can help me live my truth. Truth—I don't even know what that is, but if Jenn can tap me into it then I'm willing to let her lay her hands on me even if the idea of it makes me queasy. The laying on of hands reminds me of the evangelical church of my youth—specifically, the night that the preacher's daughter accused her dad of having an affair with my mom. She called Mom a whore, I screamed and the entire congregation encircled me, placing their hands virtually everywhere—my head, shoulders, knees—and prayed, some in tongues, for God's peace to soothe my disturbed soul.

I suppose it's conceivable that touch can heal. Jesus demonstrated his healing touch a number of times. From the lady who touched his robe and stopped bleeding to the leper whose sores instantly disappeared, Jesus rewarded those who believed. Maybe if I believe that much, I, too, will be healed.

I click onto my laptop. I want to know what sort of credentials this Jenn has before I let her hands re-wire my energy fields. Her bio says she's a homeopathic doctor who graduated magna cum laude. She's in her home office wearing a white lab coat, vials of liquid remedies lining the shelves behind her. Looks professional—harmless.

Grandpa Happy was an electrician—wired his entire three-story house. In the basement, mazes of wires intermingled, forming a web so expansive the wooden rafters could barely be seen. The concept of how electricity was transported through those wires, converging into a usable form in the outlet that allowed me to dry my hair, was elusive to me, yet plausible.

It's difficult to imagine that another person could adjust my energy field. Wires are visible—wires are tangible, but my energy seems to pulse with a current from a God who I can't see.

So where'd this Jenn get an instruction manual on manipulating energy—a scroll from the Mayans—a study of Stonehenge meridian lines?

I guess she's worth a try. Right now I'd enter a sweat tent and let a shaman chant over me if that's what it took to clear my head and help me find my path, so punch her number into my phone.

Jenn answers, her voice raspy with a slight southern drawl. I tell her I'd like to make an appointment—that Mandy recommends I see her. Jenn tells me I need to come for two consecutive appointments and have what's called a reconnection. I'm not sure what I'm disconnected from or how she's going to hook me back up, but I can't keep trying to chase the bees in my life back into their hives. It's not working. I keep getting stung, so I schedule my first appointment for Friday after school and Saturday morning.

This new venture of mine will remain a secret from my pragmatic husband—he *would* have me committed if he knew I'm seeing an energy healer. Besides, it's no more imperative a secret than the others I'm keeping.

A few appointments with the spiritual guru should be easy to pull off without him knowing. I'm on the run so much Alex doesn't know where I am most of the time anyway and as far as the three hundred thirty three bucks it costs for this reconnection—it'll be worth my handbag allowance for the month if it can connect me to happiness.

By the time the "*pop*" of the BB gun fire ceases, Alex is back and settled at the bar with his laptop. Ben stromps in asking when dinner will be ready.

I pull out my standard, "Twenty minutes. Get a snack to tide you over."

Having no idea what was going inside, doesn't stop me from confidently pushing the oven's bake button to 425 degrees. That should expedite the process a bit. I reach for a stoneware baking dish. With stoneware, you practically can't burn anything if you try. Foil over frozen chicken breasts, baked beans in a pan, cinnamon sprinkles on applesauce and voilà! The only color missing is green and I can live with that.

I'm enjoying the quietly amusing silence when a blue Thunderbird pulls in the back, and an elderly lady staggers out.

Bracing herself against the garage, she limps toward the side door—this one's got to be for Alex.

"Honey," I say, "there's a woman at the door for you." I'm not making up an excuse for him like I usually do so even though I'm elbow-deep in dishwater, I pull open the door to this sixty-year old woman who is wobbling up the steps.

She grabs the doorframe and looks through the kitchen at Alex who's in plain view.

"Hi," I say, stepping aside. "Alex'll be right out."

Alex slides off the stool with a huff. "Can I help you, ma'am?"

"Yes, oh please, Mr. Templeton. My boy, well, you know him—Bobby Barber. Well, he broke into my house. Took my money. My medicine. Everything." The lady teeters and Alex grabs her arm.

"Ok, let's get you down here where it's flat," he says, escorting her down the steps to level ground.

I shut the door, wander toward Alex's computer and notice a Yahoo email account is open. My chest is heaving, but I have to take a peek. I click on it and find what must be hundreds of messages from Stacey.

Speed-reading through several of them, I glimpse an Alex I didn't know existed—he seems to care how she feels, jokes with her. He's frisky—even charming—says he wants to nuzzle her neck, and make love to her on a bearskin rug.

Good grief! If I so much as ask him to slide inside me, he tells me that I'm disgusting. He's the one who's disgusting—living as big a lie as I am.

The messages fade into each other as I read one after the other about their riveting sex—about how they anticipate the next role-playing adventure and how their spouses are inattentive and inconsiderate. Several minutes pass before I remember that Alex could walk in any moment. I run upstairs. I have to think—to write—to pray.

I just get my journal open when Isaac bursts through the door of my bedroom, grabs my arm and pulls me along to his room.

"Mom, I saw an . . . an . . . elf," Isaac says.

I just stand, staring at him.

"Like Santa has," he says. "You know—an elf." He straightens his hand and brings it hip level. "He was this tall."

"Okay, Sweetie, it's too tiny to hurt you," I say, commending myself on the snappy comeback. I'm getting damn good at this job as border patrol between two worlds.

"You can watch TV in the basement with Ben," I say, walking toward my room. "I'm going to lie down. Got a headache."

Ten minutes later I decide my headache will go away if I get out of the house for a big. So, I grab my keys, tell Alex dinner's in the oven and head to the MuddSock library. I'm at the front desk checking out the book from Oprah's list I've wanted to read since hearing the preacher on TV talk about the power of our thoughts, when I notice the finely chiseled jaw arched over a laptop at a nook in the back. The biceps are beefy. They'd look nice framing either side of me—bracing the weight of the man they belong to, as he mounted me.

He looks up and catches me gawking. It's Logan from church.

An awkward recognition prompts me to nod. I accept the library card the clerk is handing back to me.

I'll have to go over and speak to him. It would be rude not to. This is a public place, plenty of people around. I'm not doing anything wrong—just going to be friendly. I tuck my newly rented possession, *The Secret*, under my arm—don't want him to think I'm into some sort of occultism.

As I advance toward him, Logan's cool blue eyes greet me, his wavy brown hair partially concealing one of them. The tight green t-shirt compliments his dusting of a tan and showcases his ripped abs.

He calls out before I reach his table. "Hey, Savvy. How you been?"

I clasp my newest read closer to my chest. "Busy. But I did make it to church Sunday—didn't see you there," I say, dipping my chin playfully toward my shoulder.

I can tell that having platonic conversations with men is going to be a challenge for me, but surely, I can figure out how to talk to a good-looking guy without an under-current of sex dominating my every thought.

"I just wasn't up to it," Logan says, flipping his open book over on the table and leaning back. "Heard you have some sort of spirit in your house. That true?"

Perfect. This topic will help me stay focused on God. I pull up a chair, joining him at the table that sits four. "I . . . well, I had a revelation that there is. We have water spraying all over the house and can't figure out where it's coming from."

Logan's forehead is wrinkled with awe. His eyes are focused intently on my lips and I find it difficult to concentrate. "Wow. Is it still there?"

"Father Nick's coming to bless the house in the morning."

"You called a priest? What did Pastor Todd say?"

I chuckle. "He advised me to call a priest."

Logan's Adam's apple rises and falls with his laugh. "Truly amazing story you have," he says. "There's so much we don't understand. Like this book I'm reading." He taps the hard cover. "I knew angels were here to protect us, but I didn't know they made phone calls and arranged clandestine meetings."

The emerald cover of his book looks familiar. I lean over reading the title aloud, *Angels on Assignment*. "Oh, I've read that!" I caress the embossed letters. "I was amazed, too—to learn they have specific duties. I'm usually reading at least three books at a time. Can't stay focused on just one, but I did that one."

Logan's nodding, his bangs flopping against his temple. I restrain my urge to brush them from his forehead. I remind myself I'm not doing anything wrong—a conversation in public about angels is not sinful.

I'll ask about his wife—keep things on the up and up. "Did Kerri get her dad's estate finished?"

Logan's gaze goes to the window. He seems to be trying to read the title of a book in a library a state away. "She moved out a month ago. She's been different since her dad died—says life's too short to be miserable."

I fold my hands that are lying on Logan's book, "I'm so sorry, Logan."

He places his warm hand on mine. "It's okay. Things between us have been bad for quite some time now."

His voice is smooth, velvety. I imagine him whispering perverse things in my ear, his warm breath on my neck.

I need to stop this now. I feel like I'm nearing the top of a hill on a roller coaster. As soon as I reach the pinnacle, I'm heading straight down to the hell-fire and brimstone aquarium—the one I keep hearing about from Pastor Todd who must be petrified of it himself. If he wasn't, would have at least come to my house and said a prayer.

"I'm certain that God exists and hears our prayers," I say, standing.

Logan rises as well. "I guess next time I see you will be at Luce's wedding," he says.

Luce's wedding? "Oh," I say, "so you're going?"

He winks at me, "I hope so. I'm a groomsman. Been friends with Jack since high school."

"Luce probably told me," I say, knowing that if she had I would have remembered that nugget, "but between my house and threats from a madman, I've been a little preoccupied." I lean on the chair and make a sideways funny face.

Logan crosses his eyes. "Yeah, not everyone has the caliber of excuses you do . . . uh, did you say a madman threatened you?"

"Yeah, a criminal Alex had arrested numerous times had it out for him—threatened to harm me and the boys. Even had pictures of us."

"Wow, I bet Alex was pissed. He get him?"

"Oh, yeah, but he's out already—our efficacious judicial system for ya," I say. "So, the wedding then—I'm the Matron of Honor. Guess that means you get out of escorting me down the aisle."

Logan cups his hand around my tricep. "I can think of worse duties than having you lean on my arm."

Oh good Lord! If I don't leave now, we'll be grinding out the knots in our groins right here on the table, *Angels on Assignment* vibrating with every spine tingling poke. I got to get out of here.

I glance at my watch. "Gotta run. Nice seeing you."

"Hey, I know you like to read," Logan says. "Book club meets here every Wednesday at 6:00. Next one's tomorrow night. Maybe you can come?"

"Maybe," I say, clutching the book I hope can help me attract some balance in my life.

Chapter Eighteen

BLUE GOOSE POND BLUES

I'm back home eating the last chicken breast left in the pan when Alex announces we're going fishing. I grab my favorite fishing necessity, my book, and climb into the truck with my man crew. Blue Goose pond is my preferred fishing place because it's calm, but Alex drives to the Ridgeland levy.

We pack the chairs, poles and tackle boxes to the dock where I saved the drowning girl, Madi. I read while the boys fish. *The Secret* is as esoteric as the title implies and holds my attention for several chapters before I take a break and watch the river traffic. It's too early in the spring for skiers, but a few pontoon boats are out.

Isaac's snagged his line before Ben has his hook baited. A few minutes later, Ben makes the first catch and Alex announces the competition is on. My men talk about baseball team picks and athletes I've never heard of, about the best location behind Keagan's to place a tree stand for hunting season this fall and why Smith and Wesson makes the best quality gun on the market.

I soak in the banter. We do love each other. Sometimes though, love isn't enough and as much as I wish I could make this moment last forever, I know I can't.

Waves from a coal barge lap the shore and the mew from misplaced seagulls distracts me from soaking in the good vibes of this family time. I feel sorry for the seagulls having to spend their lives flapping above the river instead of gliding above the exquisite ocean, all probably due to a storm blowing them off course. If they were migratory birds, they could navigate to the pristine Atlantic where they belong, but they're stuck here like me because they can't find their way home.

I know where my house is, but my home remains elusive. It's not just the water and weird shit that makes me feel out of place. I used to think home was anywhere Alex was, but now I know his presence, only rarely, fits me like a glove. Once I would've moved to the other side of the world to be with him, but now I know I'm growing out of him like I grew out of my jeans when I was pregnant. I feel like I'm going to give birth to something, but I'm not quite sure what.

The full moon is visible even as the sun is setting. I collapse further into the cloth chair while the sun sinks into the red horizon, feeling infinitesimal in this expansive universe. If I could see me from Pluto, I would appear smaller than a grain of sand does to me, yet I feel larger than the universe and connected to a source of power with no identifiable origin. Maybe I am home just being on the Earth.

I remember how close the moon appeared when we arrived at Hilton Head Island at three a.m. last summer—the sky void of a single light, other than the full moon that hung low like a crystal ball ready for my hands to wrap around.

Had I been able to read the moon and had it foretold the mysterious events of the past weeks, I wouldn't have believed my oracle in the sky.

I remember how much I had wanted Alex to kiss me under that magnificent moon, but when I slid my hand into his and stood on tiptoe for one, he just looked down and said, "Do you have to force it?" Then I let my heels sink into the wet sand and my hopes for romance with Alex float out with the tide.

I bet he wouldn't have needed prodded to kiss the textbook queen.

Maybe a vacation could help me relax and reconnect with Alex. Mom had absconded away with the preacher by the time I turned twelve, and I can't recall a single vacation that Mom, Dad, Luce, and me took as a family—only remember a few church picnics where Mom was probably even then pressed between the preacher and an old oak tree.

But my boys will have a broader perception of the world than I did, even if it's only as deep as the Grand Canyon. That's broader than most of the students I work with—many of whom haven't ventured further than the county line and don't realize that MuddSock Heights is in Ohio, not West Virginia.

Alex drags his chair close to mine, giving Isaac the task of watching his bobber.

Breathing in the cool April air, I touch Alex's hand with my fingertips. "Remember how gorgeous the moon was when we got to Hilton Head last year? And we could see Jupiter, too. It took my breath."

Alex inches his hand out from under mine, and pulls a can of sweet tea from the cooler. "That's your home planet isn't it?"

"Ha ha," I say. "Mine's Venus. Haven't you heard?" He's not spoiling my serene mood.

Alex sips his tea, seemingly oblivious to the allusion.

I prompt him. "The book—*Men are from Mars, Women are from Venus*."

"I don't know about you. Savvy," Alex says, shaking his head. "You're head's always in the clouds."

Rain No Evil

Maybe so. But at least I'm a literate cloud-hopper.

He probably feels stupid. Maybe he *hasn't* heard of the book. I wish I could mention a nice memory without Alex saying something crass.

I bet Logan's heard of the book—probably even read it. I stare at the water where I first saw the angel girl's head and imagine Logan's hand on mine atop the library table. I stare until the image of Logan disappears. I have to stay focused on this moment with my family—the only moment I'm guaranteed to ever have.

"How about Maine for vacation this year?" I ask. "Kennebec Valley for a moose expedition or Tennessee with a pontoon and a cabin?"

Just as I hear calliope music signaling the arrival of the Mississippi Queen, Ben belts out, "Mom, the sternwheeler!"

Alex spits sunflower seeds out of his mouth. "Stop yelling. Trying to fish here."

I wrinkle my nose and nod to Ben as I aim my cell toward the river, capturing the passing ship with people on board waving like dandelions in the breeze.

As the familiar music drifts ashore, I'm taken back to childhood. Grandpa Happy is pulling out his Polaroid One Shot and yelling, "Who's going?" He grabs his keys from the hook and scampers out the door to a car full of whichever neighborhood kids happened to be visiting. Grandpa Happy never missed snapping a picture of the grand vessel no matter that he already had hundreds.

Since the boys were toddlers, I'd pack them with me on a dead run to the river. On the way I'd describe how I'd inherited Grandpa's infatuation for the iron giant playing the unique jingle.

I watch the four story high party ship pass. It's more than a floating hotel—it's an American icon that looks like it floated out of a Mark Twain novel. The movement makes me feel unstuck. As I watch the contraption carrying souls from one place to another, I daydream of foreign lands flooded with people and creatures I've never met.

"You're going to have to let me know when to put in for vacation," Alex says. "Got to do it soon. Gilmore's already scheduled his for the last week in June."

"I thought we'd decide on the destination first," I say, watching the boys who've propped their poles and gravitated toward the cooler.

"Remember when we went to Key West and the hotel clerk told us not to throw rocks at the roosters?" Ben says, mouthful of a Little Debbie cake. "I thought he was on crack."

"How could I forget that?" I say. "It was four in the morning and thought I was just tired and delusional until you looked at me and whispered, 'Did she just say *rooster*?'"

"Why'd she tell you that?" Isaac asks.

"Roosters are endangered in Key West," Alex says. "Yeah, your mom was so busy thinking about roosters that she forgot to get her credit card back from the clerk when she checked-in. He kept it and attempted to order a few thousand dollars' worth of clothes online."

"I kinda remember that," Isaac says, staring at Alex. "Did he get in trouble?"

"The clerk's shift was over by the time we found out, but we filed a report and the police officer went to his apartment to question him. The guy wasn't home, but get this, while the officer's still at this dude's apartment, he gets a call from another policeman needing help with a DUI." Alex motions toward Isaac's disappearing bobber. "Guess who the DUI was."

"Yep, the same dude," Ben says. "Crazy stuff happens to us all the time!"

"Isaac!" Alex says, standing and pointing at the water.

"Yes, Ben, we attract crazy," I say. "Before we got to the Keys, your dad ripped his groin muscle racing Isaac on the beach."

Isaac pulls on gloves and slides the hook out of a catfish. "Last time I caught a catfish was on the Dot River."

"Where?" I ask.

"Where we stayed on the Hatfield-McCoy Trail," Isaac says, posing smile-less with his fish while I snap a picture.

"You mean the Gyandotte River?" I say. "Where you rafted down in the pitch dark after running off with strangers from the cabin next door."

"That was a blast!" He grins and I capture the rare expression.

"Well, it's not a Templeton vacation without excitement," I say, knowing there's no wacky adventure that could possibly top the freak show going on in our house and hoping it packs up and heads to the next county fair when Father Nick comes tomorrow.

At home, I'm sound asleep, when I'm suddenly being shaken awake. I roll over, shielding my eyes from the overhead light and hear Alex saying, "Wet towels . . . hardwood."

"Hmmm?" I say, shaking my head, trying to comprehend what's going on. "What's wrong?"

"Why are there wet towels on the floor in the bathroom?" Alex says.

"Guess the kids were sopping up water from somewhere," I say, or at least *I think* I say. I guess I didn't actually speak the words because I feel a hand on my shoulder. My entire body is being jarred.

I smack the hand away and sit up. "What!"

"Wish you'd keep the place picked up. You were off today and it's still a mess. You're here more than me. It'd be nice if you'd do something besides read."

"Did ya have to wake me up to just to yell at me?" I say.

"I'm not yelling," he yells, flipping off the light.

I close my eyes and imagine I'm with Huck on the river. It's so quiet all I can hear are the cicadas and a fish splashing here and there. A breeze rustles the trees as the sun shines down. I feel the churning current as the water swallows me whole.

Chapter Nineteen

JOLLY FATHER NICK

The aroma of hazelnut coffee wafts to my bedroom, enticing me to dress quicker. Wish I had Dad's punctuality gene. I join him downstairs, relishing the thought of a bicker-free breakfast since Alex left for work hours ago.

"Mornin, Dad," I say, tucking my arm under his. "They look scrumptious." I snag a raspberry-filled donut from the variety pack he's placed on the counter. "Should be an interesting morning."

Dad's spoon clinks on his mug as he stirs in creamer. "Excitement follows you, my dear. Always has. When you were still in diapers, you ran around the house like a leprechaun looking for that pot of gold."

"Still looking." I say, smiling and propping my elbows onto the counter. "Only now I know peace is the only gold I need. I'd trade all the coins in my pot for a taste of it."

Dad strokes my head with his free hand. "There's a season for everything, dear, and your season of peace has to be next on your wheel of fortune."

The boys pile down wearing their jammies and chomp into chocolate cream-filled bliss before attempting to teach Dad to manipulate the X-box controls so he can make a touchdown on Madden.

I hear gravel crunching in the driveway and peek out the kitchen door to see a hefty man reaching across the front seat of an older model Chevy sedan.

"Boys, get your clothes on pronto!" I say to the virtual football team sprawled out on the couch.

I open the door as a man dressed in black from the tips of his toes to the top of his head is preparing to rap. He removes his black ivy cap, revealing a shiny, smooth head and with a nod, extends his hand. Like the white color around his neck, an air of authority surrounds him.

"Hello," I say, stepping back to let him enter. "It's nice to meet you, uh, Father." I feel awkward—haven't addressed anyone as Father before—not even my dad. "Alex is at work. He would have liked to have met you."

Damn. Not three sentences in and I'm lying to the priest.

"This is my dad, Cal," I say as Dad steps forward and clasps our visitor's hand.

"A pleasure," Dad says.

Releasing the handshake, Father smooths his long fingers over his bare head. "We'll manage just fine without Alex. God doesn't need the help."

Seems a no-nonsense sort of fellow with a queer sense of humor; I like him already.

Father graciously accepts coffee and a glazed pastry, and plops into the recliner in the corner. "So, what's this about a spirit in your house?" he says, looking toward my plastic–covered treasures. "I see you have made good use of your table."

Dad sits on the sofa opposite me and nods for me to do the honors of initiating our holy guest.

"It started over a week ago with one drop of water in the hall upstairs. Ever since then, it's been spraying all over the house. None of the repairmen—and we've had tons of them—can find a leak. So, I was praying and God told me it's a spirit. At first we thought water was spraying out from the ceiling, but yesterday I saw it splatter from the air—like an invisible water balloon. And Isaac's seen freaky things like a girl float through the room, handprints in his wall . . ."

Dad's eyes look like full moons over his coffee cup, and I realize I may have forgotten to share a few of the goblin tales with him, but I continue. "A demon with horns, a floating eyeball, and a black figure Isaac says I walked through—even our tires are being busted by a man dressed in black."

Father Nick stops me with a wave of his hand. "Tires? On your vehicles?"

After everything I've told him, he's asking about tires?

"Yes, tires, oh and every time Ben flushes the commode down here," I say pointing toward the half-bath, "water from it hits the ceiling like a gusher." I need to slow down and let Father process the details I'm lobbing at him, but my mind's in the last lap of the Kentucky derby. No bridle can slow it down.

"I even saw a demon in my mirror!" If that doesn't persuade him that there's evil in this house, I don't know what will.

Father swallows hard on the donut and studies his long fingers that are rubbing the leather arm of the recliner as if massaging it helps him understand our predicament. His face is stoic.

Good. He's not dismissing the possibility of an evil presence.

"Sounds like you may have more than one visitor here. Like I told you on the phone, often a restless spirit is responsible for paranormal activity like what you have described with the water, but these other apparitions, well, I haven't had experience with, you say, a floating eyeball." Father chuckles like jolly Saint Nick. "That worse than seeing the whole creature?"

Rain No Evil

"Exactly what I thought when Isaac told me!" I say. We both have an odd sense of humor. Maybe it's a sign he's divinely appointed to liberate my house. "What's the difference between a restless spirit and a ghost?"

"There's not," Father says. "They're both the manifestation of a dead person's spirit into the physical realm. The restless spirit or ghost refuses to transition to the afterlife. A house blessing instructing the person to move into the light usually alleviates any further disturbances."

"Wow—that's just like the movie *Poltergeist*," I say.

Father stands and brushes the crumbs from his rotund belly into his empty mug. "In the house I grew up in the whole family regularly heard chains dragging across the attic floor when no one was up there," he says, pulling a plastic bottle from his shirt pocket. He displays a bottle that's adorned with a gold Celtic cross, explaining that it contains holy water, which has been blessed by his superior, Monsignor somebody.

"We will start the blessing where the water first fell," Father says, tucking his worn Bible case under his arm.

I lead the way upstairs, my entourage following.

"There's no getting around getting old. Knees are the first to go," Father says.

The boys scamper from their bedrooms as Father's booming voice fills the stairwell. "Nice looking lads," Father says, extending his right hand to Ben. "Now, what's your name?"

Ben returns the hearty handshake. "Benjamin, Sir."

Father looks like he's going to blow out a candle. "Oh, looks and manners I see. Good job, Mom." Father blinks approval my way. "And this young man is . . ."

"Isaac," I say, Isaac inching closer to me and accepting Father's hand.

"Hello, Isaac. You're the one seeing apparitions?"

Isaac scrunches his eyebrows my way.

"An apparition is like the handprint in the wall," I say. "It's something you see that no one else does."

"Oh, yeah," Isaac says, nodding at Father.

Dad points to the ceiling where a circular stain pattern is displayed. "That's where the first drop came from."

Father shakes his bald head, rubbing it like he's trying to bore his head into his hand. "I see. Let's get this shindig started." He slides a printed copy of something out from between the pages in his Bible, unfolds it and hands it to me saying, "You read where the 'R' is."

There's a script to this house-blessing thing? Heck, I thought Father would sprinkle his water and say the magic words himself sort of like Shakespeare's Puck.

Looking at the tiny print written in play form, I see the 'R's' alternate with the 'F's' which probably mean Father.

"What's the 'R' stand for?" I ask.

Father says, "Response. Now, Isaac, son, do you read?"

Isaac's got that puzzled look again. Father must not work with seven year olds much. The prayer I'm holding is written at adult level.

"He's only in third grade," I say, "but Ben can."

"Ok, Ben share with your mom," Father says, handing Dad a copy and pulling a pair of glasses from his pocket, letting them rest low on the ridge of his rather nubby nose. This guy's face radiates so much goodness that he could power up a light bulb with his mouth like Uncle Fester.

Father dribbles sacred water from the bottle onto his fingertips then draws an invisible sign of the cross. In a robust baritone, the words, "In the name of the Father, and of the Son, and of the Holy Spirit," ring throughout the enclosed hall.

I always wondered why Catholics draw the symbol in the air, but now doesn't seem to be an appropriate time to ask.

Father continues, "Peace be with this house and with all who live here."

Doesn't seem fair that Alex doesn't have to be here to reap the peace.

Following the prayer, Father recites something about Christ becoming man via a virgin birth and how God told the disciples to stay only in peaceful houses and eat what is given to them there.

Father clears his throat and flips his palm open like he's receiving a gift.

"Oh, sorry." I say, searching my paper for the first capital R. "Ok. Happy are those who fear the Lord."

Father's turn. "An evil report he shall not fear; his heart is firm, trust in the Lord. His heart is steadfast; he looks down up on his foes."

Our turn. I nudge Ben who nudges me back. "Happy are those who fear the Lord," we all chant.

Turning his page, Father's voice rises in progression with the invocation for God's help. "In you every dwelling grows into a holy temple. Grant that those who live in this house may be built up together into the dwelling place of God in the Holy Spirit."

Our turn: "Lord, hear our prayer." We're getting the hang of this mantra thing now.

Father belts out an, "Amen," and squeezes the bottle of holy water. Water dribbles onto the walls and floor. Father squirts his way through the upstairs and makes his way back to Isaac's room where he says, "Ah, yes, we need to say an extra prayer here."

I turn and make eye contact with the boys who are behind me and mime, "Close your eyes."

Father signs and invokes the trinity. "Any person who is deceased and hanging around this house, know that this is someone else's house and you may no longer stay here. Restless spirits abiding here move into the light, allow the light, God's light, to surround you and be at peace. You are safe in the light."

"Here," Father says, placing the bottle into Isaac's hand. "You try. Just aim and squeeze."

Isaac raises his eyebrows, staring at the bottle as if he's been asked to stick his hand in a rattlesnake hole.

Rain No Evil

"Go ahead. Give it a whirl," Father says. This holy man isn't about to take no for an answer.

Pointing the spout toward his trophy shelf where the Mickey globe used to sit, Isaac squirts the holy water onto his awards and aims toward the TV.

I snatch the bottle. "Not the TV, bud!" I say. "It's holy, but it still water. Water and TVs don't mix."

The words are barely out of my mouth when I realize we're using water to ward off water. Wouldn't that be like fighting fire with fire. How does that work? Is the holy water positively charged and the evil water negatively charged?

Father slips his glasses into his shirt pocket. "Isaac," he says, "whenever you see something that shouldn't be in here, say a prayer and squirt away. When I finish here, I'll leave this bottle with you and if you need a refill . . . well, there's plenty where that came from."

After the prayer envoy travels through the first story and the basement with Father leading the way, praying and squirting, he plants his cap atop his head and suggests that he bless the perimeter of the house since there may be unwanted spirits roaming the grounds.

We all follow out single file behind Father Nick who surveys the yard and walks to the spot by the driveway where the trash cans and a creature in black had sat last night.

"In the name of the Father and of the Son and of the Holy Spirit," Father says, signing a cross, the sleeves of his black shirt snapping in the brisk wind.

Stepping unsteadily forward on the yard that's bumpy with mole mounds, he walks under two elm trees while slinging blessed water and praying into the wind. I hobble behind him with my foot that's still sore from the gun that landed on it and hope we will be done before the dark clouds approaching from the West unleash a torrent.

Ben and Isaac are looking toward the house, probably hoping the passers-by won't see their faces. Rumors are being substantiated with each second we are out here—that's for sure.

At the edge of the yard bordering the main road, Father faces into the wind. Two teenage bicyclists twist their necks to watch our holy man's ritual. One steers into the metal guardrail and topples over.

The wind-chimes are clinking, providing a background cantata, and I'm reminded to be grateful for the change that I pray to my dear, departed grandma, is coming.

With the wind picking up, I only catch a few of Father's words like, "Surround and protect," and "Archangel Michael defend us in battle," but I stroll along behind him, hands folded into a steeple. Dad and the boys have formed a circle and are hanging back near the porch.

I turn to the sound of breaks screeching to see a man gawking my way from behind the wheel of an Oldsmobile that's straddling the center line—the first in a line of slow-moving traffic and staring passengers.

Someone's probably already sent our ritual spiraling through You-Tube cyber-space. Mrs. Z. may have activated an alert on her own hotline by now. I'd feel horrible if someone wrecked as a result of watching this bizarre parade, but as long as Father Nick encircles my home with grace and protection, I don't care what anyone thinks.

Dad heads inside with the boys. Father and I trek in the drizzling rain alongside the row of towering evergreens to the north, the three-car garage behind the house, and the weight-room.

Arriving back at our starting point, Father hands me the flask of holy water and tells me to call if I need him. As my Santa in black pulls out, the Heat Miser pulls around back—Aunt Klaire is on the scene.

I know that God has to be giving me way more credit for handling stress than I deserve because this woman may well destroy my parameters for acceptable hostess behavior.

I run inside and tell Dad that Klaire will be at the door any second.

"Sounds like a good time for a DQ run. All this praying has made me hungry," he says, tipping his cap onto his head. "Isaac, go tell your brother."

"Thanks," I say, tick-tocking my finger at him like windshield wipers.

There's a knock at the door and Dad winks at me.

"Hi, Klaire," I say, opening the door for Alex's aunt whose prickly, black frocks remain stiff even with the wind that's swirling the rain under the carport.

Clasping a red handbag she has draped over her wrist, she looks down her nose and edges through the door. A purse? She must plan on a lengthy visit.

"We were just on our way to DQ. Were you looking for Alex?" I say even though Klaire would know he's at work.

"Hello, Savannah. No, I was on my way to the bank and . . ." Klaire says, brushing donut crumbs from the bar into her hand before setting her purse on it. "I saw Father Nick gallivanting around your yard. I think all of Ridgeland did. What was he doing here?"

I hold my glass under the fridge waterspout. "He blessed the house," I say, wondering why she acts pissed when *she's* the one who suggested I call him. I turn with a smile. Maybe she just wants the credit for it. "Thanks for suggesting I call him."

"Hi Klaire," Dad says, from his roost on the stool, as Klaire brushes more crumbs from the bar into the sink as if they were glass.

"I see *I* wasn't invited to your private party," Klaire says, stroking the diamond on her hand that's more brilliant than she is. "But I see *Cal's* here."

My heart's constricting, cringing just like when I talk to Alex. I want to yell, "Get your arrogant ass out of here," but she would love that—the more conflict, the more she thrives, and I won't give her that satisfaction.

"Klaire, I didn't think to ask you to come. I mean, I know you're not Catholic so—"

"Well, hell, he's not Catholic either!" Klaire screams, sending sparks to Dad via a long, bony finger. She jams her fist onto her hip and through thin, crimson red lips announces, "Alex should divorce you—you're nuts . . . saying a spirit's in your house!"

Dad's on his feet, but I shove my palm straight toward him like I can zap him seated. I've circled this track before and it always has the same finish line—Klaire will think she is right and I am wrong, and truth will be obscured by anyone's count.

I should feel sorry for her—discernment and tactfulness isn't in Klaire's chest of mental drawers, but all I feel is disgust and rage at this foaming-at-the-mouth imbecile who thinks she has a right to talk to me like I am a measly worm in her jungle.

I draw my shoulders back and look her in the eyes. "Klaire, *you* are the one who told me to call Father Nick. because you thought he could help us."

Klaire tucks her blouse tighter into her polyester pants. "Of course, I did. I knew Alex couldn't take much more."

Ben pounds down the stairs. "Dibs on front seat, Pawpaw, and can we go driving?"

My eyes are molded to Klaire's. "Father Nick says there could be a spirit here." I allow a smirk to settle onto my face. "Does that mean he's nuts, too?"

Klaire snatches her purse off the counter and screeches, "If there *is* a spirit here, *you*'re the one who invited it!"

She storms out the door and onto a wet step that must be as angry with her as I am.

Seeing her legs sprawling in the air, her arms swimming backwards as she tries to defy gravity is, by far, the most rewarding part of my week.

Klaire is draped over a step, moaning and rubbing her hip when Dad, Ben and I reach her.

Dad offers her his hand, asking if she is all right and Ben volunteers to call 911.

"I'm perfectly fine," she says, grinding her wrists onto the concrete beneath her and buckling when she applies weight to her legs.

Dad grabs one of her elbows and I grab the other, together bolstering her ungrateful, lump of arrogance through the mist and into her car.

"Maybe you should see a doctor," I say, more to further embarrass her than out of concern.

The curmudgeon says, "I'm fine!" and stamping on the accelerator, backs out of the drive and I hope, out of my life forever.

"Wow. Was she mad!" Ben says. "She said you brought a spirit here. That's stupid, Mom." He twirls his finger by his head. "She's the one who's cuckoo."

I'm not telling Ben that Klaire may be right this time—that I may have actually, although unintentionally, invited the spirit by means of an angry prayer. I just say, "When is she not mad? Get your hoodie and get your brother. I'm definitely feeling DQ—it's either eat sugar or murder Klaire."

"Yep!" Dad says, motioning Ben and Isaac, who's just joined us, to get into the car.

Dad steps beside me. "My prayers for peace when Father was here were nothing compared to the pleas to be relieved from Klaire's company that I've prayed ever since I met that bitch when you and Alex dated in high school."

"So," I say, my chin doing the jive, "tell me how you really feel about her."

At the only ice cream shop in MuddSock Heights, I order a double chocolate rocky road for the bumpy morning I've hurdled and watch the boys roll pennies into the spiral, yellow contraption for the diabetes foundation's charity that's ironically placed inside this sugar palace.

I sympathize with the coin, on edge, swirling, knowing where it's going to end up, but having to wait out the ride anyway. Soon it will be motionless in a pit of pennies.

As I watch it spin, I glimpse my future in the vortex of movement—I'm on a patio of a house west of here—my house. There's a pond and no Alex. Just pine trees and squirrels. The picture is clearer than any photo I've seen, but it fades within seconds.

I glance around knowing no one else saw it, but half expecting someone to have their mouth hanging open like mine is. I wonder if this vision will be accurate like the one Ben had about the tire.

While we sit in the booth waiting for our orders, Dad asks me if I've told Mom about the spirit at my house. I tell him I haven't talked to her since Christmas and that Luce has decided not to invite her to the wedding. Since the wedding will take place on Dad's lawn, Luce said that Mom attending would be awkward for Dad; even though he'd said it was Luce's wedding and; therefore, Luce's choice whether or not to invite her.

The server slides a tray of food across the table. Isaac swipes his cone off and asks if the spirit is gone from our house now.

Ben rotates an imaginary steering wheel and winks at Dad from whose mustache is slathered a gob of whipped cream.

"I hope so, Isaac. I hope it's foraging for another family who needs some excitement." I say, chomping into a cocoa morsel and noticing that Isaac's eyes can't get any wider. His cone-filled hand is frozen mid-air.

I scan the restaurant for the supernatural thing that Isaac must see that I can't. "What's wrong?" I ask.

Isaac points to a spot on his forehead right between his bulging eyes.

I smack my palm to his head. "Ice cream headache," I say. "Put your tongue on the roof of your mouth."

I look around at Ben and Dad who have one hand plastered to their heads mocking me and the other holding their partially eaten parfaits.

Isaac glares at them and swats my hand away.

Mentioning Mom must have jarred Dad's memory. He reminisces aloud about a fright Mom had when they first got married. He says one night while doing dishes Mom looked out the kitchen window and saw what she thought was her reflection only to realize that the *reflection* was wearing a hat that she did *not* have on her head.

Neither of the boys has taken their lips from the ice cream they're holding. This is a rarer treat for them than the dessert—Dad sharing stories about Mom.

Dad says he took out the back door with a shotgun, tackled the window peeper and was shocked to see the face of a brother-in-Christ looking up at him from the ground. Dad didn't press charges and the pervert stopped attending church.

"Pawpaw," Isaac says, "you mean the *poor wart* went to church with you?" Dad looks at me to interpret.

"Pervert," I say, chasing my ice cream with coffee—hot and cold, just like Alex and me.

Dad sticks a peanut onto Isaac's nub of a cone. "When you gonna speaka Englisha, my man?" Dad laughs. "You quack like your speaking duck language."

Ice cream slobbers down the boys' sunny faces.

"Yep, the pervert damn sure did go to church. Sat in the pew right next to me," Dad says. "Must've had cotton in his ears during the sermon about not coveting your neighbor's wife."

"Covet means to want something someone else has," I say, handing Isaac a napkin. "It's like jealousy."

"Just going to church doesn't make someone a good person. That church was full of perverts who liked your . . . well, your mommy's mom." Dad turns to the window and watches the passing cars like it's his past he's seeing.

Neither of the boys calls her grandma and Dad's not going to use the term of endearment either. They don't know Mom ran off with the preacher soon after that, and they aren't going to find out from me today. I'll need more than ice cream for that conversation. That'll call for gin and a special package from that maroon car that frequents Ridgeland's levy.

The fact that church folks are human and often unethical, creepy and wicked doesn't bother me so much as does knowing that *I'm* living a lie—being just as hypocritical as those members of the congregation that I abhor. There has to be more to life than pretending . . . to be perfect, to be happy, to not have feelings, and to not care so others won't see my pain.

The biggest lie of all has to be the one I've told myself—that I'm not hurting anyone except myself when I lie—because I am. By pretending I can make our marriage work, I'm preventing Alex from being happy with someone else. And when I lie to the boys about my whereabouts, even if they only occasionally figure that out, I'm teaching them that the truth—their truth—is ugly and must be tucked away inside of themselves.

Timmy's in the drive with his mom when we pull up to the house. I hop out and Timmy hops in my spot. Dad and the boys take off for an obscure country road to brave an illegal ride with Ben behind the wheel.

Inside the house I tiptoe from room to room, anticipating the sound of the familiar *splat*, but all I hear is the long, low hoot of the train whistle—music to my ears. Maybe the water-slinging demon is gone.

I stare out the window as the passing train clacks memories my way. As a girl, I'd put a penny on the track that wound through the hillside behind Dad's and add the flattened coin to my collection.

Even then, the power of the penny enchanted me—how it didn't break under the weight of the steam engine rolling over it—only transformed into a thinner version of itself.

My goal was to collect 100 of them, which seemed like a million to a little girl with a Mason jar. I think I had nine of them before I replaced them with lightening bugs. I never was very good at completing anything. Maybe that's why I'm so hesitant to admit I failed at marriage, too.

I want to be like that copper coin and not let the world flatten me either. I want to allow the pressure of life to roll over me and transform me into all I'm worth—which I hope is more than a jar-full of smashed pennies.

Alex is home at 4:00 on the dot and volunteers to cook the hamburgers. Both of those things happening congruently is a pretty good indicator the world is coming to an end; so, while Alex mans the grill, and Ben prances Lazy around the pine trees, I pass baseball with Isaac and Tommy in the backyard. If this is the end, I'm having a little wholesome fun first.

Just as I'm about to call it quits, a car pulls in and out jumps Mrs. Textbook herself. I spin around in time to catch Isaac's modified curveball and yell to Alex who's on the side porch, "Visitor for you, dear!"

Alex glances up just as I throw the ball to him.

He flails his hands in front of his face and catches it. "Savvy, I wasn't even looking. Daggone, woman, if I hadn't . . . ."

"Oh, Savvy," Stacey says, tiptoeing through the grass in heels. "I'm not a visitor and I'm definitely not here to see that moron!" She flings her hand Alex's direction.

My arms remain flat to my sides while she wraps hers around me and says, "Lord, I've missed you, girlfriend!"

I can't make myself hug this woman—not right now. I have a lot of work to do before I forgive the woman who has the hole my man's sticking his dick in.

"Word has it you have a visitor all right—Casper's been spotted here," Stacey says, loosening her hold on me. "What in tarnation is going on with you, Sav?"

Alex strolls through the yard in his flip-flops and gives Stacey the proper hug I couldn't. "How you been? Haven't seen you in forever," Alex says exchanging a look with her that contradicts every word he just spoke. She was probably the "paperwork" he had to complete last night.

"I know. It's been forever," Stacey says. As she looks at my husband her eyes seem to twinkle like the tiniest Christmas lights. "We need to get together. We used to have such . . ." She glances over at Isaac who's now being led around the yard by Lazy and just out of earshot. "Such fucking awesome nights out. Remember when—"

Rain No Evil

"Hey, Stacey, I really got to get some things ready for school tomorrow," I say, walking toward the house. "I'll let you and Alex catch up."

I leave them both standing there gawking at my rude departure, but it's that or an all-out war and I don't have the energy for even a hair-pulling fight right now. Besides, I'm no better than she is. We're both white trash whores, but at least I'm aspiring to be a better person.

When I confront her—if I confront her—it won't be in front of my boys.

After Stacey leaves and dinner's over, Alex heads up to the shower—the boys and I to the basement. I toss in laundry while Timmy and Isaac gather Nerf bullets for their arsenal, preparing for the war that will break out as soon as I head upstairs.

Ben's pulling a blanket from the dresser for the rare school-night sleepover, and I'm tugging a sheet onto the bunk-bed mattress when I hear Aunt Klaire call, "Hellooo."

Well, shit! I am not entertaining her right now. She's got a lot of nerve to just barge in the house like this. "Ben, go tell Klaire that your dad's in the shower and then go tell him she's here."

Ben's back in a few seconds. "She's not there."

"Oh," I say, tossing Isaac a pillow. "Who was it?"

"No one," Ben says shrugging his shoulder. "Nobody's there."

The laundry basket in my arms falls to the floor and I run up the stairs, Ben on my heels. Sure enough—no one—and the side door into the kitchen is not only shut tight, it's locked.

As I run down the stairs, I trip over my feet and my shin slams into the last riser. I jump up and wave my finger through the air toward Tommy and Isaac like I'm lassoing them. "You hear Klaire come in the door and yell?"

They nod.

"What'd you hear her say?"

Isaac says, "Hellooo."

When he pronounces the "oo," with a drawl, I know he heard the same voice I did. I don't know what the hell is going on here now, but at least the water isn't spraying.

I can understand God letting a water spirit inside the house—even a demon—but surely God's not cruel enough to pit Alex's malevolent aunt against us.

Isaac's glancing toward the kitchen just as water shoots Tommy in the leg, soaking his PJs.

While Tommy's on tiptoe and flailing his arms like a ballerina, I hear the half-bath commode flush and Ben yell, "Awww, Mom!"

Who needs X-box anyway? I've got a water demon, a textbook hussy, and a ghost masquerading as Klaire.

I'll call Father Nick in the morning. My Santa in black better get his crucifix ready. We need a full-out exorcism.

I leave the boys shooting Nerf guns, totes piled high as shields, and hideout in my closet upstairs to decide what to do. Telling Alex about the voice or the commode won't make any of this chaos stop; so, I'll pretend, for now, that things here are sublime. Alex hasn't mentioned Stacey's visit or my abrupt departure from the reunion in the backyard. He probably knows to do so would be as dangerous as noodling for catfish.

Alex is my husband and as sick as it makes me to think of him, or any other man, touching me, I would rather feel sick than to feel nothing. I don't want to be numb to the torment—to what feels like the excruciating ripping apart of my internal organs. I have to feel all the emotions that accompany sex with Alex or anyone else. The emotions are invariably tied to my main organ, my heart, that wants to feel unconditional love—the love that childhood dreams are made of.

I have the pattern memorized. First I'll feel like an object, not a person, but a means for the male to get off. Then he'll start touching me and I'll start feeling special. Still an object—but a special object. As he's aroused I'll slowly become everything to him until I am all he can think about, and then he'll come and I'll be insignificant again.

The cycle is relentless, but at least it's a cycle and that means there's movement—and movement beats stagnation anytime. To stop moving is to die.

Alex is lying in our room watching *Sons of Anarchy* when I strut in dressed in nothing, but chaps and a black leather vest.

"Up for a Harley ride?" I say, bending over to display my ass in the chap windows.

I crawl across the bed till my long blonde curls dangle over his face. My breasts tease the vest snaps that linger open.

"What got into you?" he says, swiping my hair into a ponytail with his hands.

I'm not in the mood to talk—to explain why I'm doing what I'm doing. I just want to do it. If he pisses me off I'll stomp these red-hot heels right out of this room instead of wrapping them around his neck. He's going to have to think quick or this ride won't need a throttle.

I sit my bare ass on his belly.

"I like it," he says. "You gonna wear this on our next run?"

Good answer.

I grab his dick that's hard and poking my inner thigh.

That's more like it. Treat me like a stranger would.

Alex wraps his arm around my leg and flips me over onto my back, takes my face in his hands and says, "I love you."

Instantly, I feel special. The man touching me is not a stranger anymore. This is the man I promised to go gray with—to cherish for all my years. I want to feel this sacred to Alex all the time, but usually this Alex is a hermit with an obscure hole into which he crawls, hibernating till the conditions are to his liking.

The hermit enters me and time stands still. I promise to remember this feeling of connection to my hermit who I won't see again till the next squall is over.

As I look into the dark figure above me, one tear weaves its way across my cheek and onto my pillowcase—one more for my angel to add to my celestial jar that's overflowing with more than pennies or lightening bugs. It's chock-full of a sadness I wish I could set free like I used to the fireflies.

In the morning I'm shuffling Isaac and Tommy out the door to catch the school bus when water sprays me in the face. "I'm still here," it seems to say.

I slam the door and bark, "Screw you!"

"Who you talking to?" Ben says, walking toward the garage and munching on a sausage biscuit.

"I wish I knew," I say, dabbing my cheeks with a tissue.

Ben laughs. "You told the spirit 'Screw you.' I'm gonna tell Father Nick on you."

I snap my seatbelt and back down the drive. "Hey, if Father Nick were living here he'd be saying 'Screw you,' too. Damn demon's still here, but this thing is not going to win! Father said he will come back as often as we need him—that if the blessing didn't work, he'll come back and do an exorcism. You know what that means?"

"Heck, yeah! Are you serious? Like the *Exorcism of Emily Rose*? I didn't know they could do that to houses, too!" Ben says, excitedly.

"An exorcism can be done anywhere," I say, inching further away from my creepy house. "Anywhere there's evil."

During breakfast at school, I'm in the cafeteria that's buzzing with students not so eager to return after such a short spring break when I get a text from Stacey. She wants to go to the movies this weekend.

She doesn't know that I know she's another notch on Alex's gun-belt. I tell her Alex and I will be out with another couple that evening even though we don't really have plans.

Stacey responds that she misses me and our "just girls" times, strolling the mall or chatting at Panera.

I almost feel sorry for her. Almost.

I step into the faculty restroom and leave a message for Father on the machine at the rectory; that's what Father Nick called the church office. I don't tell him that his blessing didn't work. I don't want to offend him. I just ask him to call me.

Alex's going to be pissed that I bothered my new repairman with divine connections again, but I have to. I have to believe that Father Nick is my designated helper or I'll be joining the Bridge Jumpers Club or admitting myself to the ward where I can flap around pretending to be an airplane or a chicken laying a golden egg.

After lunch, as juniors trickle into my favorite English class, I'm at my post in the hallway when I overhear a student, Brandon, at his locker telling Terry, "My uncle said Zoey got her granddad killed."
"Hu hu how's that?" Terry asks.
Brandon removes his grungy baseball cap. "My uncle was friends with Hank and he said Hank knew Zoey was getting her smack off Cliff so Cliff probably wacked him."
The students know my husband's a cop, but if I act like I already know the scoop, they'll end up telling me what they think I already know. Terry and Brandon step past me and I ask them to hold up.
I open my door and shout over the bustle, "Bell-ringers!"
Stepping back into the hall, I notice three girls huddling by a locker and applying lip gloss. "Get a move on! You can primp later," I say. The tallest girl rolls her eyes and slams her locker shut with her middle finger predominantly high, but I'm not taking time to write that up right now. I've got enough paperwork.
I just yell, "Hey, Sabrina!" and when she turns around, my middle finger is scratching a spot on my head. "Hurry, on now," I say, smiling.
As I turn back to Brandon and Terry, I spot a couple making out in the niche by Mrs. Z's door. "Save it for the weekend," I say. "Just because Mrs. Z. has a sub doesn't mean you get to do whatever you want."
The boy drags his lips away from the girl's, and she skips into the room.
I lean toward Terry and Brandon. "Boys, look, not everyone knows about Zoey and Cliff," I say, not knowing who the heck Cliff is, let alone know that Hank had a beef with him. "The police are investigating the connection, but you know this could be just a rumor."
Terry sticks his hands into his worn jean pockets and shrugs.
"Yeah, but Mrs. Templeton, Cliff's a badass," Brandon says, shifting to one leg. "My uncle thinks he killed Hank. You know Cliff?"
I lie. "I've heard of him. Alex arrested him for domestic once, but everyone doesn't know that Zoey's grandpa, Hank, knew Zoey was getting drugs from Cliff.
"My uncle thinks Hank must have confronted him," Brandon says, "and that's when Cliff killed him."
"Maybe. It's just sad Hank had to die. You guys know him very well?"
Terry shakes his head and Brandon says, "Yeah, he'd come to our house a lot. Talk to my uncle."
"Zoey come, too?" I say.
Brandon says, "Nah, she was probably too busy getting stoned."
"Okay, boys, keep this under your hat. You don't want to get in the middle of a murder investigation; do you?"
"Heck nah nah no!" Terry stutters as they both head into the room, me

crossing the threshold right behind them to the one tiny area of the world I wield some control.

Today we join Edgar Allen Poe's character in *The Pit and the Pendulum* who must decide on death by falling into a pit or being scorched by burning walls as they enclose around him.

I'd rather be floating downriver with ole Tom and Huck, but the vessel of hate called the "Spanish Inquisition" is heralding my class to a port of desperation to which I can relate.

I'm not burning at the stake or spread eagle on a rack, but I feel bound and pulled in two directions. The love I have for Alex and the love I want for myself is competing—there's just not room for both. I can leave Alex and dive into the pit of the unknown or stick it out with him and no doubt, get burned. Neither option is enticing.

The class is watching a video clip of the history of the torture that was imposed by Pope Sixtus IV during the early 15th Century. The principal steps into my room and takes notes from a seat in the back.

Mr. Meyers, shirt soaked with sweat from the armpits to the front pocket on his shirt, jots notes as the class discusses how greed played into the church's murder frenzy. I know he always sweats this way, but it's still unnerving watching him sweat and scribble away.

"Isn't a church supposed to care about people no matter who they are?" Brandon asks as the video end. "Why'd they kill people?"

"Control, Brandon. The church wanted control. That's why people who were accused of heresy, or speaking against the church's beliefs, were killed. Then the accused's belongings were split between the church and the government." I write the word, "discrimination," on the board and ask for a volunteer to read it.

Courtney pronounces it correctly and I say, "The church is made up of people, Brandon. Just because some of the people in the Catholic Church discriminated and killed Jews, doesn't mean that all Catholics were bad people. Over the years various groups of people have been discriminated against—like the blacks in America—the Jews in Germany. But you know, for each bad thing that happens, or injustice, or unfairness, however you want to say it, there is good that comes from it—there are advocates. Who knows what an advocate is?"

Matt, who has rejoined class after a week's suspension, is painting his nails with a black Sharpie. "Matt, eyes up here. You can take care of your beauty needs at home."

The class snickers and he gives me a drop-dead look before slowly re-capping the marker. He's still not looking at the board—just scribbling on his notebook, but I can live with that.

Matt complied and Mr. Meyers will approve of how I handled that. He knows I rarely have discipline issues. I tell him it's because I care about the kids and they know it. The only time a student is getting kicked out of my room is if he's flat-out noncompliant.

I explain that an advocate is a person who supports a cause or supports someone who can't speak up for themselves, and I ask, "Who knows the famous person who advocated for black people's rights?"

"Oh," Terry shouts out. "Mah Mah Martin Luther King!"

"Yes! Great. And who helped hundreds of Jews escape the concentration camps?"

An awkward silent follows.

"Ok. Hint," I say. "You've seen the movie in history class. His name starts with an 'S' and he made a list of people he helped."

Sam, the quietest boy in class raises his hand. "Mrs. Templeton, I know. Schindler. It's *Schindler's List*. He sold his ring to pay for people and save them from the camps."

"Right, Sam. Schindler and MLK were advocates." A few students shuffle papers into book bags and sneak peeks at the clock on the wall. "Not yet," I say. "Class isn't over till I say it's over."

The student's look at me like an orangutan just ate their cell-phone.

"Tomorrow," I say, extending the lesson so there's not a second the kiddies aren't being instructed. Mr. Meyers would frown on even one minute of free time—especially, if he's writing a formal evaluation. "We will discuss how the church put Galileo through the inquisition because he had enough nerve to say the sun, not the Earth, is the center of the universe."

No reaction from my pouting class. "And discuss why the church burned thousands of books," I say.

"Cool," Matt says, pulling a plastic lighter from his jean pocket and holding it under his textbook.

Perfect. At least I got his attention, but I'm pretty sure that lighters are forbidden on school property. I glance at Mr. Meyers whose wrinkled forehead and puckered mouth tell me I'm right.

"Matt," I say, "give Mr. Meyers the lighter."

Matt huffs back and lays it on the principal's stack of papers.

The bell rings and I want to check in with Courtney—see if she's living with her mom or back with her dad, but Mr. Meyers strolls up to my desk as students rush out. "Very interesting lesson, Savannah. Stop in my office later."

"Yes, sir. I'll be in last period—planning."

"Good. It's important," my sweat-soaked supervisor says, stepping back as my next and last class of the day trickles in. I'd really like to shit, but hell, who has time for that? I figure I'm not the only teacher in public school who's constipated from the tight schedule.

Sounds like Meyers wants to talk about more than my routine observation—maybe he didn't like the controversial topic, but I know he approved my lesson plans.

I hastily call Alex and tell him Brandon's scoop about Cliff, but it's not a scoop to Alex. He had already interviewed Brandon's uncle because he was Hank's best friend, but the guy was afraid of this Cliff just like most everyone who knows him, so Brandon's uncle didn't provide enough information for probable cause to even call Cliff in for questioning.

During planning, I'm clomping through the hall on the way to Mr. Meyer's office, when my cell buzzes. I step into the faculty restroom to have a private conversation with Father Nick, whose number I'm more pleased to see than any other man in my contact list. The fact that I'd rather hear from him than a lover tells me I just might be able to grab onto those allusive morals I'm coveting.

Father says he can perform an exorcism of the house tomorrow evening. I hang up and say the word aloud to myself. "Exorcism. Exorcism."

I find Mr. Meyer on the phone in his office, but he motions me in. I close the door and sit while he tells a parent on the other end that their little angel had a gutted highlighter with Lortabs shoved in it. The eighth grader is suspended and on her way home with the PRO.

Mr. Meyers hangs up, wipes his brow with a hanky and says he's impressed by the participation he observed in my junior class.

I thank him. There has to be more.

Sweat beads are dotting his forehead again already. He sticks the end of a pen into his ear, wiggles it around and says, "A parent called the board office. Said you've been telling your students that there's a ghost in your room."

A laugh explodes from my mouth so fast that spit lands on the papers by Mr. Meyer's sweaty hand.

"Do what?" I say. "You're kidding!"

"I told the Superintendent that I would check out your class and talk to you."

I brace my hands on the edge of his desk closest to me. "Remember when I had to leave early one day last week to meet the repairmen at my house?"

He nods.

"I believe there's . . . I may have mentioned to the students that there's a spirit in my house—had nothing to do with my room here at school."

"I figured it had to do with your house," he says. "I've heard . . . well, Mrs. Z. had mentioned you had a priest there."

I bet she did.

"I appreciate her concern." I sit back. I don't want to be reprimanded for blending my personal life into my classroom. "And," I say, "I greatly appreciate your concern and discretion with this whole matter."

Mr. Meyers makes a note and says, "You know kids, Savannah, they are going to take a statement like that and contort it into a zillion fantasies. Just write up what you told me about the house repair. Leave out that you said anything to the students. I'll fax it to the Super—cover my butt."

"Absolutely," I say, getting up. "You're right. I'll take care of it. Thanks for being understanding." I hesitate, my hand on the doorknob. "My life got really complicated, really fast a few weeks ago. Feel like I'm treading water. I appreciate you not jumping to conclusions about the ghost."

A smile crosses his clammy cheeks. "I'm certainly glad I didn't see one."

At home, I'm dusting the living room when the kitchen door opens and a woman's voice says, "Hey."

"In here," I say, hoping there's a real person to accompany the voice this time.

Luce, a flowered bag slung over her shoulder, wisps in. "Thought I'd get your mind off of your crazy life!" she says, pulling out a hair-style magazine. "Look at this," she says, pointing to an up-do. "Perfect, don't you think?"

Everything from the upsweep at the nape of the neck to the tendrils framing the left-sided part, would complement Luce's exotic features. "Ah, Luce, the do is you!" I say. "What else you got in there?"

Luce empties her bag, strewing catalogs of cake designs alongside samples of embossed napkins and trendy guest favors.

I pick up a silver-monogrammed napkin. "Cool. This complements the turquoise centerpieces."

Luce smiles. "I've already ordered those," she says as water splatters the table, soaking a few catalogs, a fine mist settling on the entire table.

"Damn! Is that what you've been living with?" Luce says, covering the papers with her hands as if she expected water to spray again at any moment. "That scared the shit out of me!"

I get a dry dishtowel. "Yep and I'm sick of drying it up, but Father's coming tomorrow to do an exorcism," I say, dabbing the table as another spray hits Luce in the face.

"My God, Sav!" Luce says. "This is incredible—what the fuck's . . ."

Isaac wanders in and glances at the tux on the magazine cover. He wrinkles his nose. "Aunt Luce, do I have to wear one of those duck suits? Quack. Quack."

"Nah, you can just wear shorts," Luce says. "Shit, it's just a wedding."

Isaac busts out laughing. Isaac loves Luce cussing. Ever since she found out that cussing gets him to smile for a picture, she does it to mess with him.

"What's so funny?" Alex says.

I turn, startled to hear his voice. He's still in uniform and scouring the fridge already. Probably didn't get lunch today. "Isaac's wearing shorts to the wedding. He got Luce's official okay."

"I'm gonna wear my overalls," Alex says with a chuckle and strops down the basement stairs to remove the stiff green uniform.

Luce gathers her wedding paraphernalia, saying we need to leave so we can get to the bridal shop by 5:00.

"You still not inviting Mom?" I ask.

"Nope. It would just be plain awkward."

"True. What was it—ten years ago that she drove in for grandpa's funeral? I think that was the last time I saw her."

I grab my purse as Alex bops through the basement door, bumping into Luce who drops her bundle of papers.

Alex scoops one of the damp magazines from the floor and holds it at arm's length like he's holding a vial of the bubonic plague. "You sure you want to get married?"

Luce just smiles at him as I walk toward the door.

"Why these wet?" Alex says, shaking the one in his hand. "Thought your priest's visit was supposed to stop all this water shit."

"Don't worry, Alex," Luce says, snatching the magazine from his hand. "The priest is going to make another house call. Savvy is on the ball."

Alex smirks at me. "I told you it wouldn't work. That priest must be as crazy as you are."

I open the side door. "Got to get to the dress shop. We've—"

"Where you going?" Alex glares at me. I feel like I'm being accused of something underhanded and this time I'm really going where I say I am.

"I just said to the dress shop. We have to get fitted for our—"

"Guess there's no dinner." Alex raises his arms like he's expecting manna to pour from Heaven. "Mashed potatoes and steak would be too much to ask for," he says and gurgles out this evil laugh that makes me feel like I just gulped a flask of bleach.

Alex is his Aunt Klaire with a dick—a generous-sized one. I suppose that's my consolation prize for selling myself short.

Ben barrels through, chasing Isaac who has a guitar strapped across his chest. "Mashed potatoes? Sounds good," Ben says.

"Awesome!" Isaac says. "Mashed potatoes."

Now I feel guilty. Alex might expect the taters, but does he have to incite the kids to expect the damned potatoes too?

I want to vomit the bleach I swear I just drank.

"No, honey," I say, caressing the door handle like it's the pope's balls. I just wanted to enjoy my sister's wedding bliss since I don't know where my own eloped to. "Daddy was joking," I say. "He's going to fix you something. I'll fix you some mashed potatoes tomorrow, sweetie pie. Promise."

Alex rips the plastic off a frozen chicken entrée. "Luce, you going to be a good wife and have dinner ready every night?"

Luce looks at Alex like she sipping from the same bottle I am, walks past me and out the door.

I peer into the living room where the boys have settled into a show and let my gaze burn through Alex's head until feel a fire burning in mine.

I flick my tongue until I have enough spit to swallow and say, "Do you have to be such an asshole?"

I'm in the car before he has time to respond.

"Luce," I say, "I'm sorry. Alex thinks he's funny."

Luce starts the car and puts her hand on my knee. "Savvy, dear, I'm the one who's sorry. He's so hateful—always has been, but he's worse than he used to be. I don't know how you stand being around him. It's no wonder you have a damn spirit in your house. He is evil!"

So, Luce thinks Alex is not only mean, but evil? I recline and look out the window. I want to tell her I think it was me who let the evil in, not Alex, but that would require too much explanation.

I click my seatbelt. "He says I never cook and then when I do it's not good enough."

Luce punches the accelerator. "Sav, Alex is full of shit! I'm rarely at your house that you aren't cooking."

"I should make him some laxative-laced brownies!" I say, trying to sound impervious to the pain I'm feeling from his remarks. I'm not dampening my little sister's enthusiasm for marriage by divulging the extent of civil unrest brewing between Alex and me. Nothing she can do about it anyway. "I'm not telling him what time Father's coming tomorrow—or that he's performing an exorcism. Going to let it be a surprise. I'm not telling Dad either. I need to take care of this myself."

For the ten-minute trip Luce and I rant about teaching and rave about the latest purse styles—one of which I'm toting. Girl time with Luce is satisfying in a way that boner binges aren't. With Luce, I feel accepted and respectable.

Luce's two bridesmaids are already inside sipping on wine when we stroll into the boutique. As we shimmy into dresses, Luce chats with her friends and I feel a tinge of jealousy. Not because Luce has friends, but because I don't. I go through them faster than Dad and I do a pot of coffee—could have something to do the fact that they usually end up screwing my husband.

My social barometer is definitely out of whack, but I'm not sure I want it fixed. Being a loner makes it easier to pretend that I don't care if others like me. I can hide the real me from other people, but I'm realizing I can't hide from myself.

After the fitting, we all hit Cornerstone Quarry for a bite and secure the table close to the fire that licks the surrounding stones year-round. A young couple is sitting at the nearby table where Alex and I sat last week.

I watch the brunette bat her eyes and look away giggling as the man across from her reaches over and clasps her hand. She lifts her derriere and leans across the salsa and chips, her lips meeting his. Looks so simple—why can't I have that?

With flames flickering in the background and a long overdue raspberry daiquiri weighing down my hand, I permit myself to be whisked away to wedding fantasy land where caterers and florists reign—beats the hell out of plumbers and repairmen, floating eyeballs and demons.

Luce tells us which groomsmen will escort us down the aisle and when she gets to Logan, she pauses. "It's so sad," she says, "how Kerri left him like that. And I just can't believe she left the boys, too—all for a cowboy out in Utah who galloped her away on his white stallion."

Rain No Evil

Bridesmaid one says, "I heard she was living out there in one of those communes, you know, like the Mormons."

Luce's red-haired girlfriend says, "No, Kerri's not Mormon. She's far from that. Mrs. Zavitz, well, you know her, from your church, Savannah, she says Kerri has a . . ." She leans over so far that the candle in the middle of the table flickers from her breath. "*girlfriend* out there in Utah."

These are the kind of twisted stories people will probably be telling about me if I leave Alex—not that a girlfriend's a bad idea, although I haven't considered lip-locking a girl before. The point people miss amidst rumors is that everyone's trying to find happiness unless they already have it, and I'm sure Kerri's no different.

The decision to leave someone like Logan must have been difficult. He seems so sweet. Granted, I wish Kerri hadn't had sex with Alex during her quest for whatever she's searching for, but that happened years ago so she must still be searching. I'm seeking happiness, too, but I know that fucking her hubby in order to win sweet revenge really wouldn't feel so sweet. I'm sure I could get Logan in the sack, but I'd still be miserable and guilty.

I am, however, going to indulge the urge to catch a buzz right now. I wave the waitress down and ask for another daiquiri. Until tonight, I haven't had a drink in over five years, but tonight's a good night to fall off the wagon if ever there was one.

Luce glances around at the family beside us with the squalling kid. I guess she figures the adults are so occupied picking up every morsel the brat throws that they won't be eavesdropping on our lurid conversation. "Look," she says, "Logan told Jack that they've both been miserable for quite some time, but that he just couldn't leave her—said her leaving him might've been the best thing for both of them—that Kerri was stronger than he was for being the one to call it quits."

Maybe that's how Alex feels about me—maybe he's hoping I'll leave. Then it would be my fault the marriage didn't work, not his. I slurp through the whipping cream that's floating in the goblet the waitress just handed me and chug a long swallow of the liquid beneath.

If we split, rumors would generate no matter what the circumstances, but I don't want the truth to be that I left him for another man—if I leave Alex, it will be to find myself.

Bridesmaid one says, "Oh, but just look at what Kerri left. Hmmm . . . that Logan is a spectacle worthy of a billboard in Times Square for sure."

"Savvy," Luce says, scooping salsa onto a chip. "You're awful quiet. Something wrong?"

I'm thinking how shocked they would all look if I casually tell them that a few years ago Kerri screwed Alex and that perhaps she's just trying to be happy.

"No, just tired from everything going on at home," I say. "There's not a billboard big enough to illustrate the grand spectacle inside my house."

"Luce told me," the redhead says, coughing up a tortilla chip. "A ghost is spraying water inside your house. How fantastic!"

Each woman's gaze is locked on me. I permit the raspberry daiquiri to smooth my throat and then say, "Any phantom of mine would have to be fantastic, indeed!"

Chapter Twenty

DROWNING THE DEMON

When I get home about eight, Alex is conformed to the couch with one hand on the remote and the other holding his privates. Bet he'd jerk his hand out pretty quickly should Father Nick be visiting.

Hand-down-the- pants is a common practice by the men in this house, but tonight it strikes me that maybe I should try it—cup my special tea jar right here on the couch and keep rubbing it no matter who walks in.

Alex eyes me, gives the ole soldier one good squeeze as if to say, "Farewell. We shall finish this later," and pulls his hand up to his nose for a quick sniff.

And there it is—the reason married people don't look at each other the way single people look at each other—the reason I lock the bathroom door to keep Alex from sticking his dick in my face while I'm peeing—familiarity. Oh, and farts. Farts and familiarity can ruin the best of marriages.

I imagine Aunt Klaire's face should she be the lucky lady who had strolled in on the spectacle. The contrived image makes me laugh.

"What's so funny?" Alex says.

"Oh, just remembered something Luce said," I say, plopping onto the sofa beside my main squeeze. "You off tomorrow or do you have to work?"

"Huh?" Alex says, his hand sliding back under his boxers.

"You have to work tomorrow?"

Alex flips the channel. "I've told you fifteen times I have an overtime checkpoint tomorrow evening."

"Sorry, there's been a lot to keep up with lately." I peck him on the cheek. "Goodnight. I'm beat."

Alex says he will be up shortly so I play my timer game—face washed and lights out before he makes it off the couch. I'm not as slow as he thinks I am.

I'm asleep for what seems like a minute when I hear Isaac yelling, "Mom."

I'm in his room like I've been teleported there.

Isaac's sitting up in bed, covers pulled up to his chin and pointing to the corner of his room behind his door. "A black heartbeat," he says.

I look to where he's pointing like I'm actually going to see the heartbeat. Water's running down the wall.

"I threw holy water on it like the priest said," Isaac says, his eyes darting from the wall and back to me. "Then it turned into a circle. And a cross was in the middle."

I sit on the bed and hug him. I don't know what else to do. I rub his back and say, "You saw a heart? Like a valentine heart?

"No, heart*beat*," Isaac says, twisting out of my embrace and making an exaggerated V-shape with his index finger.

I hand him a tablet and a pencil from his desk. "Draw it."

He sketches zigzagged lines and says, "Like Grandma Lennie had at the hospital."

"Ohhh, like on the monitor grandma was hooked up to," I say, curling up closer to him. I didn't think he would remember seeing her before she died. He was barely six.

"Yeah, just like that. You know what else?" he says.

There's more? I shake my head.

"When I made the sign of the cross like the priest did, white—like white feathers—fell out of my fingers then disappeared!"

A black heartbeat had turned into a circle with a cross in the middle and something white fell from my son's fingers and disappeared, and I can't explain any of it to him. I wanted to know if God was real, but I sure didn't expect the answer to be an open invitation for an invisible water-slinging demon to camp out at my house with his entire posse.

God has to be testing me to see if I have enough faith to make it through this trial, and I'm going to prove to Him that I do. I'll sink with the ship before I cry mayday.

"Isaac, you know how different people are good at different things, like Tommy's really good at baseball and Tanner can't even hit a slow pitch, but if they're wrestling, Tanner pins Tommy to the mat in one round?"

Isaac nods.

"God gave people different spiritual gifts, too. Ben has a gift of prophesy—he knew there was a nail in the tire even though we couldn't see it. You have the gift of discernment. That means that you can tell the difference between bad spirits and good ones and that you see things other people can't see."

"Do you have a gift, Mom?" Isaac asks.

Rain No Evil

I rough his curly hair. "You and Ben are my gifts."

Isaac hunkers underneath the blanket giggling, and I sprawl across him tickling his sides through the quilt until he pops up for air.

"Sometimes," I say, "I see visions in my sleep that show me things that are going to happen."

"That's cool! Hey, see that cord," he says, pointing to the cord hanging from the vent in his ceiling. "I forgot to tell you, before you came in, it got longer." Isaac indicates a length that is practically to the floor. It would be impossible for the string to stretch that far—at least in this dimension.

"I tried to grab it and it got shorter," he says.

A laugh escapes me and the puzzled look on Isaac's face reminds me that humor, although the best medicine sometimes should be administered in private. Maybe ten years from now we can all laugh about this.

"Sorry, honey, I know you're serious." I snuggle up beside him until he's asleep, knowing that as soon as I slip out of his room, he will slip into Ben's.

Tucked into my own bed while Alex is still on the couch, probably playing with his private soldier, I write:

> Somehow I know I've prepared my whole life to tackle this trial by water.

My uninvited guest soaks my journal. I dry the page with the quilt and continue:

> I know this is a test and I have the ability to pass it. The spiritual lessons ingrained in me from childhood rivet me to my faith, even as I question the existence of the God I thought I knew and the God who surprises me anew everyday with the hurdles he's placing before me. If I lack faith, my family will be washed away—as lost as sand drug back into the ocean with the ebbing tide. I can't give up now and watch that happen even if Alex—even if the whole world—thinks I'm crazy.

Thursday afternoon when Father Nick pulls in on a wave of holy water and a prayer, Alex is on the couch with his hand down his skivvies again.

"Alex, we have company," I say, watching through the front room window as Father shuts the door to a blue Volkswagen I've not seen him drive.

Alex yanks his hand out of his underwear. "What? Who? Damn it!" he says, heading upstairs.

I smile as I head to the door, tickled to see him caught off-guard.

I ask Father if his car is broken down. He explains that he has an endless fleet of vehicles that are donated to the church from deceased parishioners and from wealthy, living ones. He hasn't bought a car since being ordained.

Alex lumbers into the kitchen, his eyes trialing up Father's pant leg until they meet the white collar at his neck. "Hello, uh, hi," Alex says. "Savvy didn't tell me you were coming."

I look at the floor. Couldn't he have a little social grace—just once?

Father Nick extends his hand, and Alex grasps it with the hand that was just fondling his penis.

"I promised Savannah we will get this taken care of," Father says, looking my way. "Want to start upstairs?"

I nod while Alex pours milk onto a bowl of Lucky Charms and sits at the table. He doesn't volunteer to participate in the ritual and that's fine by me.

If this works, I'll be wearing my own lucky charm in the shape of a Celtic cross.

Upstairs, I knock on Ben's door, and have him join Father and me in Isaac's room where I prompt Isaac to tell Father about the heartbeat and cross he saw on his wall last night.

Rubbing his smooth head, Father says, "Sounds like we're starting in the right room. Let's begin." He slips a round communion wafer from his shirt pocket and says, "This looks like bread and tastes like bread, but when placed in the mouth of a Christian believer, it becomes the actual body of Christ. We won't be consuming it today. I brought it because nothing evil can stay in the presence of the body of Christ."

I'm wondering why we need to even say a prayer. If evil can't remain where this magic wafer is then shouldn't the demon be gone already?

But I don't ask, I just grab the paper that Father's passing to me that says, "Prayer of Exorcism," at the top. I scan it for the "R," like we responded to during the blessing, but there is none. This Catholic prayer thing is confusing. I see the word "All" so I guess the boys and I are "All."

Ben steps beside me and peers at the prayer I'm holding.

Father Nick slides on his specs and begins the ritual by squirting a dab of holy water on each of us and invoking the trinity.

I trace the outline of a cross, hoping I touched the correct shoulder first.

Father raises a metal crucifix above his head, saying, "Behold the Cross of the Lord. Be scattered ye hostile powers and return not to this household."

After several variations of "Lord have mercy," Father prays for Archangel Michael to "defend us in battle."

Rain No Evil

The boys and I throw in "Amens," as prompted by the "All" on our papers. Father Nick prays. "Father, we come to you trusting in your Son's promise that whatever we ask of Thee in His name You will do. We approach Thy throne, unworthy, but trusting in Thy mercy. We request that You drive away any and all evil spirits who may infest this home. We ask that You send Thy holy angels to watch over this house and all who reside here.

"We ask You to cover these rooms and this property with the Blood of Thy Son, that You destroy all demonic strongholds and ground claimed in this place by Satan and his minions. We re-claim the ground taken by the Evil One and dedicate it to you Lord and to your Glory. We ask these things, Father, in the name of Thy Son, our Lord, Jesus Christ, who lives and reigns with You and the Holy Spirit, One God, forever and ever."

From my position at the foot of Isaac's bed I see water form in midair in the hallway and spray onto the ceiling with a *splat* in the exact location it first dropped on Ben's head.

My gaze darts to Father who's staring into the hall and rubbing his eyebrows that are as high as the arch in St. Louis.

"It's kind of like it said, Good-by," Isaac says.

"Father," I say, "it left in the same exact spot where the water first dripped. Is that a portal?"

Father tucks the consecrated host back into the tiny silver case and says, "Yes, there are doors here to worlds we cannot see. That must be one."

I'm impressed with Father's ability to accept he doesn't know everything. "So, what time is your Sunday service?" I ask as we descend the stairs. If this exorcism worked, I'll be there with so many bells on that they won't have to ring theirs.

"Mass at 9:30. You ever been to mass?" Father says, his hand bracing the rail as he maneuvers with his bum knee.

"Only with Grandma and Grandpa sometimes on Christmas Eve. They weren't Catholic though, and I didn't have a clue what was going on, but grandma said it was holy and beautiful."

We walk through the living room where Alex dredges up from the couch and shakes Father's hand. "Sorry, you had to make another trip here. Savvy's just . . . well, this water leak has gotten to her."

Father caresses Jesus' leg on the crucifix he's holding. "There's no earthly leak that sprays like that without a pipe being busted. Savannah is one sharp cookie. Better hold onto her."

Alex's cheeks turn crimson and he stammers, "Oh, glad you don't mind the inconvenience."

"Not at all. And I'd love to see you both at mass on Sunday," Father says, looking at me. "It can be confusing at first, but in short, you can kneel when we kneel. If you'd like, you may dip your fingers in the holy water font by the door, but only Catholics may partake of communion."

I walk through the kitchen with Father and extend a check toward him for $100.

"Oh, no," Father says, shaking his head.

"It's made out to the church," I say, holding the check in the air until Father accepts it. "I may see you Sunday." I can't imagine Alex going with me. He'll probably razz me about it if I go, but I'm going to start doing things that I want to do. I don't need Alex's approval in order to be happy.

Father is barely out the door when Alex nails me—how the entire community thinks I'm nuts and how I shouldn't have bothered the nice priest again who is just humoring me.

I pretend to listen, but I'm thinking that nothing he says is going to deter me from going to the Catholic Church where I just may embark on the first step on a journey to recover a version of myself that I actually like.

A priest just made our "water leak" disappear through the ceiling, and Alex hasn't even asked what Father did upstairs. I wonder if Alex will ever understand the significance of the last few weeks. I don't understand everything that's happened either, but I get the profound sense that this entire experience is going to radically change my life.

As Alex straps on his uniform for his overtime detail, I feign a headache that I've almost talked myself into having, and climb the golden staircase to solitude to write and to pray myself into a space where I feel good about myself—a space without Alex where just my breathing is enough to make me purr.

Later in the evening I'm on the commode in the half-bath when I hear a car pull in. I flush the commode that is now cooperating, even with Ben, and peek out the window where an empty, beat-up white Escort sits. I don't recognize it. Someone's knocking at the side door, and all I can see are jeans and tennis shoes.

Walking through the kitchen I glance at the steaming potatoes I was preparing to mash, per my promise to the boys, and open the door to a man with long, greasy dark hair who's sucking on a cigarette. He removes the cigarette, holding it to his side with dirt-laced fingertips, and coughs out, "Is, uh, Taze around?"

I'm not about to tell this dumbass that Alex isn't home. I keep my hand on the knob of the partially opened storm door and smile for pretense as much as for the sheer pleasure of meeting this character who, no doubt, I will soon be writing into my story,

"Taze can't come to the door right now. What's your name and I'll tell him you stopped by."

"Guess he's a lookin' for me," the man says. He swipes at the bangs that are stuck to his head and peeks up at me.

I try to exhale the disdain from my face.

"He, uh, well, he was a bangin' on my door a lil bit ago, and I didn't hear him," he stammers, managing to cough out a few hunks of smoke.

Keeping my foot propped on the door, I slip a tablet and pencil from the kitchen drawer. "What's your name and number?"

"Parker and my phone's not working, but he can call my neighbor." He rattles on while I write, "Yeah, he came by and I was a sleepin'. My neighbor told me jus' a little bit ago that he heard the bangin' and saw the policeman Templeton standin' thar."

"When's dinner?" Ben says, coming up from the basement. "And when's Dad gonna be . . ." I'm shaking my head, and giving Ben my bug-eyed stare so he retreats back to the playroom.

This Parker dude opens his mouth for round three, but I say, "Okay. I'll tell him," and shut the door.

I smile through the glass door while this crud is still talking, "Yep, I didn't want ole Taze to think I was ignoring him, no siree."

I lock the thick wooden door, snatch my cell from the counter and call Alex.

Alex is laughing when he answers. Before he gets the chance to say hello, I say, "Alex, some guy named Parker came here and says you're looking for him."

"What? You mean Cliff Parker is there at my house right now?"

"I don't know his first name—just said Parker," I say.

Alex yells, "Hey, Gilmore, that fucking piece of shit Parker is at my house!"

"He still there?" Alex shouts.

I run to the front room and slide open the drapes, squinting to make out the license tag. "Just pulled out," I say. "Heading north." My heart's beating so fast it's hard to think.

The sound of sirens race across the cell phone. "What's he driving?"

As I give the vehicle description to Alex, he relays it to dispatch. "This is C1. BOLO for a white Ford Escort heading Northbound in the direction of Ridgeland city limits. Partial license, West Virginia tags, E- echo, F- foxtrot, nine, four, eight. Alert MuddSock Police Department to cover the Ohio side of the bridge. Male driver is one Cliff Parker. Hold and detain. May be armed and dangerous."

The scanner in the kitchen is echoing Alex's voice throughout the house, and I hear the sirens, not only through the phone now, but from the two cruisers that are flying past the house as footsteps fly up the basement stairs.

I hear the echoing sound coming closer, and Ben rounds the corner with the scanner to his ear and Isaac on his heels.

"Which department, Mom?" Ben asks.

"Yes, your dad's one of them," I say, realizing I'm holding my cell that now has a dial tone.

The boys' eyes are so bright they could generate power for all of Wooten County.

"The guy they're after is the guy who just left our house." I say, feeling like I'm a drone just regurgitating information.

Ben squeals, "Awesome!" and runs out the front door and into the yard.

Isaac chases after him. "Wait up."

I collapse into a rocker on the porch.

Ben grabs a pillar and hoists himself from the ground onto the front porch. "Mom, they got him!"

"That was fast," I say as the boys huddle around my chair.

The radio dispatcher says, "Car is being detained by the MuddSock Heights City Police."

Isaac's eyes are blinking faster than our Christmas lights twinkle. "I can't believe that guy was just here!"

"Yeah and I saw him!" Ben says.

Yes, indeed. The armed and dangerous guy had just been talking to me. Just my luck, a demon leaves and a criminal shows up the same day. Thank God I hadn't let Parker inside. I think Alex called him Cliff. Where did I just hear about . . . oh, yes, at school. Brandon and Terry. They said someone named Cliff might have killed Hank.

While Ben monitors the scanner, I call in a pizza. Forget the freaking hamburgers.

I shoot Joanne a text telling her Cliff Parker showed up at my door and ask if she knows him.

She tells me that Cliff is Steven Hopper's mom's boyfriend. Joanne is worried because Cliff and Steven aren't getting along.

"Steven? Are we talking about Zoey's friend, Steven?" I text.

Joanne answers, "Yes. Last week there was a big fight between Cliff and Steven's mom. Cliff's always beating on her and this time she ended up with a broken nose. Steven jumped in to protect her and Cliff smashed Steven's phone with a hammer. I'm afraid for Steven."

While the boys catch lightning bugs, I curl my legs to my chest and think about Hank's murder.

If Hank knew his granddaughter, Zoey, got drugs from Cliff, and if Hank and Cliff had an altercation, Cliff could have killed Hank. And since Cliff's beating Steven Hopper's mom and giving Zoey drugs, Steven, who is friends with Zoey, might know that Cliff murdered Hank. Steven might want Cliff to get caught for the murder so that Cliff will stop beating up Steven's mom. If that's the case, Steven might have written the note that was in my mailbox!

It seems so obvious but, surely it can't be that simple.

Ten minutes later, I'm at the side door paying the pizza delivery guy for salvation in a box when Ben runs in, radio blaring: "C1 Control. I'm transporting Mr. Parker to the office for driving suspended. Can you get a hold of Red's Wrecker service—have his car towed? It'll be in front of the Dairy Queen in MuddSock Heights."

The dispatcher responds, "10-4, C1. Will do."

I wink at Ben, "Bet you wish you were at DQ with Pawpaw Cal to watch all the action."

I mash the cold potatoes and pop them in the microwave. Potatoes and pizza. Like grandma said—all things in moderation.

Rain No Evil

Since Parker isn't a threat anymore, I tell the boys I'm going jogging. It's me and Mother Nature tonight, no hamster treadmill for me.

"Boys, I say, "these taters better be gone when I get back. Not even a crumb left."

Ben scrunches his nose.

"A crumb?" Isaac says, giggling.

"Yes, a crumb. I just wanted to see if you were listening," I say, smiling and feeling satisfied in knowing they were. I'm realizing that I really want to be heard and recognizing what I want is a positive start to the new me.

I hit MuddSock Height's newest renovation—the paved walking path along the river that winds from the levy parking lot to a few benches in a park a few miles to the north.

As I jog, I pray for the God who I now know does hear me, to tell me what my purpose is. Surely, there's got to be a reason I was sent to this earth.

The smell of fish blows in on the cool evening breeze, bringing with it the quacking of ducks and the sound of waves lapping the rocks from the barge humming by. A peace washes over me. I feel a strength inside. My gut is telling me I co-created my purpose before I was even born. The audacity of me to think I may have input, not only into my future, but into my past—that I could have helped design the blueprint for my life—frightens and excites me.

If I inspired the problems that I would face here on Earth that means I probably developed various solutions to them, too, and I want to find a way to tap into the knowledge that may already lie dormant within me. The possibility that I have a real mission here makes me feel empowered.

When I dared God to prove he exists, He removed His protection, permitting a demon to enter my house. Maybe my purpose is to write a book about the experience.

I realize I'm half a mile past my usual turn-around, so I heel-toe a U-turn and continue embracing my epiphany.

Ever since I could read, I've enjoyed writing, and I'm good at it, but the follow-by-number essays I had to write in school choked the life out of the characters I wanted to breathe into. Now, though, I don't have to sculpt a neatly organized 3x5 that addresses a specific topic.

I can write any old way I choose—end my sentences with prepositions—start sentences with "but." No matter how quirky my style may be, it's no more eccentric than I am, and I want to share my wacky experience with the world even if the way it's written doesn't comply with the typical non-fiction genre.

With each step I take along the river, I become more passionate about the idea. My first novel is writing itself—the subject, my real life, is unfolding with every neuron that's fired. All I have to do is put it into words.

The words I write will be words Alex won't want to hear. He may not read my book anyway, but if he'd have listened the first few thousand times I tried to reach his soul with my words, the story of my life would be very different indeed. Without my desperate prayer, I may have remained ignorant as to the power of the Almighty.

I'm almost back to where I parked my car when I hear a horn beep. I turn, and in the dusk, get a glimpse of a hand waving from a truck that's pulling in beside me. The person turns down the Blake Shelton tune blasting on the radio and leans out the window.

I wish I had strapped on my mace like Dad's always telling me. He even bought me a tiny one I can strap to my wrist.

I slow to a trot and stay on the path under the lights until I'm a few feet from him. It's Logan.

"Hey, Sav." he says. "Missed you at the book club meeting."

"Oh, I'm sorry, I had dinner with Luce and the bridesmaids," I say, hoping I can talk with Logan and be as strong and true to myself as I felt just moments ago.

Logan pats the passenger's seat. "You up for a ride? I'd sure like to talk to you."

I swipe the sweat from my forehead and glance up the road. Visibility is poor so no one would notice me if I rode along. I can lend him an ear—as long as that's all I'm lending.

"Sure," I say. "Just a short ride. Got the boys at home." I round the truck and hop in. "How you doing?"

Logan drives a few feet and pulls off slowly. "Mind if we just park?"

I nod and swivel in my seat to face him.

"It's been tough, Savvy," Logan says. "I mean I love Kerri and I want her to be happy. It's just . . . I know she's not happy with me. Marriage changes things, you know. We barely see each other with my work schedule and the kid's ballgames. I just got my preaching license. I was hoping we could work things out, have my own church eventually, but now . . ."

I put my hand on his arm. "I'm sorry you're hurting," I say. "Marriage isn't what I thought it'd be either."

Logan turns to face me. There's something behind these hazel eyes that are looking at me—more than a message that says *I wanna fuck you.*

A few strands of his hair are dangling over his cheekbone, and I wonder what it'd be like to nuzzle my cheek next to his, but I can't. I want to stop this vicious cycle of fuck 'em and dump 'em.

Logan's hand is now laying on my hand that's still resting on his arm. "I'm comfortable with you, Savannah," he says, "in a way I'm not usually comfortable with a woman. You're different."

"Oh, I'm different all right!" I say, feeling proud of my quirky self.

"Don't think I'm prying, but . . ." Logan rubs his jaw with his free hand. "I've heard you and Alex are having problems. That true?"

I squirm my hand out from under Logan's. "It's complicated," I say, "but, yes, we've *always* had problems."

"Alex thinks everyone around here just loves him," Logan says, his hand going to my leg that's bare below the hem of my running shorts. "Sure, some of the thugs he arrests tell him to his face that they respect him, and he may naïve enough to believe that, but even the elite members of the community think he's a dick. No one knows how you've stayed with him as long as you have."

I sigh and take the liberty of adjusting the air conditioning to cold. "Alex is a good-hearted guy," I say, wondering why I'm defending him. "He loves his job—maybe too much. He's overbearing and obnoxious, but I love him."

I feel Logan brushing my leg. I want to stop him, but it feels so nice and tender that . . . "Logan," I say in a whisper. "Screwing around with me won't heal anything with you and Kerri. Trust me. I've tried that and . . . it's just . . ."

His arms wrap around me, and he squeezes my shoulder into his chest. I sink into his embrace, accepting his affection. This feels better than any orgasm I've ever had.

After what seems like forever, Logan releases his hold on me and touches my lip with his finger.

The image of Father Nick blazing through my yard, leading the prayer procession that just might save my marriage and my soul, makes me pull back.

Logan brushes my cheek with the back of his hand. "What a wise woman you are. I'd probably be kicking myself in the butt tomorrow."

"You have a friend here if you need me," I say, jumping out of the truck and thinking that as soon as Alex says something nasty to me, I may be kicking *my* butt.

"I'll drive you back to your car, girl," he says, waving me back in, but I wink at him and say, "Believe me, I need some fresh air."

I turn to walk to my car and hear someone growl. I jerk my head around, but Logan's window is up and he's already backing up. Either some creep's out here or . . . I take off running to my car, afraid to think that a demon could be lurking.

I'm safely inside my car when I hear a growl from the backseat. I jump out, screaming. I run to the busy gas station on the corner and look back at my car, the front door hanging open. There's no movement from inside.

There has to be a demon stalking me—first Ryan's house—then Ted's office and Joe's apartment—now the car. It's following me!

Is it a different demon than the one that was at the house?

I stand, shaking under the lamppost in the store parking lot. "Oh, God," I pray, "Please, please protect from this demon. I'm changing—I really am changing my life." I walk toward the river. "I believe that You gave me this experience to help me change—to help me to believe, not only in You, but in myself. God, I'm not giving up now. Please don't give up on me."

It's a silent night at the house —not a spirit is stirring. I think the water demon really is gone. I'm not sure if the figure dressed in black that busted the tire is the same demon that was spraying the water, but I hope they're all gone. I wonder if

I should cancel tomorrow's appointment with the energy healer, Jenn. She may notice I have a bad spirit with me, and I don't want to her to think Mandy's nuts to be my friend. Besides, Jenn will probably just refer me to a priest.

But, I don't want to tell Father Nick that an evil spirit's been following me! Sure, he's bound to rules of confidentiality, but I don't trust anyone to not spill the beans if they're tasty enough. All of Wooten County will find out. Even if Father sends it back to Hell where it belongs, the community will always wonder if evil's still on my trail. The stigma of evil will be branded on me and my family.

Maybe I should keep my appointment with Jenn. Her office is out of town so my very personal problems will be, too. She said I need a reconnection to the Almighty. I'm going to surprise her. I need a disconnection, too—from an angel of darkness.

About one a.m. I hear the kitchen cabinet bang shut. Alex is home from his jaunt to the county jail with Cliff Parker. I stumble downstairs where Alex is kicked back in the recliner with a bowl resting on his belly.

"Guess you got out of the boring traffic detail," I say, sitting on the couch.

"Parker was driving suspended so he'll be in the slammer overnight," Alex says. "Can't believe he came here. Dumb fuck. While I had him detained, I questioned him about the murder—even though I wasn't supposed to. I told him Stranahan was in the next room interviewing a snitch about the drug trade going down between him and that girl, Zoey. But he is one tough son of a bitch!" Alex points the TV remote into the air like it's a weapon. "He didn't even flinch when I jabbed the butt of the gun into his rib."

"So someone was brave enough squeal on Parker's drug dealing?"

"No, Sav, good grief," Alex says, milk dribbling down his chin. "There wasn't *really* a snitch there. That's just what I told Parker to get him to talk."

"What'd he say about Zoey?"

"He said he knows her and knew Hank, but he wouldn't admit to selling drugs to her or having anything to do with Hank's murder. Said his girlfriend's boy, Steven, is friends with Zoey. He didn't tell us that before."

"That's what I was going to tell you," I say, my fingers tap-dancing through the air. Joanne told me how Parker is dating Steven Hopper's mom. Steven's friends with Zoey and he doesn't get along with Parker because Parker beats up Steven's mom . . ."

Alex is engrossed in the milk in his bowl that's splashing near the edge.

"Go on," he says, munching. "I'm not retarded. I can eat and listen at the same time even if you can't."

I'm above this. "I squirm toward Alex and squeeze his leg. He cocks his head and squints down at me like he's wondering what I'm up to.

"So," I go on, "if Steven knows Cliff had something to do with Hank's murder, he could have been the one who wrote the letter."

"Hell, Savannah, anyone could have written the letter."

"True, but Steven had a good motive for wanting Parker to get caught. If

Parker goes to jail for murder, he'll be out of Steven's mom's life and out of Steven's house."

Alex is silent. I'll let it simmer. He used to appreciate my observations—used to say that Savvy was the perfect name for me because I was clever. I still feel clever—especially when I'm around the denseness of him.

I never feel this awkward with any other men. I don't know how to relax with Alex and just be me. When I'm honest about how I feel or what I think, he ridicules me.

I've tried creating my own reality—tried telling myself that Alex respects me and listens to me, but the reality is he doesn't—and maybe I can only manifest the life I want with a willing participant.

The news is announcing lead stories, and I ask if he's coming to bed, but he says he's to be too wired to sleep.

"You don't have to sleep," I say tracing his bare leg with my fingers, trying to connect with him the only way I know works.

He stares at images in the black box mounted above the fireplace, his choice activity when his brain needs numbing.

Me—I want to defrost mine. I'm tired of living numb.

I hop up and scamper to bed. Alex's not interested now; I won't be available later.

I marinade in the dryness of my bed, hoping that evil will soon be indelibly trimmed from my family tree, and congratulating myself for resisting the temptation of reaching out to Logan who was dangling within reach, ripe and ready to be picked.

Chapter
Twenty One

A Genie in
a Basement

B randon's the first one through the door fifth period. "Mrs. Templeton," he says, "you think the police are gonna arrest my uncle?"

Brandon looks as worried as he was after Mr. Feldman caught him smoking in the boys' locker-room last year.

"I don't know. Why? Did you hear something?"

Courtney strolls in and slings her book-bag under a desk. I ask her to stand outside the door and have the other students wait there.

When Courtney walks out, Brandon says, "My uncle says your husband didn't believe him when he talked to him right after Hank died, and he's afraid that Taze'll interview him again. My uncle's scared of Cliff. Everybody is."

Brandon spreads his hands on the edge of my desk and leans in. "Mrs. Templeton, I don't want my uncle to go to jail for lying about knowing Cliff. He doesn't know anything anyway—just rumors. I don't want Cliff to hurt him either."

"Alex didn't tell me if he's going to interview your uncle, but Cliff spent last night in jail. Alex arrested him for driving suspended, but . . ." I look at Brandon's distraught face and want to relieve his fear. "Alex doesn't want your uncle. He wants Cliff," I say, winking at Brandon.

I step into the hall to summon my students who are waiting, and Mrs. Z. motions me over.

Mrs. Z. plumps her short hair and says, "Mr. Meyers said he spoke to you about the ghost story you told your class. He said he'd mentioned that I told him about the spirit at your house and . . . well, I didn't want you to think I was spreading rumors."

"Of course not," I say. "I figured you were just looking out for my best interest."

"Absolutely, and always will." She adjusts the tight waistband of her skirt. "I'll never forget the time Alex helped us when the grandkids' four-wheelers were stolen. Alex found them and the weasels who took them."

She continues over the ringing bell, "And helped my husband out of that speeding ticket. God bless—"

"Don't want to be tardy," I say, zipping across the hall and wondering if anyone would ever talk to me if my husband didn't wield the power of the shield.

The secretary buzzes my room seventh period and tells me I'm needed in the office. I grab a tablet and a pen thinking I'll need to document a disgruntled parent who feels that their little angel isn't getting enough time to get their notes copied or their homework done. I waltz into the office, scanning for the sour-faced parent, but only see a set of very familiar, flirtatious eyes staring back.

The man behind them hustles up and shakes my hand. "Hello again, Mrs. Templeton. I was hoping to catch you on your planning."

I bet he was. His hand has already lingered on mine too long, so I snatch it away and stick my hands in my pants pockets. I don't know what to say to this man. I can't even remember his damn name.

"If you have a few minutes . . ." his voice drones on. I'm not sure what he's saying, but I could probably write the script. He has it all planned. He even remembered my planning is last period. I could also write the scene about what happens once we get to my room . . . and the one after that where I feel miserable and defeated.

"I'm sorry," I say, "I have a meeting in a few minutes." I catch the secretary's glance. She's either wondering who she's going to have to sign in for the meeting I'm referring to or she's checking this dude out for herself. "I have a phone conference shortly so today won't work for me, but thanks for stopping by."

As I open the door to the hallway, he hand's me his card and says, "Oh, sure, I understand. You can contact me at your convenience," and darts toward the door.

Walking toward my room, I feel the hint of satisfaction oozing through my blood even though I lied about the phone conference. At least I lied for a good reason.

Rain No Evil

First I turn Logan away last night and now this . . . I search the card in my hand for his name . . . Marcus. His name was Marcus and knowing that makes me feel the teeniest bit better about our previous encounter.

Saying *no* never felt so good. Now I need to keep saying no to things and people who aren't helping me to cultivate genuine happiness in my life.

Minutes later, I call Alex as I'm speeding toward Bloomingdale. I remind him that I have a doctor's appointment right after school and will be back in time for Jack's graduation dinner at seven.

This Jenn will have to be one hell of a genie in order to make any seeds I've planted sprout into a magic beanstalk.

As I park by Jenn's white picket fence, I notice a wicker angel standing guard in her front window and a ceramic green leprechaun heralding to me from the flowerpot by the door, even though St. Patrick's Day was weeks ago.

Jenn opens her side door, her whole body radiating a warmth that seems familiar, yet foreign at the same time. She's practically glowing as she leads me down the stairs to her basement office. Jenn sits at her desk, violet skirt flowing to the floor, and indicates for me to sit in the rocking chair across from her.

A funky looking tapestry of the sun hangs on the wall behind her and a Buddha sculpture sits beside a brass cat knick-knack that's waving at me from the corner of her desk.

Then Jenn smiles at me.

Just sits there smiling at me, her azure eyes glowing with a knowing and a kindness I'm trying to recognize. This lady seems familiar, yet I know we haven't met.

I'm not sure what to say. Seems she wants me to start this conversation so I do. I tell her how I think I caused an evil spirit to enter my house—maybe because I've lied and cheated, but mostly because I dared God to prove to me He was real. Regardless, a demon had been in my house spraying water all over me and my family and Father Nick had just exorcised it.

I tell her I think a bad spirit might be attached to me and how I think it's growling at me.

Jenn's eyes haven't left mine since I started talking. She must not need to take notes like an ordinary counselor and her cozy quarters lacks the cliché leather pout couch. This lady is eclectic for sure and she knows I know it. I can tell she's got a read on me.

She tells me I'm intuitive and that I "get a lot of good hits."

I tell her I used to listen to my higher-self, but think I muted my consciousness when I started prostituting my values, opting for a more oblivious perception, and that I'm here now because I want to align myself to my life's purpose whatever that may be, however scary the transition. I tell her I'm thirty-six years old and if I'm not ready now, I never will be.

If I expect her to help me improve my life I have to be honest with this lady.

I tell her that poor me is so unhappy. I justify my adultery by explaining how awful Alex treats me and how he's had other women, too. I want her to feel sorry for me so I throw in how my mom ran off with a preacher when I was a teen, leaving me and little Luce motherless.

Jenn hasn't interrupted me once. I'm sure I've rambled on—I don't easily recognize when it's appropriate to stop talking. It's not a skill I've needed much since Alex always cuts me off before I'm done anyway. At school the students listen, but my class is a structured environment, and I'm more comfortable talking with them than I am with an adult.

I take a breath and say, "So, is that all you need to know?" as if she can just hand me a *Fix Your Life* tonic and send me on my way.

Her hands brush through her butter-colored hair, and she licks her glossy lips. "We are all on this journey to learn, Savannah, and we all make mistakes along the way—sometimes we learn from them, sometimes we don't. When we don't, the universe has a way of bringing the challenges back around so we get another chance to learn the lessons."

There's no condemnation in her voice. Where's the "You need to be sorry for what you've done" sermon or the "You're-going-for-a-visit-with-Beelzebub" rail? I worm my rear back further into the seat cushion and say, "Karma is for real?"

Jenn nods and places her hands together, fingertip-to-fingertip, mimicking the crystal pyramid prominently holding its place on the front of her desk. "You understand that once we do this reconnection your life will change. Not overnight. Within a year usually. Are you prepared for the change?"

I feel like I've been here before—like I've returned home after a wayward journey through the foothills of Appalachia where I lost the conglomeration of cells that I was born with, collected them, and brought them to Jenn to help me fuse together. I know Jenn is my last chance to ascend from this pit I've thrown myself into—I can't escape without help, and she's got the ladder.

Jenn's eyes pierce to my soul. "It is often a dramatic change."

I clasp my hands and lay them on my lap. "Any change has to be an improvement," I say, laughing. Not because it's funny, but because I don't want her to know how much I'm depending on her guidance in this sun-starved forest where Alex's words—my own words—are strangling me like weeds wrapped around a gooseberry plant.

"That will depend on the decisions you make—how truthful you are with yourself.'"

She's smiling with those gorgeous, glowing eyes again. I can't be mad—she's right. I do have decisions to make—the most important being whether or not to stay married to the man I love, or leave him so I can love myself.

"I was faithful for a few years. My marriage wasn't any better then . . . we were nicer to each other for a period." I look down to my shiny red toenails feeling like a whore. "I've been with Alex since high school and I love him," I say, but even as the words come out, I know that Jenn knows divorce is in the cards—that is, if I have the courage to be honest with myself.

"Even then I didn't feel close to him," I say. "Alex is very demanding and unrealistic. The last big fight we had was because he expected me to hold a whole piece of drywall above my head by myself. I mean, I work out, but really? Then he got mad because I dropped it."

"How did you respond to his anger?" Jenn asks.

"Told him to fuck off, and then went and fucked Ryan," I say, realizing how silly it sounds for me to blame Alex for how I handled *his* anger. "I guess I just need to work on me first, and if I fix me, maybe I can fix my marriage."

Jenn stands and bustles toward an open door at the far end of the room. "Let's get to work then."

Maybe there's one of those damn couches after all.

I follow her into a small room where the only light is from a lamp on a dresser. Shadows pattern the wall beside bottles housed in cabinets and lining shelves. The bed is like the one at my doctor's office, except this one has gingham flannel sheets and a plump pillow.

"You can take your shoes off and lie on your back. The pillow is for under your knees, not for your head," Jenn says, walking toward a cabinet in the corner. "We tend to stuff emotions and traumas inside our physical bodies. Detrimental thoughts lead to disease and ailments of all sorts. I'll be helping you heal feelings you've held onto like guilt and sadness."

I slide off my shoes while Jenn inserts a CD into a player. The room is much warmer than the room we were just in so I pull my hair into a ponytail. The palliative music relaxes me—best I can gather, it's a mix of Gregorian chants and the soothing music they play at the spa where I get massages.

"We really stuff bad emotions inside our bodies like stuffing in a turkey?" I say, positioning myself on the bed.

Jenn giggles. "Sure do," she says, sitting on a swivel stool. "I'll be working on your energy field, placing my hands just above your body. You may feel warm or tingly or any number of other sensations throughout your body while I'm working on you. If you're uncomfortable at any time, just let me know. Okay?"

I nod and Jenn places my right hand on my bellybutton. She wedges her left hand under my sacrum while making loops in the air with her right hand. She's either writing a message or trying to lasso a calf.

Neither would make any sense to me, but I'm not asking her what she's doing. I know a cowboy and a beer sound good to me right now. This is weird. Maybe Alex *should* have me committed.

I'm wondering what the heck I was thinking by coming here when Jenn says, "Oh, and there are angels here who help me. You can pray while I work on you if you'd like." Her right hand is now hovering over my right hand that's still on my stomach.

Pray she says? I picture Father Nick waving his hand through the air outlining an invisible cross over his chest as if he's a symphony conductor and suddenly, I make the connection between Jenn's gestures in this house and Father's gestures in mine.

Both Jenn and Father form invisible symbols with their hands to represent the faith flowing through them, unseen, into a world they each, in their own way, are enlightening and healing. Both seem confident they are communicating with a higher power. The rituals are different, but faith unites the unlikely spiritual pair who, no doubt, have been divinely placed in my life.

Think I'll take Jenn up on that prayer suggestion. I spin a silent prayer: "Guardian angel, if ever I needed you, I need you now. I know you can hear me, and I believe you can help me to heal the brokenness I feel. Please protect me from anything not of God that may be here. I sense only good here with this lady. Jenn doesn't seem evil, but sometimes evil is disguised as good. Just help me to know the difference."

Slowly, Jenn brushes her hand from my shoulder to the end of my fingertips. She repeats this several times, and then rolls behind my head in her chair, placing her hands just close enough that I feel I have static in my hair.

I feel a little woozy, but I don't dare tell Jenn. I don't want her to stop. I want this to work.

She continues down the left side of my body. My face and hands tingle, my bowels rumble, and if I didn't know better, I'd swear someone pinched my leg. I close my eyes. A white haze floats past and a golden light flashes. There's spirits here all right. I just hope they're good ones.

After about an hour, Jenn's to my right and writing in the air again. This time as she makes her last squiggle, she flattens her hand above my belly, lowering and raising it several times as if she's tamping an invisible cork in so all the good she did won't leak out. "Now, when you sit up, you may feel dizzy or weak so take it slow."

I prop onto an elbow and turn to disembark, but my elbow buckles and Jenn grabs my arm. "Easy."

Braced against her, I slide off the bed and let my feet hit the floor. I hope whatever I'm reconnecting to is stronger than I'm feeling.

"Savannah," Jenn says, as I'm sliding on my shoes, "you said you like to work-out. You can think of these sessions like a routine that'll make you sore, but builds toward your ultimate goal—strength."

"That," I say, ascending from what I feel was a consultation with my personal oracle, "I can do."

On the way home I stop at the supermarket to buy a card for Jack. As I scan the registers and see Joe isn't working, a feeling of sadness comes over me. I want to cry, but I'm not sure why—it's not like I want to hook-up with him again. I try to define the feeling and the only word that comes to mind is "empathy." I feel sorry for Joe because he was searching for a connection—for some sort of happiness with me just like I was with him.

One thing's for sure, I have more to be happy about right now than the past demon-filled weeks. Sure, Alex nailing my supposed best friend isn't a cheery vision, but I have to believe that Alex is seeking something with his other women that he can't find with me. I can't blame him for trying to find happiness—even though I wish he didn't treat me like he hates me in the process.

Plucking my feet that seem cobwebbed to the supermarket floor, I choose the lady cashier with the frizzy black hair and hurry home to freshen up for dinner.

Alex is in the car, beeping the horn and prodding me along, but his ferocious beeping only slows me to a trot. I can only live in this moment—my now and right now I'm going to avoid any situation that will make me feel bad about myself. I'm not hurrying just to please Alex.

Turkey with the fixings at Bob Evans, coupled with the opportunity to chronicle his glory days to an enthralled audience, is the most valuable gift I could think of to give Dad for his birthday. With Jack, the new officer in the family, we have a table of seven. Alex doesn't flinch when I order two monster chocolate chip cookies for an appetizer even as the waitress is laying menus on the table. I know the value of sugar, and he knows the value of keeping peace in public.

I initiate the party with a story of a music-playing ghost who serenaded Mom, Luce, and me with "Amazing Grace," one night while Dad was working his beat in MuddSock Heights. The tune had broken the silence of the winter evening, spiraling through the staircase to our rooms where we all three lay half-asleep. Luce and I stepped from our rooms at the same time Mom emerged from hers.

As we converged in the hallway at the top of the stairs, waiting for confirmation that what we were hearing was real, I realized Mom couldn't have just turned the record on downstairs—she'd been in her room. Luce hung onto the sleeve of Mom's green fuzzy robe while I peered over the banister into a dark, empty hallway.

The music stopped and we heard the sound of paper crinkling, so Mom, one arm around Luce, one around me, led us into her bedroom and called Dad and Grandpa. Five minutes later, Grandpa was at the door, and Dad was screeching into the driveway, lights and sirens. Dad searched the first floor while Grandpa coaxed us downstairs where we found the song we'd heard, "Amazing Grace," on the turntable. Mom and I laughed—that is until Dad pointed out the power button to the stereo was off.

Ben and Isaac gobble up the last of the crumbled cookie without taking their eyes off me. Jack is nudging Luce and saying how she's never told him that ghost story when I feel a tap on my left shoulder. I jerk around, my arm bumping the gray haired waitress who's balancing a tray of drinks.

I hear a giggle to my right. "Hey, Mrs. Tah Tah Templeton," says a familiar voice.

I twist to see Terry. "Always playing tricks. That's going to cost you—think I'll have you clean all the desks Monday. You already get something good to eat or you just getting here?"

He rubs his belly and smiles, "Oh, I ate too mah mah much kah kah catfish and mashed taters." He steps closer and leans on the back of my chair.

Michele Savaunah Zirkle Marcum

I nod to the waitress who's been waiting for my order. "I'm going to have the catfish, too. Green beans. No taters."

"You gah gah get the go go ghost out of your house?"

"Hope so," I say, glancing at Alex and faking a laugh, knowing I have to downplay the comment or he'll be pissed. He'd be livid if he knew that I told my students and had to file a formal response to the allegations with the board of education. "Things good with you?"

"Mom's hoe hoe home." He laughs—his is probably fake, too.

"Enjoy your weekend, Terry," I say, steering clear of the confidential conversation. "You can fill me in Monday."

I wad the paper straw cover Isaac just blew my direction and toss it at his nose.

Our granny waitress is back already, her hair pulled tight in a bun like Mrs. Clause. She reaches around me and slides a basket of banana nut bread to the table center.

As Terry mock-salutes me from the door, Alex says, "You know how crazy you sound admitting to people you have a ghost in your house?"

"Savannah," the Mrs. Clause look-alike asks, "if you don't mind me asking, well, I heard about the ghost. Is it true?"

The waitress knows my name? I study her face and realize she goes to the early service at Pastor Todd's church. I want to tell the truth about my house spirit, but I'm definitely not dropping the word *exorcism*, especially with Alex present.

I take a swig of water to buy a few seconds, my gaze tracing Isaac and Ben's faces across from me. I know there was an evil spirit in our house and to lie about it in the presence of my boys, or of anyone for that matter, is like denying the entire experience—and I'm not denying my truth anymore.

"I'm sorry," I say. "I didn't recognize you Ms. Hunt. Yes, we had a spirit in our house. Father Nick . . ." *She's going to wonder why I've got a priest involved and not Pastor Todd.*

Alex looks up from his cell, squinting at me like he's getting a root canal without Novocain.

"Todd told me to call Father Nick because he has experience with this sort of thing. Father just came to the house yesterday. Seems it's gone."

Mrs. Hunt, holding the pitcher of water over Dad's glass and says, "My, oh my. I thought it was hearsay. You know how Ridgeland's rumor mill is."

Knowing I'm the centerpiece for many of the ones circulating in it, I smooth my hand over my shirt, letting it rest on my belly where Jenn tamped something good inside. I have the power to focus on the positive. "I sure do know about rumors, Mrs. Hunt, but would you bring me a coffee please—black."

I turning to Dad. "It's about time to plan the annual camping trip to Camp Coraltown; isn't it?"

The boys instantly start jabbering about the past Mothman hunts they've

266

went on during these outings, and Dad spouts off a few possible dates that might work.

When Isaac asks Jack if he's going on the annual guy trip this year, I turn to Alex and ask what his plans are for tomorrow.

Alex says he's helping Keagan lay tile in his bathroom, and the boys are going with him to ride four-wheelers over Keagan's fifteen country acres.

I'm relieved I won't need to make up an excuse for my morning trip to Bloomingdale for round two with someone who just may be an angel who can help me earn my own halo.

At 9:00 a.m. I'm standing at Jenn's side door, ready for the second phase toward true transformation when the clinking of wind chimes waft to me from somewhere around back. The sound that symbolizes change to me, makes me think Grandma Lennie may have been instrumental in leading me to Jenn. Grandma would like her. I whisper to my heavenly departed, "Yes, Grandma, my change is coming."

Jenn had instructed me to come on in if it the door's cracked and it is, but I hesitate. I feel like I'm entering her holy space. It's her house, not a church, I tell myself, but I'm compelled to bow my head and enter with reverence for the grace she so easily extended to me yesterday.

As I step inside and onto the landing by the steps leading down to her office, Jenn appears in the entrance to her personal living area, her aura illuminated more than it was yesterday.

Right then I know I want to look like that, too. I want to glow—I want to shine with love the way she does.

If I have to feel sore before I can exude peace and confidence like Jenn, I'm willing to participate in this alternative form of healing that I don't understand—I'm willing to give up men . . . well, maybe.

Her blue eyes crinkle at the corners as she smiles, and she waits for me to say something.

"Hi," I say. "How are you?" Okay, that was a stupid question. She's great damn it—she's the one treating me.

"Good. And how are you?" Jenn follows behind me down the stairs to her office and shoos a stoic white cat off the rocker before I sit.

"Fine. I just want to feel good about myself again—feel respected."

An odd smell vaguely reminiscent of marijuana prompts me to peer into a dish on the table to my left where smoke is rising from a bundle of sticks with celon-colored leaves.

"What's this you're burning?"

Jenn curls her tongue over her front teeth. "It's sage. It clears the area of negative energy."

Sure. Why not. No stranger than her balancing my invisible electrical currents and writing mysterious messages in midair.

Jenn adjusts the tiny golden lamp on the chain dangling from her neck. "Respect comes from within. The most important person who needs to respect you—is you."

That's going to take a lot more than a few visits here. If she can really help me to like me again, the hour trip to get here will be worth driving every daggone week.

I have more questions than she's got time to answer so I settle on one. "So, how's this reconnection work?"

"The body has acupuncture lines that were designed to connect with the earth's grid lines, uniting us with the entire universe. Over time the lines get disconnected and messages from the God-power become muddled, making it difficult to feel complete, to be true to ourselves and make decisions that are life-enhancing."

"Do you see the lines?" I ask.

Jenn leans back in her chair. "Not always. I usually sense them on a spiritual level."

"So you create new lines between me and God?"

"Yes, between you and the Divine—the source of love and grace—so you can heal," she says, as she motions for me to follow her to the therapy room.

Same protocol as yesterday—I remove my shoes and lie on the bed, gathering my hair to one side of my neck while Jenn sits on her rolling stool and writes in the air. Jenn's hand has been touching me only a few seconds, and already I'm feeling warm all over. My toes are tingling like the pins-and-needles sensation they get when I sit on them too long.

I scan the wall to my left, noticing printed symbols on posters. The swirls and zigzag symbols resemble hieroglyphics. These could be the symbols she's forming in the air above me.

Jenn's meditation melody playing in the background lulls me to semi-consciousness. With her hands above my cranium, the inside of my head feels like it's being tossed in a clothes dryer. Tumbling advances to spinning so I open my eyes and focus on a long shadow on the ceiling.

"Are you okay?" Jenn says, sliding away from my head and to my left. She places her hand on my arm, her glazed-over eyes looking down at me. She really cares. I can tell.

I'm tingling from my earlobes to my toes. I feel like I've slammed three Amaretto Sours. My head is dancing drunk, but I say, "Yep. Fine."

She must think I'm such a frail little thing, but I'm tougher than I look, and I'm going to prove it—to me—to Alex—to the whole damn world. I'm going to endure this spinning sensation and get healed.

Jenn moves her hands slowly down my left arm, extending her reach several inches past my fingertips like she's sweeping me with a whisk broom. She repeats this numerous times before brushing her hand just above my physical body from my hip bone to beyond the tips of my toes.

Rain No Evil

There's a shadow on the ceiling directly above me. As I soften my gaze, focusing on it, a ghastly, charcoaled, demon face appears and the shadow's perimeters jut out, streaking to the corners of the room. I blink and the shadow is a normal shadow again.

I wonder if Jenn saw that! But I don't ask. She probably sees spirits all the time.

Jenn is to my right tamping me closed like a good surgeon. I close my eyes letting my head feel heavy and secure. I think of all the beds I've been in—from silk sheets to nubby cotton ones that reeked of the sweat from the couples who had rented the room before me. I think of all the positions I've struck in those beds—all the emotions I've felt from the encounters—from sensual and desired to sad and remorseful.

How appropriate that I'd be healed in a bed by a lady who calls God the Divine. I'm thankful for her even though the changes she promised haven't manifested yet.

Jenn is going to teach me how to change my life for the better. Like Ben's premonitions, I don't know how I know this—I just do.

Pastor Todd would say substituting a term like *The Divine* for *God* is sacrilegious, but God *is* divine and it's obvious that Jenn respects His power. There's no way this lady's evil—darkness couldn't possibly illuminate a room like she does.

"How're you feeling?" Jenn's standing to my right and smiling down at me

"A little tired," I say. Might as well be honest. She can read my mind anyway.

Jenn extends her hand, helping me up. "Take it easy the next few days. Give your body time to adjust to the new alignment and connection you have with the universe. Just focus on living your truth."

I slip on my shoes and assure her I will. She wants me to come back next Saturday for a follow-up session to listen to a self-reliance meditation while she balances my chakras, but its Luce's wedding so I schedule the appointment for the following Saturday.

I beat Alex home and have the whole dry house to myself. Standing in the kitchen in quiet amazement, I absorb the fact that water is not spraying me.

Then it hits me—I actually kind of miss Casper's counter-ego. He gave me something to think about other than my deteriorating relationship with Alex. The evil presence captured my attention, made me focus on the spiritual aspects of life and for that I'm grateful.

I owe the water demon for alerting me to the ominous path I was on and forcing me to forge a new one kind of like Moses did when he parted the Red Sea. I only wish I'd been given a cool rod like he had so I could always clear my path.

I relax into my recliner and log into my laptop, feeling compelled to share this story about a not-so-friendly Casper and his cronies who visited my house—about a priest who sent them packing—and about a lady with divine light who, on the most guilt-free bed, I've ever lain, realigned my energy with the God source.

I'm writing in my journal, "I've went from lovers' beds of shame to Jenn's bed of hope," when Alex comes in the door.

"Sav, you home?"

"Yeah," I say, closing my notebook. "In here."

"Dad's going through drill bits like Doritos on Super Bowl day," Alex says, clicking the scanner on in the kitchen. "Came home to get more and grab a bite. Where you been?"

"Took a drive. Needed to get energized," I say, inspired by the truth I'm already speaking as much as I'm impressed with Alex's creative simile using Doritos. "I've got chicken in the oven. Should be done. The boys with you?"

"No, they stayed at Dad's I got to go back anyway and finish up. Just going to eat oatmeal and toast."

"You want to eat at the roadhouse tonight?" I say, setting a tub of butter on the counter. "Maybe go to the movies?"

He shrugs as he pumps soap into his hand over the sink.

"Mandy's still in and I thought . . ."

Alex has his finger in "just a minute" stance as he listens to the radio dispatcher giving directions to a house alarm call. "Okay. Go ahead."

"Mandy's going back home tomorrow. I've only seen her once all week. Thought we could double date. I know you don't know her boyfriend, but—"

"Sure, I don't care," Alex says, snagging a bowl out of the cabinet. "Whatever you wanna do." He tears open the hot cereal packet while I pop bread into the toaster.

Working quietly together like this is nice, but awkward. I feel like this bubble of serenity will burst any moment, liquid anger spraying everywhere.

I'd like to tell him about my experience a Jenn's, but I don't want to have to defend what I think or how I feel about the alternative treatment she offers.

"I'll see if the boys can hang with Dad tonight, and we can pick them up on the way back from the movies." I place a spoon and brown sugar beside the warm bowl of oatmeal and join him at the table even though I'm not eating. "Notice anything?" I say, my smiling eyes prompting Alex to scan me from head to toe.

"What?" he says.

"Something's missing," I say, spreading my arms wide like I'm Mary Lou Retton winning Olympic gold.

Alex scoops oatmeal into his mouth. "You know I can't ever tell when you get your hair cut."

"I didn't," I say, pointing to the table we're sitting at and the wall where our wedding picture hangs in its proper place.

"Oh, yeah, the table's not covered with plastic anymore," Alex says, laughing.

"It's like it never even happened," I say, expecting God to say, "Psych," and water to douse me any minute. "I've been writing about it. Wouldn't it be cool if I could get the story published?"

"Heck, Sav, just because that kinda shit might be real, doesn't mean I want everyone to know."

"But, the prayer Father Nick said made it leave . . ." I hesitate, expecting Alex to interrupt me, but he's just slathering jelly on his toast. "That means there's a lot of power behind him and I'd like to tap into that. I mean, can you imagine the faith he must have to be able to command a spirit to leave?" I interlace my fingers and pop a few knuckles. "I think I'll go to mass tomorrow."

Alex peers up at me from under a bushy eyebrow. "What time'd he say?"

"Nine thirty."

"I'll go," Alex says.

No way—he's going to the Catholic Church!

Alex gathers his bowl and kisses me on the forehead.

I pull my head back and look straight into his eyes. Somewhere in there is the person I married. He seems to sense my earnestness and bends farther allowing his lips to touch mine before turning toward the door.

As Alex pulls out, I tie on my tennis shoes. I want to get in a jog before my date with my husband who just may love me enough to make the change I need.

At 6:00 we meet Mandy and her beau at a packed roadhouse where dishes clank and customers chatter tenaciously in an attempt to be heard above Bruce Springsteen's "Baby, I was born to run . . ."

For the first time in a long time I don't feel like running away . . . from Alex . . . from my life. As we reach the table, I scoot into the booth beside Alex, feeling more "me" than I have since I can't remember when.

I breathe in the symphony of smells—the steak—the apple pie. I feel comforted and I'm not quite sure why. I relish the commotion of customers ordering and babies crying and the bell dinging every time the front door opens. Then I realize it is normalcy I get a whiff of, and there's not a distinct smell for that.

After we eat, I suggest we watch *The Exorcism of Emily Rose*.

"Hell no," Alex says.

Mandy winks at me. "We'll stick with *Wedding Crashers*."

And *Wedding Crashers* it is as we pile into the back row at the theater, me sitting beside Mandy, our men to either side.

Mandy's man lays his arm tenderly around her shoulders and whispers something in her ear, motivating me to place my arm on Alex's leg.

His quad is one hard muscle, not the only one I admire.

As the actors jump from one mess into another on-screen, Alex takes my hand, and I notice how tiny mine looks enveloped by his. He kisses my hand, and I feel a fresh beginning is taking root.

By the end of the movie, I'm optimistic that relationships do evolve as a result of hardships just like the characters in the imitation of life on the big screen.

Maybe Alex's and mine can, too.

At home, the boys scurry up to bed and I snap open the cabinet, making sure Pop Tarts are handy for the horn-blowing breakfast bash in the morning. Alex detests being late. On his scale of sinfulness, being late to a church is the eighth deadliest one.

In bed, I pull the quilt over my chilly bare legs and trace an "S" on Alex's chest with my finger. I stay quiet. Talking is where our problems start.

I lick his nipple, and a dab of drool slips onto his ribs, but he doesn't seem to mind my slobbers. His belly feels soft and slightly clammy against my right cheek as I wiggle down his body until I locate the McAlex Happy Meal with a prize grander than a trinket.

Rising between the most elevated cliffs in MuddSock Heights, a majestic stone steeple seems to strive to reach the heavens. As Alex, the boys and I round the corner to the oldest church in the area, the sun glistens through the trees, and I imagine it's winking at me as if it knew I would end up here eventually.

God knows everything—or at least that's what I was taught growing up. That never made sense to me then—how God could know the choices we will make before we make them. It still doesn't ring true, but I am beginning to understand that I will have to be content *not* knowing how the universal mystery called God, functions.

What I *do* know, as much as a human can know anything, is that there are forces at work in this world that I may only glimpse now and again. They can show up when I least expect them to or when called upon, and both forces, light and dark, serve a purpose. Both are a necessary component of the lessons I have been sent here to learn.

Delving into that darkness has led me to the light.

Just as I pull my lipstick out of my purse, I glimpse movement from my right. A little girl with brown curls and a yellow sundress is streaking across the road.

I scream. The car lurches to a stop.

"Damn!" Alex says. "You scared me to death, woman!"

A young man closes in behind the girl and swoops her into his arms.

I remove my hand from the dash and return the man's wave of thanks for yielding to the spunky toddler. Again, I wonder why I'm always saving babies.

Alex maneuvers into a parking space close to the door, which is easy to find since we are twenty minutes early. I fiddle in my purse buying a few seconds of freedom before entering the doors where I know everyone will inspect us—the visitors who had Father Nick exorcise their house.

I approach the boys and Alex who are waiting on me by the gothic wooden doors, Isaac squirming as Alex straightens his tie. Embedded in stone by the entrance is a plaque that reads: *Established 1808.*

That's two centuries worth of confessions and "Lord have mercies." I wonder if my family gets extra points for having the only exorcism.

In the foyer, I plunge my hands into the font of holy water until it reaches my knuckles. I'm tempted to submerge my entire hand when Alex slides his hand to the small of my back, nudging me forward. Guess I get to decide where we sit.

I lead my men into the sanctuary, noticing that most people are doing what appears to be a lunge in the aisle before they step into their pews. In the heels I'm wearing, I decide I'm not testing my balance and ending up face-first in front of these strangers.

Choosing a short pew against the far left wall for Alex and me, I direct Ben and Isaac to sit directly in front of us. This arrangement makes it much easier to shoulder-poke the boys when they slump.

The kneeler creaks as I unlatch it, drawing it to the floor. Kneeling—now, that I can do! While Alex and the boys sit on the pine seat, I bow my head, replicating the others who are resting on their knees.

There's no music or talking. A silent reverence seems to emanate from the congregation of people who are all dipping into holy water, signing the cross, or kneeling and bowing. The somber mood seems to permeate the ethers and float out the steeple as an oblation.

As I pray for God to saturate my pores with the peace I feel in this moment, I peek to my right where a prim older lady clutching rosary beads, sits swaying on her pew and mouthing a silent prayer. I return to my prayer, adding a request for Alex and the boys to be protected from evil and for cooperation and understanding to abound in our family.

The sound of organ music startles me from silent repose. I hear rustling in the surrounding seats so I slide onto the bench behind me, and laying my hand on Alex's knee, inhale a melody of Murphy's Oil Soap and incense.

A couple with five children shuffles past us and to the front just as something jars my pew. A mousy blonde-haired gentleman in gray dress pants and a plaid shirt is gripping Alex's side of the pew.

Alex asks him if he's okay, and the man responds, "Tough getting old." The old geezer reeks of alcohol and the smell destroys the bouquet of holiness I was enjoying. He stumbles forward and drags himself into the pew behind the lady with the rosary beads just as everyone stands and opens their hymnals.

I turn slightly so I can watch the entire spectacle. A tall man displaying a huge maroon book high above his head, steps forward from the entrance, followed by a young lady holding a gold cross and two robe-adorned teenagers with flickering candles. The caboose is Father Nick who's singing robustly from a hymnal partly covered by the dangling sleeves of his green robe.

They proceed toward the alter and when the choir stops singing, Father climbs the steps. The tall man places the book on the lectern while the girl places the cross on the alter table where the teens have positioned the candles.

The organ pipes fade, and Father greets his flock with, "Good Morning."

"Good Morning, Father," everyone responds.

I'm impressed. Getting students to answer my prompting in class this concisely would make me "Teacher of the Year."

I open the book everyone is looking in, but there's more than songs inside, and I can't figure out what page the man at the podium is reading from. Dad always said, "Always act as if you know what you're doing, even if you don't." So, I continue looking at the page I'm on.

A gentleman reads from Psalms about how only a fool says in his heart, there is no God.

I'm entranced, like God is speaking directly to me. Maybe there are no coincidences in life—it's all orchestrated by a higher being who provides clues—like a scavenger hunt that leads us through this maze and into the open field of freedom where we surrender to the light that is pure.

We remain standing as petitions are read for the sick and deprived people of the world.

We sit and another reading follows—this time about demons being cast into swine. I feel like God is confirming that I'm supposed to be here. Sure, scriptures are supposed to speak to the masses, but how many people in this building recently dared God to prove He is real and has seen a demon in their mirror?

The choir sings "I will raise you up on the last day," as long-handled baskets are extended through the pews by ushers.

I ponder the *raising up* that I've been told about since I was young—the rapture and how God will burst through the clouds on a white horse and people who are forgiven of their sins, been baptized and received the Holy Spirit, will fly to meet Him.

Until now I've never thought of the raising up as being any different than that scenario, but maybe the rapture is simply our ascension to a higher consciousness. Maybe we can access that particle of God within us by repairing our damaged connections and fusing them to the energy grid God created—like Jenn did mine.

We stand and three long "Hallelujah's" later Father makes his way, to the podium and reads from Luke. "Ask, and it will be given to you. Seek and you will find. Knock and it will be opened to you."

Father motions for the crowd to sit and he continues. "The word 'faith' is not used in this passage, but it's implied. We must have faith that God will provide what we ask for. Being too specific with your prayers inhibits the breakthroughs you want in your life. Always ask for God's will to be done even as you seek and ask."

I'm relieved that Father is interpreting the scripture without once screaming or gasping like the preachers I grew up listening to. Dad's probably at his church right now where his preacher is saying something like, "I'mma gonna tell ya, the world is ah ending. One sin, my brothers and sisters, will send you straight into that fiery pit where there's gnashing and grinding of teeth!"

Even after Mom eloped with the preacher, Dad's faith seemed unshaken, unlike mine.

Rain No Evil

Maybe I had affairs to experience what Mom did—so I could understand what type of love could propel a person to leave their family. But I don't want to leave mine.

I lay my hand on Alex's arm, thankful he is with me in this holy place, and thankful that Father was brave enough to wage spiritual warfare against our unseen enemy.

Ben's so low in his seat that he looks as short as Isaac so I give him a poke.

Father wraps up his speech. "Just like the Holy Spirit descended on John in the form of a dove, so too, will He descend into our hearts if we welcome Him."

Everyone stands and reads a creed—everyone except Ben and Isaac and the drunk guy whose head is drooping like a weeping willow. This dude will miss communion, but he doesn't need any more alcohol anyway. He's already had enough to save his whole family.

During communion, I inspect the stone engraving above the stained glass window beside me that depicts Jesus with a halo of light emanating around His head. I wonder if the white aura signifying enlightenment is the symbol of the same wisdom and goodness—from the same one God—as is the halos surrounding other religious figures such as Buddha. If so, then all religions may herald an element of the truth.

I want to continue paralleling the various religions, but the processional for dismissal is marching with Father trailing the group.

As the congregation disperses, I recognize the rosary lady as a co-worker from the bank where I used to work before I started teaching. She steps into the aisle and, as if we didn't have years to catch up on, asks if my house is quiet now.

I want Alex and the boys to feel as comfortable here as I do so I answer generically with, "Yes, thanks to Father."

As we pass by Father Nick who's stationed by the front door, he heartily shakes the boys' hands before taking Alex's.

Father points his finger at Isaac and says, "When you need more holy water, young man, you know where to find it."

Isaac loosens his necktie and says, "Yeah, thanks."

As we pull out of the parking lot, Ben says, "Wow! That was weird!"

"And long," Alex adds.

"I enjoyed it though," I say, turning down the radio Alex has tuned to the baseball game. "How 'bout you, Alex? You think you'd like to go back?"

"Maybe, hey, look at that rainbow!" Alex exclaims as we approach the bridge leading into wild, wonderful West Virginia.

"Cool. It's a double one," Ben says.

The arches of color bend over the bridge and seem to end on the roof of our house. I hope it's a sign that this church is the answer Alex and I need to mend our marriage.

"Breathtaking," I say. "I've never noticed that the colors of the rainbow are the same as our chakras."

"Chalk can be any color, Mom," Isaac says.

"Oh, your mom's talking voodoo hoodoo stuff, Isaac," Alex says. "Don't pay any attention to her."

"Maybe the pot of gold is on our porch," I say, figuring I may as well say something as kooky as Alex expects me to.

"Now that's the most witty thing you've said in a decade," Alex says, turning into the drive.

"Maybe it's the first time you've actually listened to me in a decade," I say, clutching my purse, ready to hop out as soon as this contraption stops and vowing to explain our body's energy centers to the boys privately so Alex can't interrupt.

I want Ben and Isaac to be willing to consider the profuse mysteries of life, even if they never understand them, and that will require more abstract thinking and less sarcasm than they are learning from their dad.

Alex pulls into the garage, and Ben says, "I'm starving. How long before dinner's ready, Mom?"

"About fifteen minutes. I put the dinner in the oven before we left. I didn't know service would be this long. Hope it's not burnt," I say, rushing into the house and yanking open the oven door, relieved to see a barely crisp meatloaf.

Alex flips on the TV and announces, "Rocky is on!"

Isaac traipses upstairs and Ben plops on the couch beside his dad.

I add a slab of butter into the instant potatoes I'm stirring and dunk my memory into sweeter times—into the squeal of grandma's mixer accompanied by her gentle prodding, "Make sure you warm up the milk before you add it to the potatoes, Savvy."

There would have been no instant mashed potatoes on Grandma Lennie's table. No indeed.

I can almost hear grandma's screen door bang shut and little Benjamin giggling as he gets chased by the Cookie Monster, played by his Aunt Luce while Dad and Alex discuss how to repair Alex's most recently purchased vehicle.

Grandpa Happy would be watching the televised golf match in his leather recliner, the arms of which were worn and dingy from the abuse over the years, but he wouldn't hear of anyone buying him a new one. "The chair has my mark," he would say. "It's like a pair of shoes—it's more comfortable with every passing year."

I turn off the mixer and walk into the living room. "Dinner's ready," I say, but Alex and Ben are riveted on the boxing story they've seen a dozen times, and neither bats an eyelash.

"Dinner's ready." I say louder.

Alex rattles his head like he's been stung by a bee. "Huh?"

"Isaac, dinner's ready," I shout from the bottom of the staircase.

Isaac appears on the top landing and says he's not hungry.

I tell him he can warm it up later, and I head to the fill my plate.

"Where's Isaac?" Alex says, shoving off the couch as Ben heads to the kitchen.

"He's eating later. Says he's not hungry," I say.

"Bullshit," Alex says, strutting to the steps. "Isaac, get your butt down here and eat."

"I'm not hungry," Isaac responds.

"I said now!" Alex says.

"I said I am not hungry!" Isaac says.

"You're so hard-headed!" Alex screams, from his stance near the stairs. "You better get down here!"

Alex screams are so loud I brace myself against the kitchen counter, preparing to run to Isaac's aid should I need to.

Ben is holding an empty plate and staring at me.

Isaac rushes past me and into the half-bath, saying, "I'm *just* not hungry."

Alex's voice trails behind. "You're a smart-ass. That's all. My dad would have knocked the shit out of me if I back-talked him like that."

Alex turns the doorknob to the bathroom, but my smart boy has locked it.

Rocky's on TV telling Adrian, "It isn't about how hard you get hit—it's about how hard you can get hit and keep moving."

Good advice, I think, jostling through the study and wondering how far I will get before Alex knocks me down, but I have to stop this before it escalates.

"Let's just eat. He can eat later," I say, returning to the kitchen and spooning baked beans onto Ben's plate.

"You *would* take up for him," Alex says, banging on the door where Isaac has barricaded himself.

I just want Alex to stop yelling and trying to make people obey his every command. I know Isaac is a kid and he has to have rules, but why is it such a big deal to Alex if Isaac isn't hungry?

The answer is control—the one thing Alex can't handle losing to others and the one thing he has absolutely none of over himself.

Alex is rattling the bathroom door handle now and insisting Isaac opens the door. I hear the door open and Alex telling Isaac to get in the kitchen, but Isaac says he's going to his room.

Alex screams, "Get your smart-ass back here right now!"

Someone runs up the steps and a door slams—must be Isaac because Alex steps into the kitchen, his face the color of the hell-fire I'm trying to avoid. "You don't ever support me. You can't be the kid's friend. You're supposed to be a parent!"

Ben says, "Isaac always has to be difficult."

I can't really be here. This can't really be my life—my mind has blistered to the popping point.

I've become an observer to my own body, as the meatloaf in my hands flies through the air and crashes onto the floor in the living room. I feel like what was left of my rational mind just exploded with the food. The area rug is splattered with the grease, chunks of meat and sprays of ketchup that accompany the marbles that just blew out of my head.

I'm paralyzed. My mind feels like a surface, sanded, and prepped for a Salvador Dali painting of melted time—time that's draped like cheese over the human landscape. My eyes are glued to the beauty of my anger that is displayed on the floor like the finest tapestry that has taken years to create.

I didn't realize I had the potential for such artwork. The dish was out of my hands in a flash just like time—time we don't see disappearing—until it's gone.

Alex sounds like the teacher on Charlie Brown. *"Wah Wah Wah."* It's as if a metal barrel covers my head. He's screaming something about me being a lunatic.

I catch a glimpse of Isaac running past me and out the door, but I'm not sure if what I'm seeing is real or imagined. Maybe everything I'm seeing is a dream. I find myself outside by the garage with my arm around Isaac as he sobs.

I'm expecting Alex to come ranting toward us any moment. If he does I swear he'll have to kill me before he lays a hand on this child. Isaac doesn't deserve a spanking.

I tell Isaac that what happened isn't his fault and I'll have Pawpaw Cal pick him up—that he can stay over there today so he can get away from his dad. I leave Isaac leaning against the garage and go inside to get my phone.

I don't know where Ben is, but I should talk to him. Maybe he should go to Dad's, too.

Alex is standing in the middle of the living room with his arms crossed watching Lazy scarf up the mess. Alex looks at me, his eyes speaking a silent message of disbelief and, possibly, a dab of fear. He looks like he just finished running the Boston Marathon, but I don't feel sorry for him. I'm exhausted, too.

I shoot an invisible arrow through his heart. I want to put him out of his misery because if he's out of his, I'll be out of mine.

I grab my phone and am outside with Isaac and talking with Dad on the phone, when Alex and Ben hop in the truck and peel out. Probably headed to a drive-thru for food.

While Isaac grabs his shoes, I scope the living room where the only indication that anything happened is the splotches staining the carpet. I get ticked at the boys for tracking in grass on the carpet; yet, here I am throwing greasy meatloaf on it.

To a stranger this could have been the result of a simple accident and it was an accident—sort of. I didn't *plan* on throwing it.

I just know that the lady whose hands just threw a flaming hot meatloaf through her house, purposefully or not, will never be the same.

I'm not quite sure who that lady is, but she's a part of me that is a survivor. She isn't afraid to make a mess—it might just turn out to be a beautiful masterpiece of a mess.

She isn't afraid to venture out on her own because the thing that scares her the most is living with the monster she is married to . . . is living like this . . . existing like this . . . growing old and gray with a miserable man who obviously can't see the goodness in the world anymore.

I feel sorry for Alex, but I refuse to become him.

In the sink, I find the dish the meatloaf was in. It's not broken, but my heart has a crack the size of the San Andreas Fault. I can't bear to scrub the dish clean. It will never get cleaned by me.

All I had wanted was for the family to eat together, but somehow, Alex has managed to strangle Sunday, the day designated to display love of neighbor and of Lord. The Sabbath should be untouchable by anger and malice, and yet, Sundays, being no respecter of persons, boasts of violent storms, hurricanes, beatings, rapes and murders just like any other day—and today a tornado just swept through my house.

The sound of traffic draws me outside onto the porch as if to suggest that something greater than me is streaming sunshine and transforming mankind's grease-splotched errors like the one on my rug. I curl my feet as tight to my chest as I can and tell myself I am going to be ok.

As if on cue, the wind chimes ding. I smile toward them with silent gratitude for the encouragement. If Grandma were still alive, she would be saying, "Well, shit, Savvy, life's too short to be miserable. You're a smart girl. You'll figure it out."

Jenn thinks I'm smart enough to make decisions that are "life-enhancing." If that means I live without Alex—without another man period—that's fine with me. I'm dedicated to following the clues out of this maze even if Alex is trying to set the surrounding field on fire.

My appointment with Jenn is two weeks away, and I don't have two weeks of sanity left.

I'll call her tomorrow and ask for the first available appointment. I know Jenn's not going to tell me to leave him—I'll have to make that decision myself, but she can help me become self-reliant enough to leave the only love I've ever known, if that's what I decide to do.

Dad waves from his truck that just turned into the driveway, and Isaac bursts out the front door with his duffel bag and hugs me.

I grab hold of Isaac's arms and look into his eyes, puffy from crying. "I promise things are going to get better. Your dad loves you. He just . . ." I rub Isaac's arm. "Just doesn't always show it."

Dad would be on the porch by now lending an ear if I hadn't told him on the phone that Alex and I had a fight, and I don't want to talk about what happened right now. It was awkward admitting that to Dad, but it did feel nice to be honest.

I have to stop hiding the pain if I am going to heal.

I'm studying the hanging azaleas, full when I realize Luce is talking to me. She's already strewn across her favorite lounge chair, back propped up with a pillow, and drinking a sweet tea. "So?" Luce says.

"What?" I say. "I'm sorry. Crazy day here,"

"Boy, you're spacey today. Where is everyone?" She gathers her long dark hair and piles it on top of her head.

"Ben and Alex are getting take out I think. You just missed Dad. He picked up Isaac." I stretch my legs to where the sun's reaching.

"Like I was saying," Luce says, "I still haven't decided on my hair. Up? Down? What do you think?"

I tilt my head high in the air, and flutter my eyelashes. "Hair will not a bride make or break; it's the sparkle in your eye that counts."

"Ah, Shakespearean humor," Luce says, offering a sitting-style curtsy.

"Luce, I'm happy for you—you know that," I say, settling back into my cushion. "I like Jack, but are you prepared to be married to a cop?"

"Hope he leaves the drama at the office," Luce says. "Oh, I don't mind if a few stories trickle home, but heck, living so far out of town, we'll probably be spared the crazies at our doorstep like you get here."

I shake my head. "Even when we lived in the country, we were barraged. Alex can't shift down from police mode when he's home. It's like the boys and I are the enemy. I hope Jack adapts to the force with his humanity intact, if that's possible."

"Me too!" Luce says.

"Alex accommodates the intruders then wonders why they bother him at home. It's because they know he's never in off mode. He's nicer to a total stranger in our yard than he is to me most of the time." I smack the wooden arm of the chair. "He won't hesitate to scream his head off at me and the boys, but let some needy criminal stop by and oh, the sweet, helpful words that are spoken then!"

Luce is not moving. I'm not sure she's breathing. Finally she gasps, "Oh, Savannah, I know. Being a policeman changed him."

My baby sister has a quiet strength I've always admired even though the compliment remains unspoken.

"I know," I say. "I love him—just tired of trying to make it work, Luce. I haven't said anything to Dad about our marriage being rocky so keep this just between us."

Luce tips her can of tea.

Alex and Ben turn into the drive and pull around back.

My stomach flips. The thought of conversing with Alex makes me want to hitch a ride out of here on the back of the train clacking by.

Suddenly, I remember something I want to share. "I had the weirdest dream last night! A demon called me on the phone. I know this was just a dream, but it was so real. This deep guttural voice just like growled at me over the phone."

Luce's face is frozen again.

"Then there's this jumble of letters on the wall behind my bed. I'm holding a flashlight and scanning the wall trying to decipher the hidden message. It started with an 'M'."

Luce squeals, "Oh my God, Savvy, you aren't gonna believe this—I had that same dream last week." Luce is flapping her arms like she's on fire. "I don't remember a flashlight, but I heard the demon on the phone. I saw words on my wall too and the word was 'Monster!'"

Rain No Evil

I scoot to the edge of my seat. We've had similar dreams before, but not about demons. I don't want to tell Luce that I think a demon is following me. I want it gone before I mention it to anyone. "What do you think it means?" I ask.

"The voice was absolutely terrifying," Luce says. "Maybe it's after us,"

"Who's after you?" Ben's says, rounding the porch with a bag of food that smells scrumptious.

"The devil—that's who!" Luce says, forming her hands into bear claws and grabbing at him. "Remember the Cookie Monster?"

Ben laughs. "The devil's already got you, Aunt Luce. He doesn't need me," he says, gripping Luce's neck with the hand not holding his take-out.

"Hey," Luce says, prying Ben's hand off. "Speaking of demons, Dad says your water demon is gone."

"The house is as dry as the Sahara," I say. I want to tell her that I saw a meat loaf fly through room, but I'm too embarrassed.

"Maybe the devil has Mom, too. She threw the meatloaf!" Ben says. "And wow was Dad mad!"

I fake smile at Luce who is slinking out of her seat. "Definitely not in the police wives' handbook of proper protocol," she says, grinning.

Luce hugs me whispering, "I'll pray for you. I don't know how you stay with him. I'd probably throw the whole damn fridge." And she's off.

I realize how much I enjoy the like-minded friendship of my baby sis. Growing up we were so different—Luce, the scaredy cat, gripping the open second story window frame from inside while I clambered out the window and down the steep roof to retrieve my baby doll's bottle that had rolled to the edge by the drainpipe—Me, boisterous, objectifying the mundane as useless. If I was a cattail whipping in the wind, Luce was a hemlock tree, unmovable, grounded.

I run inside and grab my journal, ignoring Alex who's sitting, hands-down-pants on the couch, and run back out to my spot on the porch and do the only thing I know to do—write.

According to Jenn, there's plenty of room in our cells; the ones we aren't cognizant of store our trash for us. If we neglect to filter out the negative—the bile in our lives, rather than fill our soul with joyful protein—we grow mold and create disease.

If the body has lots of hiding places, nasty molecules filling it like an expanding balloon, mine popped today.

Michele Savaunah Zirkle Marcum

He thinks he's Penthouse perfect for just gracing the boys and me with his presence every evening and with his paycheck every few weeks. When a tad of remorse sets in for one of his rages, he says, "At least I'm not out drinking every night," as if that gave him the right to be an asshole. I've always wanted to believe that he's sorry because if he's not, that makes him a total ass, and I don't want to believe I could have married the later.

But what I'm sure of today, I may question tomorrow, so I'll take root and keep my burner on simmer—not make a rash decision about my marriage. Like Alex's rage, fire can burn out as easily as it ignites.

The solitude of the library is calling so I gather my laptop and head out without any explanation to Alex who's digging along the edge of the driveway for God-knows-what reason.

A small table overlooking the river is where I land—the perfect scenic view from which to begin my novel—a novel about a house exorcism and how the experience is changing me. For the next two hours my story pours onto the pages of my laptop—liquid words filling the spongy word document and filling me with a cathartic release.

It is as if the keyboard is drawing toxins out through my fingertips, the story itself absorbing my thoughts and reciprocating an understanding that human interaction often refuses to provide.

I take a break and peruse the spiritual/paranormal section. As I glance over the titles, I feel compelled to look at the very bottom shelf. I start to walk off, but again feel I'm supposed to look at a book only inches from the floor.

Sighing, I swivel and see it—the book that's reeling me in. The title, *The Verbally Abusive Man.*

Abuse? The word seems so harsh. The word *abuse* makes it sound like I'm a victim, and I can't fit into the victim category. I'm Savannah Templeton. My husband helps victims of domestic violence. He can't be an abuser; can he?

I slide the book out and open it. I don't read self-help books, and I'm definitely not checking out a book from the local library where every desk clerk here knows me.

I tuck the book back on the shelf and take two steps, but an unseen string has attached me to the book—probably thanks to Jenn reconnecting me to my potential. I am *supposed* to read this daggone book.

I pick it up and stare at it.

"For research," I say, smiling while I'm lying to the clerk.

I'm tossing my bags in the trunk of my car when a familiar truck pulls in and Logan gets out. His black t-shirt tight around his pecs is a delight for my reading-weary eyes.

I smile as he walks toward me.

"Savannah!" Logan says, hugging me. "You're a sight for sore eyes."

"Was just thinking the same about you," I say, surprised by my honesty.

"You know you're special to me. Always will be," he says.

I want to wrap my arms around him, hop in his vehicle and ride off into the sunset.

Logan inspects his boots. "Kerri's coming back. It was weird. Just called last night out of the blue."

If a meteor had just smashed onto the library and shook the planet to its core, I couldn't feel more unsettled.

Even though I turned him down last night, he was still a possible future partner. He seemed to care about me even though we weren't having sex.

"Oh," I say, resting against the bumper.

"We're starting fresh—going to counseling," Logan says, leaning toward me and smoothing the bangs out of my eyes.

Alex and I started fresh once—twice—a million times, but I can't tell Logan that and dash his hopes. He has his own decisions to make—his own truth to live.

Logan wedges his hand into his Wranglers. "I want to thank you for what you said last night. You're right; I would have felt horrible if I had messed around on her."

I feel like all my blood just ran into the storm drain he's standing by. I have to get out of here.

"Logan, I wish you much happiness. Listen, I don't mean to be rude, but I've got to get home." I choke out a chuckle and duck into my car.

As I pull off, I see him in the rear view—just standing there with his hand in his pocket like he doesn't know what to do.

Well, I don't know either, but I'm not standing still—I know that. I'm going to keep moving even if I'm moving toward a mistake—at least I'm going to make different choices and different mistakes.

I thought there'd be a possibility of a future with Logan if I ever left Alex and that was re-assuring somehow.

Now I know what Jenn meant when she said I can't depend on anyone else to make me happy. I have to find activities I enjoy and immerse myself in them like I did today—just me and my laptop.

I think I could give up sex for the high I felt writing today—words pounding from my heart into the keyboard, each stroke contributing to my climax, the well-written scene.

Maybe someday—if I can complete a book about all this, I can actually make the world a better place—make the skeptics wonder if maybe there's something to this spirit thing.

And just maybe heal myself in the process.

Before heading home, I stop by Dad's to pick up Isaac. Dad's on the front porch swing when I pull in and Isaac, he says, is asleep on the couch.

Dad back-peddles, slowing the swing, and I hop on beside him.

"Dad," I say, raising my feet and letting him do the pushing, "Alex and I . . . well, he's hard to live with. I don't know how much longer I'm going to stay with him."

He sets his jaw and looks toward the pond where the geese are fluttering about.

"I know I haven't ever mentioned having marriage troubles and how bad things really are at home," I say, catching a whiff of lilac. "I didn't want you to worry. I love Alex and it sounds crazy, but I know he loves me, too . . . it's just . . . we don't get each other anymore."

"Savannah, I've seen the way he treats you. Luce and I've talked about it several times, but we just thought you were okay with it. We didn't want to meddle."

The geese are flying and diving into the pond, and I feel my day to fly is coming, too. "I'm not sure what I'm doing or where I'm going."

"Isaac told me what happened today. That poor boy is tore up—an emotional mess." Dad slides a toothpick from his pocket and bites down on it. "You'd think Alex could see what he's doing to these boys. Hell, you'd be better off without him, and so would the boys if today's behavior is the example he's setting."

"I've always made excuses for his cruelness," I say. "Blamed his mother because she always yelled at him, blamed his stressful job . . ."

"Let me stop you right there," Dad says, holding up his hand. "I was a cop for thirty-eight years and didn't speak to my family the way he speaks to you and the boys."

The lulling motion of my toes touching the ground as the swing sways, soothes me. "True and I'm done making excuses for him. No one knows what I've dealt with—kept it to myself for fourteen years. Thought I was just not a good enough wife—not a good enough mother, but . . ."

The screen door bangs shut, and a sleepy-eyed Isaac stumbles out.

Dad pats my leg. "Isaac, you got a good Mom here. She's going to make sure the kind of shit your Daddy pulled today won't be happening anymore."

I know Dad's pissed. He rarely cusses in front of the boys.

We pile into the car. Isaac snaps on his seatbelt without a word.

If I were Isaac, I'd want my mom do whatever she could to make my dad stop screaming too. I'm as responsible for the atmosphere in our house as Alex is—I'm his accomplice. I've permitted the treatment—not liked it or understood it, but allowed it to continue.

After a silent car ride home, I smuggle Isaac through the study and into his room, avoiding Alex who's coaching the Red's from the couch. I tuck both boys in with kisses, filing the memory in my mind under "Special." I stare intently into their innocent eyes that are peeking over the quilts I've tucked under their chins—eyes that soon may be shedding a few tears if I have to tell them Alex and I are splitting up. I stare at them forcing myself to remember the details I'm afraid to forget.

When they were babies, I imagined Alex and I tucking them in and whisking off for a glass of wine and private time—maybe an impromptu dance in the living room or a stroll in the moonlight—even a shared sitcom cuddled tight on the couch. But those moments have been rare and the boys aren't babies anymore.

I want the boys to see a happy mom—a mom who's caring, confident and compassionate.

Before today I was in a Midsummer Night's slumber—seeing what I wanted to see—a prince. But now that the mask is off, I realize I married an ordinary man playing the role of an ass.

Locking myself in my bedroom, I pull the abuse book out of my laptop bag and lock the bedroom door, figuring I'll read one chapter. Three chapters in, I'm hooked—the author could have been me.

I feel like chucking up the sandwich I just ate. I *am* being abused, but my pain comes with no bruises or broken bones. Maybe that's why I thought it wasn't abuse, but that's exactly what's been going on all these years.

I'm a victim of verbal abuse. Me—the independent, outspoken teacher who takes charge of a classroom of spunky teenagers with no problem. Me—the wife of a respected police officer who puts people behind bars for battery and domestic violence. Me—whose husband has promised to protect the citizens of Wooten County, but who first promised to love and cherish me.

I can't believe I didn't see the truth of it all these years. Alex was right—I am stupid!

I force myself up, unlock the door and slide the book under a pair of jeans in my closet then climb into bed and watch the mini-light display that's hypnotized me nightly since the night I prayed to see them like Isaac.

I thank my angels for leading me to the book that's giving me more insight into my life than any other book ever has. I petition Grandma Lennie to bend the Big Guy's ear since she's close enough to whisper into it. I can picture her telling the Omnipotent, "My Savvy sure needs help down there. Now, you surely can spare a few more angels for her; can't You? Maybe give her some more bread crumbs to follow."

On my way to the car in the morning, I hear the clinking of wind chimes. I haven't ever heard them this early in the morning. Gazing up at the sky, I imagine grandma rooting for me, using the clouds for pompoms. Changes are blowing like the clouds in wind, spiraling through the sky, not knowing where they will end up—like me.

The first part of the school day is eaten up with another end-of-the-year assembly so I take advantage of the empty classroom and read the final chapter of the abuse book. The appendix provides a contract that the author recommends that both the victim and the abuser sign. I type the contract and progress to the section that requires me to list hurtful comments that my spouse says to me. By the time I'm done, there are over sixty, and that's just the ones I can remember.

My cell rings. It's Jenn checking on me. I tell her I need an earlier appointment. I take the first slot available which is Wednesday at 2:00.

After school, I'm on the couch when Alex walks in the side door with his cell to his ear.

"Just call me if she comes to," Alex says. "Gilmore's interviewing the boy now. Keep the hospital covered, man, and keep me posted. Gonna get some dinner."

Alex snaps off his tie and places his gun on the fridge.

I smooth my hand over the contract that I need to present to Alex. He has work on his mind, and my proposal will have to wait.

"Hi, glad your home," I say. "Who's in the hospital?"

"Steven Hopper's mom got beat to a pulp," Alex says, opening the basement door. "Helluva day!"

"Oh Lord! You know who did it?"

"Probably the same ass-wipe that stopped by here—Parker. He only spent one night in the clinker for driving suspended. Damn justice system let's 'em out faster than we can get the cuffs on." Alex un-tucks his shirt from his pants. "Parker says he wasn't even home last night—was at a friend's. He's blaming Steven for beating her, and she's in a coma so she can't tell us a damn thing."

"So, Parker's blaming Steven for beating his own mom," I say, thankful that Alex doesn't physically beat me. "Wow. Steven's a sweetheart. I can't see him beating on his mom."

"Gilmore's questioning Steven now," Alex says, descending the steps.

I hear the dryer door shut. Alex is probably scavenging for clean clothes he can throw on. He yells into the playroom, "You boys are going to turn into a TV, ya know."

His comment makes me wonder . . . if Alex's example for TV watching has shaped their TV habit, how much more so will his behavior toward me affect the way they treat the women in their lives.

Alex returns wearing red shorts and an incredible hulk t-shirt with paint stains, his black dress socks still stuck to his legs.

I choke back a giggle. "Who found Steven's mom?"

Alex pops a tab off a can of sweet tea and takes a swig. "A friend of hers found her at the house nearly dead. She's in ICU. May not make it. Then we'll have two murders to solve."

"Yep, and since Parker could've murdered Hank, you could have two murders and one murderer," I say. Jenn's words replay in my head. "Live your truth," and I know I can't put off this conversation.

I flip off the TV and tell Alex I need to talk to him. I position my chair at the table to face where he's standing behind the bar. This is the moment I've postponed for what seems like an eternity—the one that will determine the rest of my life. I know the outcome depends on me not letting fear deter me.

If Alex is flippant about my wishes then our marriage is over before the conversation even begins. I refuse to be a victim any longer.

"Alex," I say, "I read a book and—"

"Now there's a surprise," Alex says rolling his eyes.

I close my eyes and flatten my hand on the table. "Look," I say, focusing again on the man behind the bar. "I need you to listen to me. This is serious and you cannot interrupt me."

Alex nods as if a crown is being placed on his head.

"The book," I say, "was about men who don't realize they are saying things to their spouse—things that are hurtful and are damaging their relationship."

Alex's mouth is snarled, but he's not talking over me.

"I think our relationship will improve if we agree to speak respectfully to each other. I've made a list of statements you say that hurt me. I want you to read them and sign the agreement if you will stop saying them."

Alex's face is expressionless. I can usually read him, but right now I'm clueless.

I rub the papers in front of me. "We can add anything that you want me to stop saying to you."

"Okay." he says. "Is that all you wanted—I thought you were going to say you were leaving me."

"Here," I say, standing and handing him two copies of the contract.

Alex reads a bit and laughs. "You want me to stop saying, 'You're so slow?'

"Yes."

"And 'You never cook?'"

"Yes. You have anything to add?" I ask.

"Nope, but you might as well cut out my tongue." Alex grins and scissors his fingers. "What if I can't do this?"

"Then I won't be here anymore," I say without hesitation. I feel like I'm watching my life unfold on the big screen.

His head pops up from the paper. "What do you mean you won't be here? Where would *you* go?"

I instantly want to defend myself—he said that like I can't possibly live without him—like no one else would have me.

Feeling for the chair, I sit down. My legs are trembling. I can't let Alex scare me into staying with him. I can be anywhere I want to be. I just want him to understand that if I stay, he will have to change how he talks to me.

"I don't know," I say. "I just know I won't be *here* anymore. This contract is my last resort to make our marriage work."

Alex's eyes are big. He's looking at me like a child does a parent when he's told he can *absolutely not* take one last ride on the roller coaster.

"You think someone out there's going to love you better than me?" he says. "You're going to be disappointed."

He's not going to skew my message. I'm sticking to my script. "I'm talking about you and me. Has nothing to do with anybody else. If you can't stop saying these statements, I won't be here. I won't be here because I'm not going to continue to live like this—not because I'm looking for Prince Charming."

"Sure! You know where you're going, or you wouldn't be saying you're going to leave. So where is it and who is it?" Alex puckers his mouth and clicks the pen against his chin. "Your bridge-jumper boyfriend? No, I saw where he's getting married to the chick from the hospital. So who?"

My heart feels like it's being twisted around a curling iron—Ryan's engaged? I remind myself that my decision to set boundaries with Alex has nothing to do with Ryan or any other man. I feel vulnerable knowing my future is unknown and I may be facing it totally alone, but I'm not letting Alex see the fear that's paralyzed the blood in my veins.

Alex thinks I have an intricate plan, and he's not going to believe that I don't, but I'm speaking my truth anyway.

I look him dead in the eyes. "Alex, I have no plans. I do want this contract to work. So it's up to—"

"Yeah. Yeah." He says, signing and laughing. "I signed as Sergeant Templeton."

"It's okay," I say, adding my signature beside of Sergeant Alex Templeton's and hoping we aren't soon signing a divorce decree. I tuck my copy under my arm with the hope that this piece of paper is as inspiring to Alex as the book that suggested it has been to me.

I yank open the basement door and announce to the boys, "Dinner's ready. Come and eat."

I hand a bowl of chili to the boys and carry mine to the table where Alex is cracking saltines over his. Isaac wants to know where the peanut butter sandwiches are.

"I didn't make them," I say, swirling the spoon in my soup. "You're old enough to make a sandwich." I like speaking my truth.

His cell rings and Alex pushes his chair away from the table. "You're kidding. This could break the case wide open."

Ben tells Isaac, "You have to put peanut butter on both sides of the bread. It tastes better. And Mom puts honey on it, too."

Still jabbering on the phone, Alex storms to the basement.

"Dad got to go?" Isaac says.

"Probably. A woman got beat up today."

A few minutes later, Alex, dressed in BDUs, steps into the kitchen and laces his boots. "Steven says Parker killed Hank. Don't know if he can prove it or if he's just saying that to get off the hook for beating up his mom." He snaps his gun into the holster. "May be out all night."

I bet I was right about Steven putting that letter in our mailbox.

About four a.m. I slip on my robe and squeak down the stairs and into the living room where Alex is staring at an infomercial about a "Shammy wow." His eyes are blood-shot and a granola bar sits atop his bare belly.

He shoots me an empty look. He's exhausted.

I sit opposite him on the couch and wait for him to say something.

After a few long seconds he says, "Steven wrote the letter—the one about the gun being in the lake."

"You're welcome," I say.

Alex scrunches up his nose.

"For suggesting it was Steven who wrote it."

The corner of his mouth curls down. "Sure, Sav, guess you got to be right sometimes."

"How'd Steven know that Parker killed Hank?"

"Steven didn't see Parker actually shoot Hank, but he's still a witness," Alex says, sucking food out of his teeth. "Said Zoey was there at his house the night of the murder, high on cocaine Parker gave her. Hank came over to get Zoey about eleven o'clock. Parker answered the door and told the old man to get lost, but Hank insisted he wasn't leaving without his granddaughter."

I sink my hands into the pocket of my robe. "Where was Steven?"

"Upstairs listening over the hallway banister. He hears the front door slam and voices outside so he watches out his bedroom window. He sees Parker gripping Hank with one hand and holding a .30-30 in the other."

Alex slurps a drink of milk. "Here's the catch—Parker had a buddy over that night, and Steven saw them both dragging Hank through the yard and into the woods behind the house. Several minutes later Steven hears a gunshot and here come the dirtballs tugging Hank back through the yard. A car speeds off. Parker and his buddy are gone until about two in the morning."

Alex pushes himself up and onto the floor in front of his seat, "Rub my neck, will ya?"

I scoot over, my legs dangling on either side of his shoulders, and stick my elbows into his traps—just like he likes. "Where were Zoey and Steven's mom while Hank's being shot?"

"Steven says they were both passed out. We have to question Zoey and Steven's mom, if she recovers." Alex squirms. "Harder. I can't even feel that."

I dig into his traps, kneading his muscle until my elbows burn. "Okay, I get it, but how did Steven know the gun was in the lake?"

"Steven overheard the two dumbasses talking when they got back—heard them mention Mud Run Lake." Alex shrugs and gets up. "That's enough. Can't feel it."

He flips off the TV and as I'm walking toward the stairs, the room goes pitch black.

My toes hit something hard—must be the footstool. "I can't see shit," I say, grabbing my toes, thankful it's not the foot the gun fell on.

"You're so coordinated," Alex says from halfway up the stairs.

I hobble up the steps saying, "Guess we need to add that to your list of banned comments."

In the bedroom, I slather lavender lotion on my sore toes. "You could have left the light on, you know. So, did Steven admit to the letter because he wanted Parker out of his mom's life, like I said?"

The headboard creaks as Alex leans back against a pillow. "Yes, Savannah, you were right. He wanted Parker to go to jail—to get away from his mom, but he didn't want Zoey in trouble for buying the drugs and he was too scared of Parker to actually put his name on the letter."

"Sure, and Steven only admitted it now because Parker accused him of beating up his mom," I say, flipping off the lamp.

"Parker's a son of a bitch."

"How you going to prove Parker beat her?"

"Parker's claiming he was with his buddy last night when it happened—the same buddy who Steven says helped murder Hank. We rounded up the ole pal and had a chat. We had him by the balls and he knew it—told him we'd be charging him with first-degree murder. The guy turned on Parker—said Parker pulled the trigger on Hank and that Parker *wasn't* with him last night. Parker's got no alibi during the time Steven's mom got beat."

"Oh, and I forgot to tell you, Diane wrote a note." Alex says, gripping my shoulder and snugging me against his warm body.

"Really?" I say, picturing that pink sash blowing around her lifeless waist.

"The note said she loved her mom, but wasn't going to let guys piss on her anymore—not even for fifty bucks."

I look toward Alex's face, barely visible except a strand of moonlight streaking across his cheek. "You think they literally peed on her?"

"Probably. If you'd see half the things I see every day—it'd make you wonder where all the good people in the world went."

"Sick bastards," I say, catching a whiff of lingering musk on Alex's shaved chest. If I saw the wickedness of people first hand like he does, maybe I would hone a shield as impenetrable as the one he has—one that keeps even loved ones from getting close.

"Sav, Diane mentioned your name. She said she was sorry she disappointed you by taking the easy way out," Alex says. "I just don't understand how people can be so weak minded."

I'm not telling him I've had a few weak-minded moments myself. I'm not going to attempt to explain that I relate to Diane's wanting to escape her life.

With Alex caressing my shoulder like he's brushing off lint, I cache this feeling of ease and fall asleep in the arms of my husband, that, tonight, feel a little less like steel and more like a down duvet.

Fifteen minutes early to school for me seems like fifty. I'm never early. I find Joanne pouring grounds into the coffee pot in the teacher's lounge, her curly hair looking especially silver. I'm sure she's earned every shiny strand.

"Getting geared up for a long last day," she says holding her empty cup like it's her lifeline.

A creamy piece of peanut butter fudge is melting in my mouth from the tray by the Mr. Coffee before I even know I picked it up. With the sweets from holidays, birthdays, and teacher appreciation week, it's a miracle any of us can waddle through the hallways without doing *The Bump* with the lockers on either side.

I fill Joanne in on the note Diane left, and she tells me that she just found out about the note yesterday from children's protective services.

Mr. Feldman opens the door for Mrs. Z. who saunters in saying, "Yes, her mom was at the store the other day just a boo-hooing for that poor girl like she had absolutely nothing to do with her death. Heavens, *she* was the reason Zoey wanted to die." Mrs. Z. grabs a donut and takes a bite so big that only half of it is left in her hand. "Isn't that right, Savannah?"

Joanne winks at me, and I nod back to Mrs. Z., knowing that she knows damn well she's correct.

"You must know every secret in Wooten County," Mrs. Z says, raspberry crème running down her chin from the last stub of pastry as Mr. Feldman dumps every paper from his mailbox into the trash.

"All the good ones," I say, letting a second piece of fudge melt in my mouth.

Joanne pours her coffee mug full, and I follow her around the corner to her office where stacks of folders are piled high on the floor, leaving a pathway to her desk.

I shut the door and slide into a chair, detailing the events that led to Hank's murder and tell her Steven Hopper probably won't be at school today.

"I knew you'd want to check on him after what he's been through," I say. "If you get a hold of him, don't act like you know any of this. Just ask how his mom is doing and see what he tells you. It's no secret the squad was called to his house—would've been broadcast across the scanner. I just want Steven to know he has people who care."

Five minutes before lunch is over, Brandon and Terry rustle through my classroom door.

"Mrs. Templeton, told you; didn't I?" Brandon says, straddling a chair backwards.

"You mean about Cliff Parker?" I say, finishing off my protein drink.

"Yep, Zoey's not here today," Terry says. "Sha sha she'll be the next one fah fah found hanging from a tah tah tree."

"Oh, Terry, don't say that." I hadn't really thought about how Zoey must feel. "You know, Zoey *is* going to have to live her whole life knowing she's responsible for placing her grandpa in the situation that precipitated his murder."

Brandon tips back on the legs of the chair. "It snowed when they killed him?"

"Put the chair down—you're going to break your neck. What about snow?" I say, taking my last bite of sweet potato.

"You said precipitation," Brandon says, the chair landing on all fours.

"Oh!" I laugh. Kids. I do love them. "Precipitation is rain or snow, but precipitated the way I used it means 'came before.' So, the situation Hank was in before his murder—like he went to Parker's trying to help Zoey and that's what caused his murder."

The rest of my favorite sophomore's trickle in for their last English class before summer break, and I have them share their summer vacation plans. A few students box up the books from the shelves. Others design encouragement cards for Diane's brother, Michael. He hasn't been back to school since Diane killed herself, and Joanne thought the contact from other students would comfort him.

Courtney's desk is sparkling from the green glitter she's sprinkled on a yellow card to Michael.

I walk over to her desk, peering over her shoulder. "Courtney, that's a beautiful angel. I didn't know you were such the artist."

Courtney flips the bangs from her eyes and holds the card arm's length.

"You should be proud of that. Michael will be touched." I lay my hand on her back. "Maybe you should consider taking graphic design at the career center next year. Lots of jobs in that field. Plus you wouldn't need to depend on a man."

I plow past a few students sitting on the floor and over to Terry and tell him that the auto store is hiring for the summer and I know the manager. If he's interested I can help him get on.

I'm a seed planter. What's harvested depends, I suppose, on the assimilation of each person to live their own truth.

Sixth period students roll in. The magic moment has arrived, my last class with students before blessed summertime.

As the students stand one after the other reading aloud their expectations for summer, I daydream about my own summer. Will Alex and I get closer—or drift to separate islands?

Looking out my window over the cow-field where cattle are grazing, I conjure up my own sun-scape—an exotic image of a private island, complete with coconuts and Gilligan. Oh, to hell with him. Delete. Make that Pina Coladas and Mark Wahlberg—add in the sound of waves lapping the palm tree shoreline, a breeze-kissed massage under a tiki hut with a tan cabaña boy doling out cocktails of grilled shrimp and . . .

The sound of the Holy Grail dinging for dismissal zips me back to reality quicker than the return trip from any vacation I've ever had, and I'm on to planning period.

Weaving around chattering students in the hall in no hurry to get to their last class, I duck into the lounge and scarf down my second cream-filled cupcake that an anonymous evil pastry bunny placed beside the fudge.

By the time the final dismissal bell dongs, my sugar's as high as the hand I'm waving to all the youngens scattering to their two months of freedom.

It's a glorious day and tomorrow will be even better—I get injected with divine energy, courtesy of Jenn whose healing power is my newfound special antidote for the poison in my life.

When the boys and I arrive home, a truck is pouring concrete onto the driveway, and my head starts spinning like the tank that's dumping the sludge. What the hell has Alex done now? There's no way he had enough money to pay for pavement. I pull around back behind Alex's cruiser.

Alex and the boys run toward a haggard-looking Keagan who's smoothing over the concrete opposite Alex. I strut the lawn toward Alex. He spots me and yells from halfway down the drive, "Careful!"

No shit, I'm thinking as I tap dance around the house through the grass until I reach Alex who's troweling the wet cement closest to the house.

"Need you to write me a check," Alex shouts over the sound of the mixer. "The guy's almost done pouring it."

I lower my head, watching my hands rub my dress pants, and imagine pushing Alex into the fresh concrete and him hardening there, mouth dried in a perpetual endless, soundless scream, with no one to rescue him—just like he makes me feel every day.

I would shine a spotlight on him in the front yard for all of Wooten County to see—a shrine of sorts to Taze Templeton who never did learn the art of keeping his mouth shut. The statue, embodying his voiceless resistance, would be a monument to my independence.

"You hear me?" Alex says, pushing the long-handled tool in his arms, smoothing the material he hasn't paid for.

He's asking me if *I* hear *him.* The tables have indeed turned.

"How much?" I ask, even though any amount will be more than we has in our bank account.

"Three thousand four hundred," he says, maintaining eye contact with the non-judgmental concrete, and I don't blame him.

I glance around to see if the boys are listening, but they're intent on watching Keagan skillfully shaping the concrete. "You know we don't have that much in the account," I say. "My gosh, nowhere near that—maybe three *hundred*."

"You know I've been saving to have this done, Savvy. I've got to pay the guy, damn it. Just get the checkbook."

My eyes rove to the blue sky, knowing the likelihood of Alex having even $200 in his rusty coffee can in the rafters of the garage is as likely as me turning water into wine.

I stomp off to the house and dig into the Snoopy satchel in my closet where I've hidden over $4,000 for vacation. I hold the bills in my hand, the hundreds, the twenties, and I realize I'm holding my independence money—money I'll need to segue toward my dream of peace—not the money that I'll spend on another family trip on which Alex and I depart delusional, thinking that a view of the heavens from an exotic location will unite us, only to return with broken spirits that match our broken bank account.

I stash the money and grab a credit card check from the filing cabinet in the study. I'll help Alex out—the idiot. But he's not using my nest egg to build a driveway that I'm probably not going to even be driving on much longer.

I scurry out and hand Alex the check.

"What's this?" he says, squinting.

Ben yells over the drive, "Can we go to Grandpa's?"

I shrug and yell, "Up to Grandpa. He's probably tired." I turn back to Alex. "It's a credit card check," I say, walking off while Alex shakes his head in disapproval.

Fifteen minutes later, Keagan pulls out with the boys and Alex joins me at the table over a bowl of soup.

"You going to tell me why you gave me a credit card check?" Alex says.

"Sure, when you tell me what you're thinking by ordering concrete we can't pay for."

Alex's face flushes the color of his cherry Kool-Aid. "I'm tired of throwing our money away on gravel. It's always a muddy mess. I formed it up Sunday when you took off. You're so selfish. You can take off for hours, but I can't even order concrete without getting the third degree."

I let my spoon slide deep into my soup. "I saw you digging by the drive-way Sunday, but I didn't know—"

"What *do* you know? You're never happy with anything I do."

"Refraining from saying that I'm never happy is on the agreement you signed. Anyway, I didn't know what you were digging for. You mentioned concreting it," I say, "but you never said anything about having it done *this week*. Would be nice if you saved up money for stuff like that."

"Would be nice if you'd save for anything."

"The agreement we made about how we talk to each other—"

"Fuck that agreement! You keep trying to change me. Well, I'm not changing and you can't make me!" Alex holds his spoon like he's going to jerk it off, chomping the crackers in his bowl, soup splashing onto his arms.

I feel woozy. This is it. This is really it. We are over.

"You can write that in your little book, you idiot! You really think people want to read about your crazy ass things that go bump in the night?"

The wood table beneath my palms helps me push myself up, out of the chair. I slip off to the bedroom. There's nothing more to say—at least not to Alex.

But I do have something to say, and I'm going to say it with or without his support or approval.

Rain No Evil

Just because he doesn't want to hear me, doesn't mean that no one does. He refuses to hear me now, but I have no doubt that when my book comes out, he'll damn sure hear me then! Mine will be the third one on the short list of books he's ever read.

Alex may read it just because he's got the starring role and not because he's searching for enlightenment, but read it he will!

After a few hours of channeling words into my laptop, I traipse downstairs for a snack. Alex slithers up behind me while I'm inspecting the inside of the refrigerator, his hand pulling me by the waist to face him.

His head lowers, and his lips touch my cheek. As he starts sucking my neck, I arch away from him and say, "If you want to apologize, I'll listen."

The man they call Taze looks like a taser has just stunned *him*. "Apologize? For what?" he says, pulling me to him.

I twist out of his embrace and grab the counter behind me.

"If you don't know, then I can't explain it," I say.

"Are you ever happy?" Alex grabs a jug of milk from the fridge, gulping it so fast it runs off his chin.

Then it hits me—all those times in the past that he came up to me after a fight, fondling me, I thought he was apologizing. He wasn't. He was just wheedling his way back into my good graces. He never believed he had anything to apologize for!

I walk zombie-like back to the bedroom, feeling as stupid as he thinks I am. Alex just wants me because I'm hot enough to flaunt around town and fuck with the lights on.

I fall into bed and into a sleep so deep that I can smell the algae in the swamp from the skiff I'm in. Alligators are circling and a baby's crying. I scan the tiny boat, but it's dark and the waning moon isn't offering much light. I hear splashing—the baby's in the water. I stretch my arm toward the sound— further—further, until I feel I'm going to fall overboard. The feel of soft skin reaches my fingertips. I latch on and pull the child close, lifting it into my arms. I swipe my sleeve across the forehead and wake screaming—the baby is me!

When I arrive at Jenn's Wednesday at two o'clock, the door is cracked so I nudge it open, yelling, "Hello," more as a question than a greeting.

Jenn says she will be down in a minute.

I make my way to the basement where the rocker cushion has a few strands of hair on it, compliments of the feline with the Cheshire grin who's squinting at me from the corner.

Brushing off the seat, I sit and scan the shelves.

Propped on edge in the bookcase against the wall is a book, *Sacred Contracts* and a DVD, *What the Bleep Do We Know?* To the right, there is an image of an emerald green mermaid staring at me from the cover of a calendar. Details of the vivid artwork are provocative and tattoo-inspiring. Should I ever get a hankering for having a permanent picture etched on my skin, this gorgeous, green beauty could be staring at me from my wrist.

Before Isaac saw the mermaid float through our bathroom, I hadn't given their existence true consideration, but now I feel that just because I haven't met the creature doesn't mean one isn't luring a vulnerable man to his death right now.

I haven't been in Jenn's office this long without her here. A handwritten, "Reiki charged" sign hangs by an array of colored candles to my left and tiny medicine bottles stack inches deep into curios. Anyone could easily swipe a small bottle or a candle. My heart clamps taut. What if she thinks I'm stealing something?

I rub my clammy hands back and forth on my legs and glance up the stairs to see if Jenn's coming. I want her to get down here so she knows I'm not taking anything.

The white ball of fur's looking at me. His blue eyes seem to pierce my skull and read my mind like Jenn does.

I've confided in her that I've shop-lifted—not because I needed the stolen item or because I couldn't afford to buy it—just enjoyed the challenge of proving to myself I could get by with stealing it.

I was an honest thief though. I'd feel so guilty I'd take the damn item back to the store the next day, wearing the stolen garment under my clothes and discarding it in the dressing room or stashing the previously taken trinket in my purse and setting it casually on a counter. The thrill of getting by with something so covert made me feel clever, and I realize Jenn's right when she says I've got a lot of work to do on myself. I want to feel clever like that *without* stealing.

I don't want Jenn to think I would steal from *her*. I could, but I'm not going to. She's my fresh start, and I'm not messing that up. So, then why did the thought of how easy it would be even cross my mind? Would a normal person waiting down here like me feel awkward like this? Would they even wonder if Jenn had considered the possibility of them stealing from her?

Jenn descends the steps, her flowered skirt draping each riser and flopping onto the next like a slinky.

My ornery eyes meet her angelic ones that glance over to the bookshelf and return to smile down at me. She knows what I'm thinking! I feel it. She knows. Guilt must be written all over my face.

But I didn't take anything—didn't even plan on taking anything. Suddenly, I know that the guilt I'm feeling is from the sheer thought of stealing. I didn't have to actually do anything wrong to feel the yucky disappointment in myself. If that basic rule applies to all areas of life then I'm going to have to learn to think differently in order to truly change.

My thoughts are creating my world—just like *The Secret* claims they do. My odd therapist settles back into her seat, dips her chin and looks at me. "How are you?"

I'm not asking her how she is. She's not just being polite. She really wants to know. The words gush out. "I can't live this way anymore. With Alex, I mean. I love him. Always will—we were high school sweethearts, you know. But he's so mean, so disrespectful. I don't want my boys to disrespect women like he does me." I swallow hard to keep tears from forming. "I love my boys, but I know I can't stay with Alex for them. I'm not doing them any favors by staying. The arguments they've witnessed . . . it's just not fair to them either. And it's not like they're babies anymore. They're developing their ideas about marriage and love and respect, and Alex and I are providing a dysfunctional example for them."

Jenn tips her spectacles forward, laying them upside down on a tablet. "When I called you Monday, you said you threw food across the room."

"You got to understand. I don't get angry like that—like I did Sunday." My hands jab the air as fast as I'm talking. "I wanted to explode. Literally. Just let my whole body combust and be done with it."

Sliding on a pair of berry colored glasses, Jenn pencils a note into a manila folder. Guess she documents my visits after all.

"I just wanted to enjoy Sunday dinner together after our first day at the Catholic Church, but all hell broke loose when we got home. Alex was screaming for Isaac to get downstairs and eat. Isaac wasn't hungry so he yelled something back and slammed his door. And poor Ben . . ."

I look down to where a tear just splashed onto my white pants and brush my fingers across my moist face. "The look on Ben's face. It broke my heart. He's so soft-hearted. I didn't want to raise my kids the white trash way, you know?"

I don't need sympathy—just someone to see my perspective. Just once.

Jenn feels my pain. I see the understanding in her eyes so I continue. "That's when I threw the meatloaf, fresh from the oven. I was gripping it with oven mitts one second and hurling it into the living room the next. It was like slow motion. I thought, *This is what a nervous break-down must feel like*."

Neither of Jenn's eyebrows has raised, and I'm wondering if I'll ever get a rise out of this woman. Maybe nothing I ever say will surprise her. Maybe she knows everything already and just waits for me to tell her my version.

I wrestle a tissue from my purse and blow my nose. "Grease and globs of ketchup and meat were all over the floor. Thank God the dish didn't hit anyone."

I shift to the edge of my seat and sit erect, looking directly into the stream of compassion shining from Jenn's eyes. "I stood there in a stupor looking at it. I never want to feel that out of control again. Ever. Whatever you ask me to do, I'll do it."

Jenn smooches her lips together and looks above me toward the ceiling. I notice she does that often, and I wonder if someday I'll be able to see what's up there, too.

Jenn says, "First of all, you can't change Alex or anyone else—just yourself. And it won't happen overnight, but you can change. Change yourself—change your world."

I want to burst out "Okay, just tell me what to do," but I force myself to be quiet and listen.

"You're reaction to Alex gives him energy—feeds his anger." Jenn leans back. "By react, I mean that you either pout and ignore him, or scream back and stomp off. Either way, he wins—he gets your energy. Instead, you could tell him that you feel hurt or sad, but he probably wouldn't hear you when he's raging, so it might be more beneficial to wait until he's calmed down and then tell him how you'd felt."

My eyes feel like they are bulging out. "What do I say while he's going ballistic?"

"Remember, you can't change his behavior. If he's screaming, that's his choice. You are only in control of your actions. Act purposefully; don't just react."

Jenn's making sense, but this is going to require a lot of effort. It's like I'm going to have to learn to speak a foreign language.

She continues, "For instance, say you're in the middle of cooking and he's yelling, ask him to leave the kitchen and tell him you will talk to him when he calms down." Jenn sees my bulging eyes and continues. "I know, he doesn't seem like the type that's going to do that, so you could leave the kitchen and find another task you want to finish or do something pleasurable like read. I know you said you like to write." She grins. "Anything that will make *you* happy and feel good about yourself."

I picture Ryan and Logan stroking my face. That made me feel good. Damn them both! I haven't told Jenn about Logan, but I want her to have time for my hands on treatment.

I pop one shoulder forward. "Oh? So screwing the neighbor is out?"

Jenn's laugh is from her belly. I'm pleased she thinks I'm funny.

"Jenn, one more thing before you work on me. A book at the library called to me. I almost didn't check it out because of the title, but I'm glad I did. It's called, *The Verbally Abusive Man.*"

Jen nods. "I'm familiar with that book."

"I read it and there was a contract inside. I typed up the agreement and Alex signed it Monday night."

Jenn's looking past me like she's gazing into a crystal ball only she can see. "He agreed?" "Yes," I say, rubbing my wedding ring as if just talking about it makes my finger ache. "But just last night he said he wasn't going to change and that I can't make him. I think that said it all. I think we are really over."

"Well, today, lady," Jenn says, swooping the side of her full skirt into her hand and walking toward the treatment room. "I am being told you need to hear a CD on strength."

"So angels told you that—about the CD?" I ask, following.

"Yes, I get sort of . . . downloaded with information." Jenn starts the CD while I slip my shoes and jewelry off.

Lying flat, I feel particularly warm when Jenn gestures to her angelic realm. The tingling along my skin is like the static electricity shock Luce and

I used to give each other after digging our rubber-soled jammies into the shag carpet.

I relax and listen to what the lady on the CD is saying about humans having four archetypes, each employed as circumstances dictate and when called upon by the individual.

Before long, Jenn has moved to my head, and I feel a stinging sensation like rubber bands are being snapped onto my skull. I try to ignore the uncomfortable feeling. I have to since this is part of the therapy. If the intensity is any indication, I must really need this treatment.

I concentrate on summarizing what I've learned so far—our Warrior's in the north, Nurturer's in the South, Sage's in the west . . . but the longer I'm here, the more my head spins like I'm drunk, except the room's not moving—my brain is. I'm aggravated from trying to focus on the words of enlightenment I'm supposed to be digesting.

I can't hear the voice on the CD anymore, only the angry ones from above my head belting out, "You shouldn't have come here!" I look up, but there's nothing up there except the ceiling tile.

I close my eyes. If I'm going to lose my mind it might as well be here—in the one bed where I've finally found acceptance.

Succumbing to the spinning sensation, I let the centrifugal force take control and hear the growling voices. "Shouldn't have come! Told you— shouldn't have come." I scan the room above me for the source of the voices I'm hearing. I peer into each corner of the room expecting to see the demon face I saw last time I was here, but there are no dark shadows or spirits that are visible.

"I'm sorry," I say to whoever is so mad at me for coming here.

I'm dazed. I sit up in bed and look over toward the blurry form of Jenn who's on her stool to my left. The inside of my head is twirling non-stop into orbit, and I'm helpless to stop the motion.

Other than the sickening echoes of garbled, growling voices that seem to be buzzing my brains out, I can't hear anything. My head is a hornet's nest.

When I look up again, Jenn is still to my left, but she's sitting in the chair draped with my purse. I push my elbows into the bed in an effort to sit up, but have no strength and collapse back onto the pillow.

Jenn's hand gently softens to my wrist that's searching for leverage. "Easy, there. No rush," she says, patting my face with a cool cloth.

After several minutes, I say, "I'm so weak."

Jenn strokes my forehead. "I know, honey."

I feel really stupid. Tired and confused and stupid.

Jenn offers her arm so I grab ahold and attempt to swing my legs off of the bed, but they barely budge. With her free hand, Jenn slides my legs till they dangle off the edge. With Jenn's assistance, I mosey out to the rocking chair where she makes sure I'm settled before resting in the chair behind her desk.

"Do you remember anything?" Jenn asks, her soft blue eyes practically propping me up from across the room.

I rub my forehead like the movement will bring my memory front and center. "I remember my head spinning and growling voices saying they didn't want me here."

Jenn says, "You sat up, looked at me and said, 'I'm sorry.' I wasn't sure what you were sorry for, but I knew you were under the influence of an evil presence. Then you went into the seizure."

My hazy memory flashes a scene of Jenn sitting in the chair beside me as I felt like I was being pushed off a mountain and spiraling into pitch black.

As I tell Jenn what I remember, my cell rings. Alex wants to know if I'm still at the doctor's appointment I told him I had. I tell him yes and that I had a seizure in the doctor's office, but I'll drive home once I feel up to it.

I hang up, place the phone in my lap and drink the water Jenn places on the table beside the sage smudge stick. "What time is it?" I ask.

"It's three thirty. I cancelled my appointments for the rest of the afternoon. You take as much time as you need. Here, take this." She hands me an oblong pill. "It may prevent you from having another seizure."

I'm tired, but my mind is calm. I feel like such a nuisance. So pathetic. A seizure! What kind of weak-ass person has a seizure—and during an energy healing session of all places?

I swallow the pill. "Jenn, I'm sorry—so sorry for messing up your day."

Jenn waves her hand. "I just want you to feel better. We'll sit here and chat until you feel like moving."

"Something's bugging me," I say. "You've told me to notice my feelings during a normal day. It's kind of weird, but I get mad when I hear people laugh—even when it's Ben and Isaac—instantly, I'm mad. I want them to be happy, so it didn't make sense until Logan popped into my life, and I realized I'm angry because I'm jealous that other people seem to laugh so easily compared to me. I want to laugh too."

"Logan?" Jenn says, the earring she's hooked her finger through glistening my way.

"Logan and I've known each other for years. His wife left him and we started talking a few weeks ago. He made me laugh. I really cared about him, but we weren't having sex. But he's back with his wife now, who, by the way, slept with Alex about five ago."

Charlie, the cat, is licking his paw from his squat under the Buddha as I ramble on.

"Does Alex know about Logan?"

"No, I've told him about other guys in the past, but I just can't tell him about Logan. It's different because I . . . I really care about him. Even after everything Alex has done to hurt me, I really don't want to hurt him."

"It's good you're paying attention to your feelings—like knowing that you want to laugh. You deserve to laugh, Savannah." Jenn says, rubbing the gold pendant grazing her neckline. "As you live your truth the laughter will come. We can't depend on other people to make us happy. They can enhance our happiness, but we have to love ourselves—all other love is icing—not necessary, but yummy."

"Well, I know I want intimacy, not just sex." I grab the wooden arms of the rocker, pushing myself out and into a wobbly stance on my feet that feel foreign. "I've monopolized enough of your time. I think I can make it home."

"Are you sure you feel up to driving?" Jenn says, following behind me as I ascend the stairs. "Promise me you will pull over and call someone to get you if you feel the least bit strange," she says.

"I will," I say, reaching the landing and turning to soak in one last ray of hope exuding from this magnificent lady in white light.

On the way home, Alex calls—asks if I have anything I want to tell him. He says I hadn't hung up the phone and he heard me talking about not wanting to hurt him.

Despite the seriousness of the interrogation that's coming, I feel at peace.

I can tell Alex didn't hear the entire conversation—just bits, so I could simply explain that I wasn't at the doctor's office—that I was at a counselor's because I needed to talk to someone about our marriage. But if I only tell him partial truths, nothing between us will change.

Alex has to know the truth—about everything—Jenn, invisible writings, needing to feel heard and Logan who makes me laugh.

I tell him we will talk when I get home, and a calmness comes over me. I'm worn out from the seizure, but the serenity I feel permeating every cell is more than exhaustion. I'm going to speak my truth and that truth will set me free—free from a life of lies, free from Alex's anger, free from self-imposed limitation—free.

Alex is frying hamburgers when I get home. Without looking up from the pan, he tells me the boys are in the basement with Cole and Timmy.

"I have several things to tell you. Not sure where to start," I say, leaning across the counter. "The doctor I went to today was actually a counselor and I told her about our relationship—how I miss laughing with you."

Alex glances at me and rolls his eyes. "Your never happy so how could you—"

"Stop right there," I say, staring his direction. "Either you're listening or I'm done talking."

Alex is silent.

I am silent.

After what seems an eternity, he jerks his head around as if he's a bobble head, and I assume that means he's ready to listen.

"The counselor lady works with the energy fields of our bodies. She offers alternative forms of therapy to help her clients heal, like—"

"Heal? Hell, you had a seizure . . ." Alex says, noticing I'm walking off.

He stops talking.

I stop walking and turn around. "I'm hurt when you interrupt me and put me down. I'm not happy, but I do want to be. That's all part of what I'm trying to heal."

Alex rolls his eyes. "Sounds quacky."

"Yes, I had a seizure, but that wasn't her fault. You know how we had a bad spirit in the house? Well, one was following me. That's why I had the seizure."

"Oh, shit, Savvy, you can't possibly believe that!"

I stare into Alex's dark eyes as if I can brand him with the truth, and I wonder how many evil spirits must be attached to him. I'd just love for Jenn to get a hold of him. I know she could help him to see himself, but he'd have to *want* to see and I think his big, bad Taze Templeton self is to damn scared to look at the enemy in the mirror.

"Yes, that's what I believe, but that's not what I need to talk to you about. We've both come clean about the affairs we've had, but I have a confession to make. Last week, I started talking to Logan—Logan from church. We ran into each other at the library and—"

"I knew it. I knew you'd have to get back at me for seeing Raven," Alex says, sucking in his jaws.

"We didn't have sex. We just talked. I enjoyed being around him. He made me laugh and I realized how much I miss that. Logan was different than the other guys I've been with.

Flipping a burger, Alex's watery eyes dart my way, then back to the stove. "How long you been seeing him?"

"A few weeks."

"That's bullshit. Had to be longer than that. You've been unhappy forever," Alex says.

I hoist myself up into a barstool. "I have no reason to lie to you. I'm done with lying anyway. We really only saw each other a few times."

"A few times and you love him?" Alex says, staring at the grease popping onto the stovetop.

I've imagined this moment for a long time—telling him I don't need him anymore—how I'm worthy of love and want more from my life than the hate I feel from him. But as I look at the man I married, I realize I have always only wanted him to see the real me, not the one he wants to conform to his ideals and to kneel, worshiping his mere presence.

The thought of hurting him feels like I'm sticking a dagger into my own heart.

"Well?" Alex is staring at me.

I clasp my hands and force the words out. "I care about him."

Alex nods.

"Logan's trying to save his marriage, and I'm trying to save mine. I love you, but things have to change if I stay."

"You don't want to stay!" he says, jabbing the spatula my direction.

Rain No Evil

I have to be calm—not just re-act to his anger. "Alex you signed an agreement a few days ago to stop being verbally abusive, but last night you said that you won't—"

"Nothing I do is good enough for you. You think someone else will love you better than me?" He clicks the burner off and slams the spatula on the counter, grease splattering up the wall. "You think I'm such a bad guy—wait till you get the boyfriend who smashes your pretty face against the wall!"

Alex opens the basement door. "Boys! Come eat!"

I hop off the stool and stroke his arm. "Why can't you understand—I do want to stay. I just can't stay where I feel so hated."

As the boys pound up the stairs, Alex yanks his arm out of my reach and squares his stance. "Just go stick someone's dick in your mouth. That's all you want."

I lower my head and turn toward the sink. I feel like I just did.

I caress the cold, hard tile countertop Alex and I built five years ago when we still had the promise of a tomorrow together. Suddenly, I feel bone tired. A deep, Rip Van Winkle kind of tired I know will require more than sleep to cure.

My dream is dead. I have to form a new one.

I will always love the Alex I married, but I love and respect myself too much to stay with him.

Ben's first to hit the kitchen. I hug him before he grabs a plate.

"Missed you, sweetie pie," I say. God, I don't want to hurt my babies. The last person I want to emulate is my mom. I said I would never leave my babies like she did Luce and me, but I see now that a decision like separating from your supposed soul-mate is not that simple, and I wonder if there's more to mom's story than I know about.

"Mom, I'm hungry," Ben says, his cool blue eyes almost level with mine.

I must have held him for a whole minute. "Sorry," I say. "You're as tall as me." I force a smile.

"Where you been, Mom?" Isaac asks as Timmy and Cole reach for plates.

I wrap my arms around Isaac from behind as he squirts ketchup on his bun. "I had a doctor's appointment and it took longer than I thought. Sorry, sweet pea."

The boys all settle at the table in the living room in front of *Whose Line is it Anyway*.

Alex shuffles next to me in the kitchen and whispers, "You know you've already decided to leave so why you going to some quack doctor lady for counseling? You know you really are nuts."

"She's helping me to like myself again—to be okay whether or not things work out between us."

"Oh, that's nice. She's telling you to leave, but she's only hearing your version of the story." The plate in Alex's hand teeters and a few chips slide onto the floor.

Even when Alex does listen, he hears what he wants. I press my hands together forming a steeple, and nuzzle my fingers to my nose.

"It's not like that. Jenn's not telling me I should leave. She's never even suggested it."

"Sure, just keep going to your crazy lady." Alex shakes his head and wrinkles his mouth like he just doesn't know what to do with me.

Got news for him. I don't need him to decide what to do with me. Not anymore.

Chapter
Twenty Two

WEDDING VOWS
AND WINDING ROADS

The rain blows east after drizzling on the white canvas tent on Dad's lawn. It's Saturday—my baby sister's wedding day.

Ushers dressed in white dry the folding chairs along the cobblestone path leading to the rose arbor. The bridal party is scattered throughout Dad's house, primping and chatting.

As I scuttle about, fetching a drink for someone here and a tie for someone there, I catch bits of conversations about everything from the weather and the Dodgers, to Casper and Father Nick's visit to my house.

Ben's the town crier, announcing new arrivals from the kitchen. In the event he doesn't know the person, he describes their appearance like, "An old guy with a crooked back and a cane," and "Some big dude with a stiff mustache all curled up at the ends like a cartoon."

By four o'clock the seats are almost completely filled with friends and family. From my bedroom window view I see Kent strolling down the aisle and to his right, his wife, on the usher's arm. They settle into chairs, and Kent leans in close to her, whispering, sharing the way married couples do. She smiles adoringly at him as his arm slips around her shoulders.

She wouldn't be smiling if she knew the hand hugging her shoulder had been squeezing my bare ass a few months ago. I haven't seen him since then. Don't want to. The thought of him touching me makes me cringe.

I wrap my hands around my arms, warming them in a soft embrace and reminding myself that I don't have to let anyone touch me.

Because You Loved Me floats in soprano to my room—my cue to meet my groomsman and line up at the side door. As I'm turning to leave, a lady who just sat down in the back catches my eye. She looks like Mom except her hair's cut in a bob, not piled on her head like ice cream in a cone, and it's a smooth ash blonde rather than the frizzled gray I remember, but if it's not Mom, it's her twin.

The way the woman bites her lip and keeps tucking her blue skirt under her legs as she adjusts her sit bones in the chair, she's anything but comfortable here. I'm pretty sure it's Mom.

It's not like Luce to forget to tell me something as important as inviting Mom, but I'll be cordial. This is Luce's big day, and I'm not going to be selfish and ruin it. Mom sure didn't attend *my* wedding, but then again, she wasn't invited.

I stroll down the hallway, heels clicking with every step. My assigned groomsman steps forward and offers me his arm for our trip down the yellow path of daises.

Just like Luce, choosing flowers instead of a red carpet—that would be too pretentious for a unique country girl like her. I hope getting hitched to an officer, even one as sweet and level-headed as Jack, doesn't make Luce a crass, close-hearted cheat like me.

Wish I was on Logan's arm, but he's paired with another lucky bridesmaid. Besides I would feel like everyone could see my thoughts—me wanting his hand over my thumping heart. His wife, Kerri, is probably in this crowd somewhere, but I don't see her, and I don't want to. I would feel bad for caring about her husband even though we didn't so much as kiss.

I focus on the lavender hyacinths cascading from crystal vases on either side of the lectern where a Bible lays. I remind myself that it was little more than a month ago I was on my knees in the shower begging God to help me believe in His divine existence. He granted me an experience that did just that. Now, I have to forgive myself and trust that whatever I do, wherever I go, I will have everything I need for this inspired journey God's got me on.

Stepping out the back door, my shoes sink into the moist ground a bit. My escort steadies me with a steel grip.

Just as I promenade past the back row, I lock eyes with the lady in the light blue skirt. No mistake about it—it's Mom. I return her smile and proceed down the aisle, thinking how ironic that Luce's marriage is just beginning as mine's ending.

Watching Luce and Jack say, "I do" propels me back to my wedding day. Alex sobbed so hard that when he pulled back from kissing me, a slime of snot linked our mortified faces. We had joked that the video could've won the grand prize on *World's Funniest Videos*.

I'm not laughing now—seeing Luce dive kiss first into her dream when my fantasy reel is running the credits. Literary junkie me, I do appreciate the irony of the circle of life that seems to be sucking me into a tornado as I brace for a landing into unknown territory.

Rain No Evil

Luce and Jack's picture-taking session is quick, and within thirty minutes, they're smashing cake into each other's mouths under the tent where the crowd is gathered, drinking margaritas. Keagan is scolding Isaac for tossing cheese cubes at Ben.

The caterers dole out cake while a line forms along the path to the buffet where Dahlias hang damp from lampposts and rock-filled beds brim with pink peonies.

With a sliver of vanilla cake and a full goblet of Chardonnay, I take my seat next to Luce at the bridal table.

Luce leans close, speaking loudly over the band. "What's Mom doing here?"

I stop chewing the creamy, iced piece of heaven in my mouth. "You didn't invite her?"

"Hell, no. To Dad's house?" Luce swigs a long swallow of wine. "Can you believe the nerve!"

"Well, no sense to make a scene now. She'll probably leave soon," I say, hoping to put Luce at ease. I swipe a falling tendril of hair from her temple. "I'll keep her occupied so you won't have to deal with her okay?" She tips her head my way and sighs.

With butter-cream icing still melting in my mouth, I step into line for some beef and veggies, planning to locate Mom and find out who the heck invited her. Dad's taking my place beside Luce, when I feel a tap on my shoulder.

I turn to the strangely familiar face of my mother. Her blouse complements her gray eyes that are crinkled on the edges like a homemade pie. She smiles and steps toward me, her foot unsteady in the heels.

"Hi, Savannah. You look wonderful," she says, reaching out and wrapping her arms around me. She's shorter than I remember.

"Hi," I say. I haven't seen this woman for ten years, and I can't call her Mom like we chat every week. It was courageous of her to come uninvited. "Are you still living in Tennessee?"

She looks down rubbing her hand in long strokes as if petting a cat. "Buck moved out four months ago. We're getting a divorce. I might move back this way."

I don't know how to respond. I can't imagine her living close to me.

"Savvy, I'm really sorry I wasn't there for you on your wedding day . . . and all the other days." She looks across the lawn toward the horizon, pools forming in the lower lids of her eyes. "I missed out on a lot, I know. I messed up. I love you girls." She swallows hard. "Hope you can forgive me."

Forgive? How can I forgive her—forget the pain she caused me, Luce, Dad when she absconded away with the preacher? I'm not prepared to forgive her for anything right now.

Alex and his Aunt Klaire step into line behind us, jabbering about the Catholic Church, and I step forward grabbing a paper plate. "Are you going back to Tennessee tonight? That's a long trip."

"No, I stayed with Sarah last night. Remember Grandma Lennie's dear old friend, Sarah—she'd bring no-bake cookies over?" Mom smiles as she steps back in time. "You'd gobble those cookies up and then grab grandma's hand, swinging her around, dancing to Blondie. Oh, what was that song . . ."

"*Dancing Queen*," I say, joining Mom on Grandma's green shag rug for a second.

Mom steps forward, handing me a napkin with Luce's new last name, "Newbury" scrolled in silver. "Yes. *Dancing Queen* and that's what you were to grandma—her little dancing queen."

"Yeah, Grandma said I was her exercise," I say. "I can see Grandpa Happy in his brown plaid pants leaning against the doorway watching us twirl under each other's arms. We made his pant scraps into a fabric cross that hangs in Isaac's room."

Mom laughs. "Really? Sounds like you made good use of those ole pants. Wish Mom and Dad could be here today—see Luce so happy. Sarah and I've had a lovely visit down memory lane, too. Her daughter and I were good friends—went to high school together, but then she moved, and after I moved . . . well, I lost touch with everyone except Sarah. I'm going to stay with her again tonight and head back in the morning."

Must've been rough on Mom to leave all her friends for Buck. She must have really loved him.

I start to ask if Sarah's the one who told her about the wedding and to find out why Sarah's not here because *she* was invited when I hear Aunt Klaire say, "She brought that evil into your house—now you've gone Catholic with her?"

Klaire has to be talking about me and she says we've "Gone Catholic" as if we've gone rogue. She hasn't seen rogue till she's seen me pissed—the dark side of me roaring like a wounded hyena.

I step past the rolls, putting a few more inches between Klaire and me, and amuse Mom with an anecdote of Isaac calling MuddSock Heights, "Muddy Socks."

As I scoop barbeque onto a lettuce leaf, Klaire says, "She's a witch. You should divorce her."

With the silver spatula in my hand suspended above the beef, I look back at Klaire whose black-bean eyes are boring a hole in Alex's forehead.

A witch! Really? I can't ignore this, but I don't want to make a scene either. I could pierce her malevolent heart with this pointed silverware in my hand, but . . . I slap the spoon into the bowl, flinging my plate onto the table and stomp my stilettos solidly between Klaire and Alex.

I punch my finger into her boney shoulder. "*You* are the witch," I say in a forceful voice I can't believe is mine.

Klaire sticks her neck high like a giraffe reaching for a limb or whatever they eat. "You'll leave your kids just like your mom left you."

I make a fist and stick my fingernails deep into my palm. I want to hit her so badly. Just once. But it's Luce's day. I lower my voice and say, "I'd rather have no mother than to have one like you."

I pivot on my four-inch spikes, leaving Alex saying, "Now, ladies" and trying to avoid eye contact with the many eavesdroppers.

Ladies my ass! Klaire started this and I could finish it by dunking her head into the punch bowl till her snobby snoot puckered like a fish, but instead, I trot to the bathroom—a serene retreat. Between the maroon curtains I see the pond rippling like my swirling thoughts.

I wish I *were* a witch—I'd turn her yacking duck lips into concrete so her filth can't fill the air—reach my ears. If I had that power, I'd smack Alex's together, too.

I'm going to divorce the big dick. He won't get a chance to divorce me—that's what I should've told Anaconda Klaire.

And how Mom must feel. She must have heard Klaire's slam to her motherhood—not that it's a lie necessarily. She *was* absent during most of my teen years, but just because she ran off with the preacher, doesn't mean I'm leaving my boys for some man, and Klaire had no right to suggest I would.

I feel bad for just leaving Mom standing there listening to God-knows-what dialogue passing between Klaire and Alex and me. Mom wouldn't defend herself from the verbal darts if her life depended on it. She's as quiet as a snowed-in countryside in Maine.

Not me. I'm not living cowered on my haunches, praying for someone to rescue me from my choices—good or bad. Nope. My days of waiting for a knight to save me are over. God gave me a mind—think I'll use it. I'm not allowing Klaire's insidious quacking to make me miserable on this joyous occasion—and I'm not hiding out in the bathroom!

As I stomp through the kitchen to rejoin the party that's just winding up as the sun winds down, Kent saunters through the side door.

"Savvy," he says, practically singing my name. His long stride brings him to within a few feet of me. His eyes roving over me, making my blood cake. I feel as if he is actually ravaging me on his office floor.

I step back placing the granite island between his bulky body and mine that, suddenly, feels as buoyant as a sailboat and able to catch the next breeze..

Kent walks his fingers across the bar as he steps toward me. "When you coming to see me again?"

"I've been busy," I say, tugging up on the low neckline of my gown and remembering I need to speak my truth. "Kent, I'm not screwing around anymore."Kent stands stone-faced. "Too bad Alex doesn't hold such high standards. I hear the backseat of his cruiser gets more poontang than it does criminals in cuffs."

Isn't he the clever one! Kent thinks he can talk me into screwing him just because Alex is messing around. I recognize the manipulative tactic, but I do want to know who Kent's heard Alex is seeing. Maybe Alex is seeing someone I don't even know about, and Kent will tell me if he thinks he might get up my skirt again.

I bat my eyelashes, looking coyly up at him as if his dick were down my throat. "True. Maybe I should reconsider. So who's Alex's new weed monkey?"

Kent's laugh is deep. "Weed-monkey? Is that what they call the police whores?"

Kent rubs his hands together in circles like he's actually getting somewhere with me. "Stacey Chutney I hear. She's a friend of yours, isn't she?"

She used to be, but my idea of sharing with my friends doesn't extend to sharing my husband—even if he is a dick.

"Kent," I say , "I've got to catch up with Luce."

I'm keenly aware Kent's entranced with my ass that's swaying as I walk toward the door.

Maybe I should have told Kent he's never satisfied me sexually—not one orgasm—and that the thought of his wrinkled hands on my skin makes me want to shake like Lazy does after a bath, but that would be mean.

I have to learn to be honest without intentionally hurting others. This living my truth thing is going to require me to change my perspective of every situation. Guess Jenn's going to be in my budget for a while.

I can still hear grandma's sweet advice. "Always be lady-like, Savannah," and I've followed that advice for years. No matter how desperate or heartbroken I've felt inside, I've abided by society's rules of etiquette, hoping that people saw the lie I want them to.

Turns out, the community knew the truth all along, that my marriage is a farce. Ted knew about Alex fucking Stacey, Logan knew my marriage rocky and Dad and Luce recognized the crudeness behind Alex's jokes.

Mom's at a round table in the back when I return to the party, and the band's playing *Celebration*, by Kool and the Gang, to a rambunctious group of dancers on the grass dance floor.

Alex is sitting with his Aunt Klaire near the food table. I'm thinking how they are good company for each other and how both their faces look like they've been chiseled from a glacier when suddenly, I feel guilty like I sent badness to them somehow.

We all have lessons to learn. I'm helping them learn theirs, and they're helping me learn mine. I might as well start on this new me now.

I take a deep breath and picture Alex and Klaire blissful and smiling.

I know I have to be secure within myself—so secure that when someone like Klaire lambastes me, I recognize the statement as the other person's desire to control me—just like Alex has tried to do for years and just like Kent and . . .

"Savvy," Mom touches my arm, and I realize I'm staring at Alex and his aunt who no doubt are spreading gossip about some poor soul—probably me. "Are you all right, honey?"

Mom's blue eyes are dim with her own despair, but I see the same caring in her eyes that shines through Jenn's. I don't have the heart to ask her who invited her. Klaire's already hurt Mom enough, and it doesn't really matter who invited her. She must want to be included in Luce's life pretty badly to brave crashing this shindig anyway.

Growing up without her was lonely and I didn't understand why she left. Now that I'm searching for happiness myself, I feel a bit of compassion for her and realize that her leaving didn't mean she hated me or Luce or Dad. She was searching for something just like I am—maybe love—maybe acceptance. How can I blame her for that?

"I'm going to be alright," I say, laying my hand on Mom's shoulder. "I'm starving. Think I'll get . . ." Mom is pointing to the setting beside her plate. A dab of each entrée and side is on it, even rolls. She doesn't know I stay clear of grains, but how would she? Last meal we had together was Grandpa's funeral dinner twenty years ago.

Scooting my chair a little closer to hers, I smooth a napkin over my lap and say, "Mom, when you're back this way, maybe we can hit the mall."

Her hand flies to cover her open mouth like Tom Selleck has just proposed to her during the opening act at the World Series. "Savannah, I would just love that."

I stick my fork into the green beans and ask her if she's spoken with Luce.

Closing her eyes, Mom shakes her head.

A few bites in, Alex is standing beside me with his hand extended and saying, "Come on. They're playing our song."

My dress swishes around my ankles to the tune of *You are my shining star, don't you go away.* "Since when is this our song?" I ask.

He smiles down at me, his hand on the small of my back. "Since I don't want you to go away."

I want to vomit. My stomach is churning with the music, but I know it's not the dancing that's making me sick. Our song has been sung. There is no more us. He's had fourteen years to be the person I wanted to shine for, and instead he's thrown his crusty blanket of hate over my light.

He doesn't follow through on his promises, but I'm following through on mine. I have to prepare to leave.

Alex bends down close to my ear. I can feel his breath on my neck and I feel suffocated. "Savvy, I was going to surprise you, but . . . I'm taking you to Hawaii. Thought we'd fly into California . . ."

The room is spinning now like it does at Jenn's. He really thinks a trip is going to fix us. I try to focus on what he's saying.

"Dad's going to watch the boys for the week. I got a great last minute deal."

Thinking of spending a whole week with him makes me feel totally spent, like I have no energy for even one more breath.

"So, can you be packed by Monday morning?" Alex looks down at me with the soft brown eyes I fell in love with on the gym dance floor when all we had was a dream and a package of condoms.

How can I possibly leave him now when he's at least attempting to make an effort to make me happy?

"Huh?" I say, stumbling.

Alex grabs my arm. "You okay? We're leaving Monday morning for Hawaii. You gonna be ready?"

"Oh, I got dizzy. Must be the wine."

Alex plants his hands tighter around my waist and slows the circle he's spinning me in.

"Monday?" I say. "That's so soon."

"I know. I really feel like we need the break. Especially after the whole water thing. Just you and me. No kids . . . so?"

"I guess," I say, "I can pack."

The song ends and I cradle Alex's jaw, planting a kiss on his cheek in the hope that it takes root and that he always feels the love I have for him whether I go on this trip or not.

A lady darts over, arms open and engulfs me in an embrace like we're long lost friends. She looks familiar. She rares back and I recognize Klaire's friend, Ruthanne. Seems like eons ago I was confiding in her right there in line at the pharmacy.

"I heard a priest got rid of your demon. Amazing!" Ruthanne says, popping a handful of mints into her mouth. "You certainly have a story to tell, my dear. Was it scary?"

Indeed, I do have a story, but as I'm trying to focus on her words, my mind is already boarding a plane to Hawaii—a plane where I sit feeling like the test dummy in a Roswell UFO—just waiting for the crash I know is coming.

"So was it . . ." Ruthanne is saying, "was the exorcism scary?"

Alex is to my right holding a plateful of meatballs so still that he may have just seen Medusa and turned into stone.

"No," I say, turning back to Ruthanne, "the priest brought the body of Christ with him, said a few prayers . . ." I feel a hand on my shoulder and slight shove. I plant my feet firmer. "There was a *splat* in the hallway and it was gone."

"Oh, dear, well, thank God, it is," Ruthanne says.

Alex is urging me forward. I take a few steps, knowing with each step the invisible energy lines to my vocal chords are severed a bit more. I slide out of his grasp and lay my hand on Ruthanne's arm.

"Ruthanne, I'm very thankful it left, but I am also grateful it came. It taught me a valuable lesson." She's staring and I keep talking. "I'm the reason it came. I asked God to prove to me He was real, and He allowed an evil spirit to antagonize my family so He could prove it."

Ruthanne covers her mouth with a hanky. "Klaire did say she thought you had brought it in, but I just thought she was joking."

"Savvy's joking, too. She's had a bit too much wine," Alex says, stabbing a meatball with his fork and twirling it by his temple in circles.

I lean toward Ruthanne. "You can believe what you like, but the house exorcism is no joke to me."

I shake my rear through the crowd of guests gyrating to *She's a Brick House* until I reach Luce, who's inspecting a package on the gift table.

"Where'd you run off to?" she says, ripping a card open.

"To the bathroom—had a few interesting conversations along the way, but those are Sunday front porch-sitting material, not wedding entertainment."

Luce punches my arm and laughs. "Oh, I just bet they are. I saw Klaire just yammering away to Alex."

A little boy about seven years old runs up to where I'm standing and slides under the table, using the cloth cover for a shield as a girl about his age rounds the buffet table with her hand on her hip, no doubt scouring the dance floor for the inconspicuous character at my feet.

"So'd you find out who invited Mom?" Luce says.

"I didn't have the heart to ask, Luce. She seems genuinely glad to be here— happy for you. Even apologized for not being at my wedding."

The little girl runs off holding hands with another girl, and I nudge the boy with my foot. "All clear, dear."

The table skirt rises and a pair of button brown eyes peer up at me. The boy's wearing an Elvis grin. "Thanks, how'd ya know?"

I squat to his level. "Girls are always chasing boys, sweetheart. Always know where the nearest table is to hide under."

Luce pulls a check out of the envelope and hands it to me. "Give this to Dad. He's holding the money. I'll go speak to Mom. If you can, guess I can, too."

I smile. My forgiving attitude is catching. I'm already changing my world.

I'm awake early. Today I have to decide if I'm going on this trip, believing that Alex is truly committed to change, or if I'm going to accept the truth—that he's oblivious as to the need to change. I can't go with him just because he thinks a plane trip and a different view of the skyline is going to make me accept that he talks to me like I'm the lady who simply cleans his commode, not the one who nurtures his life.

I lay my hand on Alex's back, hoping with each inhale that if I leave he'll be able to breathe in the awesomeness of possibilities that is obscured with me here—to break habits that aren't life-enhancing for him—habits that he may only be able to break with the drastic scenario of me leaving.

His transformation may begin with me living my truth.

One of the hardest parts of divorcing him will be dealing with the boys' feelings— making sure they know Alex and I both love them. And that, even though I love their dad, it's no longer a romantic sort of love.

I shower, put on my makeup sans the mascara that may run should I cry later, and fix a breakfast fit for my three kings—omelets, fried potatoes, and pancakes with strawberry eyes and a blueberry-shaped mouth, just like Mom's Paddiwinks.

Even though the topic of separation doesn't usually carry the pomp of celebration, today is a day of liberation for me. I'm setting myself free from the control Alex has had over me. I'm cutting the noose around my neck, and I choose to celebrate the freedom. No more whining around, blaming Alex for my unhappiness.

I light a vanilla candle on the bar and say a prayer—to Archangel Michael to provide stamina for my journey to independence—to the Blessed Mother Mary to guide my path in motherhood even if it will be on a single lane.

Isaac's up first and wants to eat, but I hand him a glass of orange juice and tell him we will wait on his Dad and Ben. This is one morning we will all eat together. After I tell Alex how I feel, the ambiance of all four of us sitting at the table may never be the same again.

Ten minutes later Ben pounds down the stairs and into the kitchen. "Smells awesome, Mom."

I pop a strawberry in my mouth and handing Ben one, hear the shower running—Alex is up. "We'll eat in just a few," I say, squirting whip cream into the shape of a mustache onto my masterpiece.

When everyone's around the table, I ask Alex to say grace.

Alex raises his fork like it's a gavel. "Please bless the meat. Let's eat."

I'm savoring the table talk and grasping my fork like I'm holding the hand of a friend during their last breath. Ben's asking when Alex is going to take him and Isaac four-wheeling at the Hatfield-McCoy trail again. Alex's rattling off the maintenance that must be completed on the Honda before they can ride while Isaac jumps up and down in his seat and asks if Timmy can go, too.

I listen and eat and watch. I commit each detail to memory while the eggs stick to the roof of my mouth.

I focus on the way Isaac picks the green peppers out of his omelet—the way Ben adds chocolate milk to his mouth before swallowing his food.

Seems like I was just spooning mush in their mouths that they would just spit out—like I was just removing small objects from their grasps so they wouldn't get choked. Protecting my boys has been my life, and I want to protect them from the pain that speaking my truth will cause them.

I could stay silent—go on this trip and continue to live with hope that Alex will change or that I'll find a way to cope with him that won't compromise my morals.

And I *would* keep my feelings to myself—if I were the same person I was just a month ago. Before demons and exorcisms. Before Father Nick and Jenn. Before God proved to me that I don't need to see something to believe it's real.

Happiness in my future is unseen, yet I feel the certainty of its existence within the stillness of my mind.

I've changed. I don't want to live a lie anymore—pretend that I'm content with having a roof over my head and a husband who's not hugging a barstool every night.

To stay here would be to accept the version of me that Alex sees—whatever that may be—probably a wicked woman who doesn't understand him. But I've booted the evil from my reflection. With Jenn's help, I've snipped the cords that connected me to a demon and kept the scars as reminders of the lessons I've learned.

As I look across the table today, my husband looks different—his mouth, slightly drawn up to the left. The same wrinkle is creasing his forehead, but he looks like a stranger. A stranger—like I never knew him at all—only got a glimpse of his glorious soul and that was a long, long time ago.

My stranger says, "You all right, Sav? You look funny."

I nod and sip coffee while Isaac squirts more maple syrup onto his already soused eggs and tries to no avail to entice Ben to taste it.

It's surreal—the most easy-going meal we've shared at this table in months—the Last Supper of sorts for us. I can only hope my family's resurrection will be as miraculous as Jesus'.

Rain No Evil

I stop rinsing my dish to answer the knock at the door. Cole comes in and spots the warm pancakes on the bar.

"You're the best, Savannah," he says, scraping one off and eating it whole.

The boys run outside to play, leaving their dishes in the sink.

I stand by the counter, my hand braced on the bar. "Alex, you know the agreement you signed last week that—"

"Good Lord, do we have to talk about that shit again?" Alex says and swallows the last of his grape-juice.

"No, actually we don't," I say, conjuring the peace I feel when I'm sitting by the levy watching the river flow. "I just need to tell you that I understand that you aren't ready for the commitment of that contract. That's not where you are right now."

The candle flickers to my right reminding me I have heavenly helpers. "Alex," I say, "I appreciate you planning the Hawaii trip, but I feel that a vacation isn't going to help."

Alex chews silently, alternating glances between his plate and me. "I want to feel a connection to you, but the starting point of that is the agreement that—"

"Sav, if you don't go I'm done trying." Alex gets up and scrapes his leftover pancake into the sink.

"I thought you were done the other night when you said that you weren't going to change, and I couldn't make you."

"You don't know what you want," Alex says, walking past me. "You want to screw half the county and come home to me."

I'm not listening to him telling me what *I* want. I don't want to screw half the county and he's never going to understand that.

I look at the flickering candle on the counter and the flame dies as if it was snuffed out. I don't want the hope inside of me to die with it. "I will pack," I say, heading upstairs to dig out my suitcases.

I'm going to pack, but I'll need more than sunscreen for this trip—I'm packing for a journey that will last the rest of my life.

Alex and I are done. I'm jumping off the roller coaster ride. I'll strap Alex in as best I can, but for me I'm shooting out of this cannonball and into the wide-open sky.

After calling Dad and telling him he will have company for the indefinite future, I spend the afternoon packing and washing clothes. The biggest suitcase gets tucked into the trunk first. I pack another and another. First mine, then Ben's, then Isaac's, rotating from one room to the other, finding smaller bags I can squeeze into my truck and the floorboards of my car.

The boys and Cole are roving the area on bicycles, and Alex is washing his truck, not paying attention to how much I'm loading into the car.

I place the last bag that will fit in the backseat and still leave enough room for Isaac then I head inside to stand in my kitchen for one last time.

Looking out the kitchen window, cradling my coffee and watching Alex spraying his vehicle, scrubbing the windshield like he will be able to see everything he needs to see with it clean, I wonder why he can't see that his entire life is about to shift.

His view is obscured by his ego, not the bugs on his window. He may never see himself the way I do . . . or life, the way I do.

I can't just tell him I'm leaving and walk out. No, I've lived here unheard for fourteen years. I'll leave my thoughts on paper for him to refer to as much as he wants.

I run upstairs and scribble a letter.

Alex,

You've been my best friend and I'll miss you, but we both deserve to be happy and neither of us are. I hope you find comfort in knowing I truly tried to connect with you and understand you, but I have exhausted my every effort, and I believe you feel the same.

I remember you looking at me during a Mother's Day service in college and saying, "Happy Future Mother's Day," and I know you meant that. It was one of the sweetest things you've ever said to me. And a few summers ago when the family was all out in the backyard, you grabbed me and swung me over your shoulder and I felt so happy. You were playful and I knew as you were swirling me that I wanted more of those moments. I also knew I would always remember that moment and I always will.

I'm focusing on the future and I hope you do the same. I wish you every happiness that life can offer you.

The boys will deal with this much better if we are respectful of each other during this transition.

It may be hard to hear this, but I do love you. I just can't make this work.

Love, Savy

I hear a door slam downstairs, and I tuck the note under his pillow. I glance out my closet window. The boys' bikes are lying on the ground and Lazy's fetching a stick Cole's throwing. When I get to the kitchen, Alex is washing his hands. "What's for dinner?"

Rain No Evil

The question throws me off guard. I won't be here to cook dinner anymore. I look at the stove, and it already feels like I'm standing in someone else's kitchen. "Alex, I'm not making dinner," I say, pouring my cold coffee down the drain. Alex gulps a glass of sweet tea and shakes his head. "Of course you're not,"

"Alex I'm leaving," I say, clutching my purse handle.

The stranger's face is gone, a fearful-eyed, high school sweetheart stands staring at me.

"I want you to be happy—I do," I say. "And I love you, but I can't stay."

"I always knew you'd leave," Alex says, hunching over and untying his tennis shoes. A drop splashes to the floor and this time, it's not from a demon. It's from my fallen angel who I wish would wrap his arms around me and tell me he will change—tell me he will chop his tongue off in a guillotine if that's what it takes to make me stay.

But my voiceless angel bustles upstairs where he will find a handwritten note, and just maybe, let himself cry.

I scramble outside and send Cole peddling home and tell the boys we're heading to Pawpaw Cal's.

As the crescent moon hangs low over MuddSock Heights, looking like it's trying to snag the steeple on the Catholic church, I sit at Ridgeland's levy with Ben and Isaac and tell them their dad and I are getting a divorce—not because we don't love each other, but because we want each other to be happy and we aren't happy together.

I roll the window down and tell them I'm sorry—that I had hoped it would not come to this—that we could make it work.

Isaac says, "When we going to see Dad and our friends?"

I turn to the backseat. "We're staying at Pawpaw's for now. You'll get to see your dad almost every day. We don't have a schedule yet, but we'll work it out.

"But, Mom, you just said you still love each other, so why can't you still try?" Ben asks, looking like he's stuck at the top of the Ferris wheel I just got off of.

I curl one leg under me. "We love each other in a different way than we used to, bud, and believe me, we *have* tried. If there was any way possible we could make it work, I wouldn't be here telling you this right—"

Instantly, the humming of a passing barge transports me to another time. I've been here before. This already happened—these same words Ben and I just exchanged, the smell of the fish, the moonlight reflecting off the river, the sound of the barge—all of it. It already happened!

"Mom?" Ben's staring at me.

"You know what déjà vu is, Ben?" I ask.

"No," he says.

"It's when you feel like something's already happened—like you've lived it before. I just had that feeling. I've had déjà vu before, but never this strong," I say, stroking the rosary beads hanging on my rear view mirror.

"I know we've been here and done this before. Sounds crazy, but after everything we've been through, maybe nothing is crazy, huh?" I say, leaning across the console and hugging Ben. "I love you guys. Everything is going to be all right. It'll be different, but just know you're loved . . . very much."

If a time warp actually exists, it's in Jenn's basement.

The cruel, unreasonable world seems to not exist at all—like it's been sucked into a black hole and up through her floorboards has risen an Atlantis, pristine, sublime and as non-dimensional as the cosmos.

Doesn't seem like just yesterday I left my husband, but I did, and I'm thankful Jenn worked me in. Feels like an elephant just stomped across my chest.

Shooing kitty off my chair, I tell her I left Alex.

Jenn sits back, a somber expression on her face.

"I knew I had to, but I feel sorry for him because he doesn't see his part in the split, and I don't think he wants to."

Jenn cradles her elbows with both hands, and the golden aura around her expands. "He may get a different perspective with someone else—later on with another woman."

"Guess we can still care about each other, and not be together making each other miserable," I say, kicking off my shoes. "I need to love myself again and I just can't do that with him around."

"Savannah, you know, you may or may not find another love of your life. I'm not trying to scare you. I just want you to be prepared to be alone and be all right with that—to be happy whether there is or isn't another karmic relationship for you."

"I was unhappy and alone anyway," I say nuzzling into what has become one of my favorite chairs in the world—second only to Dads. "My chances for surviving on my own far outweigh the possibility of me surviving another year with Alex. I'm going to focus on healing me, and if I never fall in love again, well, I'm okay with that."

"You will feel like you're on a teeter-totter for a while," Jenn says. "Like you're trying to stay balanced. How are the boys?"

"They took it okay, but I'm sure they're in shock and will need a lot of reassurance as the days go by," I say, picturing all three of us sitting at the levy. "Oh, and when I told the boys about the divorce, this intense feeling of déjà vu came over me—stronger than I've ever had. I knew I'd had the exact same conversation. Even the sounds and the smells were the same. How do you explain that?"

"Time is an illusion," Jenn says, stacking her hands one above the other. "The past, present, and future are occurring simultaneously. You know anything about Einstein's theory of relativity?"

"A little, it's based on the premise that we can change our past and our future by changing our now."

"Exactly. The infinity symbol represents this well. The first loop on the lemniscate represents the past; the second loop, the future and where they intersect, the present. It's as if you are riding a train and nearing a station, if you look to your left, you would see your past—to the right, your future," Jenn says, turning her head from side to side. "Your location on the train is your *now*."

I tip my head toward the spot above me where Jenn's always peering at angels I can't see. I pass a silent request to them to help me understand this quantum physics concept that's more above my head than they are. "If that's true, then the future already exists, so how can what I do now effect the future?"

"Our perception is our reality. Each person perceives the world in his own way. Our current perception is the only thing we have the ability to change, but when we change our perception, the past, the present, the future—they all change simultaneously."

She must see my scrunched up face, smiles, and says, "In our three dimensional world, I know it's hard to grasp the time thing."

"Jenn," I say, cupping both knees with my hands, "whose voices did I hear before I had the seizure?

Jenn is staring into the space above me. Probably asking if it's all right to tell me the entire truth—asking if I can handle it.

I shoot a quick prayer to whoever's hovering up there and insist that I indeed can and *must* know. After everything I've been through, I deserve to know.

Jenn leans on the desk. "The spirits that were talking to you weren't acting in your best interest, and they didn't want you here because they knew they would have to leave. Savannah, they . . ." Jenn knocks her clasped hands on the desk like a gavel. "They were attached to you."

Her gaze is tender. She doesn't want to frighten me, but if I got this right . . . "Jenn, are you saying that they were *in* me?" I say, trying to conceal the fear in my voice. I want all the facts.

"No, but they were embedded in your auric field and fed off of your energy. They enjoyed watching you when . . . during your sexual encounters."

Jenn is speaking slowly like I'm a lip reader.

I smile despite the deafening heartbeat in my ears. "Did I bring any of the voyeuristic crew here today?"

"No, dear. They're all gone." Jenn says. "I don't want to scare you, but they have been known to return so be careful what you open yourself up to. If a situation doesn't feel right, live your truth and you will stay protected."

During the healing session, I close my eyes and see white flashes of light that I now believe to be my guardian angels. Jenn's hands are several inches from my bare arm, yet the heat from them feels like I'm standing near a campfire. After a soothing meditation, a deep sense of contentment replaces the sense of loss.

Before I leave, I hug Jenn whose saintly soul saved mine.

Travelling back across the winding West Virginia highway, I wonder why I've had such preposterous experiences as I've had this month when surely, I'm not the only person in the world to ever get angry with God—not the only woman in history to have an affair, yet I haven't heard of other people having a demon spray them with water and attach to them in order to watch them have sex. Maybe God gave me the unusual experience in the hope that I would write about it—that is if God hopes for anything.

Before going to Dads, I pull in MuddSock Height's parking lot, bright with the afternoon sun. As I grab my baseball cap from the seat where my notebook lies, the air sparkles like I just shook a tube of glitter.

I brush my seat with my hand to remove the dust that should be there, but there are no particles on the seat. If fairies exist, maybe they're trying to get my attention. Maybe they're trying to tell me that the book I'm writing will help me heal. It may even help others to heal or to believe in a higher power, and that would be the best gift I could give the globe.

I open my notebook and write:

> Heal myself, heal the world
> And let it rain no evil!

A few minutes later, I'm jogging the path along the rippling river, wondering what awaits me in the future.

Will I become Catholic because of the unmistakable power that God demonstrated through Father Nick?

Will I extrapolate every bit of information I can from Jenn about the Divine and energy healing?

Will I really complete a manuscript and sell a million books?

As I breathe in the moist air on this clear night when every star in my celestial view is visible, every boat afloat, reflecting light onto the water, I know that whatever I choose to do, my future—the future that is occurring now with each thought and with every single intention I'm creating in this moment—is creating the me I want to be.

If life's a test, I want to pass. I want to learn my lessons and move on to the next dimension, enlightened. I want to find my way home.

A warm breeze carries the smell of honeysuckle my way, invigorating my heightened state of awareness. The familiar whistle from a train that's clacking along the rail in front of my former home in Ridgeland blows low and steady across the river to my ears, and I realize—I *am* home.

My ever-present—ever-changing—soul home.

THERE IS NO END☺

CPSIA information can be obtained
at www.ICGtesting.com
Printed in the USA
FFOW04n1729230616
25321FF